NEW YORK REVIEW BOOKS
CLASSICS

T0000948

TELLURIA

VLADIMIR SOROKIN was born in a small town outside of Moscow in 1955. He trained as an engineer at the Moscow Institute of Oil and Gas but turned to art and writing, becoming a major presence in the Moscow underground of the 1980s. His work was banned in the Soviet Union, and his first novel, *The Queue*, was published by the famed émigré dissident Andrei Sinyavsky in France in 1985. In 1992, Sorokin's *Their Four Hearts* was short-listed for the Russian Booker Prize; in 1999, the publication of the controversial novel *Blue Lard*, which included a sex scene between clones of Stalin and Khrushchev, led to public demonstrations against the book and demands that Sorokin be prosecuted as a pornographer; in 2001, he received the Andrei Bely Award for outstanding contributions to Russian literature. His work has been translated into more than thirty languages. Sorokin is also the author of the screenplays for *Moscow, The Kopeck*, and *4*, and of the libretto for Leonid Desyatnikov's *The Children of Rosenthal*, the first new opera to be commissioned by the Bolshoi Theater since the 1970s. He has written numerous plays and short stories, including the O. Henry Award winner "Horse Soup," which will appear in *Red Pyramid*, a volume of stories forthcoming from NYRB Classics. His most recent novel is *Doctor Garin*. He lives in Vnukovo and Berlin.

MAX LAWTON is a novelist, musician, and translator. His translations of Sorokin's stories have appeared in *The New Yorker* and *n+1*. In addition to eight of Sorokin's books, forthcoming from NYRB Classics and Dalkey Archive Press, he is translating two books by Jonathan Littell. He lives in New York City.

OTHER BOOKS BY VLADIMIR SOROKIN

The Blizzard
Translated by Jamey Gambrell

Blue Lard (forthcoming)
Translated by Max Lawton

Day of the Oprichnik
Translated by Jamey Gambrell

Dispatches from the District Committee: Selected Soviet Stories
  (forthcoming)
Translated by Max Lawton

Ice Trilogy
Translated by Jamey Gambrell

Marina's Thirtieth Love (forthcoming)
Translated by Max Lawton

The Norm (forthcoming)
Translated by Max Lawton

The Queue
Translated by Sally Laird

Red Pyramid: Selected Stories (forthcoming)
Translated by Max Lawton

Roman (forthcoming)
Translated by Max Lawton

Their Four Hearts
Translated by Max Lawton

TELLURIA

VLADIMIR SOROKIN

Translated from the Russian by
MAX LAWTON

NEW YORK REVIEW BOOKS

New York

THIS IS A NEW YORK REVIEW BOOK
PUBLISHED BY THE NEW YORK REVIEW OF BOOKS
435 Hudson Street, New York, NY 10014
www.nyrb.com

The publication was effected under the auspices of
the Mikhail Prokhorov Foundation TRANSCRIPT
Program to Support Translations of Russian Literature

 transcript

Library of Congress Cataloging-in-Publication Data
Names: Sorokin, Vladimir, 1955– author. | Lawton, Max, translator.
Title: Telluria / a novel by Vladimir Sorokin; translated by Max Lawton.
Other titles: Telluriya. English
Description: New York: New York Review Books, [2022] | Series: New York
   Review Books
Identifiers: LCCN 2021024674 (print) | LCCN 2021024675 (ebook) |
   ISBN 9781681376332 (paperback) | ISBN 9781681376349 (ebook)
Subjects: GSAFD: Dystopias. | LCGFT: Dystopian fiction.
Classification: LCC PG3488.O66 T4513 2022 (print) | LCC PG3488.O66
   (ebook) | DDC 891.73/5—dc23
LC record available at https://lccn.loc.gov/2021024674
LC ebook record available at https://lccn.loc.gov/2021024675

ISBN 978-1-68137-633-2
Available as an electronic book; ISBN 978-1-68137-634-9

Printed in the United States of America on acid-free paper.
10 9 8 7 6 5 4 3 2 1

TELLURIA

I

"'Tis time to shake the Kremlin walls!" Zoran wandered back and forth under the table with great focus, driving his fist into his palm. "'Tis time! 'Tis time!"

Goran jumped up, climbed onto the bench, sat down, and began to wiggle his little feet into his old boots in a practiced manner. Hemmed with an even beard, his crooked-nosed, low-browed face radiated calm certainty.

"Not shake, but crush," he pronounced, "and not the walls, but their rotten heads."

"Like pumpkins! Like pump-kins!" Zoran smashed his fist against the table leg.

"We'll crush 'em."

Goran extended his hand demonstratively and poked his finger through the smoky stench of the packhouse. And there, seemingly at the command of his tiny finger, two biguns removed a crucible with the capacity of a hundred buckets and filled with molten lead from the furnace and carried it over to the casting flasks, a peal of thunder seeming to escape from their bellies. Even the steps they took with their bare feet made the packhouse tremble. A human-size glass clinked around in a glass-holder on the table.

Zoran began to awkwardly clamber up onto the tall bench. With his feet still dangling, Goran helped him up. Zoran climbed from the bench and onto the table, straightened up, walked over to the edge of the table, and stood there, clutching at the lapels of his short coat with his little hands. His narrow eyes gazed into the crucible and his auburn locks fluttered in the heat of the furnace.

The biguns brought the crucible to the casting flasks and began to tilt it over. The lead, hissing and buzzing, was poured into a wide gutter, raising up plumes of gray smoke. Immediately, dozens and dozens of piercingly white little streams of lead diverged from the gutter and began to spout and drip into the casting flasks. The half-naked, sweaty biguns in their canvas aprons continued to gingerly upend the crucible.

The lead flowed and spread, disappearing into the earth-colored casting flasks, flowed and spread ... Zoran and Goran watched: the first standing tensely at the edge of the table and the second with his feet kicking around on the bench. The biguns' monstrous biceps went crimson and shined with sweat. The plumes of smoke rose toward the hole in the packhouse's ceiling. *Great words to suit our great cause* ... Zoran thought. *Wet-Earth Mother* ... Goran remembered.

The crucible tilted farther and farther over. It seemed there would be no end to it. Goran's little eyes filled with tears. But he didn't blink and didn't wipe them away.

Finally, the leaden lava went dry. The biguns lowered the crucible down to the stone floor with a roar.

Zoran wiped at his eyes with his palms. Goran pulled out a pipe and began to light up.

"Well done, comrades!" Zoran shouted with all his might, trying to make himself heard over the noise from the furnace.

But the biguns didn't hear him. Disseminating the stench of the hastily assembled smelting hearth with their enormous bodies, they moved into a corner, picked up buckets, and began to drink thirstily. When they had each finished three buckets, they took off their aprons, pulled on their chlamydes, and walked over to the table. Their figures blocked out the light from the smelting hearth. The shadows of the biguns fell across Zoran and Goran.

"Well done!" Zoran repeated, his contented eyes glittering brightly. Even in the shadow of the biguns, his face was also shining.

Puffing on his pipe, Goran climbed up onto the table, walked over to Zoran bowleggedly, and stood next to him.

The biguns silently extended their enormous palms covered over in brownish corns to the littluns. Goran took two hundred-ruble bills out of his jacket pocket and slowly laid one into each palm. The first bigun immediately closed his fist around the bill and stuffed his fist into his pocket. The other brought the bill to his face and narrowed his already swollen eyes.

"Good?" his lips pronounced.

"Good," Goran chuckled, baring his smoke-stained teeth.

"The very best there is, my big comrade!" Zoran encouraged him. "Thank you from our workman's Moscow!"

"We'll call on you again soon." Goran let forth a puff of smoke.

The bigun grunted and put away the hundred-ruble bill. And held out his hand once again. Zoran and Goran stared at it. The biguns looked at the littluns. The bigun's hand reminded Zoran of Russia, which had, not too long ago, stretched all the way from Smolensk to the Ural Mountains. Zoran, a Moscovian, had only ever seen *images* of that country. It was as if the bigun was teasing him.

He carries Russia in his pocket? flashed through Zoran's head. *The trolls decided to rip us off,* Goran thought.

Several agonizing seconds passed. Zoran's red brows began to curve defiantly and Goran's hand reached toward his pocket. But the biguns suddenly grunted mischievously, threw their hands back, and slapped their palms together violently.

The sound was deafening to the littluns.

The littluns shuddered.

The biguns laughed. Their laughter thundered against the corrugated roof of the packhouse.

"A joke?" Zoran raised his eyebrows.

"A joke..." Goran nodded gloomily.

The biguns turned away and walked over to the door. Reached the door. Hunched over. Crawled through the door on all fours. The door slammed shut.

"Jokers, huh? They're good guys!" Zoran walked around the table excitedly, clutching at his lapels.

"Good guys..." Goran muttered and pulled an expensive lightning discharger out from the pocket of his jacket. "I had half a mind to light 'em up..."

He spat. Laughed. Paced around with his bowlegged gait, as if he were on the verge of performing some ancient dance. And abruptly gave the single human-size glass on the table a sharp kick. The glass flew from the table, slipped out of the cup holder, dinged against the bench, and shattered.

"Let's go! Let's go have a look!" Zoran bustled about, attempting to climb down.

"They're still too hot. Let 'em cool down."

"Let's have a look! Have a look before the *people* come!"

They slid down onto the floor and walked over to the casting flasks. There were twenty of them. They reminded Goran of the old capitalist sinny about alien monsters laying precisely these sorts of *earthy* cocoon-eggs. Unpleasant critters had then hatched from the eggs.

Zoran ran over to the toolbox, grabbed a sledgehammer, but couldn't make it budge. Found a hammer, raised it over his head like a banner, ran toward the casting flasks.

"O-one!" he hit a casting flask with a running start.

Shards of the casting flask flew to the ground.

"O-one! Two! Three!" Zoran was attacking the casting flasks with furious and persistent blows, as if it were his last chance to do so.

This is just how he does things . . . Goran thought gloomily, knocked his pipe against a casting flask, then began to clean it out with an *empty* tellurium nail.

Tiring himself out quickly, Zoran handed Goran the hammer. Goran put away the pipe and began to hit the casting flask—patiently and with great force.

After the sixth blow, the casting flask cracked and began to fall away. A casting was shining inside it. The littluns began to crush the fragments of the casting flask with their feet. Still steaming, the fresh casting fell to the floor with a clang: there were forty brass knuckles. Goran pulled iron tongs out of the toolbox, grabbed the steaming-hot brass knuckles, and picked them up.

"Won-der-ful!" Zoran squinted. "A popular weapon! En-tire-ly app-ro-pri-ate!"

He held out his hand and spread out his fingers, measuring them up. These brass knuckles were intended for the *middle class*—for ordinary people, that is to say. The brass knuckles would be like a ring on the little finger of the bigun who had cast them and wouldn't even fit on the foot of the littlun who had paid for the casting.

"Eight hundred," Goran recalled.

"Eight hundred crushers! Now that's power!"

"Eight hundred heroes." Goran nodded gravely.

"Eight hundred dead ghouls!" Zoran shook his fists.

A smartypants beeped in Goran's pocket. Dropping the tongs with the brass knuckles, he took out the smartypants and stretched it out in front of him with his habitual sharpness of movement—as if it were an accordion. The head of a medieval knight rose up in the semitransparent smartypants.

"The biguns left and there're no scotch eggs," the knight-errant reported.

"And the people?" Goran asked.

"They're here."

"Five at a time."

"Got it."

Goran put away the smartypants. Clutching at his coat, Zoran walked impatiently around the empty crucible. Goran took out the pipe, jumped up, and sat down on a casting flask.

That should warm my ass up . . . he thought and, filling the pipe, asked, "When's . . . the second casting?"

"On the eve of the big day." Zoran slapped his palm against the crucible. "Yes! On the very eve!"

"The Leader knows best." Goran nodded.

Twenty-three minutes later, five people with proletarian aspects carrying bags and rucksacks came in without bothering to knock.

2

MY SWEET, most venerable boy,

I have arrived in Moscovia. Everything happened faster and more simply than usual. Though they say that entering this state is much easier than leaving it. In that fact lies the metaphysics, if you will, of this place. But to hell with that! I'm sick of living based on rumors and conjectures. Us *radical* Europeans are biased against and wary of exotic countries up until the moment of penetration. To put it more simply—until we become intimate with them. Which I indeed became. Congratulate your old tapir! Oh yes. On my first night, a charming, sixteen-year-old *Moscovian* became the narrow gates through which I was able to immerse myself in the local metaphysics. Because of this boy, I learned a lot about Moscovian ethics and aesthetics. Everything is more or less civilized, though not without some wild *game*: for example, just before we got intimate, the boy hung towels from both mirrors in my room, turned off the light, and lit a candle. Which he had brought himself. And I (don't get mad) allowed myself to enhance my performance with tellurium. In the morning, I then heard (and saw) how charming, little Fedenka prayed for a long time in the bathroom in front of a small foldable icon cast in copper (what we call *skladen*) that he had erected on the shelf in the corner of the shower in place of the shampoo. It was touching to such a degree that, spying on this kneeling Adonis in his checkered undies through the cracked door, I immediately *wanted* him. Which happens to me in the mornings, as you know, rather rarely! Without waiting for the end of his prayers, I forced my way into the bathroom, laid bare the throne of my concubine, and penetrated into his depths with my

8

demanding tongue, calling forth a surprised exclamation from him. You can imagine what happened next ... I'll tell you with complete sincerity that it's wonderful when the day begins with a prayer, my friend. Such days almost always *come off* and imprint themselves in one's memory. And my first day in the Moscovian state was no exception. Having paid my brown-eyed Fedenka (3 rubles for the night + 1 ruble for the morning = 42 pounds), I had a pretty decent breakfast at my inexpensive hotel, the Slavyanka (tea from a samovar, *syrniki* with sour cream, *kissel*, rolls, and honey), then set off on a stroll. The weather didn't disappoint: clear, sunny, and fresh. October is a lively month in the Moscovian capital with some yellow leaves still on the trees. You know that I'm no great fan of *attractions* as such and have never been a good tourist. Your friend likes to try everything with his own tongue (don't hem and haw, you cynic), not trusting the whims of the masses. Upon my first taste, I didn't really like Moscow; a combination of mawkishness, untidiness, technology, ideology (communism + Russian Orthodoxy), and provincial mustiness. The city seethes with advertisements, cars, horses, and beggars. To put it in gastronomic terms, Moscow is an *okroshka*, a cold summer soup made from kvass, raw vegetables, hard-boiled eggs, and boiled meat. A particularly important issue here is the air. In Moscow, only statesmen and rich people travel with gas or electricity. Ordinary people and public transport use biofuel, which is essentially potato pulp. Thanks to the potato, Moscovia hasn't gone hungry since Ekaterina II. The potato exhaust gives the local air a cloying and musty taste that spreads all through the city. And when you try the main Moscow dishes with your tongue—the Kremlin, the Bolshoi Theater, Saint Basil's Cathedral, and the Czar Cannon—this, so to speak, not-very-appetizing sauce spoils the ensemble and leaves you with an unpleasant aftertaste. But, I repeat, this is only on the first day. By the second day, I had already grown used to it, just as I grew accustomed to the stenches of Cairo, Madras, Venice, New York, and Bucharest. Alas, odor isn't the issue here. Moscow is simply a strange city. Yes, a strange city in all its particular strangenesses. Least of all do I wish to call it a capital. It's difficult to explain this to you, as you've never been here and are entirely indifferent to the history of the place. But I'll still try, thanks to the fact that I have an hour and a half before my potato taxi will come and take me to Vnukovo Airport. And so: it makes little sense to root around in the prerevolutionary history of the Russian Empire, which showed the world Asian-Byzantine despotism in combination with indecently dimensionless colonial geography, a harsh climate, and a submissive populace, a large portion of which lived like slaves. The twentieth century is far more interesting, starting with a world war, during which the monarchic titan of Russia began to stagger, followed by a bourgeois revolution that surged forth rather naturally, after which the titan began to tumble over. Perhaps it'd be better to say "titaness" (grammatically speaking, Russia is a feminine noun). Her imperial heart stopped. If she, this gloriously merciless giantess wearing a diamond tiara and a mantle of snow, had properly collapsed in February 1917 and disintegrated into a collection of human-size states, everything would have turned out more or less in keeping with the spirit of modern history, and the nations that had been oppressed by the czar's power would finally have gained their postimperial national identities and begun to live freely. But everything happened differently. The Bolshevik Party did not allow the giantess to fall, compensating for its small numbers with its beastly bite and inexhaustible social activity. Having successfully pulled off a nighttime coup in Saint Petersburg, they stopped the falling corpse of empire just before it hit the ground. I see Lenin and Trotsky precisely as tiny caryatids, holding up the dead and beautiful giantess with furious grunts. Despite their "fierce hatred" for the czar's regime, the Bolsheviks ended up being neoimperialists to their core; after they won the Civil War, the corpse was rechristened as the "USSR," a despotic state with centralized governance and a rigid ideology. As befits any empire, the USSR began to expand and to seize new lands. But Stalin turned out to be the purest imperialist of this new imperial circumstance. He didn't become a caryatid, but simply decided to raise up the imperial corpse. This was called *kollektivizatsia + industrializatsia*. He did so for ten years, raising up the giantess according to the method of ancient civilizations that necessitated laying stones underneath a statue in order to successfully erect it. Instead of stones, Stalin used the bodies of citizens of the USSR. As a result, the imperial corpse assumed an upright position. They then applied makeup to its face, rouge to its cheeks, and froze it. The freezer of Stalin's regime worked without fail. But, as everyone knows, no technology shall serve us forever—just remember your wonderful red BMW. After Stalin died, the corpse began to thaw. They just managed to get the freezer running again, but not for long. Finally, the body of our beauty melted for good and she once again began to topple over. New hands rose up to catch her and post-Soviet imperialists were ready to turn into caryatids. But, at that moment, a wise group finally came to power, one led by a man who was unprepossessing at first glance. He turned out to be a wonderful liberal *and* psycho-therapist. For a decade and a half, this toiler of the fall talked constantly about the revival of empire, while doing everything he could to make the corpse land successfully. And that's what happened. After which another life melted into being amongst the shattered bits of the beauty. So here I am, my dear Todd, in Moscow—the former head of the giantess. After this definitive collapse of the empire, Moscow went through a lot: famines, a new monarchy and the bloody oprichniks, estates of the realm, a constitution, the International Trade Union Confederation, a parliament . . . If I were to try to define the current state regime of Moscovia, then I would call it enlightened theocra-tocommunofeudalism. To each their own . . . But I embarked on this historical digression only to try to explain to you the strange strange-nesses of this city. Imagine that you've been abandoned by Providence on an island of giants, caught in bad weather, and forced to spend the night in the skull of a long-deceased titan. Shivering and soaked, you climb into it through the eye socket and fall asleep beneath this ossuary dome. It's easy to imagine that your dreams would be filled with rare visions not devoid of heroic (or hypochondriac) gigantism. Moscow is essentially the skull of the Russian empire and its strange strangeness lies in these ghosts of the past, which we call "imperial dreams." They're saturated with potato exhaust to boot. Dreams, dreams . . . Russia has always lived sleepingly, waking up for short periods of time at the behest of conspirators, rebels, and revolutionaries. Wars can't even manage to torment her with insomnia for long. Barely having woken up to scratch at the unquiet places on her body, the giantess wrapped herself in snow and fell asleep once again. Her snores shook distant provinces and the functionaries of those provinces also shook, awaiting the frightful visit of an inspector from the capital. She loved the colorful dreams she so often had. But her reality was quite gray: a gloomy sky, some snow, the smoke of the Fatherland combined with a blizzard, the song of a coachman transporting Decembrists and/or sturgeon . . . It seems that Russia always woke up in a beastly mood and with an awful Moscovian headache. Moscow was ill and demanded German aspirin. And still, despite all its pathologically political unprepossessingness, this city is not devoid of charm: the charm of the dream of a long-dead great state that unexpectedly comes to you at night. But this charm is difficult to describe, because the Russian state dream has its own particular . . . etc. For that reason, I'm not going to waste more of your attention or the energy of my gouty fingers, but upon my arrival, I'll try to tell you about and show you, if not all of Moscow, then at least the Czar *Cannon*. When we're deservedly back together in bed. I'm generally pleased with my trip. You can stick the next pin onto the old family globe. In the winter, you and I will fly to sweet Vietnamese baby dolls. And in the spring, we'll visit postwar Europe. Before my taxi arrives, I'll still have time to smoke a *papirosa* and drink a bit of Russian cranberry vodka.

Until we meet again in our *native* neoimperial skull, full of brain fog and Anglo-Saxon sobriety.

Yours,
Leo

3

By the grace of the Sovereign Top-Manager, *ad majorem gloriam* the CPSU and all the saints, for the happiness of the people by the will of the Lord alone, at the behest of world imperialism, as per the request of enlightened Satanism, by the burning of Russian-Orthodox patriotism, having a solid consensus and peace of mind built on financial expertise and based on capitalistic concepts, for the full historical, hi-tech right of the Russian State to crush and to unify, to call for and to direct, to gather the whole world together and to inflict punishments in the holy places of the great holdings of the international cathedral and Soviet pseudoscience, by resolution of the house committee, by the Stakhanovite initiative of the nationwide nanotechnology of the Holy Spirit, in connection with the further deployment of democratic events in hermitages and labor collectives, in houses of tolerance and child-care facilities, in detachable hideaways and tearaway crashpads, in Streltsy settlements and building cooperatives, in the editorial offices of widely circulated newspapers, in catacomb churches, in military martial arts, in the halls of power, in genetic incubators, on cots in the slammer, on the bunks and shitholes of the camps of our vast Motherland, to the operating-system clipboard by default, for it knows how to make noncommercial use and bring about a hostile takeover thereof, how to effectively run over, bend, wring out, sweep away, lower down, and snuff the victorious glory of the Russian Army in the crappy, plus in light of the secret installations of the Central Committee and the All-Union Central Council of Trade Unions, having crushed their fierce adversaries and the black ravens of the whole of progressive humanity with a Komsomol liar from the affiliated company using the right dudes from the Russian-Orthodox bank, preserving and enhancing the imperialist traditions of knightly hi-tech in special zones of national trust on the shores of a great Russian river, in monastic cells and monarchic editorials, in communistic dispatches from prison and in theological announcements, in sexual decrees and in black budgets, in daughters needlessly murdered for currency interventions, for bread and for salt, for whispers and for screams, for hence and for thence, for the presidential motorcade, for zoological anti-Sovietism, for the white birch beneath my window, for proletarian internationalism, for cock and for balls, for dollars and for euros, for iPhone 7s, for vertical authority and for the proper storage of the common fund, contrary to blood and soil, in spite of the black border and the white brotherhood, for the inexhaustible spiritual glory of androids, retirees, National Bolsheviks, grain growers, weavers, polar explorers, bodyguards, homosexuals, political strategists, doctors, anthropogeneticists, militants, serial killers, cultural figures and public servants, *okolnichi* and Metropolitans, strippers and Chippendales dancers, the mute, the deaf, and the dumb, the taxed and the taxer, the old and the young, all honest people bearing the name Vasily Buslayev, Sergius of Radonezh, and Yuri Gagarin, those who hate the enemies of the falsifiers of Russian history, indefatigably struggling with communism, Russian-Orthodox fundamentalism, fascism, atheism, globalism, agnosticism, neofeudalism, devilish confoundments, virtual witchcraft, verbal terrorism, computerized drug addiction, liberal spinelessness, aristocratic national patriotism, geopolitics, Manicheanism, Monophysitism, and Monothelitism, eugenics, botanics, applied mathematics, the theory of large and small numbers for peace and prosperity all around the world, for the Kingdom of God within us, for *that dude*, for the Lord Jesus Christ, for newlyweds, for the light at the end of the tunnel, for the Day of the Oprichnik, for the glory of mothers with many children, for those at sea, for the academicians Sakharov and Lysenko, for the Tree of Life, for the Baikal-Amur Mainline, KAMAZ trucks, and the Gulag, for Perun, for tellurium nails, for the smoke of the Fatherland, for youthfulness, for creativeness, for iconoclasticness, for the

TB and the ROC, for an honest name, for a cow's udder, for a warm stove, for a tallow candle, for a full glass, for a tinted window, for blue fog, for Father Makhno, in the name of the ideals of humanism, neoglobalism, nationalism, anti-Americanism, clericalism, and voluntarism, forever and ever. Amen.

4

SHE LEFT the entrance to her building at a quarter past six and my
heart skipped a beat; seeing her for the first time at a distance, I was
shocked, I couldn't have imagined that she would be so delicate and
miniature, not even a schoolgirl, but almost a Thumbelina, a little
girl from an ancient fairy tale, a miraculous elf in a little gray hat and
a short black cloak walking toward me along Gorokhovsky Lane.

"Hello!" Her little voice—boyish, unrefinedly enchanting, and
one I'd never confuse with any other—had been sounding in my
telephone all week, this ridiculous, damned, rubber-stretched week
that had almost driven me crazy, the week of our tormenting, idiotic
nonmeeting.

My hands stretch out toward her, reach her, touch her, hold her . . . I
want to convince myself that she's not a ghost, not a hologram in a
loudly crumpling cloak.

"Hello," she repeats, bowing her head and looking at me sullenly
with her miraculous greenish-gray eyes. "Why are ye so quiet?"

And I keep quiet. Smiling like an idiot.

"Did y' deign to wait long?"

I joyfully and negatively shake my head.

"I'm verily slammed with Humaniora." Squinting over at the
trash-covered lane, she fixes her scarf. "I can't fix my mind on what
to do. 'Twas only on the third day that those snooze-o-trons deigned
to hand out study guides. Can ye imagine?"

I can't imagine anything or anyone but you, my joy.

"Were ye truly not waiting long?" She wrinkles her delicate eyebrows sternly.

"Not at all," I pronounce, as if I'm just learning to speak.

"C'mon, let's go breathe some oxygen." She clings to my sleeve with her small hand and drags me along behind her. "I think yer replier is full of *baichi**—I call her and stick to the script: Please tell him that I'm unreachable, for Mom and my smartypants went sour a few days ago. Seems like a simple request, right? And she says to me: Sweetie, I have no one to pass the message to. Thy will be done, oh Lord, but is sticking in a red splinter verily most difficult?! *Yuivan!*† She's a mischief maker! Punish her!"

"I'll certainly punish her."

I walk alongside my joy like a zombie.

She holds my hand, her half boots clopping against the pavement and shattering puddles half-frozen overnight. It's too bad she's in her plainclothes and not a uniform. She's even more enchanting in her uniform. I saw her for the first time in her uniform on her school playground. Standing in a chalk circle, the little girls were playing their favorite game. A red ball flew up into the air, they shouted *her* name. She rushed to catch it, but didn't manage right away; the ball smacked against the pavement, bounced up, then she grabbed it, pressed it to the bosom of her brown uniform next to her EZ‡ badge, and shouted "*Shtander!*" And the fleeing schoolgirls froze, paralyzed by this harsh German word. She threw the ball at a lanky pal and it hit her on the head, which made her gasp loudly and unhappily, before she burst out laughing at what she'd done. She covered her mouth with her palm and crouched down on her lovely legs, shaking her little head with its charming braid, muttering something apologetic, fighting to suppress her wondrous laugh . . .

Her lips—exquisite, slightly turned out, and crowned by a tiny line of golden fuzz—let fall miraculous words:

"Everyone's lost their minds, I swear. I'm standing in line for beef yesterday on Apothecary Street when suddenly someone knock-knocks

*[Chinese] idiot
†[Chinese] idiocy
‡Eastern ZaMoscvorechye

'pon my back. What could it be? A hand holding a note: 'I'm mute, I humbly ask ye to buy me three pounds of beef tongues for the sake of Our Lord Jesus Christ.' And the main thing is it's not at all possible to make him out. Neither face nor body! I solely see yon hand! Where was the actual individuum?!"

She stops after this sentence and stomps her heel against the ground.

"He was probably blinded by your beauty, so he hid himself behind the backs of the other queue-standers," I joke awkwardly.

"What does beauty have to do with it! It was a trick, don't ye get it?! Some crook had fashioned a hand out of a stolen smartypants!"

"Ah, so that's what happened..."

"That's exactly what happened! And yon hand was calmly walking itself down the line. Maybe it was asking for alms and maybe it was sliding into peoples' pockets. And that was that!"

"Give me *your* hand," I say suddenly and take her little hand in its glove.

"Wherefore?" She looks at me sullenly.

I roll up the sleeve of her cloak and press my lips to her childish wrist, to its delicate veins, to its intoxicating warmth and tenderness. Without resisting, she looks at me silently.

"I'm crazy about you, Miss..." I whisper to the veins. "I'm crazy about you...crazy...crazy..."

Her fairy-tale, elven wrist is no thicker than two of my fingers. I kiss it, lips pressed against skin like a vampire's. Her second childish little hand touches my head.

"Ye went gray decidedly young," she pronounces quietly. "Forty-seven and almost all salt and pepper? Were ye at war?"

No, I wasn't at war. I embrace her and lift her to my lips. Suddenly, she slips nimbly out of my embrace—like a lizard—and runs off down the lane. I set off after her. She turns the corner. I lag behind. She runs excellently.

"Where are you going?" I follow her around the corner.

Her little black cloak with its gray hood flashes forwards. She runs along Old Basmannaya toward the gray hulk of the ring wall separating Moscow, where I live, from ZaMoscvorechye, where she lives.

She runs over, puts her back up against the wall, and spreads her arms out.

I rush over to my agile elf.

Her body is very small against the background of the twelve-meter-tall wall, which hangs over her like a murky, gray wave. I get frightened: What if this concrete tsunami suddenly drowns my joy? And I never get to hold her in my arms?

I sprint over to her.

She stands there with her eyes closed and her arms spread, pressing them against the wall.

"I love standing here," she pronounces without opening her eyes, "and listening to Moscow buzzing beyond the wall."

I lift her up like a feather and start to whisper into her big, child-ish ear.

"Have mercy on me, my angel."

"And what do ye want?" Her arms wrap around my neck.

"For you to become mine."

"Yer kept woman?"

I can sense a little laugh knocking around in her belly.

"My beloved."

"Ye want a secret date?"

"Yes."

"In a hotel chamber?"

"Yes."

"How much will ye pay?"

"Ten rubles."

"That's a lotta money," she pronounces into my cheek soberly, but with a kind of unchildlike sadness. "Can I . . . get down?"

I let her down. She straightens her beret. Her face is now right next to my solar plexus, where sporadic bursts of atomic desire are detonating.

"Shall we?" She takes me by the hand, as if I were her classmate.

We walk along the wall, kicking at trash as we go. She is swinging my arm. In ZaMoscvorechye, it's just as dirty and unkempt as it's always been. But I don't care about trash or ZaMoscvorechye or

Moscow or America or the Chinese on Mars. I marvel at the focused face of the one I long for. She thinks, then decides.

"Ye know what," she pronounces slowly and stops. "I'll do it."

I rake her up into my embrace once again and begin to kiss her warm, pale little face.

"Well, hold on . . ." She presses against my chest. "I shall solely be able to come next week."

"You're heartless!" I get down onto one knee in front of her. "I won't survive until next week! I'm begging you: anytime tomorrow at the Slavic Bazaar."

"Humaniora," she sighs. "I must needs write something and turn it in the day after tomorrow. Otherwise, they'll do something nasty to me. I've been on the black list since first quarter. I must needs fix that."

"I'm begging you! I'm begging you!" I kiss her old gloves.

"Believe me, I would hang Humaniora if Mama didn't suffer so much when they punish me. Her heart is most sensitive. And I don't have anyone other than Mama. Papa didn't come back from the war. My older brother didn't either. Devil take Humaniora . . ."

"When shall I be able to rejoice in you?" I squeeze her little hands.

Her grayish-green eyes squint thoughtfully at the wall.

"Perhaps . . . on Saturday."

"On Friday, my angel, on Friday!"

"No, on Saturday." She determinedly puts a period to our discussion.

Internally, she is much older than her childish years. These children of war grow up young. Her father died near Perm. We were different at their age . . .

"Okay, on Saturday. Does six suit you?"

"Mhmm . . ." she hums almost boyishly.

"There's an excellent restaurant, they have fantastic desserts, soft drinks, cakes, impossible chocolate towers . . ."

"I love pistachio ice cream, cocoa with cream, and white chocolate." She straightens my crooked scarf. "Get up, it's dirty here and yer wearing nice clothes."

Getting up off of my knees, I suddenly notice an *empty*, blackened tellurium nail next to me in a pile of trash. I pick it up and show it to her.

"You're all living the good life in ZaMoscvorechye!"

"Wow!" she exclaims, takes the nail, and twirls it around in front of her face.

I take her by the shoulders.

"So, on Saturday at six?"

"At six," she repeats, looking at the nail. "Yeah . . . someone's getting lucky. When I grow up, I'll definitely *test* it."

"What do you need tellurium for?"

"I want to see my brother and my daddy."

Someone else might have said they wanted to meet a handsome prince. This is what war does to children . . .

Three trucks filled with PodMoscovians in yellow robes pass by. They're singing something in the last truck.

With a sigh of envy, she throws the nail at the wall, sighs, and touches one of my buttons.

"I'm going."

"I'll walk with you."

"No, no." She resolutely stops me. "I'll go alone. Farewell already!"

She waves her little hand, turns around, and runs away. I accompany her with the gaze of a hungry lion. My doe is running away. And each glimpse of her knees and ankle boots, each sway of her cloak, and each shudder of her gray beret brings closer the moment when I, in the half dark of our chamber, having sucked at the hard candies of her body until my head spins, smoothly sit this ZaMoscvorechian elf down on the vertical plane of my passion and start to rock and cradle her over waves of tender oblivion, forcing her schoolgirl's lips to repeat that wizardly word: "Humaniora."

5

"RICHARD, steaming-hot red alert!" Zamira's voice sings out in Richard's right ear.

Moving through a deafening carnival crowd, he hears the beeping of numbers in his right ear, each of which also flashes red in his right eye, then begins to report.

"And so, dear viewers, this is Richard Scholz from RWTV* reporting live from Cologne where the long-awaited Cologne carnival continues in full force. We've been waiting for this Pink Monday for three years in order to take to the streets of our hometown. For three years, the people of Cologne have been effectively forbidden from doing so by their invaders, who consider our carnival to be 'the breath of Sheitan.' And now that *we* have triumphed, some members of our young government have already developed a dangerous syndrome: a short memory. They don't want to remember, they dismiss our concerns, they say there's no need to stir up the past, that we need to live in the present and move into the future like this joyful carnival crowd. But this is a dangerous tendency and it is our duty to say so until this 'short memory' syndrome relinquishes the ministers and the parliament. The carnival is fantastic! And I'd like to remind you at precisely this moment, on precisely this joyful day, remind you so that you and your children might never forget that, three years ago, nineteen transport Hercules took off from Bukhara at dawn on a quiet May morning and dropped off the airborne division known as the Taliban

*Rhenish-Westphalian TV

in Leverkusen, a suburb of Cologne. And so began three years of the Taliban's bitter occupation of Northern Rhine-Westphalia. So began another life. The Taliban forces were well prepared to seize power, having carried out large-scale underground work using radical Islamists from the local population, then . . ."

"Get to the point, Richard!" Zamira's voice sings out in his ear.

"And we all remember what happened next: executions, torture, corporal punishment, a ban on alcohol, cinemas, and theaters, the constant humiliation of women, depression, a stifling atmosphere, inflation, collapse, war . . . Let's make sure that, in our young state, in the Rhenish-Westphalian Republic, this never happens again, that the Wahhabi-Taliban hammer never again hangs over the Rhine, that we create a free state in which to live with our children, looking to the future with optimism, but always remembering, remembering, and remembering our great poet's words about the war . . ."

A choice of four quotes by Celan, Brecht, Heym, and Grünbein appear over his right eye.

"'We drink the black milk of dawn in the evening, at night, and at noon.' For three years, our people drank the black milk of occupation and many Westphalians dug themselves those very same 'graves in the sky / in which we shall have space to lie,' so let us bow to those graves and to those heroes of the Resistance so as to move forwards into a new future with neither fear nor reproach—"

"Look out, Richard, the president and chancellor are on your left!" Zamira's voice buzzes like a wasp in Richard's ear.

"Friends, ahead of us and to the left, I see our president, General Kazimir von Lutzov, and Chancellor Shafak Bashturk. As I have already said in previous reports, they joined the carnival crowd on Appellhofplatz and walked here—to the Old Market—along Brückenstrasse. Before they reached the market, they were on foot and it was extremely difficult to reach them even for me, the ex-Wushu master of Cologne, but now that they've started riding horses, wonderful, knightly war horses—the president on a white horse with a cross-emblazoned white blanket and the chancellor on a black horse with a half-moon-emblazoned green blanket—this is symbolic, my friends, this is wonderful and relevant, as it symbolizes not just the politics of our state, but the alliance of two cultures, two civilizations, and two religions—Catholicism and Islam—an alliance which helped our state to overcome an insidious and powerful enemy and helped us to survive a brutal war. The president and chancellor are animated, cheerful, and full of strength, they throw candy to the crowd from enormous horns of plenty, they look like the actual knights, which they, in fact, are. All of us remember General von Lutzov's famous winter campaign, how he advanced on Cologne from the Dutch border, and we haven't forgotten the wartime reports: the liberation of Oberhausen, the gory battles near Duisburg, the brilliant Düsseldorf operation, and—the event that is already considered to be a deeply important moment in contemporary history—the Bochum *coup de main* formed by General von Lutzov's army that broke the Taliban's back and the enemy's subsequent retreat—their flight, to be more precise—became inevitable, when the Taliban cutthroats ran for the eastern border in total panic and their ideological mastermind, the so-called Burning Imam, found his—"

"That's enough about the president, Richard. Move on to the chancellor."

"—well-deserved death on the streets of Troisdorf, a town destroyed by the Taliban. And, at this time, Shafak Bashturk, the future chancellor of our state, conducted heroic and painstaking work in the Cologne underground, creating his own army of the Resistance, forging the Excalibur of victory in the cellars of the city, and ensuring the fall of the Taliban. This heroic individual, a denizen of the Ruhr Valley and a former heating engineer, became a living legend during the occupation, an underground hero who rallied a coalition of like-minded Muslims burning with hatred for this barbaric Taliban regime. The price on his head promised by the Taliban didn't just go up every month, it went up every day! His army, the Serbest El,* deprived the

*[Turkish] the Free Hand

invaders of a quiet life. Thanks to the wisdom and heroism of the soldiers of the Serbest El, the ground literally burned beneath the sandals of the Taliban and their—"

"That's enough about the past, Richard. The present! The present!"

"—and their days were numbered. But now we can all rejoice, not only in this military victory, but in this carnival, the first in three years, this miraculous, joyful, beautiful, boisterous Pink Monday, look how many shades of pink are in the festive crowd and how many children are dressed up as flowers with their heads made to resemble pink buds! These are the children of our future, the children who are destined to become the citizens of our young state and to keep the peace won by their fathers in the fields near Duisburg, in the suburbs of Bochum, and on the streets of Cologne. May they be happy! The president and chancellor are throwing candy out into the crowd from golden horns of plenty—does this not represent hope for peace, prosperity, and well-being?"

"The public, Richard, interviews!"

"Friends, the time has now come to speak with those participating in the carnival." He turns to a middle-aged couple dressed up as medieval jesters. "Hello! Where are you from?"

"From Pulheim! Hello everyone! Hello Cologne!"

"Just seeing you, it's obvious that you're thrilled and happy to be here today!"

"Of course! The carnival is back! It's awesome!"

"The carnival is back! And with it, a peaceful life belongs to Pulheim once again."

"Oh yes! It's a symbol! We won! Our son voluntarily enlisted in von Lutzov's army."

"Is he still alive?"

"Yes, thank God! Unfortunately, he's now in Oslo on business, he really wanted to be here with us. And he *is*!" The couple stretches out a smartypants and calls up a hologram of a young man. "Hello, Martin!"

"Hi, Mom and Dad! I'm right there with you! Hi from Oslo!"

"Hi, Martin, this is Richard Scholz from RWTV! You're really going to regret not taking the time off from work to be here and breathe in the fresh air of freedom!"

"I'm really really gonna regret it . . . That's exactly goshdarn right! I already regret it! I'm an idiot, no doubt about it! Wow! I can almost taste the air!"

"It's just amazing how nice it is here, son! It's like we're all gonna be connected forever!"

"Awesome! I can hear the voices of the people of Cologne and it's driving me crazy here in quiet Oslo."

"Martin, your parents just told us that you were in General von Lutzov's army. What cities did you liberate?"

"I managed to fight only in Duisburg and Düsseldorf because I got a concussion just before the Bochum *coup de main* and stopped being part of the process, so to speak."

"Were you there on the first Victory Day in Düsseldorf?"

"Of course! It was awesome! Von Lutzov is a great man. I'm happy that we have a president like him!"

"He's riding a white horse right over there!"

"Wow! Awesome! Dang, what an idiot I am not to have stayed!"

"You're with us, son, you're here!"

"That's Shafak Bashturk, Mom! A hero of the underground! Oh man would I love to shake his hand. Wow! Now I'm gonna go to a bar and get drunk!"

"Just don't drink Norwegian aquavit, son! It causes depression!"

"Only beer, Martin!"

"I know they don't serve any Reissdorf* there, son."

"Only drink local beers! Only local ones!"

"Got it, Dad."

"Tell me, Martin, is everything in Oslo still as calm and quiet as it was before?"

"Yeah, the Norwegians were lucky. Everything got done here without any bloodshed. The war didn't reach 'em, the buildings are

*A kind of beer

still standing, and only a couple of missiles fell. Not like it was for us. Wow! I can see trolls and gnomes! That's awesome!"

"We're going to head over to the trolls now! Good luck to you, Martin!"

Three biguns dressed up as trolls are carrying gnomes throwing candies out into the crowd on their shoulders. Richard makes his way over to them.

"Richard, stop! The trolls can wait. Sabina Girgich is right behind you," Zamira buzzes in his ear.

Richard turns around and moves backwards through the crowd. Tall and muscular, Girgich is walking in a group of her Amazon companions, who are just as tall and muscular as she is. They are dressed up as the elven warriors from *The Lord of the Rings*.

"Hello, Sabina! This is Richard Scholz from RWTV. Our viewers and I are happy to see you, the heroine of the Bochum *coup de main*, here in this festival crowd!"

"Greetings to all ye who are worthy." Sabina raises her hand proudly—with a sense of her own worthiness.

Her friends also raise their hands.

"How's your new hand?"

"It's still not mine, but it does everything I make it do." Sabina smiles.

"My dear viewers, if anyone doesn't remember the story of Sabina Girgich—and I'm sure there are only a handful of you who don't— then let me remind you: the Bochum *coup de main*, the university building where the Taliban's last pocket of resistance was located, the humanitarian corps, the commander of the third regiment George Maria Hutten's jeep, a grenade thrown by the Taliban, and Sabina Girgich grabbing the grenade with her hand, saving the commander and losing that hand. And before that there was a battle near Hustadtring, during which Sabina knocked out a Taliban armored personnel carrier in her wasp. She's a hero! It's an honor for the carnival that heroes like Sabina Girgich and her warrior friends are participating in it! Are you happy today, Sabina?"

"I'm happy that evil was defeated and that the black tower with the All-Seeing Eye collapsed. We knocked it down!"

Her Amazon companions let forth a war cry.

"Wonderful! The Sauron of the Taliban has been defeated and the people rejoice! What would you like to wish our viewers today, Sabina?"

"I wish all of the inhabitants of our Rhenish kingdom a Golden Wind, a Clean Shore, and a New Dawn. Here's to our New Dawn!"

"To the New Dawn!" the Amazons shout.

"The wonderful war cry of the Bochum Valkyries! We haven't forgotten it! Have you already been back to your native Bochum, Sabina?"

"My house on Auf dem Aspei was destroyed by orcs, my beloved Brust was incinerated in the goblin's crematorium, my wingèd Sylvia met with Eternity, and my golden-haired Masha fled to America. But I still have the Rod, I've removed the White Veil from the Jade Gates, and I believe in the Overcoming of the Gray Mist. Just as before, we're floating down the River of Pure Love."

Sabina's companions let forth the Cry of the Valkyries.

"Wonderful! I'm sure that your River of Pure Love flows exclusively into the Rhine today! Sabina, you wonderful Amazons, be happy! On behalf of all of our viewers, I kiss your beautiful, updated hand, the hand of a new and peaceful life!"

He gets down on one knee in front of Sabina and kisses her hand.

"To the right, Richard! To the right, to the right!" Zamira buzzes. "It's Tsvetan Mordkovich!"

"Look who's right next to us, friends! Tsvetan Mordkovich, the renowned ace fighter pilot, the aerial hussar who defended the sky of our country, bringing down stinging blows from the air! Hello, Tsvetan!"

"Hello!"

"You're here with your family and it's so big!"

"Yep, the whole team is here today!"

"What can you, a hero of the skies, say to our viewers?"

"I'm very glad to be here today along with everyone else…"

"Finally back down to earth, right?"

"Yes, back on earth with my loved ones and everyone else I was protecting."

"Thanks to you, we can safely walk around on this earth today without fear of being bombed or of explosions and whistling bullets. Air raid sirens no longer howl out over Cologne. This is thanks to your aerial feats, Tsvetan! You personally shot down four Taliban planes, four vultures tormenting our peaceful skies…"

"Yes, I managed to do something. The main thing is I wasn't shot down. The sky helped."

"And the sky is something else today, Tsvetan! Like we put in a special order for it—not a cloud in sight!"

"The sky is beautiful and we're all very happy…"

"That the dark clouds have dispersed, right?"

"Yes, that everything's A-OK now…"

"That there's only sun in the sky, right? And no black silhouettes!"

"Yeah, a peaceful sky's a great thing."

"Well put, Tsvetan. Do you want to say hello to your fellow soldiers from the Westphalian Falcon Squadron?"

"Oh yeah, my dudes! Oh yeah, you aerial hussars! I remember and love all of you! We did it! Long live the carnival!"

"Long live the carnival! Thank you, Tsvetan. Now, my friends, we'll go over to the trolls!"

"Stop, Richard, Fatima's taking over, you're free to go."

Richard removes a piece of smart plastic from his shoulder and puts it away in his pocket. He makes his way through the crowd with some difficulty, exits onto Filzengraben Strasse, finds his auto-mobile, unfastens it, stands on it, then rolls along the embankment all the way to his home. He enters the building, goes up to the third floor, opens the door with a key, walks into the entryway, and takes off his jacket.

HIS WIFE SILKE'S VOICE (*amplified by a speaker*): It's you?
RICHARD (*hanging up his jacket*): It's me.

SILKE'S VOICE: Do you want to eat?
RICHARD: Very much so.
SILKE'S VOICE: Eat without me, then.
RICHARD: You already ate?
SILKE'S VOICE: Not yet.

Richard walks over to the small kitchen with its old furnishings, opens the old-fashioned refrigerator, gets out a bottle of beer, opens it, and drinks from its neck. Looks into the refrigerator, grabs a rice bowl filled with not very fresh chicken salad and a couple of sausages. Puts the kettle on, puts the sausages into a saucepan, and pours boiling water over them. Eats the chicken salad standing up, nibbling at the rice bowl and looking out the window. Outside the window is a narrow courtyard with an old chestnut tree, rusty bicycles, and overflowing garbage bins. Having finished the chicken salad and the bowl, he takes the sausages from the saucepan and eats them quickly, washing them down with beer. Having emptied the bottle, he puts it into a plastic box for empty beer bottles. Picks up an apple, takes a bite, walks out of the kitchen, walks down the narrow hallway, walks into the bathroom and urinates, holding the apple between his teeth. Then freezes, as if he were completely paralyzed. Spits out the unfinished apple into the toilet, groans angrily, leaves the bathroom abruptly, slamming the door, buttoning his pants on the go, and muttering to himself, "Shit, shit, shit!" Begins to almost run down the hallway and enters the only other room in his apartment. The room is lined with antique furniture, which, judging from its appearance, often gets moved from place to place. Some items are wrapped in plastic. There's a glass house on the oval dining table. This is Silke's house— she's a littlun, a pretty blond with a tight figure. Her height doesn't exceed that of a three-hundred-milliliter beer bottle. Silke is working out on a miniature ski simulator in the attic of the house. She's wearing athletic gear. Rhythmic music rings out audibly through the little house. Richard runs up to the table, rests his hands on its surface, and hovers up over the house.

RICHARD: Silke, I need a nail!

SILKE (*continuing to work out*): That's good news.

RICHARD: I need a nail!

SILKE: This is so boring, darling.

RICHARD (*shouting*): I need a nail!

SILKE: You're making the roof shake, Richard. It could fall off.

Restraining himself with great difficulty, Richard sits down in a chair and places his clenched fists on the table.

SILKE (*continuing to work out*): You look super aggressive. You're exhausted, I get it. I was watching your coverage.

RICHARD: Gimme a nail.

SILKE: Calm down, darling.

RICHARD: Gimme a nail!

SILKE: I'll be done in three minutes, then I'll come to you and we can calm down together.

RICHARD (*slaps his hand on the table*): I need a nail!

SILKE (*continues to work out*): Richard, you don't need a nail.

RICHARD: Gimme a nail!

SILKE: Did you take your medicine, Richard?

RICHARD: Open the door, Silke!

SILKE: I won't open it.

RICHARD (*losing his temper*): I'm gonna smash your little shack to shit!

SILKE: No, you won't.

RICHARD (*hysterically*): Open up, you witch.

SILKE: Take your medicine, darling. You only took it this morning.

RICHARD (*grabs a chair and swings it back*): Just watch out, bitch . . .

SILKE (*moving calmly and measuredly*): I'll watch out, I'll watch out . . .

Richard throws the chair at his bed with a howl: Collapses onto the floor.

SILKE: You're just tired. I never liked that carnival. It's exhausting.
RICHARD (*his head hanging down impotently*): Gimme a nail...
SILKE: Take your medicine. You'll feel better real quick.
RICHARD (*screams*): Turn off that goddamn music!

Silke turns off the music, gets off the ski simulator, and hangs a towel around her neck.

SILKE: Darling, I understand how hateful it is for you to spout all of that patriotic nonsense. But why are you taking it out on me when no one in the world's closer to you than me?

Richard is silent.

SILKE: You did everything super professionally. I'm sure they'll confirm you.
RICHARD (*his head bowed*): That decision doesn't depend on the quality of my work.
SILKE: *Everything* matters during the trial period.
RICHARD: In my case, it only depends on that bitch.
SILKE: They're only interested in your *psychosoma*. Everyone already knows what a pro you are.
RICHARD (*shakes his head*): Well, they can go fuck themselves...
SILKE: They've already fucked themselves, Richard...they fucked themselves, then they unfucked themselves. You have to take that into account, darling.

Silke goes down to the second floor, enters a transparent shower stall, gets undressed, and stands underneath the shower.

RICHARD: We're still not gonna have money for another month.
SILKE: Does that scare you? We won't die of hunger.
RICHARD: I need a dose.
SILKE: That's what you should've started in with. Not "We have no money."

RICHARD: Just one. And I'll come to my senses.

SILKE: No, you'll lose control and they won't take you back.

RICHARD: One dose! I can't lose control from one dose!

SILKE: One dose won't be enough. And we don't have enough money for five, as you yourself just explained.

RICHARD: If you sell one nail, we'll have five hundred marks.

SILKE: To buy you a dose for twenty marks? Wonderful arithmetic, darling.

RICHARD: We don't even have two marks! It's never been like this before! And I'm still in debt!

SILKE: Everything'll fall into place when you're confirmed, darling. Take your medicine.

RICHARD: Gimme a nail.

SILKE: You know that the nails are our nest egg. If I give you a nail, you'll just buy five hundred doses. And the whole rigmarole we know so painfully well will start all over again ...

RICHARD: I'll just buy one, one single dose! I swear!

SILKE: O, swear not, ye glorious knight!

RICHARD: We don't have any money! The situation is critical! Not a single pfenning!

SILKE: No one has money right now. As our president says: the postwar reforms are slowly, but surely gaining momentum. And the price of nails is creeping up. Eight percent in three days. In a couple of months, my tellurium inheritance will have doubled.

RICHARD: One nail, Silke! We have eight of 'em! Just one! And we'll feel normal again!

SILKE (*gets out of the shower, dries herself off with a towel*): I feel totally normal. So stop asking.

RICHARD: Are you ... that much of a bitch?!

SILKE: You chose to be with me.

RICHARD: Can't you see that I'm sick?

SILKE: Take your medicine.

RICHARD (*screams*): You can stick that shitty medicine you know where!! I'm sick! Seriously!

SILKE (*puts on her bathrobe*): Are you strong or weak, Richard? When you carried me across Bochum in your pocket when the city was burning, I knew that you were strong. And when we were hiding in the basement. And when you roasted dog meat. And when you ran through that tunnel. And when you fought off three invalids. You were strong. I was proud of you. Insanely proud. You weren't thinking about drugs back then. But when the war ended, you became a pussy overnight. What's with you?

RICHARD: I just need one nail. One! To come to my senses.

SILKE (*screams*): I'm not gonna give you a nail!

Richard sits in silence: Silke goes down to the first floor, walks into the kitchen, drinks some water, sits down at the table, puts her feet up onto it. Just sits there drinking water.

SILKE: In a month, you'll be working for the state and they'll pay your salary. And we'll have money.

RICHARD: I . . . need . . .

SILKE: You need a dose. Fine. I have a stash.

RICHARD: What stash? Like . . . your grandma's diamond ring? No one needs any dumbass diamonds these days!

SILKE: That's right. No one wants diamonds right now. So no . . . it's not the ring.

Silke stands up, walks upstairs to her bedroom, sits down on the bed, bends over, pulls a suitcase out from under the bed, and opens it. There's a vibrator in the suitcase.

RICHARD: The "violet lotus"?

SILKE: The "violet lotus."

RICHARD: What . . . you don't need it anymore?

SILKE: I have three other vibrators.

RICHARD: But you said that . . .

SILKE: This is the best one? Yes, I said that six months ago. But everything changes, my darling, time passes, and old desires with them. New ones come into being.

RICHARD: And you think that it'll ...

SILKE: They'll snatch it out of our hands.

RICHARD: But logically speaking, wouldn't vibrators be in demand *during* wartime and not afterwards?

SILKE: That's true for people. But it's the other way round for littluns.

RICHARD: I'm still not getting it ...

SILKE: You're obviously exhausted from the postvictory carnival. I mean, think about it, men come back from war to their wives and lovers. They're heroes. They bear the powerful erections of victors. And the littluns? They didn't fight, they just sat in ratholes shaking with fear. The thunder of victory set to rumbling, so they crawled back into the light. But they left their *potency* in those ratholes. What can such a lover do? Just get drunk and tell his girlfriend about great feats performed by biguns, maybe give her a foot massage on a good day.

RICHARD: Maybe ... you're right. (*He laughs relievedly.*) You're smart, Silke!

SILKE: A smart bitch, right?

RICHARD: You ... (*He sighs.*) You know you're all that I've got.

SILKE: I know.

Silke picks up the suitcase, walks down the stairs, walks out of the little house, and steps out onto the table.

SILKE (*hands him the suitcase*): Littluns will give you at least eighty marks for this at the flea market.

Richard holds out his hand, but Silke hides the suitcase behind her back. Richard freezes.

SILKE: But someone called me a bitch pretty damn recently ...

RICHARD: Forgive your idiot.

SILKE (*walks over to the edge of the table*): On your knees!

Richard gets down onto his knees. His head is level with the tabletop.

SILKE (*sticks her knee out of her bathrobe*): Kiss it!

Richard stretches out to her with his lips and kisses her knee. Silke hands him the suitcase.

RICHARD (*whispers*): Do you want to work out on my tongue, darling?
SILKE: Oh no, darling. Everything in time. Tonight, in the evening, we'll set up jumps with obstacles . . . (*She looks around.*) Eesh, there's shit everywhere again. I can't stand your mess!
RICHARD: I'll clean up everything. (*He takes the chair away from the bed and puts it next to the table.*)

Silke takes a broom from her entryway and begins to sweep the table. Richard puts the suitcase with the vibrator away into his pocket.

SILKE: Buy yourself some food too. Buy me yogurt, nattō, protoplasms, and juice. And please—don't buy two torpedoes. Not today, in any case.
RICHARD: Alright, my dear. I'll only buy one. I swear! (*He holds up two fingers.*)

He makes his way over to the hallway, but suddenly stops and turns back to Silke.

SILKE (*continues sweeping*): What is it now?
RICHARD: Show me.
SILKE: Now?
RICHARD: Now.

With an unhappy sigh, Silke drops the broom, walks into the house, walks up to the second floor and into her bedroom, walks over to what looks like a gun cabinet, and puts her hand to the lock. The cabinet opens. Inside, instead of rifles, are eight tellurium nails. Silke takes a nail out of the cabinet, takes off her robe, puts the head of the nail to her naked breasts, and takes aim at Richard.

SILKE: Bang!

Richard stares at her, then turns and walks away.

6

THE GLORY of the partisan detachment named in honor of the hero of the First Ural War Miguel Eliazar thunders through all of Ural. Created by the underground regional committee of the Communist Party of Ural only six months ago, the detachment became a combat formation to be reckoned with during the struggle against Barabinskian White Guard invaders. The backbone of the detachment is made up of genuine patriots of an insidiously enslaved Motherland, professional soldiers, who fought not just in the Second War, but, as a rule, in the First War as well. They fought in the besieged city of Nizhny Tagil, went on the attack near Karabash, and experienced the full weight of trench warfare near Magnitogorsk. The firmament of Ural has been abundantly watered with the blood of such distinguished fighters as Fyodor Loza, Victor Katz, Volisha Mouret, and Harry Quiller. The detachment is led by the communist Alisher Isanbayev, also the bearer of a state order. Under his command, the partisans carried out 213 military operations not only against the Barabinskian Tatar invaders, but also against the rabid dog Karop's regime, against Wahhabi separatists, and even against Mongolian imperialists, who were reaching for Uralian lands with their bloody tentacles.

We're sitting with Captain Isanbayev in a narrow trench, dug out only this morning. It's nighttime now and the detachment is resting after a three-day passage. The commander is restrained and laconic. His harsh face is lit sparingly by a smart bulb. Dotted with scars and outfitted with a dyrolone cheekbone and the piercing gaze of a red binocular eye, Captain Isanbayev's face is the face of the Uralian

People who have rebelled against their invaders, the face of a war of liberation that has spread with the speed of a forest fire, not just to the foothills of Southern Ural, but also to Northern Ural. Taking a sip of his beloved oolong from a worn-looking regimental mug, the commander calmly recounts bold raids behind White Guard lines, the demolition of roadblocks and railroads, a recent bout of hand-to-hand combat with the Wahhabis, and a surprise attack on a Mongol landing party. I write down the captain's laconic replies in the old-fashioned way—with pencil on paper. Smartypantses are strictly forbidden by the detachment.

"These warriors have earned themselves eternal glory," the captain says, remembering a beastly September sortie against a Karopian roadblock. "The five of us didn't just manage to cut down eight Karopians, we also snatched a *smart* head. For as long as the head was alive, it served us well; for four days and nights, it guided our Karop-fucking."

The commander winks at me mischievously with his single eye. Scorched by the flame of war, this laconic man has lived through a lot. His detachment leads a harsh life of fighting—performing daily feats of glory in the name of their future republic and of the future triumph of justice and socialism.

I ask about their provisions, about their relations with the civilian population, and about the leadership role of the underground regional committee. The commander answers in great detail, but complains about nothing—not about interruptions in the supply of ammunition and medicine, not about skirmishes with local kulaks, and not about two regional committee messengers who were blown up by mines. Captain Isanbayev and his warriors are prepared for any and all difficulties.

"Everything can be overcome when there's a goal to be attained. We're fighting for the USU, everyone knows that," he says. "The impoverished locals are with us, that's the main thing. The local peasants've had it up to here hearing about the Barabinskian 'economic miracle' when they're carrying all the brutality of land reform on their own backs."

Captain Isanbayev's detachment is locked in a fight to the death for the United States of Ural. Those three letters—USU—mean a lot, not only to these warriors, but also to the Uralian peasantry, to Uralian miners, and to all of the honest workers of Ural who yearn for a fair life. It is for their sake that feats of glory are performed and for their future happiness that partisan blood is spilled. USU is the free future of Ural…

I ask the commander very detailed questions about the party leadership. The detachment has a strong, unbreakable connection with the underground regional committee.

"The secretary of the regional committee Bo Zuo-Fei is doing everything he can for us," the captain says. "He's an intelligent man, attentive, honest in the party way, and principled. We keep nothing from him and no 'toads at the well' bother us. The tellurium nails always arrive on time. And I have all of the regional-committee directives right here." The commander taps his finger against his binocular eye.

Then I ask the commander my long-prepared "uncomfortable" question.

"And what about the Cubans?"

The partisan's face grows stern and he looks off to the side, where holograms of Che Guevara, Liu Shaoqi, and Eliazar shine on a rough log wall.

"We're ready to welcome anyone who wants to fight for freedom into the detachment," the commander replies. "Just not those who stained themselves with double-dealing during the First War. My warriors and I don't recognize the amnesty granted to the Cubans."

"But Comrade Captain, your position is at odds with the July directive of the regional committee," I remark.

"On this question, yes," Isanbayev retorts fiercely. "My warriors and I remain faithful to our oath. When we triumph, then the Communist Party of Ural can judge us."

The conversation is over. The commander has to get at least a little sleep after such a difficult day. Yes, there are no easy days for Partisan Detachment No. 19…

I say goodbye and leave the trench. Impenetrable forest darkness is all around me. I hear only sentries in the pine trees communicating with each other by way of birdcalls. I feel my way over to my hole. It will be hard to fall asleep after such a tense day, a day that, after my midnight conversation with the commander, seems to have been almost impossibly long ...

A war of liberation is making its way down the roads of Ural with its heavy, but victorious, stride.

There shall be no peace here for the enemies of working people—neither day nor night. The partisan bullet shall find them everywhere and nothing shall save the Barabinskian invaders and their Karopian henchmen from a just punishment.

The grapes of the people's anger are ripening.

The harsh Uralian forest is stirring.

7

"COUNT, my good man, czarist Russia was knocked over by the English using German hands and gutted by Stalin's yid commissars. They sold the offal to the capitalists for currency and stuffed the insides with Marxism-Leninism."

The prince was the first to reach the fallen elk. He looked at it, handed his rifle and cartridge belt to his huntsmen, and waved his glove: the hunt was over. The handsome, mustached trumpeter brought his horn to his lips and blew. Encouragingly valedictory sounds rang through the autumnal forest. The huntsman pulled a cleaver from a leather scabbard and ably drew it across the elk's throat. The animal's dark blood surged steamingly onto the carpet of fallen leaves. The hounds were no longer barking, but whining and yipping in a small pack. Their three keepers led them away.

"Russia keeled over on its own, Prince." The count handed his carbine to a very young huntsman, tried to take out his cigar case, but instead took out a tellurium clip, cursed, put it away, felt around for the cigar case, took it out, opened it, and lit a small cigar. "Its insides deigned to rot so much during the nineteenth century that no bullets were needed to knock it over. The colossus keeled over from a single German pellet."

"It was the Krauts, the underground yids, and the English who knocked it over." The prince began to look around without listening to the count. "Trishka! Where are you?"

"We're here, Your Excellency." Gray-haired Trifon ran over in his silly dolman.

"Set up a bivouac o-o-over there." The prince gestured with his goatee over toward a lonely oak.

"Yessir!"

The count took a small, flat flask of cognac out of his jacket pocket, unscrewed it, and handed it to the prince.

"Russia couldn't withstand the blow of the German military machine in fourteen. How do your yids have anything to do with that?"

The prince took a sip from the flask.

"Here's to the hunt . . . All right then, my good man, here's a popular riddle from the Soviet era: Six commissars are sitting around the table, but the riddle is, 'Who's sitting underneath the table?' The answer: the twelve tribes of Israel. Have you seen the lists of commissars' names? Ninety percent of them were yids. The leaders of the Cheka, the NKVD, and the Joint State Political Directorate—who were they?"

"Yids." The count nodded, taking a sip from the flask. "And so what? Yes, they were quick to take on the dirty work. It turned out they had stronger nerves than Russians. And fewer prejudices."

"Dirty work: murder, in other words!"

"Yes, murder . . ." The count glanced thoughtfully up at the high autumnal sky. "What would we do without it? Hecatombs are indispensable. Overpopulation. Everyone wants a good life."

"After Russia had keeled over onto its back, the Bolsheviks raped her with industrialization." The prince reached for the flask. "And she died. Stalin's troglodytes danced their boogie-woogie over her beautiful corpse for seventy years."

"At least they fed the poor. How many people were starving in Mother Russia under the czar?" The count sneered.

"Surely you're joking . . ." The prince waved his hand. "Fed the poor! After they shot them, that is."

"No, Prince, the first thing they did was feed them."

They suddenly fell silent, watching as two huntsmen began to nimbly flay the fallen elk. They smelled offal in the air. Trishka ran over with skewers.

"Just not the liver!" ordered the prince.

"The heart, your excellency?"

"And the fillet."

"Yessir."

A duck and a drake flew over the clearing.

The count took a sip from the flask, looked at the elk's half-closed eye, and began to speak thoughtfully:

"In each eye, a deer is running. In each glance, a spear is flying..."

"What?" the prince asked.

"A Khlebnikov poem came back to me... But if we're to speak seriously, I have more complaints about the Russians than I do yids or Germans. Nowhere on earth is there a people more indifferent to their own fate. If this is a national trait, then such a nation deserves no sympathy."

"As Stalin said, 'I have no other people.'"

"We should've started to repopulate Russia with Krauts when the time came, we really should've. The Bolsheviks didn't realize this. Catherine II started the process, but there was no one left to finish it..."

"Russia came into being so as to..."

"—so as to teach the world a great lesson. The lesson was read out. The world heard. A lesson to make one's hair stand on end."

"God rest her soul." The prince took a sip of cognac. "But everything's all right now."

"In what sense?"

"Russia's image is all right. And more generally—everything's fine! In any case, I'm happy with *our* state."

"Well..." The count looked around with a smile. "The Kingdom of Ryazan is a bit more respectable than the Uralian Republic, of course."

"Woah there! To whom do you deign to compare us? With the 'Bughouse'? After the accession of our Andryushenka, everything will be even more respectable in terms of economy and culture, most venerable Count. And not just Tverian or Kalugian culture! *Chez vous* in Moscovia as well."

"These days, Prince, it's only the dead who don't kick at my Moscovia. And how they used to grovel at our feet for *yarlyki*..."

"I've always hated your Moscovia! Since I was a child!" The prince waved his hands. "But reproach me not. When post-Sovietude collapsed, I was a teenager. I didn't truly understand. But I fierce-ly hat-ed Moscow! And my grandfather hated it when he went there to shake the money tree! And my great-grandfather when he had to head there for *shabashka* work! Yessir, a hereditary hatred! Even later, when Moscovia held out an olive branch, when it was struck by famine, when wide prospects were soiled over with potato fields, and when the city smelled of cannibalism... And when the communokingdom came into being, I began to hate it even more. A New Economic Policy, my left foot! We should give PodMoscovia to the Chinese! And build a wall around it! Yessir, now that would be smart! I hate Moscovia!"

"Be careful that *ours* don't attack *yours*."

"We have six delightful little hydrogen bombs, my good man! Such beautiful bombs! Painted by artisans to look like matryoshka dolls! If anything happens, we'll toss one of them to the Moscovians! Yessir! As a gift!"

"As you wish, Prince... I just want to tuck into something tasty."

"To fuck into something *what*?"

"You misheard me. To tuck... to tuck into something tasty."

"Of course! By all means! Let's head for the bivouac."

The prince took the count by the arm and led him to the oak tree. The count's massive figure hung over the small, mobile figure of the prince. Deaf in one ear, the prince was speaking louder and faster than usual.

"You're younger than me by half, Count, there's much you don't understand. Think about it, my good man, in what language are we speaking?"

"In Russian, it would seem."

"Yessir! Exactly so! In Russian! And not in a post-Soviet pidgin dialect of our great language! It took thirty years to find our way back to a clean stream. *Ordo ab chao*. The state is a language. Whatever that language is, such shall be the order of the country. And who was the first to understand yon principle? Us—the Ryazanians. Who was the first to reform their language? Who banned pidgin dialects of Russian? Foolish foreign words? All of these *rebrandings*, *holdings*, and *marketings*? Who set the example for everyone else? For your Moscovia as well? We did!"

"My deceased daddy always used to say how if they used the word 'internet' at school, they had to kneel in peas..."

"Yes, they had to kneel in peas or they were whipped! But what's the result thereof? Our ears are captivated by vibrant, proper Russian speech! Civic order! In our state, at least...Don't you agree?"

"About civic order...I'm not sure. People speak correctly, I won't argue about that. But those doing the speaking..."

"Leave you with some questions?"

"Frankly, it's not the people as such, but their appearance. Too many ugly mugs."

"And that, Count, my good man, is the legacy of the Soviets."

"I'm not sure...you can't blame the Soviets for everything..."

"The total genocide of the Russian people carried out over sixty years must not be forgotten. The Bolsheviks extinguished the leading lights of the country in order to clear the field for yid cockleburs and yokel saltbush. And Mother Saltbush just keeps on making babies! It's hard to pull her out by the root!"

"Mhmm...ugly mugs, endless ugly mugs all round the globe..."

"Come again?"

"I was just remembering a Pasternak poem..."

"And the architecture? The attention paid to one's domicile? In what era has that ever been at play for the Russian people?"

"Never. The people always lived in a stable, while the elite built themselves devil knows what."

"Without any understanding of what they actually want: Versailles, the Palace of the Soviets, or—"

"The Empire State Building."

"I'll ask you then, Count: When did this new conception of the domicile first appear among us?"

"When we split up."

"Yessir! When we split up, my good man! That's when we started to pay attention to our domiciles! To our cities! Today, in my city, there's not a single building constructed without intentionality! God is the city architect! We all bow down to Him! Yessir, He's been granted special powers! The face of the city! Of my ci-ty! I live in it and shall be held responsible for it before history—before world culture—if you'll forgive the pathos!"

"I shan't . . ." The count smirked, taking a drink from his flask.

"How do we build our cities now? At-ten-tive-ly! Responsibly! Taste! Heritage! Caution! Diligence!"

"Diligence . . ." the count repeated, glancing into the darkening forest. "Now, diligence is the eternal companion of the Russian people."

"It 'gan to smell of Old Rus' on the Central Russian Upland after the collapse alone."

"I agree. Before that there were other smells . . ."

"Just so! Sit down, let's have a drink, and I'll tell you one story in particular."

They sat down on a rug beneath an old oak that had already lost its foliage. The prince's regimental table was standing on the rug and covered over with traditional bivouac chasers, as well as pepper vodka in a round green bottle braided with copper wire. No servants were allowed on the hunt, so the prince filled the silver shot glasses himself.

"Here's to the hunt, Count!" The prince raised his glass with his slightly trembling, thin-fingered hand.

"Here's to the hunt, Prince!" The shot glass disappeared into the count's broad hand.

They drank and began to nibble at the chasers. In the meantime, Trishka had agilely stuck pieces of elk heart and fillet onto skewers and begun to roast them in the tongues of flame flashing up from the campfire.

"After post-Soviet Russia collapsed and the states of the so-called post-post-Soviet space had started to come into being, our first ruler Ivan Vladimirovich once invited us, the new Ryazanian nobles, to pay him a visit. An exchange of opinions, a banquet, Serbian folk songs, in short, all the usual things. And then, just after midnight, when only the chosen circle remained, he led us...where do you think he led us?"

"To the maidenry?"

"That would be very banal, my dear...He led us to the billiard room."

"I thought he preferred *gorodki* to all other games?"

"Just so! So he took us to the billiard table, picked up a ball, and said, 'Now, oh gentlemen of the new nobility, I offer you a graphic representation of the, so to speak, phenomenon of twenty-first-century history.' He picked up one ball and dropped it into a pocket. The ball fell in without incident. Picks up another ball and asks, 'Now I'm going to aim this one into the same pocket: What's going to happen to the ball?' We answer all together: 'It'll fall into the pocket.' He drops it, then pushes a button on a remote control. Just before falling into the pocket, the ball explodes, breaking into little pieces. And pieces of ivory, my precious man, lie before us on the table."

"Beautiful."

"That's right, Count, beautiful! And Ivan Vladimirovich asks us, 'What would have happened if this ball hadn't broken up into little pieces?' Our answer: 'It would have fallen into the pocket.' And he asks, 'So, it would have disappeared from the table?' 'Yes, Your Majesty, it would have disappeared from the table.' 'That's correct, my dear, loyal subjects. So,' he says, 'this table is world history. And that ball was Russia. Which, beginning in 1917, was inexorably rolling toward a pocket. That is to say: into the nonbeing of world history. And if it hadn't fallen to pieces six years earlier, it would have entirely disap- peared. Its fall from the table doesn't represent geopolitical collapse, but internal decay and the inexorable decomposition of the populace into an impersonal, ethically unhinged biomass, a biomass that knows nothing but theft and groveling, having forgotten its own history, living in the sordid present alone, and speaking in a decayed language. As an *ethnos* (forgive our ruler's Greek, my dear man!), the Russian people would have disappeared entirely.'"

"Disintegrating into other *ethnoses*." The count nodded heavily. "I completely agree. But, Prince, listen—"

"You listen to me! Post-Soviet rulers, sensing their, so to speak, imminent undoing, let forth a nationwide call for help: Let us search for a national idea! They announced a competition, gathered together scholars, political scientists, and writers—My dears, give birth to a national idea for us! And they started to rummage through ideological haylofts with a *smalloscope*: Where is it? Where is our national idea?! The fools didn't understand that a national idea isn't a treasure hidden behind seven seals, isn't a formula, and isn't a vaccine that can inoculate a sick population overnight! A national idea, if there is one, lives within every person living under said state—from janitors to bankers. And if there isn't one and they persist in trying to find it, we can assume the state is already doomed! A national idea! When did a national idea start to grow in every Russian person? When post-Soviet Russia broke into little pieces! That's when every Russian remembered that they were Russian! That's when we remembered not only faith, history, czars, nobles, princes (counts too!), and the customs of our ancestors, but our culture and language as well! Our great, noble, and *correct* Russian language!"

Tears shone in the prince's eyes. Trishka brought over the skewers of steaming meat.

"As for the collapse's timeliness, that's obvious, no one can argue with that." The count took a skewer and sniffed at a piece of steaming elk's heart. "Post-Sovietude was an occupation zone and it was impossible to effectively manage it ... But Prince, as for the national idea ... tell me, Brother Trifon, what is *your* national idea?"

Having laid the skewers onto a plate, Trishka looked at the count with an astonished smile, as if the count had just said something in pig Latin.

"What is the main idea of your life?" the count asked, enunciating each word distinctly.

"Idea?" Trifon asked and looked at the prince.

The prince kept silent and filled the shot glasses.

"Our idea, Your Excellency, is to serve our master," Trishka pronounced.

With his heavy gaze, the count looked attentively at Trishka's broad, weathered, smiling face. Then he turned his gaze to the prince. Having finished pouring, the prince handed a glass to the count with an expression on his face that suggested he'd heard nothing. The count took the glass of vodka into his broad palm slowly and silently.

Not receiving any response from the count, Trishka ran to the campfire and began to put more meat onto the skewers.

The prince took a bite of the hot meat, chewed, and swallowed.

"M-m-m...excellent! And the smoke! The taste of smoke! Good work, Trishka! Laymen roast meat solely upon coals. But a true hunter must make friends with open flame...Well then, Count, my dear, what shall we drink to?"

"To what? M-m-m...to what indeed..." The count stared heavily at the prince.

Their gazes met.

Lord, how unbearable these Moscovians are, the prince thought. *How they shy away from everything sincere, honest, and unmediated. They have nothing but tellurium on their minds...*

How backwards everything is here among the Ryazanians, the count thought. *Their brains are overgrown with old moss. You can't even break through it with a tellurium nail...*

The pause stretched out. The prince was waiting.

"Let's drink, Prince, to..." the count began uncertainly.

But suddenly, in the eiderdown-lined inner pocket of his suede hunting jacket, his Breguet began to play a romance from *Tannhäuser*.

"To music," the count pronounced, rejoicing internally at the intercession of his father's old Breguet. "For it is higher than politics."

"Wonderful!" The prince smiled, his face brightening.

Their glasses came together.

The romance of Wolfram von Eschenbach swam almost inaudibly through the invigorating forest air.

The smell of roasted meat was inextricably intertwined with the smoke coming from the campfire.

They could hear a growing chirp off in the distance, and a small, silver drone soon flew over the bare crowns of the trees and melted away into the autumnal sky.

8

THE WIND of holy war howls over Europe.

Aiya!

O ye ancient stones of Paris and Basel, Cologne and Budapest, Vienna and Dubrovnik. May fear and awe fill your granite hearts.

Aiya!

O ye paving stones of Lyon and Prague, Munich and Antwerp, Geneva and Rome. May the weathered sandals of the proud warriors of Allah walk all over you.

Aiya!

O Old Europe, cradle of crafty humanity, stronghold of sinners and adulterers, refuge for apostates and embezzlers, haven for atheists and sodomites. May the thunder of jihad shake your walls.

Aiya!

O ye cowardly and crafty husbands of Europe, who exchanged faith for the everyday, truth for lies, and celestial stars for pathetic coins. May you flee in fear down your own streets when the shadow of the sacred sword falls upon you.

Aiya!

O ye beautiful and weak women of Europe, ashamed to give birth, but not ashamed to do the rough work of men. May you tumble over backwards and let forth lingering cries when the hot seed of valiant mujahideen flows into your wombs like lava.

Aiya!

O ye swarthy Europeans who call themselves Muslims, who have defected from the old faith in favor of the sins and temptations of a new century and allowed the infidels to tempt you with treacherous tellurium. May you cry out when the imam's hands tear the filthy nails, carriers of illusions and doubts into feeble minds, out from your heads. And may these nails fall from your free heads and onto the paving stones of Europe like dry leaves.

Aiya!

9

SOLOVYOVA, the secretary of the city committee, impatiently fixed her complex hairdo. Sitting behind her big desk, she became more and more visibly nervous as she played with an *empty* tellurium wedge.

"Victor Mikhailovich," she began, "don't you understand the people can't wait anymore? They don't just have to work, they have to relax, raise children, wash clothes, cook food . . . !"

"I understand that very well, Sofya Sergeyevna!" Kim brought his sleek arms to his chest, and his diamond family ring sparkled in the light. "But it's not possible to jump over one's own head, as the ancients used to say. There will be no Sovereign Funds until January! That's the objective reality."

"You had funds in July." Malakhov stood up and walked along the windows. "Sizable funds too! Enough for blocks, self-generator, mounts, and foundations! Gah . . . sixteen wagons!"

"Oh, Sergei Lvovich, here you go again with your endless explanations . . ." Kim spread out his hands and sighed exhaustedly. "I guess I'll sit down and write another report."

"Christ . . . not another report . . ." Malakhov waved his hands, having lost patience. "Get out! Go give *them* your report!"

He nodded toward the bulletproof window behind which a crowd of demonstrators dappled the square in front of the monument to Ivan III. The black figures of the Special Purpose Police Unit hemmed in the statue.

"No, no, I still can't manage to get it straight in my head." Solovyova leaned back into her armchair, nervously mashing at a smartypants rolled into a cylinder with her left hand and playing with the tellurium wedge with her right. "How is it possible to withdraw from a rolling agreement? Nataliya Sergeyevna! You've been our lawyer for three years already! And you overlooked the cancellation of the contract by the Nizhny-Novgorodians!"

Tired after three long hours of discussion, Levite put out her thin cigarette.

"I'm the only one to blame."

"She's not to blame for anything!" Malakhov almost screamed, standing by the window and jabbing sharply over his shoulder with his thumb toward Kim. "That's who's to blame! For everything!"

"Of course, I'm to blame! Of course—me, me, me!" Kim almost sang, folding his arms across his chest and counterfeiting a lachrymose expression on his broad, tanned face. "I'm the one who brought the contract with the Nizhny-Novgorodians to fruition and I'm the one who went to Tula and I'm the one who set the fire and I'm the one who approved the quarterly plan without an angle!"

"The quarterly plan was approved here!" Solovyova slapped her palm against the table so violently that the mormolon beetles in her hairdo began to stir. "You raised your hand too! Where was your gift of fore-sight-ed-ness?!"

"He foresaw everything." The overweight Gobzev laughed gloomily. "He foresaw everything he'd need for the Perkhushkovo construction with fantastic precision. Now there's a skyscraper in Perkhushkovo. With no demonstrations and no Special Purpose Police Unit. The result of his, so to speak, foresightedness."

"So, shall I resign, comrades?" Kim asked in angry surprise. "Or continue to build barracks for our workers? I don't un-der-stand what I'm to do!"

"You need to honestly tell us how you allowed the Tulians to fuck up the Nizhny-Novgorodian train of sixteen wagons," Gobzev pronounced.

"Sofya Sergeyevna . . ." Kim stood up and began to button up his silver-tinted olive jacket.

"Sit down!" Solovyova ordered.

Kim continued to stand there tensely. Solovyova squinted her already-narrow eyes at him—they were made up with Iranian ocher.

"Tell us, Comrade Kim, who are you?"

"I'm a Russian Orthodox communist," Kim replied seriously and shifted his gaze to the wall above Solovyova's head, where there hung a living portrait of Lenin constantly writing and, in the corner to the right of it, were affixed a massive icon and a glowing icon-lamp.

"I don't believe you," Solovyova pronounced.

There was a tense pause.

"I don't believe that you didn't know about the break initiative of the Tula city government back in July."

His face impenetrable, Kim silently and sweepingly crossed himself before the icon and began to speak loudly—to the whole office.

"With God as my witness, I tell you that I didn't know!"

A tired stirring began to take hold of those sitting at the table; someone sighed in relief and someone else exhaled indignantly. Solovyova stood up, walked right over to Kim, and stared fixedly into his face. He didn't look away.

"The party congress will be in six months, Victor Mikhailovich," Solovyova pronounced.

Kim was silent.

Solovyova silently unbuttoned her jacket, bared her right shoulder, and turned to Kim. A living tattoo seethed in crimson on that shoulder: a heart and crossbones. The heart shuddered rhythmically.

Kim stared at the heart.

"When the Sovereign announced the Third Party Call, I was twenty. My husband was at war and our kid was three. I was working as a nominator. My salary was twenty-five rubles. Not even enough for food. I dug a garden in Yasenevo and planted spuds. I worked nights too—kneading smart dough for Chinamen. I get up in the morning, can't see anything after kneading all night. I turn on the beef-o-matic, feed my kid, take him to his kindergarten, then I go to work. And after work, to the district committee. Until ten. Then I go to the kindergarten and Garik's already asleep. I pick him up and take him home. And do this every day, there aren't weekends during wartime. Then, one wonderful day, I get a spark: 'Your husband Nikolai Solovyov died heroically liberating the hero-city Podolsk from Wahhabi invaders.' That's when I made this living reminder for myself, Victor Mikhailovich. And I moved from the department of technology to the department of social construction. Because I made myself a promise: to make our postwar life happy. So that my son grows up to be a happy man. So that his peers are happy. So that all the working people of PodMoscovia have inexpensive apartments. So that our young Moscovian state becomes strong. So that no one ever dares to attack it again. So that no one gets a death notification like I did ever again."

She went silent, walked away from Kim, buttoned up her jacket, and sat back down at the table.

"What should I do?" Kim asked dully.

Solovyova unhurriedly lit a cigarette and tapped her red fingernail against the table.

"Right here. Tomorrow. Nine thousand. In gold. First-coinage gold."

"I won't be able to get that together by tomorrow," Kim answered quickly.

"The day after tomorrow."

He shrugged uncomfortably.

"Also unrealistic, but—"

"But you'll do it," Solovyova interrupted him.

He went silent, shifting his furious gaze away from her.

"And reclamations or rubbings-out!" She leaned back in her armchair.

Clasping his hands over his groin, Kim nodded furiously.

"Nine thousand," Solovyova repeated.

"Can I go?" Kim asked.

"Go, Victor Mikhailych." Solovyova looked at him coldly and exhaustedly.

He turned sharply and walked out, slamming the door behind him.

"We need to drive that nit out of the party," Murtazov spoke gloomily, having been silent for a long time.

"Drive him straight to hell." Gobzev shook his massive head.

"At the very next meeting!" Malakhov slapped his smartypants onto the table.

The smartypants squeaked and began to light up.

"No need," Solovyova pronounced seriously, looking out the window at the crowd of demonstrators. "Not yet."

Having extinguished her cigarette in businesslike fashion, she stood up, fixed her jacket, touched her hairdo, calming the still-stirring mormolon beetles, and spoke loudly—to the whole office.

"Well then, comrades, let's go talk to the people."

10

SOMEONE opened the door very slightly and very cautiously.

"Yes, it's me," Bogdanka said, barely moving his lips.

The door slammed shut. Bogdanka didn't hear, but rather felt with what terrible difficulty Vladimir's hands were attempting to unfasten the door chain.

I said "It's me," didn't I? Everything's fine! he wanted to scream through this accursed, beastly old door, upholstered with devil knows what kind of crappy material back in preimperial times or maybe post-Soviet times or perhaps even Soviet times.

But he restrained himself with his last bit of strength.

Vladimir swung the door open, as if this were his older brother who had come home, the brother who had disappeared without a trace during the Second War. Bogdanka leapt into the warm darkness of the entryway, and no sooner had Vladimir slammed the door shut and locked it behind him than Bogdanka slid down the wall and onto the floor, neglecting to even take off his jacket.

"What is it?" Vladimir hunched over him uncomprehendingly.

"N-n-nothing…" Bogdanka whispered, smiling to himself, "I'm just tired."

"Were you running?"

"No," Bogdanka admitted honestly, took a matchbox out of his pocket, and held it out to Vladimir.

Vladimir took it quickly and walked out of the entryway.

Bogdanka stayed seated for a little while, then threw his jacket to the ground, unwound his scarf and threw it on top of his jacket, pulled off his boots, which were splotched with PodMoscovian filth, stood up, walked into the bathroom, opened the tap, and eagerly drank the tepid, undelicious water. Standing upright once again, he looked at himself in the mirror. A gray, haggard face with dark circles underneath its eyes was looking back at him.

"Good evening," the face's weathered lips pronounced, attempting to smile.

Bogdanka pushed himself off of the yellowed sink and walked into the room.

Twelve people were sitting silently in a circle on the living room carpet. At the center of the circle, the matchbox, now open, lay on top of an extremely battered copy of *Three Kingdoms*. A silvery tellurium wedge sparkled inside it.

Bogdanka sat down in the circle, unceremoniously displacing Felt Boot—from PodMoscovia—and Vladimir's *second* girlfriend, Regina—from ZaMoscvorechye. They paid no attention to Bogdanka's rudeness. Their eyes were glued to the tellurium.

"And? Did the idiots get what they wanted?" Felt Boot tried to joke nervously.

Everyone was silent.

Vladimir sighed impatiently.

"Well then, let's ... goddamn, could you not stare like that ... ?"

"Ladies and gentlemen, we must needs cast lots so that everyone is satisfied without even a shadow of resentment, so that no one even slightly hints at any form of dishonesty, at any kind of rigged game, at anything unclean, petty, or rotten, at someone else's wickedness ..." the feeble, slender Snowball began to speak feverishly.

"No resentment and no cheating ..." the eternally angry Mavrin-Pavrin shook his bulldog's head.

"Wait, what kind of resentment could there be?" muttered the very rotund Li Guaren, who was dressed poorly and sloppily.

"I get offended easily ..." the stooped-over Bedbug muttered almost inaudibly.

"We're not talking about that! Decidedly not about that!" Bondik-Dei slapped his knee.

"No, let's establish terms! Let's, let's, let's!" Self nodded grimly.

"Listen! We didn't get together to scam each other!" Vladimir raised his voice and everyone could feel that he was on the point of exploding. "You're at my house, ladies and gentlemen. How fuckin' dare you even mention scamming each other!"

"Vladimir Yakovlevich, we're not talking about scamming each other, which would of course be impossible among us, people of *compos mentis* who are unique, responsible, and intelligent; I simply wanted to warn everyone against—" Snowball was beginning to chatter away, but got interrupted.

"Cast lots! Cast lots! Cast lots!" Vladimir clapped his hands in a furious frenzy.

Everyone glared at him.

Avdotya, the chubby woman sitting next to Vladimir, embraced him tightly.

"Volodenka . . . it's all good . . . it's all glorious . . ."

He began to push her away, but Amman reached out his large hand and took Vladimir by the shoulder.

"Vladimir Yakovlevich, I'm begging you. I'm begging you."

His deep, authoritative voice had a strong effect on Vladimir. He fell silent, stirring languidly in Avdotya's arms.

"Ladies and gentlemen," Amman continued, looking at the people around him with his intelligent deep-set eyes. "We are gathered here today in order to *test* the new. It is the new that lies before us."

As if on command, everyone began to stare at the matchbox.

"It cost us a lot of money. This is the rarest, most expensive, and most illegal product in the world. None of us have ever *tested* it before. Therefore, let us not allow this day to turn bitter. I suggest we cast lots."

"Let's draw matches! If that veritably be a matchbox . . ." The always melancholy Rodya Schwartz grinned bitterly.

"Thirteen little pieces of paper and one lucky winner." Amman ignored Rodya's quip.

"I don't have any paper at home," Vladimir muttered.

Amman lifted up the matchbox, tore a page out of *Three Kingdoms*, then put the matchbox back down.

"Scissors."

He was handed scissors. Then began to carefully cut the yellowed page into strips of equal width.

"Bring me a garbage bag," Vladimir ordered Avdotya.

She jumped up awkwardly, which set her sizable body to trembling, ran into the kitchen, puttered around, then came back with a black plastic bag.

"I hope you have a stylus, Vladimir Yakovlevich?" Regina asked.

"There's one here somewhere," Vladimir muttered, before angrily adding, "but I'm warning you: I'm not trained to write with it."

He stood up, rummaged through his drawers for a long time, found a time-corroded pencil, and threw it to Regina. Regina caught, sniffed, and licked the pencil with a nervous smile.

"You know, ladies and gentlemen . . . I also . . . don't really know how . . ."

"I'll write." Amman took the pencil from her, wrapped his fist around it, and began to write coarsely and clumsily on one of the strips: TELLURIUM. Dropped the pencil and began to carefully fold the strips of paper and stuff them into the black bag. His big, strong hands were steady even at moments like this. When the last strip of paper had disappeared into the bag, Amman shut it, shook it for a long time, then opened it very slightly.

"Around the circle, counterclockwise. The man of the house goes first."

Suppressing his excitement with some difficulty, Vladimir shoved his hand into the bag's black mouth, dug through the strips of paper, pulled one out, and glanced at it. Crumpled it up and threw it furiously into the air.

"Son of a harlot!"

Unperturbed, Amman offered the bag to Avdotya. She pulled out a blank piece of paper and smiled with relief, snuggling up to Vladimir.

"Get lost . . ." He pushed her away, jumped up, and went to get a drink of water in the kitchen.

The bag moved around the circle. But it didn't even make it halfway: the round-backed Bedbug drew the lucky ticket.

"Tellurium," he pronounced with a sickly smile and showed everyone his strip.

"Tellurium," Amman agreed and, with obvious displeasure, plucked the piece of paper from Bedbug's thin fingers. "Bedbug will be *testing*, ladies and gentlemen. Well then . . . call the craftsman."

No one stirred. Bedbug's victory excited some and drove others to a state of stupefaction.

Snowball rushed over to Bedbug.

"Bedbug, my dear, darling Bedbug, you're on top today, you're a *chuanchi*,* a demiurge, you're Architecton . . . don't you see that you're going to stand so tall you'll prop up the clouds with your head and the world will lie at your feet, the world will be like a lizard, like an amphibian, like a dog licking your hands and feet . . ."

Bedbug laughed silently, his back becoming even more rounded, swaying and pressing his bony fist to his thin, acne-covered forehead.

"Bedbug, you bitch, respect plus Envyville," Felt Boot said old-fashionedly. "Say what you will, ladies and gentlemen, but I was entirely sure either Rodka or Bedbug would pick the lucky strip."

"Stop jokin' around, man." Rodya Schwartz sadly slapped Felt Boot on his shaven head right next to its mormolon plate.

"A bedbug's a bedbug, what do you expect . . ." Mavrin-Pavrin sullenly slid behind his mask.

"Why the fuck're there thirteen of us, I still don't get it, it's unlucky!" Self scratched at his needle-marked hands.

"Do you have sixty?" Li Guaren asked him, grimacing like a *soft* clown. "Or twenty at least?"

"Nope. I don't even have four rubles and sixty-two kopecks."

"The money's already gone?!" she exclaimed.

Everybody laughed. Unexpectedly, this burst of laughter calmed them down. Some of them were nursing a drink. Sniffing at something, Mavrin-Pavrin chilled out and threw a *warm* pill to Regina. Regina *grimaced* at him.

*[Chinese] knight

"Let us rejoice for Bedbug, ladies and gentlemen," Amman pronounced. "Where's the craftsman?"

Coming back from the kitchen, Vladimir took out a key and unlocked the bedroom door. A scrubby man with a wide face, close-set eyes, and a bag over his shoulder came out through it.

"Alisha," he introduced himself with a half bow.

Amman directed him silently to Bedbug. Alisha put his bag down on the table in a businesslike manner, pulled clippers out of it, walked over to Bedbug, got down onto his knees, and began to shave Bedbug's head.

"This is why I haven't gone to the barber for so long," Bedbug pronounced, fiddling his thin fingers.

"Hold your head up higher," Alisha requested.

"I still don't understand: Why isn't it possible to use a wedge twice?" Avdotya asked, contented as she embraced Vladimir.

Snorting contemptuously, Vladimir rapped his finger on Avdotya's forehead.

"Due to its interaction with fatty acids in the brain, tellurium loses its purity and becomes a salt," Alisha replied as he worked. "The process is so chemically volatile that the layer of salt grows rather thick. But that's not the only issue. There are inexplicable things too. The crystal lattice changes its polarity, for example. Generally speaking, no one's ever managed to clean up a nail and drive it home a second time."

"Nor shall they ever manage to," Rodya sighed.

"Instead—a lethal outcome," the flushed Mavrin-Pavrin added.

"The diaphragm of the neuron and the tellurium atoms interact rapidly," Alisha continued. "But only if the nail is beaten into the right place. The tellurium is oxidized and the diaphragm loses its fatty acids."

"Yes, yes, yes!" Snowball feverishly affirmed. "It's a stunning, unbelievable process my friends, the lipid diaphragms of the neurons literally lick the tellurium atoms from the metal with their fatty acids, lick like tongues, lick, lick, then oxidize them, while they themselves rapidly soften and another process begins in the neurons, in the brain and—O ye lucky being—the person enters into their desired space! How wonderful, ladies and gentlemen!"

"There's nothing wonderful about it." Felt Boot was rolling himself a cigarette. "Six chernovetses for a single nail . . . the world's going insane."

"You're not just paying for the nail," Regina interjected.

"One must needs be able to beat it in, yes?" Avdotya nodded stupidly—as if she were both interrogating and expressing understanding.

"Some people hammer it in themselves," Felt Boot muttered, "without a *carpenter*. And it works out."

"Without a *carpenter*, you can beat yourself straight to the saints and all the angels," Rodya smirked.

"It goes in crooked and you're fucked." Self spat onto the carpet. "Nail-pullers won't help."

"It's so delightful, my dear ones!" Snowball chattered. "Yon product is like fugu—dangerous and delightful—and twelve percent mortality is nothing to sneeze at, it's a sign of divinity, isn't that so? The Divine lifts up and smashes down, resurrects and annihilates into roadside dust! The gates that leadeth into Heaven are so very narrow that to the chosen alone shall it be given to penetrate them!"

"Are you from the mountains of Altai, my friend?" Amman asked Alisha.

"I'm a Yakut," he replied calmly as he finished shaving Bedbug's head.

"And where did you—" Bondik-Dei began to say.

"There," Alisha cut him off. "That's where I lived and studied."

"And how many times have you *carpenteered* before this?" Self squinted evilly at Alisha.

"This shall be the one-hundred-and-fifty-fourth time," Alisha replied and began to wipe Bedbug's head with rubbing alcohol.

"Motherfuck . . ." Vladimir cursed enviously.

"This, Volodenka, is how Mother Moscow got hooked on tellurium!" Avdotya giggled, squeezing him tight.

"These aren't mere cubes and spheres..." Felt Boot lit his cigarette. "Sixty per dose... for that, you could buy thirty cubes, twenty spheres, and eight pyramids. A six-month high."

"The cube is a fantastic product," Li Guaren expressed. "I wouldn't exchange it for any wedge."

"And no one's suggesting you do, madame!" Self snapped.

A lot of them laughed.

"I'm going home." Li Guaren stood up and stretched affectedly.

"Yes, yes. Drive out a wedge with a wedge..." Self was still agitated.

"We're going too, good luck." Felt Boot got up and took Bondik-Dei by the hand.

"Happy trails, Brother Bedbug," Bondik-Dei *threw* at Bedbug.

"I too, I too, ladies and gentlemen, am going, though, I'll admit it honestly, I'm burning with the most terrible, the most incinerating curiosity." Snowball jumped up. "All of my insides, my whole immortal essence shudders with the desire to climb into Bedbug's skull, to experience yon divine transfiguration to which no *radiance* shall ever be equal, I'm not even talking about flights and arrivals, yes, yes, to climb, and if not to climb, then, at least, after all of this, to interrogate the venerable Bedbug about his experience, to rejoice in his joy, in his celestial communion, to dissolve, even for a moment, into his extrasensual confession, and, being so dissolved, to burn with blackest envy and, immediately afterwards, like the Phoenix, rise up from the black ash of envy in the whitest clothes of joy and cheerfulness!"

"The seance can last for as long as five days," Alisha warned, pulling on a pair of rubber gloves.

"I know—O venerable one—I know, most precious Alisha!" Snowball confirmed. "'Tis precisely this knowledge that forces me to leave the very place of power, for my heart would not withstand the trial of those five days! 'Twould burst apart from envy like a Palestinian fig. So farewell, my dears! Farewell, Vladimir Yakovlevich!"

He took a low bow and left.

Mavrin-Pavrin and Self followed him out without a word. Rodya left the apartment with a sad smile on his face. The only people remaining seated on the carpet were Bogdanka, Vladimir, Avdotya, Amman, and Regina.

"We need a bed." Alisha straightened up.

"In the bedroom." Vladimir nodded with tired indifference.

Bedbug wandered into the bedroom like a sleepwalker. Alisha, Regina, and Amman followed after him. Bogdanka, Vladimir, and Avdotya remained seated on the carpet.

"Let's go watch, Volodenka." Avdotya stroked Vladimir's drawn cheek.

"I don't want to," he muttered.

"Well, I want to." Regina stood up and walked into the bedroom.

Bogdanka followed her out. Staying seated for a little while, Vladimir eventually stood up and walked into the bedroom. Bedbug was already lying on the bed rolled onto his right side. His eyes were half closed. Alisha stretched out a smartypants and wrapped it around the crown of Bedbug's shaven head. The image of Bedbug's brain appeared atop the smartypants as a floating *map*. Alisha held his hands out over Bedbug's head and froze for several long minutes. When those minutes had elapsed, Alisha quickly removed the smartypants from Bedbug's skull and made a green mark on it. He then took the wedge from the matchbox, cleaned it with rubbing alcohol, pressed it to the spot, pulled a hammer out from his bag, and, with a quick, strong motion, drove the wedge into Bedbug's head.

11

O, CONSUMMATE State!

You shine over us with your visible and invisible sun, warming us and scorching us. Your rays pierce us. They are powerful and omnipresent. No one can hide from them—neither the just nor the wicked.

And why should they?

Only the cunning escape from your radiance, hiding in the dark corners of their own vanity. They cannot love you, for they can love only themselves and those similar to themselves. They are afraid to give themselves to you; but what if you were suddenly to take away their vanity? And destroy the dusty little worlds of their cunning? Their teeth are clenched with greed and egoism. Life for them is a constant gnashing of teeth. Conceit is their throne. Fear and envy are their eternal companions. Their faces are immersed in themselves. They are complex and full of fear. They are opaque. With the complex objects of their domiciles, they are obscured from your light. Your light burns them. Their thoughts are the shadows of eternal doubts.

Woe unto you, the complex and the opaque.

Burn, then, you who are doomed and condemned! Smoke up, o dark thoughts of the old doubts of humanity! The light of the Consummate State shall turn you to ash! Weep and cry out, you who are cunning and vain, writhe with burning and hide yourselves away in your dusty domiciles. You are condemned to be turned to ash. You are the past.

We are the present and the future.

Only us—the simple and the transparent—are capable of loving the Consummate State. Only for us, the transparent, does its sun shine. Our life is joy, for rays of the state's light pass through our bodies.

We shall not interfere with your rays, O Consummate State! We shall swallow them with greedy joy! You are the Great Hope. You are the Great Order. You are the light of our lives. In every atom of our bodies sings forth the joy of our complicity with this Great Order. Our faces are joyful and open. We believe in the Consummation of the State. And it believes in us, relying upon our faith.

Man's highest joy is life lived for the sake of the Consummate State. Its Great Building is made of us. We are the shining bricks of its greatness. We are the comb filled with the honey of statehood. We are the backbone of the State. In each of us sings forth the energy of its power. In each of us lives the idea of the Great Consummation. Each of us is ready to sacrifice themselves in the name of the State. Our flesh is the foundation of its edifice. Our love is its columns. The Great Building surges forth unto shining heights. Its peak is made of the purest tellurium. It is radiant and blinding.

O, how magnificent and consummate this structure is! There's nothing like it in all of existence. It was created and built for our happiness. And our happiness lies in the greatness of our state.

Its consummation is our joy.

Its power is our strength.

Its wealth is our peace.

Its wishes are our labor.

Its safety is our care.

O glory be to you, Consummate State!

Glory for centuries and centuries!

12

THE FACTORY outpost's where we live. Right on Similar Road, where the monorail ends, that's where the outpost is. The factory's three stops later an' it's real good an' big. A lotta diff'rent self-generatin' stuff gets made there: glue, felt, rubber, plastic, gaskets of various calibers, an' even self-generatin' toys. 'Bout fi'teen hundred reprobates work there. Five hundred of those is nonresidents, just like the Sovereign said it oughta be, an' all the Chinamen are BeyondtheSecond-Wallers. The Chinamen reside in their dormitories an' come here fur nu'in more than work. So we got the Chinamen workin' an' then ours who come to work from the outpost. It's a mix of ZaMoscvorechians an' BeyondtheWallers at the outpost at an ideal ratio of one to three. There oughta be three times less of us ZaMoscvorechians an' more BeyondtheWallers—three times more. There're twelve buildings we live in at the outpost. Good buildings—they been redid not long ago. No one's crib is none too big, but they is warm an' comf'trable. An' in crib number twenty-seven, in the third house, the bastard Nikolai Abramovich Anikeyev lives 'n resides with his household. He came to us at the factory 'bout a year ago an' got hisself set up. He's a Yaroslavian an' came with some other people from there. When he got here, he registered as not havin' a household so as to rent a mere corner an' not pay fur a crib. That's what he told everyone: bach'lor, I'm a bach'lor. He told me that too when he invited me to the dance. I danced with him an' I liked him too. Curly haired, wide in the shoulders, jaunty, knows 'ow to dance, a dab hand of a dancer ye might even say. They'd start playin' a lil' jig an' he'd walk forward right away jus' like a peacock, horseshoes ringin' on his boots, fixin' his cowlick, shoutin': take a gander, PodMoscovia, at how these Yaroslavian devils strike fire from the ground! So we got acquian'ed, 'came friends, an' started conversin' conversations in the workshop. He worked on felt an' I worked on toys, the one of which is right next to th'other, just through the rubber workshop. Soon as I'd take a smoke break, I'd get a spark: Les go have a smoke, Marusya. 'S not like I fell in love right away, he was just an int'restin' fella, tha' much was clear. We only had maidens an' broads in the workshop an' what was there to talk about with them, seein' as we lived together 'n all. An' this here fella starts tellin' me his life story, how he was drafted into the army, how he fought fur Ural, how he got wounded by a burstin' bullet, how he was lyin' there with his leg all split up in a military hospital, how the gangrene set in an' he set to ravin', so they cut off his leg, wanted him to check out, but he insisted otherwise, sayin' that he'd open up his veins an' he weren't goin' out of there one-legged like ... But, as usual, there weren't no new legs in the hospital. A doctor came over to him whisperin': If ye get me a lil' *terlurium* nail, ye'll have yer leg. He wrote to 'is parents, who killed two calves, sold their radio, rented to the neighbors, an' sent money, then he bought the nail, the doc sewed 'im up, an' signed him out— he got back into formation, found his way to Ural, fought how was s'posed to do, got a medal, then deserted with ev'ryone else when Mishutka the Bloody got overthrown. Nikolai Abramych was a real dab hand at tellin' stories too, he'd tell ye diff'rent things an' it was like it was happ'nin' right in front of yer eyes. He told me 'bout his family, that his daddy was a baptized Jew, a most faithful believer, he'd gone t'all the holy places, he'd even been to Athos an' prayed fur 'is son, an' this *daddy-prayer*'d saved 'im twice, once when they were goin' on the attack an' his machine gun got hit by bullets three times but he di'n't, an' the second time when he was scrappin' with two ZaUralians in a trench two to one an' it was real slippery, but he still cut 'em both down. An' he told me 'bout his brother, that he got hitched up to a Chinawoman an' went away to live in Krasnoyarsk, where 'e put down roots an' got real settled in; he 'n 'is wife keep syaoshitan, bought two auto-mobiles, 'ad three kids, 're waitin' on a fourth, an' he's goin' to visit 'em fur Christmas. That's how he an' I were conversin' conversations. Then he invited me out to our tavern. Got me some wine an' fed me with meaty food an' sweet stuff too. An' when he was walkin' me home, he pulled me into some pine trees an' started kissin' me all over. I di'n't resist 'cuz I liked him okay. He kissed me, then let me go. An' on the next day, he gave me a lil' ring with a turquoise. Then we went to the cinema an' he really got up all on me there too 'fore he calmed down. An' the next day, when our maidens went to market, I gave myself to him. An' from that point forward, Nikolai an' I were lovers. We engaged in love in various places, wherever we could. Durin' Dormition, I went with him to the market, to the Sparrow Hills, he spun me round on a carousel, we flew on a spaceship to Aldebaran, wandered through the blue mead- ows, wet our throats with Bavarian beer, an' he fed me some sweet stuff an' gave me two livin' handkerchiefs. I lost myself in my love for him. He b'came not only a lover, but a true friend. I waited fur him to propose t' me, but he kept 'is mouth shut an' said it weren't time yet, we must needs take root an' save up some money, he said. I'd already sparked my mama onto what was goin' on, would tell how, what, 'n where ev'ry day. She calmed me down sayin' that the fella's in a new place, still ain't got his bearin's, an', perhaps, ain't sure 'bout me yet, so I shouldn't keep botherin' him for nothin'. A lil' time passed an' autumn was already over. Three maidens from our workshop got themselves hitched up. An' then Nikolai's wife came—a real bolt from the blue. She di'n't come alone, but with their six-year-old daughter too. That's how it turned out. They moved to a family crib right away. An' soon as I gleaned this fact, it was like lightnin' 'ad gone off in my head an' wouldn't stop flashin'. I couldn't eat or sleep. It was like I couldn't see nobody on account of the lightnin'. I had one thought in my head—go to him an' sort this out. I started sendin' him lil' notes: Kolya, darlin' I wanna see ye. But he extinguishes all of 'em, he's as silent as if he were at the bottom of a well. I wait for a smoke break an' he's not there. When the day was startin', I tried to go into his workshop myself, but the foreman kicked me out—yer disturbin' the work, he said. I walk up to him in the cafeteria an' he starts slurpin' up his cabbage soup. Hello, I say, Nikolai Abramovich. He looks at me like he'd never set eyes on me before. 'Lo, he says, Marusya. Wherefore did ye deceive me, I ask. "Ain't no wherefore." He turns away an' keeps slurpin' up his soup. That's when the lightin' went off in my head again an' I grabbed a plate of meatballs an' threw it at his head. An' walk myself right out of the cafeteria. Then I go into our toy workshop, take the "Gramps's Mushrooms" kit for kiddos off of the conveyor belt, an' there're tiny lil' mushrooms in there, they need to be cultivated, an' I grab a handful of 'em, swallow 'em, open up a bubble of self-generatin' water an' drink it up. Livin' water's totally tasteless. I walk out onto the street an' into our chapel, cross myself, an' bow down: Forgive me, O Lord, fur my sin. An' then it was like the plastic'd exploded in my stomach an' I lost conscientiousness. I woke up in the hospital. I'm lyin' on a table an' the doc shows me a Boletus with a head that's all humanlike an' soiled in my blood, plus a penny bun that's just as big: Well, ye little idiot, the doc says, ye wanted to grow Gramps's Mushrooms in yer stomach? Ye can invite me over for some mushroom soup, then! An' he says: The factory insurance'll pay for the treatment, but forty-six rubles 're bein' kept from yer salary for the new stomach. Ye can start workin' again in a week. I wanted to scream, but I di'n't have the strength for it. I say only one thing: Why'd ye bring me back to life, doc?

13

THE NAKED Dorothea of Charlottenburg—the thirty-seven-year-old widowed queen of a troubled kingdom, the Princess of Schleswig-Holstein by birth, Duchess of Grunewald, Landgrave of Feldafing and Darmstadt, and Princess of Mlet—is chasing me down a palace enfilade flooded with moonlight.

Having rolled out of the royal bedroom, I cut through the night air, which smells like parquet polish, fireplaces, hemp, and rotten furniture. Rooms flash by: bathroom, audience room, the green office with the low divans, on the lemon silk of which we so love to play tepel-tapel...*

"Bleib' stehen, du, Scheisskugel!"

So now I'm a *Scheisskugel*...Just a half hour ago I was *"mein Damsel-toy." Bam!* She swings a butterfly net at me as hard as she can. And misses! I'm flying through the palace in a zigzag. The net slams into something behind me like a high-explosive bomb. The queen has a heavy hand. *Slap! Slap! Slap!* It's a carpet bombing! Active protective measures are required. I bank to the left: vase, ottoman, column, harpsichord. Heavy steps, elephant, elephant, heavy slap, breathing, lion, lion, hotly. *Bang!* A vase. Rolling around, but not broken. *Boom!* The lid of the harpsichord, flooded with moonlight: ring, ring, fuck, fuck, fear, fear. Bach? Bach? Bach? Handel!!!

I muster my final forces. And that I still have the strength after this unhinged evening! A miracle! A miracle!

Bam! Bam!

*An active game played by enserfed phalli—reminiscent of leapfrog

Doorjamb.

I skirt round it, breathing heavily.

I fly

into

the Oval

Hall.

Open space. Window. Moon. I shove off, zooming familiarly across the chessboard marble. *Mein Gott*, how many *lively* games we've played upon it in the last two years! And I always end up as a black knight on B8...A "little hobbyhorse," like that bastard Beanpole-2 says when I don't agree to a Marshall Attack in the Spanish Game...

And behind me, an elephanopotamus across the marble; the queen speaks.

"Halt! Halt, Miststückchen!"

I'll slip, I'll slide into the tapestry room. Wrap myself in one of them, farther away from her fury, lie down and fall into a deep sleep. Suck on this crooked Russian *dick*...

And like all that which is crooked, I lose my balance while banking. Motherfucker! My head smashes into a table's gilded leg. Sparks, sparkles, sparklers. Legs, legs, and the gilding is peeling off of 'em. Wonderful legs. All that's left of you is horns...

I writhe between the table legs, moaning.

"Nun, komm 'schon, leetle fool!"

The queen slams down her hoof. The vases tremble in horror. I hear her *juice* drip down onto the parquetry. That's right—Vagina Avida.

"Ach, du kleine Sau!"

The queen is furious.

Flying into the red office, I hear how she grabs the net by its gauze tip and begins to sprint heavily, as if she were about to pole-vault.

"Haaaaaaaalt!!!"

Dorothea's chesty voice carries through the nocturnal palace. Bass, bass. Roar, roar. The Chinese vases are humming with the echo. Vaginal Jericho. And, right away, off in the distance, a weak, pitiful voice comes from the bedroom she's abandoned.

"Dorothea, Feinsliebchen, wo bist du denn?"

The gutless nonentity, the *dickkkkkless*, heartless, endl…oh woe is me, I'm entangled in a rug like a postwar bedbug. Damn Turkish rugs! Cheap and hairy! The Persian and Chinese rugs have long since been plundered by the court bastard.

She overtakes me on the threshold of the Porcelain Room. The net's handle whistles, then a blow. I fly into the fireplace. Ash. Ashes to ashes?

"Achoo!"—that was me.

I jump out of the maw of the fireplace, horrified to notice how the queen—enormous, her breasts dangling like kettlebells—thrusts the bulk of her buttocks back and winds up with the net as if she were playing golf. And the queen plays golf beautifully. Her abundant shoulders shine with sweat and the moon sparkles in her disheveled hair.

Sw-i-i-i-i-i-ish!

A miss.

I rush between the vases.

Sw-i-i-i-i-i-ish!

Bam!

A vase is smashed to smithereens.

I jump onto a porcelain dragon, then higher, onto a parrot, a basilisk, a Buddha, onto…*Bam!*

She knocks me down like a spring woodcock in Grunewald. Tumbling through the dark air, I am earthbound. Then into her sweaty palms.

Queen Dorothea's feverish face hovers over me.

"*Pass auf du, kleiner* Russkiy Buzzturd, *das hast du dir selbst eingebrockt!*"

Curtains.

An end to all ends.

An end to all ends.

An end to all ends.

Sooner or later, it was going to come to this. Alas. As the deceased eunuch Kharlampy used to say: 'Tis not the longest and stoutest of you who shall suffer, but the smartest and most sinuous. The old man turned out to be right … And I'm smart. Even Shorty-3 admits it. I'm sinuous and *convoluted*. I'm fluid and dynamic. I dance a *juicy* samba and a *slippery* lambada, I twist like a dervish from a sexual desert and spin all five vaginal rings round me like hula-hoops. I'm resilient. If you were to attach a bowstring to my five-pointed body, the arrow would fly through the window of the queen's bedroom, whistle out over the rose garden, then fall into the green labyrinth of the palace garden. And our beanpoles would follow it with the envious gazes of their jaundiced little eyes. If you were to pull me back and let me fly, I would knock out whatever brains remained in the head of the queen's latest lover. Her current lover, for example. Conrad of Kreuzberg! How menacing that sounds … And what a nonentity is covered over by this loud name. "He who freed Neukölln from Salafi savages!" And the grateful Turks kissed the hands of their liberator … As is always the case in *recent* history, laurels are awarded only to the most incompetent. Oil on canvas, a juicy painting of court life: *Queen Dorothea of Charlottenburg Sodomizes Conrad of Kreuzberg with Me.* And this nonentity politely moans into a pillow. It was the Chinese wingèd battalion that freed Neukölln, even Beanpole-8 knows that. As befits a coward, Conrad of Kreuzberg hammered a tellurium nail into the crown of his head for courage and sallied over to Kreuzberg with a detachment of local marauders on his two-story-tall cart horse when all the corpses of the Salafis had been removed—when even the ruins of buildings had been swept away. He rode along Karl Marx Strasse and the Turkish women threw roses under his Beowulf's hooves. A hero! I'd already stopped being part of the *process* and run away, though certainly *not* as a result of moral considerations: like all *members* of the royal harem, I don't care whom I sodomize—a coward or a hero, a murderer or a righteous man … It's a job. There are simply … limits. A limit. Maybe I'm just tired. Not physically though, not physically … Am I depressed? Maybe. A troubled soul? Could be. A difficult character? Of course! How dangerous it is to be among the *toys* for too long! Even more dangerous than reading too many books. I'm an individual. That says it all. There are *things in themselves* that are also hard to explain to oneself. Especially when you're hanging in the punishment cage at night...

The harem sleeps. Or, as Pushkin might say: The harem slumbers, knowing not sadness...

From the cage, our community of *units* is clearly visible. Thirty-two beds on thirty-two peckers. Five of which are empty: mine, Beanpole-7's, Beanpole-4's, Fatso-2's, and...God...what's his name... Shorty-4's. This is how the queen fills in for my absence. But it will be difficult for her to replace me.

The harem sleeps. The fatsos are snoring, the shorties are snuffling, the beanpoles are sibilating, and our collective bodies twist into a phallic Swastika giving itself silently to Morpheus. Six of us who are crooked. But all of us, I must admit, are worthy individuals, though not without our whimsies. Crooked-1 loves to lather himself up for a long time, but washes rarely. Crooked-2 can't stand coconut oil. Crooked-5 has a panicked fear of deep throats. Crooked-4 has one of palace mice. And I...fear a great deal. Fears, fears. They lie at the foundation of any real elite. So that even this "idle little hobbyhorse" has its raison d'être. And I ha-a-ate the Marshall Attack! Better the tedious Caro-Kann or the rotten Pirc Defence than that *black* longing 'pon the board. Generally speaking, the crooked much resemble chess pieces or seahorses; that's axiomatically true. And fears...who doesn't have them, *verdammt noch mal*?

Fatso-3 laughs in his sleep. He's happy...You could say that our fatsos are a fine selection of exclusively *sanguine hedonists*. Maybe because they're not circumcised, unlike us and the beanpoles. They stretch out their hoods like Franciscan monks and go to sleep. The fatsos are rarely made use of. They're given food and drink till they're stuffed. A walk in the fresh air, dynamic games, swimming...How could he not laugh in his sleep? Beanpole-1, for example, often cries in his sleep. And he's not alone. During my first months here, I often woke up in tears. For some reason, I was always dreaming of the orangerie in Sheremetev Palace—palm trees, succulents, butterflies and beetles with whom I found a common language...swallowtails eagerly landing upon my lilac-colored head, their wings fluttering. I don't just know how to speak the language of insects, but also how to sing. It's true that not everyone in the harem shares my taste for such songs. They warned me: We'll smoosh you like a mosquito if you keep buzzing like that, Crooked-6. To be honest, collective life is hell. But loneliness isn't heaven either, that's for sure. As soon as you imagine yourself sleeping in a jewelry box under a Turkish widow's bed or in a light-skinned widower's suitcase as he roams about the world and scribbles his graphomaniacal *Confessions* by night...you start to feel the fear.

Someone farted. Again. And another little one. Mhmm...it's probably already two in the morning. It'd be nice to get some sleep before tomorrow's *dressing down*, but for some reason sleep just won't slide into my little *head*. I don't sleep all that soundly here, I must confess. The problem isn't nightmares or the awful "night terror" so endemic among *us* and described by one English psychiatrist in his famous monograph *The Megacastration Complex of Transgenic Phallic Organisms*. No, the black vagina dentata doesn't knock at the door of my dreams, thank God. But insomnia, the harem, fat bodies packed together...Early-morning wake-ups have been my scourge for the last six months already.

At night, from here, from above, our bedroom has a most pacifying aspect. The peckers are sleeping, having laid their lilac heads to rest upon their pillows. As if there were never any nocturnal disputes, fights, or brawls. As if people here never "did the dark," never sluiced urine from their chamber pots over their companions' sleeping bodies, never put a hornet or a little bear into someone else's bed...

Overall, the summer has passed by in peaceful fashion. The fatsos have calmed down, the shorties have stopped singing "Silent Night" before their *retreats*, Beanpole-3 got sick of jumping off the balcony, and Crooked-4 got sick of beating up Crooked-1. No one is especially jealous or reproachful of anyone else. In part because our queen loves and is open to so many different kinds of relations; today she sodomized Conrad of Kreuzberg with me; tomorrow the Countesses of Nuremberg—twin sisters—will take her with a duo-pitchfork; and the day after that, no one shall prevent her from raising up the countesses on a sexto-pitchfork with the help of two beanpoles, two crookeds, and two shorties or from simply holding a broad-minded sex party with games of tag, flagellatio, Abyssinian guardsmen in powdered sugar, and champagne. There's enough work for everyone, even Fatso-2.

The clock whispered half past two.

Anyways, how did I end up in this cage? Why the hell did I sprint off like that? Stupidity? Old age? I'm four years old. That's middle-aged, not just for peckers, but for most littluns too. That means it's a typical age for a midlife crisis.

I try to doze off, but don't really manage to.

The clock whispered three. And, as if on command, four of our *wrung-out* colleagues return to the seraglio from the bedroom. They walk slowly and unsteadily, heads hanging down. Judging by their aspect, the queen overdid it after she lost her use of me. The unpleasant Shorty-4 approaches.

"Rejoice, oh crooked one! Vagina Avida ordered that you and the rest of the Russians be given away to Saatgut.*"

That's no joke. That's worse than a widows' auction or a brothel. That's a *milked* fate. Life in a laboratory. Hellish work with no artistry to it. Test tubes + *cum*post. Rivulets of tortured sperm. Until you die.

And I'm the idiot to blame. I grew fat and debauched in the palace—became a *bold* shithead.

The shorty collapses into his bed and Beanpole-4 drinks thirstily. I ask him to give one of the Russians a kick.

Soon, three of my countrymen are standing drowsily below me. I make a declaration:

"They're giving us away to Saatgut!"

From my cage, I can see how picturesquely they go stiff. The citizens of Calais as depicted by Salvador Dalí...

A short debate ends with a unanimous decision: to flee.

Wither?

It's unclear...

Certainly not to Count Sheremetev... Four years ago, he made a

---

*An institute/laboratory for semen collection in the eastern sector of Berlin

worthy gift to Queen Dorothea: four Russian peckers in beautiful lacquered boxes painted by Palekhian craftsmen. I don't believe that yon nobleman would be overjoyed at our illegal return to our native incubator.

Shorty-12 (who goes by the name of Petya) tells us that a train harnessed to a three-story cart horse is headed to Bavaria for Oktoberfest tomorrow. An idea came to us: to get into the giant's ears and make it to Bavaria in those. We'll have to pay, of course. Various things have accumulated in our trunks during these long years of labor. Of *peckerish* labor. OK, we'll make it to Bavaria. And then what? Where shall Brother Pecker find peace? In Telluria perhaps... A laughable thought! Good for laughing until we cry. Even though we have no tears left...

Well, never mind. An upstanding dick must be brave in love *and* war—brave until the end.

14

"YOU DIDN'T get tailed?" Kholodov asked as Masha Abramovich burst brashly into the entryway.

"No!" she replied in her maniacally focused manner. And off comes her downy shawl, down comes an ejaculation of snaky hair, and out wafts her perfume, as overwhelming as she is.

Masha's eyes are shining brighter than usual: stubborn anthracite. With his big hands, Kholodov takes off her white coat of self-generating fur and throws it onto a mountain of clothes; all his clothing hooks are occupied, everyone has gathered here. Quorum! Her greedy eyes flash comprehendingly. Masha's slender figure in the half light of the musty entryway: a black arc—the fury of new spaces and desires. Kholodov just barely managed to restrain himself from caressing it.

"Everyone's here!" Her head jerked affirmatively in an old mirror.

"Everyone." He looked at her from behind like a grim rapist.

She slid away from his body, flew down the hallway, and tore open the living room door.

"Hello, comrades!"

Kholodov followed her gloomily.

Warm living room, candelabras, illuminators, a steady glow in the half light: it was Wednesday, so there was no electricity.

"Hello, Comrade Nadezhda!" Voices came toward her from all sides.

Masha's eyes suck in and glide out: Nedelin, Rothmanskaya, Maul, Veksha, three *little* comrades from Bolshev, Ivan and Abdullah from the factory, the black-bearded Timur, the nondimensional Wazir, Rita Gorskaya, Zoya Li, the birch-bark Mom, Kholmsky, Bober, and . . .

"Nata!" Masha rushed over to her, grabbed her, and pressed her comrade to her flat chest.

Nata the White, alias "the Bee"—Nata's free and Nata's here!

They embraced, the branches of their strong arms intertwining.

"Take your places, comrades." Nedelin adjusted his pince-nez and the small jacket lying across his shoulders.

Masha is onto the carpet at the feet of the shaven-headed Nata and squeezing her hand, which is covered over in scabs and swastikas.

"Sister Nadezhda always keeps pace with the essential." A littlun from Bolshev smiles a quiet smile.

"Glory to the Cosmos!" Masha puts her hand to her chest and bows.

Everyone smiled.

Nedelin's icy eyes melted a bit.

"So, let's continue. The main thing: Goran and Zoran."

The living room stirred uncomfortably. Waiting for a question.

"Yesterday, they cast another batch of brass knuckles. They've now cast a total of . . ."

Mom stroked the smart birch bark stretched over his knees.

"Six thousand two hundred and thirty-five brass knuckles."

"Six thousand two hundred and thirty-five," Nedelin repeated what the bark had said. "What does that mean, comrades? Six thousand two hundred and thirty-five demons possessed by Socialist-Revolutionary propaganda going out onto the streets and destroying all of our painstaking work in a single blow."

A pause hung over the living room.

"Comrade Mikhail, don't you allow for the possibility that there might be honest workers among those six thousand?" Kholmsky leans forward, compressed and springy.

"Most of them *are* honest workers," Nedelin parried him coolly, before immediately standing up and going on the attack. "It is precisely their honesty that shall aid them in discrediting a grand idea. It is precisely their honesty that shall bring them into the line of fire and put all of us under arrest. It is precisely thanks to this honesty that they fell under the influence of the adventurists Zoran and Goran! It is precisely their honesty that has differentiated them from us! From me, from all of you, from the decision taken by the congress, and from the Proclamation of the Twenty-Five!"

"Can it really be their honesty?!" Wazir thundered.

"Precisely my question, Comrade Wazir! Can it really be their honesty?" Nedelin raises his voice. "Perhaps a different term is needed here."

"Credulity!" Nata squeezed Masha's hand.

"Impatience!" Rothmanskaya raised her thin brows.

"Readiness for revolution," Maul enunciated as if to highlight the complexity of the words.

"Unmanageability." Zoya Li shook a butt out of her long cigarette holder.

"Now we're getting somewhere!" Nedelin raised his finger, glancing at the beautiful Zoya. "Unmanageability. Tell me, comrades, who is to manage the working masses?"

"We are!" Masha almost screamed.

"We're the ones who're incapable of taking advantage of the credulity of the working masses!" Rothmanskaya twists around in her armchair like a snake that has just been bitten by a scorpion.

"It's a sin! A great sin!" thundered Wazir.

"Not a sin, but a provocation!" shouted the dark-faced, light-haired Abdullah.

"No, a sin! A sin!" Wazir threw his massive hands into the air. "We fell into sin ourselves, suckin' Yakshi, but didn't manage to pull the workers down with us! Our credulity plus their credulity must be multiplied by the Idea so that they become One—like two streams of water! Then seethe with precipitous grease! And begin to spill over! Spill over their banks! In a great flood, suckin' Yakshi!"

"It's very banal to frighten us with arrest, Comrade Nedelin." Rita Gorskaya grins.

"We're not bombers, glory to the Cosmos." Zoya Li opened her fan.

"Nor communists." Bober grinned.

"Unfortunately..." Maul grunted, mashing his cigarette.

"Ladies and gentlemen, credulity is not a sin, but a crime," the thin-faced, sharp-bearded Kholmsky began. "'Tis a crime when a Futurist going out into the people is incapable of using yon people's innate credulity. In any case, Comrade Nedelin, this is your miscalculation. And a miscalculation by the entire congress."

"This was the program that you created!" Masha cried out, delightfully feeling the blood of rage flow into her cheeks. "A program for capitulators! A program for needy do-nothings! They shall have need of us, Comrade Futurists! Of us!"

"I think they've reached the end of that need!" Veksha waved the stumps of his hands. "No one had need of Goran and Zoran, they simply cast brass knuckles and bore into the workers!"

"They poured and bored, suckin' Yakshi!" Wazir thundered.

"And swerved round us on a bend." Kholodov nodded gloomily, looking at Masha, as if he were searching for her bittersweet approval.

"We lost, comrades." Zoya Li fanned herself sarcastically.

"We gave up another round to the Socialist Revolutionary riffraff!" Masha won't calm down, her cheeks still blazing.

"That's a total defeat." Mom nods his head gloomily.

"I don't consider it so." Nedelin straightened up in his chair with such calm in his face that everyone went quiet. "We have a secret weapon," he said, glancing over to the right. "Comrade Timur."

Handsome and exquisitely dressed, Timur began to get up as if he were preparing to be coronated. He always called forth unquiet and overwhelming interest from Masha, as she didn't understand the essence of this beautiful person, and yet, for some reason, she always resolved not to get closer to him. This wasn't professional caution—it was existential. Timur did his work as an underground propagandist irreproachably, calmly, and with well-honed professionalism. The underground soon became attached to him like a knight's armor and the Futurist Party became the sword shining in his fist. He burnt his Aryan bridges. Acted decisively: he fenced, struck, fell, then retreated to a carefully chosen position. But calmly—without any pathos, paranoia, or hysterics.

Holding high his beautiful head with its beautifully trimmed black beard, his neck enthroned by a high, snow-white collar, his long, thin arms stretched out along his slender body, which a blue three-piece suit hugged tautly, Timur began to speak.

"Comrades! In the thirteenth century, the Mongols entered Europe after conquering Russia. Economically, it was an incomparably daintier tidbit than the semideserted *peasantries* of Russia. The knights of Europe gathered together an army and, near Budapest, there was an epoch-deciding battle between the nomads and the Europeans. The nomads utterly destroyed the Europeans. Europe lay before them. But they didn't even enter Budapest. After camping for a little while beneath its walls, they turned around and headed back to the steppes of Russia. For what reason did the army of Khan Batu neither enter nor conquer Europe? The Mongols explained it in this way: There's not enough room for our horses in European cities. Having been born on vast steppes, they felt insecure on city streets. They didn't understand urban spaces. It follows that one cannot conquer or attempt to possess that which one doesn't understand. Attempts by the Europeans to conquer the Russian steppes also demonstrate the syndrome that is the total opposite of claustrophobia: agoraphobia. This was precisely the phenomenon experienced by the armies of Napoleon and Hitler as they advanced east. These boundless spaces frightened the Europeans. They didn't understand how one could possess the steppes, how one could civilize and cultivate them. That's why they were defeated."

Timur fell silent, touching his hips with his long, strong fingers and rocking gently. And continued.

"I just *tested* tellurium for the nineteenth time. And I've overcome the dark veil."

The assembled company stirred.

Raising his hands abruptly, Timur grabbed his hair. His wig slid off his shaved head. A wound was drying out above his left ear.

He closed his eyes and began to sing in a low, clear voice.

Among fields, forests, mountain ranges,
A crystal palace rises like a crag,
It is enormous, beautiful, transparent,
The hundred thousand faces of its light
Overwhelm the heavens,
Crystal columns rise up through the air,
Pillars propping up the wondrous vault,
Its deathless stronghold with transparent floor
Rooted in the ancient mountains' granite.
Soon as a ray of sun burns through the sky,
The sunrise heralds the fine hour,
The wondrous palace wakes up, comes to life,
Fills up with endless buzz of voices,
And people by the thousands, much like bees,
Begin a hard and wondrous day in hive.
And all who live here are so gorgeous,
Marked by special, elevated beauty,
Their faces seem to show nobility,
Love and truth, sincerity and passion,
Their bodies, also consummate and gorgeous,
Full of mobility and strength.
Their blood is free from foreign intermingling,
It pulses solemnly in all their hearts,
Which are ready to fight furiously
Or burn fev'rishly with life's passion.
They are most clever, consummate in spirit,
And speak 'tween themselves without words,
They know no human form of dress,
Their consummate and able bodies
are born naked and so must live,
For joy, for happiness, for love,
For them the day begins with prayers:
Prayers to the shining, sunny day,
To trees, grass, mountains, valleys too,
To beasts and birds and fish and worms.

They pray to nature without words,
Their prayer sings forth in every atom,
It pierces mountains of leaves and granite,
And streams to the blue of sky.
Their beautiful bodies are bowed low,
Bent over as their thoughts do also ring
With endless chorale of grateful chants.
And so they meet the start of each new day,
As if it were the first and last on earth.
And just when a collective wave of prayer
Has irrigated ev'ry atom with its shine,
The palace, like a lily made of crystal,
Opens up to meet the power of the day
And thousands of divine creations
Descend into the Nature that's been blessed,
They now shall fill it with their labor.
Their hands are filled with strength and power,
With energies that bring forth fire.
They know not alienation from all Nature,
That destructive distance and hostility
With which—alas!—inglorious *other* people
Allow themselves to rape the world round them.
They have come to be at one with nature
To bring forth the happiness and joy of being.
Nature gives itself to them with no violence,
They take only what they need
For creation and fulfilling lives.
For they create such wondrous things,
Not knowing any formulas or science,
No worlds of reason filled with ghosts.
They need no *complex* mechanisms,
Need no machines that rattle violently,
No blast furnace, no factory, no *works*.
For they create with touch of hand,
Transform the structure of all matter,

Create that which they need on earth.
They hold dominion over matter,
Create their world, like a sculptor with his clay,
A wondrous, consummate, and endless world,
A world filled with endless possibility.

Timur stopped singing and opened his eyes. The assembled company had been listening intently—barely breathing. Even the flames of the candles and the candelabras seemed to have been created by the same hands he described in the song.

Timur looked out in front of him, penetrating the surrounding world with his gaze and seeming to actually see what he'd been singing about. He was *showing* something to his comrades in this great cause. His lips began to stir, and his voice, now weak but still clear, came to life once again.

Themselves, they also make by hand,
Not knowing any terminal disease,
Nor bod'ly weakness, nor resentment,
All so familiar to people round the world.
They know not fear, nor pain, nor sorrow,
All of this has fled from their imperishable hearts.
Having made their nature consummate,
They have defeated death forever.
Time to them is now completely subject,
For them, there is no past nor future,
There is only *now* in all its glory,
It stands before them like a gold cathedral
Where the solemn mass is carried out
By and for great beings who have conquered death.

Timur fell silent and closed his eyes once again.

Everyone continued to sit motionlessly. Suddenly, a woman's voice cut through the quiet of the living room.

"He was there!"

It was Sister Nadezhda who'd made this exclamation.

And, as if on command, all of them came to their senses, began to stir, and moved over to Timur, who rose up over them.

That night, Nata and Masha were lying in bed after innocent, sisterly caresses and speaking quietly, in a half whisper. A curtain of stars floated across the ceiling.

"Timur passed beyond the curtain," Masha kept repeating as she looked at the stars.

"Passed into that which has come true." Nata was playing with Masha's hair.

"Into the great!"

"Into the real!"

"And that means a lot for us."

"A lot. More than just hope."

"Timur drew back the curtain and saw a palace. A palace! A crystal palace, Nata!"

"A palace of the consummate!"

"A palace of the eternal!"

"Of the immaculate!"

Masha closed her eyes. Nata embraced her, pressing herself against her comrade's body.

"Futurum!"

"Incarnate!"

"Imperishable."

They froze in this embrace for a long time.

"Nata," Masha whispered as if she were revealing a great secret. "I want Timur as a brother. But I'm afraid."

"He is whole," Nata sighed. "He needs neither brothers nor sisters. He needs only one thing."

"Futurum?" Masha pronounced with delight and resentment.

"Futurum," Nata sighed with hope and delight.

And the sisters smiled in the darkness.

15

Ariel placed his hand on the white square of the door.

"I'm listening, Ariel Aranda," a voice rang out.

"I have it," Ariel pronounced.

"If you have it, then come in," the voice replied.

The door slid off to the side. Ariel stepped into the dark entryway. Barely had the door closed behind him when a light flashed on and two German shepherds ran over to him, growling.

"*Suelo!*" the voice pronounced, then the dogs lay down and stopped growling.

"Walk forwards and don't be afraid," the voice ordered.

Ariel moved down the hallway with the dogs moving alongside him. The hallway flowed into an archway, which opened up into a large hall with a dark-red floor and filled with low Japanese furniture. It was cold and smelled of sandalwood in the hall. Ariel walked through the hall and his old, but brilliantly polished, army boots stepped across the wide, soft carpet with tones of burgundy, violet, and black. The carpet led into a comparatively small room with silken wallpaper of a greenish pastel tone. A low table appeared, behind which was sitting a bald carpenter with a homely aspect and a standoffish face. The dogs ran into the office and lay down around the table.

"The figure of your age—fourteen—so impressed me that I told you to come in," the carpenter immediately began to speak in his quiet, natural voice. "I've beat in two hundred and forty-five nails, but this is the first time I'm seeing a client of your age."

"Mr. Carpenter, I'm begging you to make an exception," Ariel pronounced his pre-prepared plea.

"Beg, then. What else can you do?" The carpenter grinned, as he sipped at a decoction of burnt rice from a flat mug.

"I've come from Almería."

"Are bombs still falling there?"

"Rarely."

"What's the situation with foodstuffs?"

"Not great."

"Have you come to Barcelona to eat?"

"I've come to beg you to make an exception, Mr. Carpenter."

"Are you a parrot?"

"No, Mr. Carpenter."

"It's true that you don't look like a parrot. You look more like a crow that got sucked into the turbine of a bomber jet, then spat out."

"I'm really begging you. Here's the nail and here's the money." Ariel showed the money in one hand and the nail in the other.

"Are you a magician?"

"I'm a warrior."

"I see that scar on your lower cheekbone. Is that from a bullet? Where'd you get it?"

"Shrapnel. Near Cádiz."

"How long did you fight for?"

"A year and a half."

"A hero, then. But the war is essentially over."

"I'm not fighting anymore."

"Thank God."

There was a pause. Ariel stood there squeezing the tellurium nail in his right hand and a hundred-thousand peseta note in his left.

"Do you know the Carpenters' Codex, soldier?" the carpenter asked, sipping at his decoction.

"I know about the restriction on *working* with people under seventeen."

"Then why have you come?"

"Because I'm older than that."

"You pressed your hand to the door. Here"—the carpenter called up a hologram of Ariel's hand and his whole life story together with it: his biography, a record of two childhood illnesses, two injuries at war, and one medal. "You're fourteen."

"I'm older, Mr. Carpenter."

"You're fourteen."

"I'm twenty-one."

"What makes you say that?"

"I'm a grown-up."

"Because you were wounded?"

"No. Because I killed nine Wahhabis, severely wounded four, and lightly wounded eighteen."

"And you're sure that your brain matured seven years because of that?"

"I'm twenty-one, Mr. Carpenter."

"You're fourteen, soldier."

"I'm begging you, Mr. Carpenter."

"To beat it in?"

"Yes."

"That particular sinny is forbidden to children under the age of seventeen."

"I'm really begging you."

"In your case, the chance of death would be fifty-two percent. Do you know that?"

"Yes."

"It's not for children."

"I'm a grown-up, Mr. Carpenter, my brain can take it. Believe me! Believe me! It can really, truly take a lot. It's a grown-up brain. More grown up than me."

"That was well put."

There was another pause. The carpenter sipped at his decoction.

"But the codex is the codex, buddy."

"But Mr. Carpenter—"

"Sorry, buddy. It has nothing to do with you and nothing to do with your corpse, which I'd know precisely *what to do* with. Like you warriors, us carpenters have no fear of corpses. It's all because of our codex."

"But, Mr. Carpenter…"

"Come back in three years, buddy. And I'll beat one in. With a discount, as if you were an old client."

"I really need it now."

"In three years."

"Mr. Carpenter—"

"I won't keep you any longer, soldier."

Having heard this last sentence, the dogs leapt up and began to growl quietly as they stared at their master's visitor.

Ariel walked out onto the street and wandered aimlessly. He thought of all the Spanish, English, and Chinese curse words he knew and mumbled them under his breath. But this didn't really help and, soon, tears began to run begrudgingly down his swarthy cheeks. He licked them up with his tongue, reaching up to the scar on his lower cheekbone with it as he continued to wander and mumble. Approaching an intersection, he stopped and noticed that he was still squeezing the nail in his left hand and the money in his right. He put both away into separate pockets, pulled out a smarty, and unfolded it.

"Did you hear everything?"

"I heard everything, Comandante." The smarty looked at Ariel with its tigerish eyes.

"What is to be done?"

"There are two options, Comandante: One, wait three years. Two, make use of the services of riveters. I recommend option one, Comandante."

"Stick your advice up your smart ass."

"Sir, yes, sir, Comandante." Its tigerish eyes flashed.

Ariel put the smarty away into his pocket and moved decisively down the street.

A riveter was soaping up Ariel's head using an old shaving brush with a cracked bone handle. The foam was warm, though there was no hot water in the garret where the riveter had been living for three months. Generally speaking, it was rather gloomy, dirty, and dank there, plus it smelled of pigeon droppings. The riveter heated a mug of water with the flame of an oil lamp.

"With a carpenter, you'd be running a fifty-two percent risk of death, with me it's sixty eight," the riveter began to speak in a quiet, passionless voice as he lathered up Ariel's head.

"I know," Ariel replied.

"I've only ever done four youngsters."

"And how did it go?"

"Only one bit the dust. That's a fantastic average."

Ariel didn't reply. The riveter put the shaving brush down onto a pile of bricks, picked up a straight razor, and began to shave Ariel's head. When he'd finished, he wiped off Ariel's head with a wet nap, sanitized it with rubbing alcohol, unfolded a GPS, stuck it to his head, determined the spot, and marked it. Removed the GPS from his head, sprayed his hands with antiseptic, and began to rub them together.

"You know that young people's legs really set to work after the *slaughter*, right?"

"I know."

"I'll lock the door and you'll be in here for the first two hours. Just don't break it down. And then you can go wherever you want."

"OK."

"Do you know how to remove it?"

"Spray it, pull it out slowly, spray it again, glue it shut, and apply ice."

"Attaboy, you know just what to do."

"Everyone knows what to do."

When the antiseptic on his hands had evaporated, the riveter wiped down Ariel's head with alcohol again, then sprayed the spot.

"Should I lie down?" Ariel asked.

"Sitting is better."

The riveter opened an oblong metal box, in which the tellurium nail Ariel had brought floated in a disinfectant solution, took out the nail, put it to the spot, took out the long-prepared hammer, and, with a single blow, beat the nail into Ariel's head.

And Ariel found himself in the city of battle. And people were killing each other in this city. And many people were lying dead upon the ground, but many were still living as well. And fury filled the hearts of the living. And they killed the opponents of their faith. And Ariel took up his weapon and walked along the streets of the city with it, sowing death. And he began to kill his enemies. And they wanted to kill him, but he was nimbler than his enemies because he didn't fear them. And many fell by Ariel's hand. And he made it to a street where stood a burning house. And he began to walk toward the burning house. And enemies blocked the path to yon house. And they were trying to kill Ariel. But he turned out to be nimbler than these enemies too and he killed them. And he walked up to the burning house. And walked into the burning house. And there were two enemies in that house. And they were hidden so as to try to kill Ariel. But he turned out to be more cunning than his enemies and he killed them. And there was an animal in that house and the animal was crying out, for it feared the flames and could not get out of the house. And Ariel picked up the animal and carried it out of the burning house in his arms. And he released the animal into freedom. And the animal went off to find its territory.

The prostitute came quickly, sitting on Ariel and clutching his shoulders with her small yellow fingers.

"*Olé, mi niño! Me has dejado planchá!*" she screamed in her ridiculous Andalusian and, almost immediately, deftly slid off of the prone adolescent, wiped herself with a towel, perched on a wicker chair, pulled a thin cigarette out from its pack, and lit up. She was Vietnamese but had been born in Andalusia.

Ariel lay smiling at the ceiling with its old-fashioned fan spinning around.

96 · VLADIMIR SOROKIN

"I don't get so worn out with a grown man as I get with you!" she laughed, breathing heavily, but still managing to smoke.

Ariel was silent.

"Do you want some beer?" the prostitute asked.

"Yes."

She opened a second bottle, filled two glasses, stood up, sat down on the bed, and placed one of the glasses on Ariel's chest. He took the glass, pulled back his head, drank it all in one go, let his head back down, and returned the glass to his chest.

The prostitute sat there smoking, drinking beer, and examining Ariel.

"We look alike," she pronounced with a grin. "Like two *dudes*. Have you ever been with a *dude*?"

"No."

"I have," she answered with affected seriousness, then laughed.

Ariel smiled silently.

"Are you going to come today?" she asked, taking his taut penis in her hand.

"I will," he replied.

"Because I have to work tonight."

Ariel was silent.

She finished her cigarette, put its butt into an ashtray, and touched the head of the tellurium nail with her finger.

"Is this what makes you so hard?"

"I dunno."

"What do you mean—you dunno? Tellurium's not really an aphrodisiac."

"I dunno."

"Ah, but I know. Even though I've never tried it. Horrible to think how much dough these nails cost... And people rarely fuck when they're *testing* it. You know why?"

"I dunno."

"Stop repeating yourself! Because it feels better than fucking. Where are you now?"

"I'm there."

"Is it nice there?"

"It's hot," he smirked and covered his eyes.

"Ocean? Sand? Palace? Servants?"

"No. Burning houses."

"Is it a fire or something?"

"Yeah, a fire."

"Are you a pyromaniac?"

"What's that?"

"Do you love to burn down houses?"

"Not particularly."

"Got it. Okay, *chaval*, get warmed up by the fire, then you can come and I can go."

"Hold on"—he abruptly grabbed her arm—"hold on, hold on."

"Did something happen?"

"Now...now..."

His eyes still closed, Ariel's whole body tensed up and he lifted his legs into the air.

"You're so handsome." The prostitute hunched over and kissed his belly. "Obviously you're fucking someone in a fire. Is it, like, the president's daughter? His wife, maybe? She's still got it! Great tits!"

He sighed with relief, opened his eyes, and relaxed, breathing evenly and wiggling around on the sheet.

"That's it. I set it free."

"What?"

"The blue kitty."

The prostitute looked at Ariel silently.

"A house was burning on my left. And there was a kitty inside of it. Under a bed. It'd gotten scared and hid. And it was crying. I wanted to save it right away, but there were two Wahhabis in the house. So I didn't go into the house. And the kitty kept crying. I could hear it. Clearly. But I still walked away."

"And then?" the prostitute asked.

"Then I went into the house, killed the Wahhabis, and set the kitty free."

Ariel was smiling joyfully.

"But I didn't know that it was blue!"

"Does that change anything?"

"No, no…"

"What an interesting trip you're having, *chaval*!" The prostitute hemmed and scratched herself.

"Blue…" Ariel repeated.

He breathed in joyously, closed his eyes, took the glass off of his chest, and put it down onto the floor. He exhaled, opened his eyes, stood up, and walked over to the shower. The prostitute followed him with her boyish gait, taking broad strides with her thin, crooked legs. In the bathroom, Ariel was hopelessly trying to urinate into the sink. His penis was erect. The prostitute embraced him from behind.

"Are we gonna come?"

She was a few centimeters taller than Ariel.

"We shall," he said, looking at himself in the mirror as if he were seeing himself for the first time.

Ariel was sitting on the ground in the aisle near the vestibule in the incredibly crowded night train from Barcelona to Cartagena. Other people were slumbering next to him with their luggage. Ariel had no desire to sleep. After the tellurium, he felt very good. He was filled with that which was good. As if he had been pumped full of fresh, new air. With ozone consisting exclusively of molecules of a glorious future. Every thought and every movement of his body brought Ariel pleasure. The new ozone was singing in the blood running through his veins, buzzing in his muscles, ringing in his bones, and singing in his brain. And it was a song about the future. There was no space left for the past in Ariel's body. And, from now on, he *knew* how to live.

The smarty in his pocket vibrated softly. Ariel pulled it out and unfolded it on his knee. Its tigerish eyes stared at him.

"You asked me to remind you, Comandante."

"Remind me."

A hologram of the blue kitty with the address of its owners rose up over the smarty.

"Mine was a lighter shade," Ariel said.

Another kitty arose.

"That's more like indigo."

Other kitties began to appear—light-blue kitties, indigo kitties, violet kitties—but Ariel just kept muttering "no."

The smarty's tigerish eyes blinked.

"Comandante, the color you're looking for doesn't exist in Almería, Malaga, or Granada."

"Does it only exist in Cádiz? Show me then."

More holograms of kitties arose. But the necessarily tender shade of light blue was nowhere to be found.

"Why aren't there any kitties of this shade in Cádiz?"

"There are four possible reasons, Comandante: the kitty was a one-time gift; the breeders of the kitty have perished or become refugees; the mother of the kitty died or became a refugee; the breeders of the kitty no longer trade in kitties."

"So what should I do?'

"You can try to find that exact kitty."

"Which will have become a grown-up cat in a year." Ariel grinned. "You're as stupid as ever."

"You selected me to be like this, Comandante." Its tigerish eyes blinked.

"How much does it cost to clone a kitty?"

"Between thirty and eighty thousand pesetas, Comandante. There are two laboratories in Almería. Shall I do some price comparisons?"

"Do that."

"Sir, yes, sir, Comandante."

An unshaven man sitting next to him with a soldier's knapsack between his legs shuddered and began to murmur in his sleep.

"There's something else." Ariel took the baseball cap off of his shaven head and scratched at the skin around the bandage with great pleasure.

"Yes, Comandante?"

"Make your eyes more catlike."

"Like these, Comandante?"

Instead of a tiger's eyes, a blue kitty's eyes now blinked forth in front of him.

"I said more catlike, not more kitty-like."

In the dark air of the train car, air that smelled of too many people, a cat's eyes blinked slowly.

16

From: S. I. Ivanov,
Third-Class Lathe Operator,
Russian Orthodox Foundry

To: B. I. Usakhyov,
Director of the Russian Orthodox Foundry

DECLARATION

I am asking to be allocated 120 rubles for the purchase of a tellurium nail and 50 rubles for the services of an Altaian carpenter so that he might beat the nail into my head and so that I might meet with my deceased brother Nikolai who dead sixteen days past and took a set of liquid cutters from our workshop for the secondary manufacture of large shining crosses so as to sell them and continue his binge with that money and it was from that that he dead, and our workshop is already stood still for two weeks by fault of my brother and it's unclear where, why, and how he hid them from his wife who was loath to hit him and not let him drink, and the cutters cost 2,560 rubles, and the factory doesn't have the money to buy a new set for the lathe workshop in this quarter, but brother didn't have time to sell the cutters, that's agreed on in the city, he hid them, we were looking with our relatives and a district officer but didn't find them because brother wasn't himself and he had the shakes he could've shunted them off Lord knows where, but I can find out where he hid them when they beat a tellurium nail into me and I meet with brother and axe him direct and he won't be drunk up there and he'll account for where he shunted the cutters off to. I had a conversation with the party committee as represented by P.A. Barybin and he gave me his support for this project as it will aid our workshop and the factory as a whole because the factory is suffering losses and burying the honor of the party and every ruble matters. I also spoke with Father Mikhailov the rector of our factory temple he said he won't bless my getting beat but he won't stand in my way and then I can read the penitential canon for a month or so after, and go on foot to Optina where I can confess to my sins and partake of the Holy Mysteries. My meeting with my deceased brother will very much aid our workshop and our factory and it shall also help our family to restore the good name of my brother Nikolai.

Yours,
S. I. Ivanov

17

I HAD WANTED to leave in the early morning tomorrow, as had previously been my intention, but, again, nothing went my way. Is that not how my life simply *is* now? Everything trundles past me and how I would've liked it to be; all through external compulsion and the snow ends up in one great lump. I told Gavrila to load up our things as soon as the sun rose. I began to get ready promptly after dinner, wrote my farewell letters, wiped my traces and tabs, *washed* my smartypants, ordered that my chests be taken downstairs, then forbade Vasilisa from knitting and playing and told Eropka to sleep naked in a mitten—so that they both might rise painlessly at dawn. Prayed, fixed my mind upon the eternal, and went to bed early. Just as I fell asleep—a call. Matilda Yakovlevna: they're searching the Akhmetyevs' house.

What a beastliness, this bit of news! These days, 'tis not given to us to know from which direction the poison arrow shall fly. As the deceased Darya Evseyevna used to say: friendship with the *okolnichi* won't save you, Nikita Markovich. As if she'd divined it in the water. I got up, dressed myself, and lit up the news bubble: Mr. Akhmetyev's arrested, along with his wife Nataliya Kirillovna, both daughters, and their son-in-law. "Most insidious enemies of the Moscovian State." If He went after the Akhmetyevs, 'twould seem that a new wave of red won't wait long to wash over us. Tomorrow night, they'll take Solonevich, Vasily, and Gerhard. Then they'll come for the Moscovians on the city committee. I'll be stretched across the rack too. I wouldn't find suffering for Yurochka too terribly *much*, but my intended business would then grind to a halt. "Most insidious enemies of the state..." That beast made a vow to the Metropolitan that there'd be no new purges. Never trust a pig that tells you it's done eating shit. His promises have now fled from the list of that which I believe; I should never have accorded any trust to that two-legged degenerate and have yet again proven myself to be a gullible fool. And not solely me—the entire circle of widows. "I touch not the widows of mine enemies." Of course not! "If the wolf has sated itself with human blood just once, so shall it sate itself once again." And for the last year, the ghoul's lived solely on the blood of His subjects. He drank, drinks, and shall drink our blood until He tumbles down into His grave. That's the truth. I thought I'd leave without burning any bridges: the thought of being able to return someday warmed my heart. But now I shall have to burn everything, to chop it up while it's still alive, and to flee without looking back. I didn't mince my words: Load up our things, Gavrila! Half an hour to warm up, five minutes for packing! To flee means to flee, after all. I rolled up my smartypants and flushed it down the toilet so that the oprichniks might search for my traces anon. And I took the smart birch bark alone; that shall be enough for my diary. The gates are wide open and the servants howl. I pass through as if I were an inspecting commanding officer: farewell and hold no rancor toward me! And we rolled off at one in the morning under the lupine sun. My auto-mobile smoked its way through my native ZaMoscvorechye, Vasilisa in tears, Eropka whimpering into my bosom, and me sitting still as a stone—not a single sob. We pass by our Church of Grigory of Neocaesaria—the church wasn't stirring. Here is where you kissed me on the lips and made me your wife, Yurochka. Farewell, church. They say that it was from this spot that Vasily the Dark, having escaped from Tatar captivity, first lay eyes on the white stones of the Kremlin upon his return and wept with joy. But I cannot see the sinister Kremlin from here and I shed no tears. Farewell, oh my ZaMoscvorechye! Farewell, cruel Moscow. Farewell, hopeless and inhuman Moscovia. Farewell, friends and lovers. Farewell, Kremlin ghoul.

Farewell to all and for all time!

October 2

The auto-mobile bucked, sneezed twice, then went silent, rocking with inertia. Strapping and in a black sheepskin coat belted round with a red girdle, Gavrila waited for the auto-mobile to stop, slid out unhurriedly, and, paying no attention to the honks and curses of those driving past, walked to the end of the auto-mobile's train with his swaying gait.

Despite the late hour, the Moscovia-Ryazan Way was lively; state auto-mobiles running on gas and diesel rattled down the left lane, which was indicated in red, private scooters and auto-mobiles took up the first and second lanes, riders on horseback took up the third, and long-range two- or three-story cart horses hitched up to freight trains took up the fourth, which was wide and adjacent to the side of the road.

The beginning of October was cloudy and dank. A cold wind blew down from the north, promising an early winter.

Gavrila walked over to the last of the three trailers, unfastened the burlap, and began to pull out a bag of potatoes. A wooden brake squeaked behind him, following which there was a quack and a cracked voice began to speak.

"Can't ye pull over like a normal human being, ye ragged wolf?! Ye stop in the middle of the road like a bitch and we're supposed ta just go around ye?!"

"Oh, you'll go around, you unmagnificent failure," Gavrila answered in his bass voice, easily swinging the bag over his shoulder and refastening the burlap.

"May devils tear ye into little bits, ye son of a bitch!" the man cried at the top of his lungs.

"And may you be taken into the asshole of the earth, old man." Gavrila carried the bag calmly, waving his left hand.

"May ye ride a Chinese pig!"

"Take a breath through your ass, old man, and keep on drivin'," Gavrila replied, walking over to the auto-mobile and dropping the bag from his broad shoulder with deliberate ease.

The disgruntled man began to go around the stopped auto-mobile, cursing Gavrila as he drove. But Gavrila had stopped paying attention; he pulled a key on a rope out from his girdle, undid the lock on the neck of the intake valve, pushed back the iron lid, untied the sack, and deftly poured potatoes into it. As usual, several of the potatoes didn't fit. With a practiced motion, Gavrila pulled his lash out from underneath his box, threw the extra potatoes there, then put the lash back. Then he shut the intake valve, put the key back into his girdle, turned away from the auto-mobile and toward the road, hunched over, and noisily blew his nose from both nostrils onto the ground.

A scooter passed by with an open hood, under which the recently shod horses fought ably against their load, one of them persistently neighing in its thin voice; its coachman was cross-eyed and half-asleep.

Gavrila wiped his nose with his broad hand, wiped his hand off on the bottom of his sheepskin coat, sat down atop the box, and began to slowly roll a cigarette in the shape of an "L," looking off to the sides from under his thick, black brows, as if he weren't planning on going anywhere. As always, the way smelled of horse manure, sharp diesel exhaust, and far-too-sweet potatoes. Having finished rolling up his cigarette, Gavrila bent it into the "L," pulled out a flint, and lit up. A stream of blue gas set the rice paper alight. Gavrila took a drag, put away the flint, then turned the key in the ignition. The autonomic cracked, shredding the potatoes into a pulp, and the main sputtered, then growled loudly. Gavrila waited for a moment, exhaling smoke through his nostrils, then half opened the flap. The growling of the engine gave way to its usual rumble. Gavrila undid the hand brake on the auto-mobile, switched the speed, squeezed the coupler, pulled on the gauntlets, took up the principle wrapped in self-generating insulation tape, and gently pressed the coupler's pedal. The auto-mobile began to move smoothly.

"Hold forth!" he muttered the parting admonition he always said—even back when he was a coachman—puffed at his hand-rolled cigarette, and began to slowly increase the pace.

October 3

We dragged our way toward Ryazan all night. I had spent too long under lock and key, hadn't seen anything of the outside world, hadn't left Moscow for eight months already, and couldn't imagine what on earth the Ryazanian Way could be like. I thought we'd roll like the wind all night to push Moscow out of our hearts all the faster. What a thought! On this four-lane road, even at night there's such pandemonium, one can hardly believe it: people go and go and never get tired of going. An army of travelers! Because it's cheaper at night—the toll fares are half as much as during the day. At first, everyone drives more or less as they're supposed to, everyone in the proper lane. But yon order comes to an end as soon as you pass by the ring road: three-story cart horses here, riders there, and auto-mobiles all the way over yonder—all mixed up as if 'twere Babylon! And all for that same old reason: manure from the long-range cart horses. A problem. Heaps of it all over the place and not even close to all of them are fresh. An antediluvian abomination . . . The lawlessness and pandemonium are a function of those heaps. Indeed, how is it possible to go round these great masses of shit at full speed without inflicting damage or surprise upon others? It'd be easy to get flipped over around here, one never knows. Shame and ignominy. 'Tis the state vehicles alone that are unaffected by this, flying in the red lane on the left side without even glancing at us. Nobles have been considered to be second-rate in the Moscovian state for three years now. Vasilisa crosses herself and curses. Eropka slid out from my collar and is now tugging at my earrings cheerfully. I'm not up for cheerfulness right now: our state of affairs is disheartening . . .

The ghoul purged the Council of Roads twice—imprisoned them, made them destitute, sent them to Kapotnya to the swamp of many mazuts, and ordered that the boss be publicly whipped. They whipped him and he screamed a little bit on Bolotnaya Square, but then managed to squeeze his whipped ass back into his old chair. And nothing changed. Just as they didn't used to clean the roads in Moscovia, so too do they not clean them now. They rake up the Metropolitan Ways, but all the other roads are Augean stables. "Once there were whorish-ness and hope, anon there's hopeless whorishness," as the deceased Yurochka used to say. And there is no Hercules within our state who might make everything clean. Nor does it seem there shall be. Alas!

We made it to the Moscovian border by morning. As soon as I saw the walls, the gates, and the eagles, my heart set to trembling: What if they don't let us out? What if He already gave the order to his oprichnik hounds? For dogs take more pleasure in hunting rabbits on the run . . .

We drove up to the gates and the common line to get away from the state ghoul is a verst long. It seems I'm not the only one tearing off into freedom. We turn into the special line, as the prince's coat of arms still shines on the auto-mobile for the nonce. We drive up to the barrier. A sotnik stands there with six archers. I give him my documents. He asks for what reason I, Princess Semizorova, a mem-ber of the Party, am leaving the limits of the Moscovian state. I give him my preprepared reply that I am going to China for medical tourism. He tells me the new rate of the state exit tax. Leaving Mosco-via now costs a thousand golden rubles. For up to six months of absence, yon sum shall be returned to the citizen in full. And after those six months, one gold ruble shall be deducted every day. This is the current system.

I gave him a purse with the gold and was given a receipt.

I realized that they had been given no orders relating to me. I was relieved. Everything is as it was before. I maintained my outward calm. I gave him a silver ruble to not inspect. He asked about contra-band: gasoline, memory, wedges? My tellurium wedges are scattered in the ZaMoscvorechian snow, as I'd thrown them out the window. Voluntarily. Otherwise I'd be smuggling them in my vagina, as I usually do. But enough . . . enough sleeping with a ghost . . . The sotnik was surprised we were exporting so many potatoes in the trailer as, he said, they're cheaper in Ryazan. I expressed that we still must needs make it to Ryazan. The fool nodded his head and raised the barrier.

With divine aid, we departed from yon ghoulish kingdom.

October 4

Eropka the Jester awoke in the princess's bosom at a pothole's impact: the scooter had been jostling in the line to the entry gate of the Kingdom of Ryazan for a long time. Grunting, the jester climbed up the bone buttons of her blouse, squeaking out a song as he maneuvered beneath her light fur coat of shorn mink.

"Tralala, tralala, the cat's house is up for sale."

Slumbering in her deep armchair, the princess reached out.

"Eropushka..."

It was stuffy in the cabin; all three windows were misted over from the breath of the princess and her servant Vasilisa. Vasilisa was sleeping in the armchair opposite. Barely had the princess unbuttoned the collar of her fur coat when Eropka stuck his long, red nose out through it.

"There we are!"

"Why will you not sleep, Eropushka?" The princess began to further unbutton her fur coat.

"Oh Mama! I got all sweaty in your bosom, it's like a sauna in there!" Eropka clung to the shoulder of the coat with his short white fingers, grunted, pulled himself up, and sat down directly across from the princess's face.

This was a littlun with a big head that looked like a potato tuber and large, chubby, white hands like those of a five-year-old child's. With its exorbitantly long nose, long, pinched mouth, and swollen slits for eyes, his face was always laughing. His red hair was neatly trimmed in a circle and his large ears jutted out. He was dressed in a spotted white kosovorotka belted round with a loop of coral beads and flannel bloomers tucked into fashionable ankle boots with silver tips that jutted upwards. Eropka wore a massive gold ring with the monogram of the Prince and Princess Semizorov on the index finger of his right hand—a gift from the princess's deceased husband.

Having taken a seat on his mistress's shoulder, Eropka pulled gently at her earring, as was his habit, and began to squeak.

"A bad dream came to me, oh light of mine,* Varvara Erofeyevna."

"What was your dream, you little fool?" The princess spoke with the jester without shifting her exhausted, pale, and beautiful face with its thin lips and greenish-brown, deep-set eyes.

"Let me catch my breath, then I shall tell you anon."

The princess took out a narrow boxwood cigarette case, removed a cigarette from it, and put it between her thin lips. Eropka immediately reached his chubby hand into his pocket, pulled out a tiny lighter, clicked it, and held it up. A narrow blue flame seared the tip of the cigarette. The princess took a drag, then quickly exhaled a narrow stream of smoke.

"It seems to me that you've been lighting up painfully often, oh Mama..." Vasilisa muttered from her chair without opening her eyes.

With a small bruise underneath one eye, her high-cheeked, masculine face remained immobile.

Eropka took out a handkerchief, stuck his nose into it, and blew noisily, shaking his head comically as he did so. Then he wiped at his sweaty forehead with the same handkerchief.

"A dream came to me that an Altaian carpenter beat a little nail into the crown of my head and I became a bigun."

The princess smirked wearily.

"How many times can you have the same dream..."

"He's lying," Vasilisa pronounced without opening her eyes.

"As soon as dawn comes, I'll swear on a foldable icon!" Eropka squeaked solemnly, threatening Vasilisa with his crumpled handkerchief.

"And what is it about your dream that's so frightening?" Her cigarette smoking, the princess wiped the condensation off the window with her hand and squinted at the road, where various means of transport and horses of every possible size gloomily towered forth.

"Oh Mama, 'twas frightening that as I began to grow, the clothes on me broke and burst at a pace with my enlargement. And at yon moment, I'm not standing in just any place, but in God's temple."

*An archaic Russian form of affectionate address.

"Oh Lord..." Vasilisa muttered, then yawned with her whole mouth gaping open.

"Not in your temple though, but in our temple—where they used to still baptize littluns. And it was as if our entire *brood* from that era was standing round me, all sixty-five littluns. And Father Paisus is delivering a sermon. About humility and things both large and small, saying that a little person was also capable of creating big things. And as I stand there listening, I suddenly begin to grow. And everyone begins to look at me, but I don't know what to do. And, as luck would have it, oh light of mine, Varvara Erofeyevna, my pecker sets to rising."

Vasilisa giggled and opened her eyes.

"And it grows and grows, stretches out so much that it stands directly before Father Paisus's face like a battering ram, a touch more and it'll knock him over! But even so, I just stand, stand, stand there, neither alive nor dead, and then—boom! I wake up."

Vasilisa laughed.

"What a load of nonsense!"

Curling out her lips and not turning her beautiful head, the princess blew a stream of smoke toward Eropka as she often did. Grunting, he moved onto the princess's neck and grabbed her by her two ears from behind, as he often did.

"As soon as we get past the border, tell Gavrila to stop off at a decent tavern," the princess said to Vasilisa, paying no attention to Eropka's relocation.

Vasilisa's high-cheeked face went dark.

"'Tis not necessary, oh Mama."

"Give the order without fail." The princess put out her cigarette butt in the wooden ashtray and closed her eyes.

October 5

The country of Ryazan met us with a clean road and delicious pies. I had grown peckish from all my worries and ordered Gavrila to pull off at the first acceptable tavern. And the Ryazanian tavern didn't keep us waiting—it immediately sailed out of the morning fog that'd settled round us past the outpost and the tall ratniks with luminous cudgels. A floor cloth came out, bowed, and invited me into the Lords' Hall and Gavrila and Vasilisa into the Hall of Bastardry. I drank my fill of green tea with honey and ate a half vatrushka and a pair of sturgeon pasties. Not able to restrain myself, I ordered a glass of rowanberry vodka. Thank God Vasilisa didn't see. Just a little glass. After such worrying, dispensations must be made. Eropka soaked a crumb in vodka, sucked at it, and sang me a song about a kitty. And on the bubble, they're playing an old Soviet sinny about a Hussar maiden. In Ryazan, morals are less rigid—incomparably so. After they shook off that Wahhabi henchman Sobolevsky six years ago with Chinese help, everything began to go smoothly for them. They even clean their roads, not at all like in Moscovia . . . I wanted to call Marinka Solonevich from the tavern, but changed my mind; what if after we've driven through Ryazan, he gets to me in cheerful Tataria? I restrained myself with the help of a second glass. And a third one too, which flew by with all the sweetness of a spring swallow.

And I felt terribly well.

Vasilisa and Gavrila were drinking a fourth cup of tea with gingerbread and raspberry jam when a lanky and preoccupied floor cloth from the Lords' Hall came into the Hall of Bastardry.

"Your mistress is makin' a fool of herself in there."

"Oh Lord," Vasilisa sighed.

Gavrila quickly put a half-eaten piece of gingerbread into his pocket, stood up, and crossed himself in front of the iconostasis.

"It's my fault," Vasilisa muttered with fury in her voice, then jumped up and hurried off behind the floor cloth to the Lords' Hall.

Princess Semizorova was standing on a table, clutching herself by the elbows and swaying. Her eyes were closed and her cheeks were sickly red. A plate crunched beneath the heel of her boot. Three customers looked up at the princess dumbfoundedly. With a glass in his hands, the drunk Eropka sat imperturbably enthroned on a pillow.

"Oh Mama…" Vasilisa sighed mournfully and malevolently, letting fall her long arms.

"The wo-o-o-oorld has fa-a-a-a-allen do-o-o-o-own upo-o-o-on you like a we-e-e-e-edge of whi-i-i-ite li-i-i-i-ight," the princess sang violently without opening her eyes.

18

Sweaty Robin didn't have to wait for long. Even without any *touchings* or "hello!" in the parking lot, I could still hear him as if from inside a well. That which a *smarty* hears, even an idiot can understand. What a position! Now all the idiots have *smarties*—they mold them over their domes like a Jew with a *kippah*—and then they sweat. Sweat isn't tears. And a grave isn't a sanatorium for incompetent nail-pullers. What a story! So changing a *smarty* for a smarty just means losing nails. That's why Robin molded it over himself back at the station. So much experience! He was riding on the tram, sweating, and not paying any attention to his surroundings. What a system! Look around today, choke tomorrow. And he who chokes must be taken to the lazaretto. They need healthy guys for the *hardware* business. Islamic Stockholm ain't Protestant Bucharest. Here, they won't let you look around for long. Blixtnedslag! Why shoot? Blood means tidying up. The Swedes have a simple law—turning blue is better than blushing. Here, they respect visiting *lightning rods*—there was a lot of electricity left over after the war. Enough for everyone. They'll sort it out with the avatars later—real slowly. The Swedes have no reason to rush these days. The *blue original* is a hindrance to no one. It doesn't get dirty or ask for self-generating porridge. It won't get *warm*—stay blue! What a principle! And Robin takes other principles into account. So it's better to sweat than to turn blue. Robin and the Swedes got ambushed in the *new* parking lot. Better. Deep and furious, there are no fields and the *eyes* are bedaubed. No options. Who will give rotten guarantees as regards the *new*? The biggest idiot? Our closest friend? He who shows his fangs? The maws of Stockholm are fastened shut and there are no idiots. So sweat and *think*. Just sweat wisely, don't fiddle with the *hat*, and do touch the fuse. What trust! That which we entrust to a *smarty*, we take away from an idiot. What a routine! Business trip, jewelry work. Robin couldn't keep *flies* in his nose even before the war, but it's even worse now. He sat still for six minutes and the smarty warns him: They're coming. Two white SUVs. As if to a wedding. The fields are clean. The avatars are *clear*. I didn't go out, but tossed the *little ball*—guys, I'm alone and without *relatives*. They understood and picked it up. Now, nails are a nonexclusive product. After all that commotion, everyone just wants a happy life. What a rebirth! A hardware store ain't no antique shop. That's why the prices are *icy*, and not *ironclad*. Ice ain't iron, you can melt it. But in order to melt it, heat is required. When you have *heat*—stoke it and let it flow. No—take it, blow on your fingers, and get outta there! In terms of *heat*, everything's cool with Robin. He started to throw around hot *splinters*. The Swedes don't even frown—stick it in, man, we've got thick skins. He beat it in at 24 percent. They didn't even frown. That's the locals for you. No masquerades for them, that's not in their blood. And lengthily airing out the tongue isn't their style. Robin said so—they did it. That's it. Oh, the North! Robin got out of his *hole*, threw off the fields, and lit up the *hallway*. The Swedes are peace itself. He walked over to the jeep and glanced inside. Three armored trunks with a thousand nails each. What an arsenal! As Bucharest carpenters say: enough for the house *and* the birdhouse. He took a sample and verified its *acidity*. The purest tellurium. Took out the smarty so that the Swedes would touch the *possibilities*. Unrolled it. And right when they touched a finger to it, Ibrahim and his Norwegian Arabs came crawling out of the walls. What a surprise! A third player. Neither Robin nor the Swedes expected anything like this. And the Norwegians immediately laid on heavy fire from two trombones, then fanned out lead peas. The jeeps burst apart like spheres. The Swedes—splattered across the ceiling. To Valhalla! They really didn't see 'em coming. How could they've? Everything was clean on the trace—never been cleaner. Robin checked three times. The Swedes too. A magic trick? Technology! Ibrahim wasn't made with a finger. It turns out they'd been *building*. A team of dark build-ers ordered to build a flat hallway. A month of work—twenty thousand new krones. What a job! But it was worth the bother—three trunks worth one and a half millies! Ibrahim *knew*. And Robin didn't know that he *knew*. Robin is more or less alive, but with one less leg and with his guts in his hands. He was ready for everything, everything except for Ibrahim. And didn't think to think of him. Though he was *thinking*. What a shock! And Ibrahim won't finish him off, he walked off like a businessman, took the three trunks with him, then labels, then molds the *signs*. Robin's just lying there. Still conscious. Not a word to Ibrahim. What would he say? If someone violates the contract, just shut up. Silence is gold, not tellurium. *Stupid* Robin's holding his guts. He thinks—I'll buy myself out of this. They'll tuck my guts in and sew me a new leg. What else would he be thinking of? Certainly not about when they met in Bucharest and drank tea, ate pilaf with lamb and lokum, or Ibrahim telling a parable about a lame dervish and a white mare, or when they laughed at their down-stairs neighbor: I'm going to call the police, it's *too quiet* up there! Especially not about how Ibrahim *showed* him, gave him, and out-weighed him—then they even prayed together to Allah. When you're holding your guts in your hands, it's better not to recall such things. Lie down and watch. As the Norwegians take inventory of the trunks, Ibrahim says: Open one. They opened it. He took out a nail and walked over to Robin. Thank you, man, he says, for having the right *approach*. It's good, he says, that you didn't look around on the tram. You're now entitled to a bonus. And he beats the nail into Robin's forehead with the grip of his pistol. Robin stayed there lying down on the floor. No new leg or old *flames* for him to wait for now. What an act of vengeance! And they took the chests, clambered out through the breach, went up on the hooks, severed the guard, sat down on their *camels*, and "the tired caravan heads off into the distance."

19

THE BUS always gets me to the hotel by six for the first shift. Today too, it got me here on time. Real early, still dark, and you can't see nothin'. I walk into the staff room, change, pretty myself up, and even have time to knock back some tea and exchange a word with the other maids. Frankly, I'll admit it, I've only got two real friends here—Oksana and Tatyana. Fortunately, we're usually on duty together on the first shift, but today neither of them are here. Oksana's kid took real ill and Tatyana's husband just got back from a crusade. At six thirty, my shift begins. And my day with it. Our hotel—the Slavyanka—isn't too big, but it's comfy, and the main thing is it isn't altogether most expensive like other hotels in Moscow. You gotta look in Za-Moscvorechye for the cheap ones 'cuz here in Moscow you won't find a chamber for less than fifty rubles per night. But here, a one-person chamber costs forty rubles per night. That's real manageable, I'd say. It's because the boss man is wise and God-fearing, and not a grasper or a bloodsucker. He loves the guests, always walks out to meet 'em, and when he hired me, the first thing he asked was: Avdotya Vasilievna, do you like servin' people? A question I pretty much didn't expect, I hadn't prepared for it or anything, so I just spoke my mind: I love it! And that's the truth. Some people force themselves to serve, but I'm always ready to do nice things for other people—I don't must needs force myself to. I always clean up real nice without any carelessness. I don't have a family and probably won't have one either, as I'm not most beautiful in terms of my face. To put it better—I'm totally ugly. My body ain't much to look at either—chubby, short-legged, and big-boned. If I end up having someone, it won't be for another twenty or so years, when I get up into my fifties. That's what a Chinese fortune-teller told me. She said: In your life shall appear an older man when you yourself are already not at all young, and you shall live together, and everything shall be granted to you. God willing, that's what's gonna happen. But for the nonce, I live with my mom in PodMoscovia. We're renting a two-room apartment in sunny Solntsevo. It's a bright apartment, but it really is small. Mom's already seventy, she gave birth to me real late 'cuz God's will can accomplish anything. She gets a pension for Dad, who was a policeman and got killed when the war started. Mom's pension is twenty-six rubles and my salary is sixty. We pay fifty for the apartment. We have enough to live on and Mom sets a little aside. Riding to work is real convenient for me—first I go to the University by monorail, then I switch to a bus. These days, I'm usually on the morning shift, but before this, I would always work the night shift, which started at eleven thirty. I couldn't keep that up for long. Not because I couldn't sleep, but for a totally different reason. I have one joy in this life—the love of others. If a person isn't given their own love, they feed on the love of others. Or God's love. But I have no plans to run off to a monastery, am generally unprepared for a monastic life, and love my human life. I love human love mortally, to the point of insanity—so much so it turns my heart cold. That's why I work in a hotel. The thing I adore most in this world is listening to how people love each other. So I work the night shift less because I'm trying to keep my heart in one piece. On the night shift, I was only concerned with one thing: how I might overhear the love of others. All of my thoughts were about that and only that, my mind totally focused on it alone, and all of my knack and understanding worked to track down and eavesdrop until I couldn't take it anymore. I walk through the hallways at night, my legs shaking, my hands shaking, and my heart pounding with expectation. The sweetest thing will be when I see the couple from the restaurant walking up to their chamber in each other's arms after dinner. My heart immediately skips a beat and I follow behind them like a lunatic. My legs are trembling and my mouth's all dry, I head up in their wake and I see what chamber they go into, and right away I'm laboring to get into the neighboring chambers. As long as there are no lodgers in them, that is. That's the main condition for secret eavesdropping. And it almost always turns out my way, as if someone were helping me—my beloved, hot-wingèd Angel of Secret Love. And in the neighboring chamber I take my lil' eavesdropping device out of my bra, put it to the wall, and listen, listen, listen . . . This little device can hear clean through anything, through any kind of brick or concrete, you can even hear the rustling of the sheets, not to mention the voices . . . And, in this world, I needn't anything more than these minutes. I listen, completely paralyzed, as if I were drinking divine nectar. It all began when I was a little girl. Once I was staying with my godmother at her dacha for the summer, when her lover came to visit her. Her husband earned his living by way of the forest and had shoved off to Arkhangelsk. Her lover came to her at night. And I heard from behind the wall how they'd please each other. I liked eavesdropping so much that I spent all my energy just waiting for her lover to come again. And, a couple days later, he'd come again. And please my godmother all night long. I clung flat against the wall, picked up a glass so I could hear better, put that to the wall, then listened to their moans. My godmother went so far as to wail with pleasure and plea: What're you doing to me, Sashenka? And I just stood there as if I'd turned to stone and it was so nice that I couldn't hear or see anything around me, and even if the whole world had collapsed, my entire soul would have remained paralyzed in those sweet moans. There's been nothing more powerful than that in my life. I've never had any loves . . . who wants an ugly woman like me? Twice I slept with men when I was drunk— once with a kid and once with an African security guard—and I didn't like it. I've watched a lotta porn, but didn't like that either—for, can that whorishness verily be compared to this whisper? There's nothing sweeter than lovers moaning behind a wall. That whisper would penetrate me to the point that I'd come home from the hotel in a terrible state, Mom asks: Dunechka, what's with you, can it be you've fallen ill? And indeed—I had fallen ill, I was barely able to move my own legs after my shifts. I come home, collapse onto the bed, but I can't sleep—all of the lovers' whisperings are singing in my head. And my heart begins to ache, so I take medicine, get some injections, but then I decide—I'm not gonna run myself to ruin, you can't put such strain on your heart. I made a deal with my boss so that I would do the night shift solely once a week. And that's just right: it's no good stuffing yourself with sweets every day. I wait for that night all week. I work four days on the first shift and I come in at night on Friday. Friday's a good day for lovers too, I must needs solely catch 'em on time. A lot of people come to the Slavyanka for love, though we're not a house of meetings. I thought I might somehow get a job in a house of meetings, but stopped myself in time: I'd have died eavesdropping there, my heart would've gotten shredded. Here, I had just the right amount of joy, my cup didn't overfloweth. Once was enough to get my fill of eavesdropping for the whole week— till I couldn't take it anymore. And I love the first shift in the morning, when everyone's gone to breakfast and I slip into a chamber where lovers were loving the night before, get down onto my knees in front of the bed, plunge my face into the still-warm linens, and just stay like that...yeah, just stay like that. The bed's still so warm and it remembers all the moaning. So, today, I'm walking down the hallway on the second floor and I see two people coming out of chamber 206—a respectable-looking, gray-haired foreigner and one of our little boys, slender and wearing a silk kosovorotka. The boy is just a cherub. They set off for breakfast. I saw right away this wasn't a father with his son, but two lovers. It'd seem the visiting gentleman had rented out this li'l one for the night. I walked into their chamber. An empty bottle of champagne in a bucket, two glasses, an *empty* tellurium nail in one of them, and golden candy wrappers. The bed's all crumpled and beaten up. One pillow on the floor and another in the middle of the bed. It'd seem the foreigner'd placed a pillow underneath the cherub in order to love him up more comfortably. I get down onto my knees and stuff my face into the pillow on the bed. And just stay like that.

20

"ROBOTS!" Kerya the machinist bellowed out so loud they heard him in the third car.

Their hearts skipped and tripped and skipped a beat: a psychic attack!

Though they'd been expecting it for a long time, the cry made the hairs of the whole Profiteering Brotherhood of the Bag stand on end.

They all began to bristle up.

"Robo-o-o-ots!"

"Rebo-o-o-ots!!"

"Anaspheres!!!"

Click-clack. Bang-clang.

The brothers from Tambov in the second car leapt up and the brothers from Orlov in the first car roared. But the brothers from Voronezh in the third car were the *baddest* and they didn't get scared— if you're from Belogorye, you're ready for anything.

Everyone rushed to his rod.

Martin stuck himself to a machine gun and Makar loaded a clip into a rifle.

"At the ready-y-y-y!!"

The brothers boomed and thundered in the cars. And the cars swayed like a longboat.

Stomp-stamp.

"Weapons ou-u-u-ut!"

They clacked.

They jerked.

They pressed themselves to the windows armed with whatever they had.

And through the windows—only steppe. Hazy heat. And a flash on the horizon as if someone had built a steel barrier: a chain of...

Robots.

They take broad steps. All-encompassing steps. Pummeling steps. In great numbers—no economy to 'em.

The Brotherhood of the Bag exhaled, fogging up the glass.

"Anaspheres!"

"Sixth model, let's make 'em piss blood!"

"Te-le-col-u-u-u-umns!!!"

"The Kerch jerk-off set loose the oyster mushrooms!"

"Time to meet the psychic attack!"

And Bogdan's voice—stentorian, authoritative, and overwhelming.

"Win-dows down!"

They unlatched the latches. Barrels through the windows. At the ready!

"Bring us forward just a touch!"

And the locomotive was already bringing them forward *just a touch*—there's not been enough coal for high speeds since Nalchik. The train's loaded up to the brim: ghee, lard, wheat, salt, Kerch herring, seeds, and Caspian roach. A lotta goods! And the steam train is like the little engine from the fairy tale. Even at this pace, it's clear it'll puff its way home... The bagly society was hungry for a powerful machine—the Simferopol bandits racked up the price four times; they could smell the want, that was clear.

Moving slowly and expecting a psychic attack. And the robots unarmed—why fill the goods with holes if you can lift 'em whole?

Bogdan: "Don't shoot without my command!"

But the bagmen's nerves give out.

Crack-bang! Crack-bang! Crack-bang!

The Voronezhians in the third car couldn't restrain themselves.

They knocked over a dozen silvery robots. But for what? The chain closed again. Many robot links in the chain.

And now the Tambovian oil carriers don't restrain themselves.

"We're ruined, brothers!"

"Save yourselves!"

"We're dead!!!"

But Bogdan extinguishes the wicks of the panickers. A fist in someone's ugly mug and a Mauser in someone else's mouth.

"Get to your places, ye *knights-who-can*, it'll be because of you if we fall!"

A knee into someone else's ass.

"To the loopholes, shmack-givers!"

Panic is suppressed aboard the train.

And the robots are real close. They shine unbearably in the sun.

Bogdan—loading the Mauser.

"Ready!"

The robots within sight. They surround the train and throw their net around it like a fat whale.

"Fire!!!"

Crack-bang! Crack-bang! Crack-bang!

Tak-tak-tak-tak!

Pfiou-pfiou-pfiou!

A good third of the psychic attack mowed down. But two-thirds reach the train. Hijacking!

Telecolumn 2049, or Anasphere 6000+ robots are programmed for one thing: climbing onto trains and throwing goods out the window. They have no other goals. They never work against the strength of the living. This is what makes them frightening—they don't aim at the bagmen, but eagerly reach for the bags.

And again.

Crack-bang! Crack-brack!

Tak-tak-tak!

Point-blank now.

The faceless, hook-handed, silvery robots climb through the windows. Attempting to melee with them would be useless. Shooting point-blank in the train cars would be dangerous—wouldn't take long to massacre each other. Only with a sledgehammer to the dome can a robot be crushed.

"Sledgehammers!!!" Bogdan thunders.

The brothers pick up the sledgehammers already lying in store. And aim for shining silvery domes.

But the robots know their iron business: rob the train and to the bagmen—zero attention. As if they weren't there at all. Bags of grub through the windows. And other robots under them—to catch and drag the bags across the steppe. Some jump out the windows squeezing a bag in their arms.

The shining ants drag away bags of oil, lard, and perfumy seeds…

Kerya the machinist curses and the little locomotive puffs forward with its final strength.

The robots rummage around, combing through the train shamelessly and wordlessly.

Those who didn't get their shining skulls smashed in—out the window with their quarry.

The bagmen bid 'em farewell with curses and tears.

'Tis only Bogdan who imperturbably paces about, twisting his bald head from side to side with a tellurium nail shining from its crown.

"Make ta-lly of our losses, brothers!"

Make tally… Oh they make tally, but who shall compensate these losses? All that remains is to watch one's beloved bag of Caspian roach from Odessa march off into the distance.

And that's how it is… the bagman's harsh lot.

21

OPEN SPACE flashed forth in Magnus the Hasty's single eye. And not an ashy, plasticine, peeling space like the Lausanne Christmas carousel after it was incinerated by the Taliban. And not fragmented brick and granite like the Geneva downtown after it was bombed by Sheikh Mansour's squadron. And not the *alp*ine spurs of Switzerland. Here, in the southern part of what was once France, in the middle of the summer, the space was tricolored, like the flag of the new Republic of Languedoc, which had united four provinces: these colors were plantlike, stony, and divine. It didn't smell of ashes here. Other smells whistled into Magnus's nostrils as he jumped over the Swiss border: lavender, oil refineries, cheese factories, gas terminals, and comfortable, sun-kissed towns. Magnus skirted round big cities, not wishing to be distracted. He was in a hurry. The sun beat down. Violet fields of lavender stabbed at his eyes. Dust swirled down stony roads. But this was not the brick dust of the destroyed cities of Switzerland. It was pleasant to breathe in the dust of Languedoc. Magnus's high-speed boots, which he'd had fixed up in Salzburg for one hundred thirty-seven pieces of gold directly after the Battle of the Three Peoples, were bringing him directly to his goal: La Couvertoirade.

All roads led to the castle—all Provençal, Languedocian, and South Pyrenean peasant fingers pointed southwest. Pushing off of the dusty stone, Magnus leapt up over the landscape. The towns and villages untouched by war shocked him. Frozen time. It smelled of prewar Europe. The smell of childhood. Magnus leapt up, hanging over hilly meadows filled with grazing sheep, cows, and horses, with tiled houses and stables, with the awnings of smokehouses and cream-eries, with antiaircraft complexes, with solar panels, and with peasants looking up at him as they shielded their eyes from the sun, as if he were a hawk or a drone. He leapt up, hovering for a long time and wasting his fuel uneconomically—as if he wanted to be encased in this moment as if in amber so that he might remain within it for all time. But his heavy high-speed boots invariably brought him back down to earth.

La Couvertoirade.

This was already the second month Magnus the Hasty was hur-rying to make it there. He had to make it on time. Before tomorrow morning. No matter what!

It could not be otherwise.

And he was already very close. The hot day passed in leaps and bounds. His tight overalls cooled him down, ably sucked away his sweat, supplied him with vitamins. Magnus felt no fatigue. Generally speaking, he was a strong and hardy individual, despite his shortness and skinniness. And he just leapt better here than in Austria or Switzerland. Having fortified himself with fresh bread, warm cu-cumbers, boiled goat's meat, and sheep's cheese in sleepy Riez, Mag-nus delightedly drank his fill of spring water, filled his boots with gas at a tiny gas column, and leapt west off to the place where, behind an uneven bluish-green horizon, the sultry sun of a new republic was going down, a republic that had defeated the Salafi barbarians. Mag-nus liked this sun and didn't hide his only eye from it behind dark glass.

Magnus the Hasty's pupil was full of sunlight.

This light promised a *meeting*.

And this promise wasn't long in bearing fruit. When the stuffy night had covered the Pyrenean foothills, when it no longer smelled of lavender, but of honeysuckle, acacia, and wisteria, and the cicadas had begun to sing, an enormous hologram flashed forth in front of him in the evening sky: the eight-pointed cross of the new Knights Templar.

Finally!

"La Couvertoirade…" Magnus sighed into the air and smiled wearily as he leapt.

The cross hovered above the castle towers, rotating slightly around its axis.

Magnus leapt so high that swifts fluttered nervously around him, their day's flight coming to an end. The warm evening air whistled through Magnus's dirty hair for one last time. He came down onto the cobblestones of the wide road leading to the castle, turned off his boots, and began to walk, laboriously moving his massive feet.

The castle was *impending*, the cross rotating and hovering above it as if it were the held breath of the citadel's heroic denizens.

The calm that had filled Magnus for the whole of his one-and-a-half month journey was replaced by an excitement that waxed with each step: the growing legend of a New Europe, a hope for all European Christians, and a stronghold of spiritual feats and fleshy heroism towered up before him.

In order to calm himself, Magnus began to pray aloud.

The road was cut off by a moat. The ring of a low rampart rose above the moat and encircled the castle. Directly in front of him, a raised drawbridge became visible.

Magnus stopped at the edge of the road. A scanning beam immediately shone out from the watchtower and an amplified voice asked him a question.

"Who are you, traveler, and what has brought you here?"

Magnus pulled more air into his lungs and loudly pronounced the sentence that had been leaping within him for the whole duration of this month and a half.

"I am the carpenter Magnus the Hasty and I have come on the invitation of the grand magister."

A long minute passed.

The drawbridge began to silently descend.

"Welcome to La Couvertoirade, Magnus the Hasty," the voice pronounced.

Magnus stepped out onto the black, ribbed surface of the draw-bridge and began to walk across it, his high-speed boots stomping.

I made it . . . he thought and smiled, overwhelmed with a feeling of long-awaited, unbelievably pleasant relief.

The gates opened and a light flashed. Magnus entered the castle. Three ratniks in light armor crossed with weapons belts came to greet him. On each belt hung a short-barreled assault rifle, a pistol, a short sword, three grenades, and a *liquid* axe. The faces of the ratniks were stern and indifferent. The oldest ratnik held out a luminous smarty in his hands and proffered it without speaking.

Magnus silently lay his right palm on its shining surface. A holo-gram containing all existent information about Magnus arose in the chill air. Studying it briefly, the ratnik nodded and rolled up the smarty. Another ratnik turned a lever. The hydraulics came to life, the lattice rose, and the second set of gates began to move apart—tall, thick, wrought iron gates studded with spikes. Two more ratniks were waiting behind the gates.

"Follow us," one of them said.

Magnus followed them as if they were his dear friends or family, smiling and stomping his boots. They crossed the castle's inner court-yard, around the perimeter of which were more than a hundred auto-mobiles, went through a set of gates, walked down a stone pas-sageway illuminated by the greenish flame of artificial torches, and began to go down into the basement. In a small, round hall, a man with gray canvas clothes and a red Templar cross sewn onto his chest was waiting for him.

"Welcome, Magnus the Hasty." The man bowed his head slightly. "I am Leonard, the cellarer of the castle."

Magnus bowed to the man.

"I shall take you to the other carpenters. There, you shall be fed and given the opportunity to rest until tomorrow."

Leonard led him through the corridors. Unlike Magnus with his loudly clanging boots, Leonard moved almost completely silently. They approached a door, the cellarer placed his hand on a white square, and the door opened. Magnus walked through the door and the cellarer remained outside. This hall was lit up by the same greenish artificial flame. In the middle of the room was a long table with wine and modest nibbles to accompany it. Five men were sitting around the table. When they saw who'd come in, they got up from their seats and walked over to him. These were the Carpenters of Western Europe—famous men. Magnus knew three of them personally—Sylvester of Florence, Nikolya the Hairy, and the Hugo of the Oily Hands. Two of them—Theodor of Constance and Aris the Wedged—were known to him by reputation alone.

"Ba-a-ah! Who is this I see? Magnus the Hasty!" exclaimed the fat, golden-bearded Hugo, shaking his long dreads with mormolon snakes woven into them. "You've been *hastily hurrying* to make it here for a long time!"

"Magnus!" The stern Nikolya thumped him on the chest with his fist, blackish-gray hair grown round his head and nearly covering his eyes.

"There were rumors you'd be late." The thin, clever-faced Sylvester shook his head.

"But we crushed them!" Hugo chuckled, embracing Magnus with his ring- and bracelet-covered arms.

"In the most merciless way!" Nikolya showed Sylvester his tattooed fist.

"I couldn't let the magister down," Magnus pronounced, freeing himself from Sylvester's embrace and removing his combat rucksack from his shoulder.

Strong carpenter's hands reached out for the newcomer.

"Welcome, Magnus the Hasty." The fair-haired, light-bearded Aris squeezed Magnus's hand forcefully. "Rome still remembers the ringing of your titanium hammer."

"Greetings and joyful be, Aris the Wedged." Magnus squeezed the carpenter's hand in response. "Your glory precedes you. From Prague to Vienna, you've paved a broad tellurium road."

"I offer my heartfelt greetings and highest respect to Magnus the

Hasty." The short, stocky, shaven-headed Theodor walked over and offered his sinewy hand to Magnus. "Your mastery becomes more consummate from year to year."

"Only so as to match yours, Theodor of Constance. The heads of the nails beaten in by you are blinding to me."

"Oooh! 'Tis not without reason they still dub you Magnus the Eloquent!" Hugo chuckled.

These carpenters of the European South spoke Euro—a mix of French, Spanish, and Bavarian. Since his Swiss tour, Magnus had come to miss this language, a language with which his life was inextricably interwoven.

"Gentlemen, let us allow the guest to remove his boots!" Hugo thundered.

The carpenters placed a chair in front of Magnus. He sat down, unfastened his high-speed boots, and took his exhausted feet out of them with enormous pleasure. The boots were immediately taken away and a basin of water was placed before Magnus. Aris and Theodor got down onto their knees, unlaced Magnus's high, soft boots, removed them, took off his sweat-soaked socks, placed Magnus's feet in the water, and began to unhurriedly lather them with fragrant lavender soap.

"I can see by your feet that you came galloping here straight from Switzerland." Hugo winked at him, holding a towel at the ready.

"Yes. I had to interrupt my tour," Magnus replied quietly, as if he were afraid to interrupt the ritual of the washing of the feet, which was so pleasant to him, especially now, at the end of this long day and at the end of his journey.

"What's new in Switzerland? The Lucerne squad didn't bend your nails?"

"No. But they didn't sharpen them either. During the tour, I was *overlaid* in white, then they removed the *trace*."

The carpenters exchanged knowing looks.

"The Swiss have never liked *tour*ists. Not before the war and not now," Nikolya the Hairy pronounced furiously. "Not before the war, not during the war, and not now. What buffoons!"

"'Twould seem the War of the Swiss Carpenters didn't teach them anything." Aris nodded, washing the soap suds from Magnus's feet. "To remove a *trace* from an indigenous European ... well well ..."

"They don't even wanna learn," Magnus remarked, closing his only eye at the excess of pleasure and fatigue. "For them, the main thing is profit."

"The Swiss are clinging to direct deliveries." Sylvester shrugged his thin shoulders. "That's as clear as day. And wherefore the codex doesn't interest them. Only direct deliveries."

"Direct? The Persians are still acting as intermediaries for them! The same people who bombed Basel!" Nikolya shook his mane.

"The Kazakhs are the ones doing the deliveries," Theodor expressed, not looking up from the ritual. "Straight from Telluria through a *backlit* corridor."

"And the Persians!" Nikolya wouldn't let up. "General Halatbari's Persians. The same ones who beheaded the Hungarians, they *repainted* the archives, and beheaded Old Man Maurice."

"There's no problem with the tellurium in Switzerland," Magnus pronounced. "There's a problem with the carpenters."

"It's that they're shit!" Nikolya growled, shaking his head and setting his four mormolon collars to ringing. "They were shit and shit they've remained! That's where the magister should be called in with iron and fire! These can't be Christians! To remove a *trace* from a European! Six months haven't even passed and they've already shriveled up!"

"The magister knows of their sins, Nikolya." Hugo placed his weighty palm on his companion's hairy shoulder. "The time shall come when they pay for yon arrogance and avarice."

"'Tis apostasy, not avarice, Brother Hugo!" Nikolya thundered.

Hugo nodded gloomily.

"Greed bordering on God-forsakenness," Aris pronounced.

"If it were up to me, I'd hang all of the goons in the Lucerne squad, but before doing so, I'd beat their golden hammers up their asses." The frightful Nikolya couldn't calm himself down.

This threatening sentence set the carpenters into motion: Sylvester walked over to the table and began to pour wine from a jug into goblets; Aris and Theodor took Magnus's clean feet out of the basin; and the fat Hugo got down onto his knees heavily and began to gently dry Magnus's feet with a towel.

Then Magnus was taken to his cell, a modest space, but comfortably laid out. He took off his thick, dusty overalls, took clothes out from his rucksack—tight-fitting beige kidskin pants, red boots with copper heels, and an embroidered, collarless silk shirt—and changed with great pleasure. First hanging a necklace of white gold with pearls and mormolon around his neck, he then put a ring with a diamond cross onto the ring finger of his right hand and walked out of the cell, his heels clomping cheerfully.

The other carpenters awaited him around the table.

"Forgive us, Brother Magnus, that we saw fit to repast without you," Hugo rumbled. "But 'twould be an honor for us to drink wine to your health and to the strength of your hands."

"I hold it as an honor to raise my glass in such company," Magnus replied.

Praying to God quickly, he plunged his hands into a silver chalice, took the towel proffered to him by Sylvester, wiped off his hands, then accepted a full glass.

"To your health, Magnus the Hasty!" the carpenters pronounced in unison, all holding forth their goblets.

"To all of your health, my friends!" Magnus clinked goblets with them.

"And may your hand be strong!"

"And may all of your hands be strong!"

The local wine, last year's marcillac, refreshed Magnus, and he happily drained the glass to the dregs. Nikolya removed the lid from a tureen, Aris held out an empty bowl, and Hugo generously filled it to the brim with peasant bean soup made with smoked brisket and seasoned with herbs and garlic. This was a good ole' *garbure*, consummately satisfying the hunger not only of peasants, but also of travelers. Despite the fact that the soup was only lukewarm, Magnus found it to be incredibly delicious and each sip thereof increased his strength.

As they drank their wine, the carpenters first talked quietly amongst themselves, then went silent. They sat motionlessly, their hands on the table and their eyes cast downwards, as if some form of paralysis had descended onto them. The only audible thing was Magnus eating his soup. Finally, that ended too.

He wiped his mouth with a napkin, pushed aside his empty bowl, and glanced at his hushed comrades. They looked at him. He wanted to ask a question, but something prevented him from doing so. Silence reigned beneath the stone arches of the hall. It wasn't an oppressive silence; on the contrary, it was a gracious silence full of the expectation of the great and the important, that for which all those sitting around the table had prepared themselves. One wouldn't want to break such a silence. But Sylvester had to do just that.

"One must sleep before *slaughter*," he pronounced quietly and distinctly.

None of the carpenters replied to him.

The first to get up was Hugo. Without saying anything, he turned and shuffled heavily to his cell, his dreads shaking. Everyone rose from his seat just as silently and dispersed off toward the cells. Magnus too got up and went to his cell. Once he arrived, he got down onto his knees before a crucifix and thanked the Lord as briefly as possible—as always—for food, shelter, and easy trails. Then he undressed, tumbled into the narrow bed, and immediately fell asleep.

And a new day began.

As soon as the village roosters cried out and the sun flashed forth on the horizon, all 312 knights gathered in the castle temple, the grand magister leading them. Alverius the chaplain, clad in a snow-white cassock and a shell of fibrous armor marked with scars made by Salafi bullets, began to recite a mass. His voice, sublime and sonorous, echoed through the temple above the kneeling Templars.

"Dominus vobiscum!"

"Et cum spiritu tuo!" the knights responded like the ocean surf.

The liturgy had begun. Six carpenters were also in the temple standing in a row, their arms folded and their heads bowed. Magnus froze, as if he himself had dissolved into the words and sounds. He'd been waiting for this for such a long time. The organ rang out and they began to sing the Sanctus. And the carpenter Magnus the Hasty sang with everyone else. Time no longer existed for him.

He came to his senses when the chaplain addressed the herd with a short sermon. Alverius spoke of a feat to be performed in the name of Christ, of the preservation of belief and believers, of the end of days, and of the heart of a warrior of Christ, a heart that must contain the meekness of an angel and the fury of a lion. Then began their communion. The first to approach the chaplain was the grand magister. Having taken communion, he went out through a low arch. All the knights did the same—taking communion from the hands of the chaplain, then passing through the same arch, walking through a corridor, and finding themselves in a large refectory, where there were five long wooden tables with benches next to them. The tables had been laid out in a special way so as to resemble the Roman numeral III with a line both below and above it; during refections, the chaplain invariably sat at the center of the upper line and the magister at the center of the lower line. Servants were standing along the walls. As soon as the last knight had taken his place, the doors were closed.

And so began that for which the six carpenters had so hurried to La Couvertoirade. The servants dressed them in traditional rubber carpentry aprons and brought them copper basins with water and soap for washing their hands. In the total silence that reigned, it was audible to all those seated just how the water flowed into the basins and how delicately and meticulously the carpenters washed their hands. When there was no more water in the jugs to be poured into the basins, their hands were dried off with towels, and rubbing alcohol was poured over them. After which a servant carrying an elongated case on a velvet cushion walked up to each of the carpenters. All the cases were different shapes and made of different materials—Hugo had a rough, iron case; Sylvester had a case of lacquered ebony; Theodor had a case of Japanese pine; Aris had a copper case; and Nikolya had a light aluminum case. Magnus's case was made of cypress. The servants opened the cases. Inside of each of them was the carpenter's primary tool—his hammer. The hammers were as different as the characters of the six carpenters. The handles of the hammers of every carpenter in the world were necessarily made from Canadian ash. But each carpenter chose for himself the metal to be used for the head. The fat Hugo had discovered his preference for black gold long ago; the wise Sylvester preferred platinum to all other metals; the fierce Nikolya used soft, untempered iron; Theodor, like Hugo, worked with a gold hammer; and Aris preferred copper. Magnus's hammerhead was titanium.

Picking up their hammers, the carpenters raised them very slightly into the air, just as Prussian marshals used to raise their batons, and froze. The servants left with the empty cases. The chaplain approached the carpenters. He walked slowly down the row they'd formed, peering into the face of each *craftsman*. His thin, swarthy face with its six scars exuded faith and an awareness of the foretoldness of that which was happening. As he walked, he locked eyes with each of the carpenters in turn. It seemed as if he were bidding them farewell. But in reality, he was making a choice. And, having stopped in front of Magnus, he chose.

The carpenter froze.

The chaplain laid his napalm-burnt hand on Magnus's shoulder.

"Magnus the Hasty, in the name of Our Lord Jesus Christ, I bless your undertaking of this great deed!" the chaplain pronounced loudly in his high-pitched voice.

I made it on time, oh Lord! Magnus's heart shuddered triumphantly.

First bowing to the chaplain, he then walked along the wall with hammer in raised hand. Two servants carrying plastic containers followed behind him. Magnus reached the back wall, turned left, and began to walk along a table of seated knights, moving behind their backs. Having reached the middle, he stopped. In front of him was Geoffroy de Payns, the grand magister of the Templar order. The magister sat motionlessly, his clenched fists resting on the rough wood of the table. His battle armor, adorned with gold and mormolon, was magnificent. Dents from bullets and scratches made by Salafi sabers and axes only enhanced its splendor. His perfectly shaven head, seeming to have been cast from some noble metal, was striking in its beauty.

A great man sat before Magnus. He and his knights had been the very stronghold of Europe on which the Salafi hammer broke. They smashed the enemy in Toulouse and Marseille, liberated Nice and Perpignan, and sank Salafi ships near the Hyères islands. It was he, Geoffroy de Payns, who had raised the proud flag of Languedoc over the towers of their new capital, he who had instilled hope into the heart of a bloody Europe, and he who had brought together the efforts of all European Christians and defended Christian civilization on the continent.

Magnus exhaled silently, closing his eyes and taking control of his feelings. He had cultivated this ability spectacularly. The servants opened the plastic containers with quiet pops. Each of them contained a tellurium nail in disinfectant solution, a smarty rolled up into a tube, and hemostatic tampons. Magnus made a sign to one of the servants. The servant picked up the smarty, unrolled it, and molded it to the magister's head. The smarty squeaked, brightened up, then a green dot appeared on its surface, swam over the head, and stopped. Magnus nodded. The servant removed the smarty from the magister's head. A faint mark remained at the necessary spot. Around it was a crowd of twelve nail scars—what'd been beaten in before. Magnus picked up the nail, put it to the spot, then froze.

Everyone in the hall was looking at him.

Magnus's single eye looked out across the hall. In his thoughts, the carpenter was asking for strength from the Lord.

But that didn't last for long. A quick swing of the hammer and a blow. The nail went into the magister's head all the way up to its head. His body shuddered, his armor snapped, and his fists unclenched.

The grand magister let forth an enormous sigh of relief. And the hall exhaled with relief along with him. The five carpenters standing by the wall smiled restrainedly at Magnus. Having put the hammer that'd done its job back into its case, Magnus took a tampon and dabbed at the miserly drop of blood that'd welled up from under the head of the nail. Not seeing the magister's face from behind his back, he felt the power of his gaze now that the tellurium had taken hold reflected in the three hundred pairs of knights' eyes in the hall. And this reflected gaze made Magnus's heart skip a beat. All this *eyesight* formed a single, solved puzzle.

"Languedoc . . ." the carpenter's lips whispered involuntarily.

Everyone in the hall came to life and bustled about. The carpenters scattered across the room and dozens of servants followed after them with containers held at the ready. And that for which these five craftsmen had so rushed to the citadel of the New Templars began. The containers clapped open, tellurium nails flashed, and the first hammer blows rang out. And the knights bellowed out their first exclamations of delight as the divine tellurium entered their smooth heads.

The carpentry work had begun. Magnus stayed standing behind the magister's back, for he had come here only to fill this single great and noble head with tellurium. Such was his mission. Standing motionlessly with his arms stretched along his body, he watched his colleagues work. And with each blow of their hammers, professional delight filled Magnus's soul.

How ably and properly the carpenters did their work!

The fat, heavyset Hugo of the Oily Hands did the deed with a fearsome expression on his heavy face, putting nails to heads and beating his hammer as if he were an ancient sculptor creating living monuments to a great era with his own hands.

Sylvester of Florence acted with graceful precision, his thin surgeon's fingers casting a spell with their quickness and economy of motion.

Nikolya the Hairy conducted the *slaughter* with the calculated fury of a warrior fighting against a mighty enemy for a new, happy, and fair world.

Theodor of Constance did his work as if it were so simple, ordinary, and unpretentious that it had already become a familiar business to everyone else, a business that shouldn't encourage the slightest fear of fatal *misfire*.

Aris the Wedged hunched over the knights' shaved heads as if he were a medieval alchemist hanging over rows of distillation retorts in which a miraculous elixir—long awaited by mankind—was brewing . . .

Magnus watched. Did he envy them? No! He was content and satisfied. His hands, unlike the hands of the other carpenters, were motionless, but he'd already done his work: atoms of tellurium bombarded the neuronal membranes inside of the grand magister's head. And this was extremely important not just for the 312 knights of the order. But also for all of Languedoc. For all of Europe.

Hammers rang out.

Silvery metal entered into heads.

The knights trembled, cried out, and let forth moans and involuntary exclamations. It seemed that an end to this would never come. But, when a little more than an hour had passed, the last nail had already gone into the last knight's head. And the carpenters, their work completed, walked over to the wall, gave the servants their hammers, and just stood there. Everything had come to pass. And again, as with the previous twelve times, not one of the knights was hurt, not one of them fell over writhing in pain, and not one of them curled up on the floor, his eyes rolling around in his head. And not one of them died, as those who are unlucky oft die from tellurium.

Here, everyone was lucky.

In La Couvertoirade, they had already grown used to this miracle.

Everyone sat motionlessly for a minute. And then the grand magister rose up from his seat and began to speak in a loud, authoritative voice.

"Oh brothers in Christ! Oh knights of the order! The enemies of the Christian world have not yet been laid to rest! Crushed by us in Marseille, they retreated, spilling their black blood onto the earth. But their hatred for Christian Europe did not run dry. Having escaped from captivity, Ghazi ibn Abdallah is again gathering troops to attack us. As before, our enemies shall endeavor to enslave Europe, to destroy our temples, to trample our shrines, to impose their faith with iron and fire, to establish their cruel regime, and to turn all of Europe into an obedient pasture of slaves. Until today, we've only managed to parry their blows. But each time they've been destroyed by the soldiers of Christ, they've again amassed their forces and invaded. So would it be seemly for us, the defenders of Christ's faith, to sit and wait for a new attack by these barbarians?"

The magister paused, looking around at the knights. They were frozen, awaiting the words that had long nourished their hearts. Some began to rise up from their seats.

"Nay! 'Twould be unworthy of us to remain on the defensive!" the magister almost screamed, and the hall exploded into a roar of voices.

The knights stood up from their places. The magister raised his hand, asking for silence. The roar immediately vanished.

"The best defense is to attack!"

And the hall exploded again.

"Let us remember Hugo de Payns, Raymond of Toulouse, Conrad III, Godfrey of Bouillon, and Friedrich Barbarossa! They didn't wait for the Muslims to attack, but went east so as to protect Christian shrines, so as to crush the barbarians and defilers, and so as to affirm the borders of Christian civilization. So let us follow their example!"

Exclamations of affirmation filled the hall and rang out beneath its arches.

"Today, we shall strike the main Salafi nest—Istanbul! We shall unleash all of our might upon the enemy! We shall cut down the barbarians with the sword of truth! Let us show the infidels all of the valor of the warriors of Christ!"

The stone walls and ceiling of the hall rang out. And, again, the magister raised his hand. When it was quiet, he began to speak again.

"I, Geoffroy de Payns, the grand magister of the Templar order, announce the thirteenth flying crusade! Together with us shall fly the warriors of Belgium, the Netherlands, Charlottenburg, Bavaria, Silesia, Transylvania, Wallachia, Galicia, and the White Sea. Together with us shall also fly Louis Braveheart with his wingèd legion of Rioja Falcons! The fifth column of occupied Istanbul shall also be with us! Together, we shall deliver a crushing blow to the enemy! For so desires God!"

"So desires God!" the hall thundered.

"So desires God ..." Magnus whispered, frozen with delight.

And immediately the main bell of the castle temple began to sound the alarm.

The magister turned sharply and moved toward the exit. Magnus saw his profile—long, sharp nose, deep-seated eye, sunken cheek, thin lips, and small, willful chin. The magister walked through the arch along with the chaplain and the knights that formed his guard. Their armor and the heads of the nails in their heads shining. The other warriors also took their leave of the refectory. Magnus stood still, fascinated by the people moving past him, a group so large one might call it a horde.

The knights took their leave.

Silence fell in the hall, a silence broken only by the bell. Penetrating the narrow windows, sunlight fell on empty tables, shining onto the occasional drop of blood on their surfaces.

Shaking off his paralysis, Magnus walked over to his companions. They exchanged long, understanding looks. Words would've been inappropriate.

Having left the refectory, the knights went down into the castle temple's basement, where, in the empty stone space, spread out between two sheets of bulletproof glass on a heavy frame of levitating superconductors, the shroud of the Savior hovered—a sacred mandilion and holy relic taken from the infidels during the cruel Battle of Turin. The knights lined up and each of them in his turn kneeled down, kissed the shrine, walked out through the low arch, went upstairs, then found himself in the castle courtyard. There, already laid out in its entire forty-meter length, was the famous catapult of the Templar Order—a complex, metal structure reminiscent of an MRLS. Next to the catapult, three-meter-tall robots armed with automatic cannons, rockets, and flamethrowers were crowded into stern steel rows. A red, eight-pointed Templar cross shone on the chest of every robot. The grand magister was the first to climb into his robot. Having sat down in the cockpit, he buckled up and took hold of the control levers. The robot's hermetic helmet closed and the magister's willful face flashed onto the robot's head behind a thick layer of glass impenetrable to both bullets and shells. The military chaplain and the six knights of the guard did as the magister did. The other knights began to hastily climb into their robots, their buckles and helmets snapping. Taking heavy steps on ancient cobblestone with steel feet, the robots moved toward the wide elevators. The elevators hummed and began to take the robots up to the catapult. When they had gotten up top, they lay down in rows on the catapult's platform. When the first fifty robots had lain down, solid-propellant rocket launchers were attached to their legs.

The enormous mass of the catapult began to turn southeast. The bell rang. The signal resounded, fuses flared, and quickly, one after the other, fifty trains of fire carried these steel warriors of Christ into the indigo Languedoc sky with a thunderous roar. As if comets were carrying the knights off to their distant goal on the shores of the Black Sea. In these moments, hundreds of such comets flew from launchers near Liège and Breda, from the forests of Siewierz, from South Carpathian peaks, from the shores of Lake Starnberg, and from the Solovetsky islands.

The thirteenth flying crusade was gaining strength for a devastating blow.

Outside the walls of the castle, the crowd let forth a joyful cry. Thousands of Languedocians had come here this morning to see their heroes off to holy war. In the knightly robots' steel rucksacks, there was room for more than just ammo. There was also food carefully prepared by local residents and brought from nearby *locales*: cheese, warm homemade bread, sheep's butter, baked tomatoes, artichokes in olive oil, ham, salt cod, figs, apricots, and, of course, the invariable peasant's *aligot*—mashed potatoes with cheese and fried pork sausage. These kind, touching symbols of human warmth and domestic comfort were being carried away by merciless steel giants, as, during their first bivouac, the food would be responsible for renewing the knights' strength and reminding them, exhausted as they would be from battle, of the simple Christian people of Europe for whom they had set off to perform their great feat...

Another salvo echoed out in La Couvertoirade. The earth shook. Another fifty comets soared into the sky and flew southeast. Standing in front of the narrow refectory window, Magnus saw the crusaders off with a gaze full of hope and faith.

"La Couvertoirade ..." he pronounced and smiled happily.

22

LATE FALL. A cloudy, dank morning. A copse of birch trees on the border between Tataria and the Kingdom of Bashkiria. Two travelers with dog heads, Roman and Foma, are sitting next to a campfire heating water in a pot hanging from a camping tripod. Roman is broad shouldered, stocky, covered with smooth gray fur, and has old scars visible on his snout. He's wearing a worn jacket made of waterproof fabric, cotton pants, and high lace-up boots. Foma is lanky, stooped, narrow shouldered, covered with smooth black fur, and dressed in a long-tailed thick woolen coat lined with wadding. On his feet, he's wearing wide snow boots made of self-generating rubber.

FOMA: It's burning rather lousily. We should've thrown in more wood.

ROMAN (*laying birch twigs into the fire*): S'all wet.

FOMA (*looking up at the sky*): Mhmm…the abyss tumbled down right onto our heads.

ROMAN: Thank God the rain stopped when night fell.

FOMA: It'll snow soon.

ROMAN (*sarcastically*): You really know how to cheer a guy up, Foma Severyanych.

FOMA: Always at your service, Roman Stepanych.

A swirling gust of wind drives the smoke from the fire directly toward Foma.

FOMA (*turning away unhappily and rubbing at his eyes*): How disgusting... Are you against me, oh Mother Nature?

ROMAN (*rakes the badly burning birch branches toward the pot*): Isn't it time to plop it in?

FOMA: Don't neglect the sequence of the recipe. The water needs to boil first.

ROMAN (*yawns nervously*): I've a deadly hankering for some chow.

FOMA: Don't diminish yourself with such expressions, my friend. It'd be better to simply say "I'm hungry."

ROMAN (*displeasedly*): I'm hungry.

FOMA: I am too, I must admit.

A pause. The travelers sit in silence.

FOMA: There's no need to look at me with such hatred.

ROMAN (*annoyed*): Because of your wisdom, we're stuck performing this ridiculous ritual.

FOMA: It's a process, not a ritual.

ROMAN: It's madness. Your madness.

FOMA: No one has yet seen fit to do away with the laws of chemistry, most venerable Roman Stepanovich.

ROMAN: Demagoguery! You insist on even the smallest of change.

FOMA: The world rests on the order of things.

ROMAN: Your rhetoric isn't gonna make this damned water boil.

FOMA: But perhaps it shall remind you of how to be patient.

ROMAN (*reaching resolutely for a rucksack*): I'm done with this, god-dammit! Y'know what, I've had enough of this symbolic godbothery...

FOMA (*raises his four-fingered hand covered in smooth black fur with a silver ring on its third finger in warning*): *Pacta sunt servanda*, Mr. Bard. I urge you not to commit any irreversible act. By refusing to follow my recipe for the soup, you shall not only be depriving us of a nutritious meal, but also wounding me very deeply.

ROMAN (*irritatedly grabs the rucksack and throws it at Foma's feet*):
Fine, do what you will . . . (*contemptuously*) Mr. Philosopher.

FOMA (*pulls the rucksack closer*): I shall do exactly that. And you shall
end up thanking me, as you always do, in decadent trochees.

ROMAN (*spreads his hands, which are covered in thick gray fur*): Why,
by your wisdom, did we refuse the carrion?!

FOMA: My precious one. You've already asked me this question.

ROMAN: Carrion is sweeter and softer than any other meat. And you
don't must needs boil it!

FOMA (*unties the rucksack*): I agree.

ROMAN: And there were heaps of it there!

FOMA: I'll not dare to disagree with that.

ROMAN: There was young and old carrion, something to everyone's
taste! Plus all the organs. What could be sweeter or healthier than
decomposed tripe? Liver? Heart? My God! There were so many
bodies. We could've taken whatever we wanted . . .

FOMA: Yes, yes . . . Their bodies wormed at by decay and the moon
illuminating them scantily . . .

ROMAN: We woulda long been satiated!

FOMA (*nodding*): Yes, having stuffed our stomachs with rotted human
offal, we would be satiated, satisfied, and benevolent. And, for a
little while, it would seem to us as if earthly life were a blessing.

Roman looks at Foma furiously.

FOMA: There is simply an outrageous concentration of anger and
irritation in your gaze, my friend. Can it be that Mr. Poet is getting
ready to grab hold of the neck of the poor wandering philosopher?

ROMAN: I'll never forgive you for yesterday's trick by the field.

FOMA: There was no trick at all. We simply passed by the field of
battle in honorable fashion.

ROMAN: Like total cretins . . .

FOMA (*not ceasing to dig around in the rucksack*): You curse me for
watching out for your future, my priceless friend and companion,

Roman Stepanych, oh light of mine. Once again, I deprived you of the possibility of getting down on all fours. Which is to say: of falling to the beastly, chthonic bottom instead of moving, so to speak, upwards, *per aspera ad astra*, toward bodily and spiritual consummateness. You write wonderful Romantic poems and listen to the music of the spheres and the singing of the angels. And still, you passionately wish to stuff yourself with carrion. This is such a contradiction in terms that it makes my blood run cold! As a thinking animal, I cannot allow this. If your ethics are silent, then at least your aesthetics should revolt and scream at the top of their lungs: Basta!

ROMAN: Your demagoguery makes me feel even more nauseated than hunger does. What kind of goddamn aesthetics are at play in the question of food?! I just wanna chow down!

FOMA: Is that the title of your new poem?

ROMAN: We're creatures of a dual nature and should preserve this duality, not destroy it.

FOMA: If you and I had different professions, if we were intercontinental drivers, for example, I would gladly nourish myself with carrion. But as a *total* post-cynic, I'm a staunch opponent of bestialization. If I were a simple antediluvian cynic (or even a post-cynic), I'd get down on all four paws and tear out the tripe from fallen Wahhabis with great pleasure.

ROMAN: The consumption of carrion doesn't contradict my profession.

FOMA: In the context of your own existence—true. But, my precious, besides your own *psychosoma*, there's also the cultural context to consider. Tradition, heritage, the image of the poet... Believe me, a poet who writes of "the mysterious ovary of spring sunsets" and nourishes himself with rotted human offal shall call forth bitter feelings in his two-legged readers. I don't think Pushkin would've welcomed the existence of such a poet.

ROMAN: Baudelaire would've welcomed it eagerly.

FOMA: Listen... As animals, we were created under a particular influence. GENENG didn't have any luck with wolves—dogs turned out to be better anthropogenic material. Unfortunately.

ROMAN: Fortunately.

FOMA: And if we are indeed anthropogenic or, as your friend with the donkey head used to say, anthropoloyal, then we were created for lofty goals, which we must endeavor to meet, dammit!

ROMAN: Unlike you, I'm entirely content with my nature. And I'm not planning to improve *any* part of myself. My dream is connected with human nature, not with my own.

FOMA: I'm aware, my friend. But, believe me, you and I are full-fledged victims of anthropotechnics . . .

ROMAN (*interrupting him*): Your damned water's boiling.

FOMA: Ah, yes . . . (*he takes a man's head wearing a helmet out of the rucksack, removes the helmet, and drops the head into the pot.*) And just like that . . . Boil away, oh ye head of a Tatar warrior who died defending his homeland from Wahhabi barbarians.

ROMAN (*looking into the pot*): Is that all?

FOMA: Is it not enough for you?

ROMAN: It sure isn't!

Foma takes a human hand out of the rucksack and drops it into the pot.

ROMAN: And the second one?

FOMA: One hand is more than enough, my friend. We have a long passage ahead and all of the fields of battle lie behind us. Ahead are barrows alone, as Gumilyov the Younger would say. War breathes down our necks. So we must needs economize the human protein we do have so as to be able to go further. (*He twirls the helmet around in his hands, finds the bullet hole in it, and sticks his claw through it.*) Voilà, *mon cher*! The bullet found its hero. (*He twirls the helmet around on his claw.*) How does it go again . . . "I left my home, he says, and went to fight and give my land . . ."

ROMAN: "To the Salafis." Don't quote mediocre Soviet poets.

FOMA: Are those Soviet verses? I didn't know.

ROMAN: There's no need to know.

FOMA (*adjusting the campfire beneath the pot*): I was sure that it was a hymn written by some Barabinskian partisan in the Joan of Arc Squadron, a detachment into whose hands I wouldn't much like to fall.

ROMAN (*looking impatiently into the fire*): And for how long do you intend to boil it?

FOMA: Not for long, my friend. A short thermal processing in an infusion of birch rot, giving the human meat a slight aftertaste of entropy.

ROMAN (*sniffs*): I smell nothing more than wormwood.

FOMA: You're having olfactory hallucinations because of your hunger. I would never put wormwood in my soup. For, verily, our nomadic life is bitter enough without wormwood.

ROMAN: Ain't that the truth.

Foma takes two metal bowls out of the rucksack and hands one of them to Roman. Foma takes one of the bowls and puts it down on his knees.

ROMAN: I've been dragging this head with me in the rucksack all the way from Bugulma. If you start to really think about it, it's kinda crazy.

FOMA (*stirring the contents of the pot with a spoon*): My friend and comrade in anthropotechnical misfortune, most respected Roman Stepanovich, you know very well that my backbone, which at one time sustained several monstrously merciless blows from a baseball bat, is not in any condition to bend beneath the burden of yon rucksack. I would carry all of our doleful freight on my back with great pleasure, would carry the post-cynic himself, but am in no physical state to allow myself that, for, without even having taken two steps, I would tumble down to the musical accompaniment of the crunching of my spine with the cry of a fatally wounded swan who shall never again be able to pull Lohengrin's boat behind him—in sooth, nor his own mortal body neither.

ROMAN (*not listening to Foma*): All the way from Bugulma! Like sleepwalkers we walked past the field of battle that'd been served to us by Fate; a field of the dead, the delicious, the soft, and the delightfully odorous...We kept moving, carrying this pal-try, sense-less, id-iot-ic, fresh head in a bag!

FOMA: Don't speak ill of fallen heroes. Five minutes and you'll be sinking your fangs into the head. It'd be better if you would respond to this more or less intelligible question: Shall we drink?

ROMAN: If we're going to eat, then I wouldn't mind drinking too.

Foma takes a flask out of the rucksack, unscrews it, and hands it to Roman.

ROMAN (*mockingly*): To your backbone. (*He throws his head back and pours the flask between his jaws.*)

FOMA: I thank you, my dear and faithful friend.

ROMAN (*jerks, yaps, and grits his teeth*): O-o-o-of!

FOMA: Alcohol is always apropos, isn't that so? Although for real dogs, it's poison. It's hard to imagine life without alcohol. That would truly be a dog's life. That's probably why all dogs have such sad eyes. (*He takes the flask from Roman.*)

ROMAN: I've known of a few cases of canine alcoholism. But they were rare...

FOMA: I'm sure that the dogs were doing it out of solidarity with their owners—a situation even captured in Russian cinema from the Second Time of Troubles. I remember some alcoholic general forcing his mastiff to drink cognac. And the mastiff drinks and staggers. A rather gloomy sinny...Prosit! (*He pours alcohol between his jaws.*)

ROMAN (*pats himself on the stomach*): Now I'm ready to eat a whole warrior.

FOMA (*squeals and yawns nervously after drinking*): Wonderful! Oo-wo-o-o-o-of! (*He growls.*) Halt, oh time!

ROMAN (*impatiently*): Well, drag the head on out!

FOMA: Yes, yes, yes...(*He takes the head out of the pot and plops it down into his bowl.*) Well there, the main dish is ready. (*He sinks his claws into the head and tears it in half.*)

ROMAN: You're not so weak after all.

FOMA: Strength from my human-crippled spine flows into my hands. (*He hands Roman half of the head.*) Dig in, my friend.

ROMAN: Aha ... (*he seizes the head and begins to gnaw at it hungrily.*)

FOMA: You forgot to pray to Saint Christopher.

ROMAN (*now greedily perched over the head and gnawing at it*): M-m-m ... Next time ...

They eat in silence for a little while.

ROMAN: M-m-m ... Love and food have a devilish way of bringing one back to life ...

FOMA: I hope that's not a quotation?

ROMAN: M-m-m ... delicious ... glory be to Saint Christopher that you didn't overcook the head ...

FOMA: No need for that ... m-m-m ... sublime ...

They eat in silence.

ROMAN: The brain's so sweet ... such a smell ... it makes your head spin ...

FOMA: I'll leave it for dessert ... the ears, the ears ... so delicious and such a delight ...

ROMAN: For dessert ... m-m-m ... I shan't do the same ... one must needs eat the most delicious bits first ... here and now!

FOMA: You're a real poet ...

ROMAN: The real is for real poets ... *et après moi* ... m-m-m ... *le déluge* ... m-m-m ... the brain ... divine brain ... and how many of them are still lying on the field of battle ... brains lying on the field of battle with no concept of shame ... m-m-m ...

FOMA: Those are ... m-m-m ... rotten brains. Weak brains. Forget about them. We ... m-m-m ... must needs become consummate and break away ... m-m-m ... from chthonic worlds ... move upwards ... m-m-m ... upwards ...

ROMAN: You're ... m-m-m ... a provocateur ... you're ... m-m-m ... a

dangerous neo-Hegelian ... you ... oof, how delicious ... Owwww!
(*He screams and stops eating.*)

FOMA: What on earth?

Roman puts his fingers into his mouth and pulls out a bullet.

ROMAN: Devil take it!

FOMA: Ah, there you go ... the brain's got stuffing too.

ROMAN: I nearly broke my teeth.

FOMA (*laughs*): It isn't an empty head you've been lugging around,
my friend!

ROMAN (*twirls the bullet in his fingers and looks around*):
    A paltry bit of lead
    Rudely cut short his train of thought,
    And 'neath the cover of wet night, he
    Was smitten on the spot.

FOMA: Yes, yes, my friend. A paltry bit of quick matter put a full stop
to yon defender of Tatarian democracy's book of life.

ROMAN (*throws the bullet into the dry grass*): It's overwhelming all
the same.

FOMA (*continuing to eat*): What?

ROMAN: In our most pleasant moments, something necessarily reminds us of Eternity ... reminds us with total existential mercilessness. It's always like that.

FOMA: *Morti proximus*, of course ... As a poet, you should be more
prepared for that than anyone else.

ROMAN (*eating the last of the brain*): M-m-m ... I'm always ready ...
but ... it's still overwhelming.

FOMA: Empiricism?

ROMAN: Yes ... m-m-m ... even squeezing ... m-m-m ... your lover
in your arms and shuddering with love ...

FOMA: With ejaculation?

ROMAN: With love! With love! Even then we catch ourselves
wondering ... m-m-m ... if she isn't an old woman with a scythe
whom ...

FOMA: Whom we're pumping full of cum?

ROMAN: You're disgustingly...m-m-m...theoretical...

FOMA: It's my profession.

ROMAN (*cracking bones*): M-m-m...in my opinion...human skulls are becoming...

FOMA: All the more fragile?

ROMAN: Mhmm...A person crumbles far more easily...

FOMA: Because man is losing his nature.

ROMAN: Or his image, rather.

They eat in silence.

FOMA: Now it's time for the brain! (*He begins to eat the brain.*) O-o-o-o-w-w-w!!

Roman stops eating and looks at Foma. Foma sticks his tongue out from his jaws and touches it with his hand. There's a drop of blood on his tongue.

ROMAN: Have you already forgotten how to deal with bones, Mr. Philosopher? There it is: your upwards trajectory!

FOMA: I pricked my tongue.

ROMAN: That's symbolic.

FOMA: It's not a bone. (*He pokes around in his half head and pulls a tellurium nail out of it.*) Devil take it! It's not a bone at all.

ROMAN: Tellurium! Oh dark harpies of sorrow! It's tellurium!

FOMA: There was a nail in the head! And it pricked my tongue! The slightest hint of a puncture!

ROMAN: How mercilessly Providence japes with us! Oh ye gods!

Foma holds the tellurium nail in his hand. They stare at it fascinatedly.

FOMA: My damnèd hunger made me inattentive. I didn't notice the nail! And you were rushing me along so brutally...

ROMAN: In what worlds did this warrior dwell as he made battle with the Wahhabis?

FOMA: No one shall be able to give us an answer to that question, my friend. Not even this *empty* nail.

ROMAN (*takes the nail out of Foma's hand and twirls it around in front of his face*): Oh ye gods! How mercilessly you jape with me!

FOMA: Has envy begun to stir in your heart?

ROMAN: Yes! And I won't hide it. In poetry, I envy only myself, but in life ... O fallen warrior! You went out to fight your enemy after having beaten noble metal into your head, metal which equipped you power and resilience and filled you with courage, resoluteness, and the noble fury of holy war! Tellurium made you Ilya Muromets, King Arthur, Attila, Frederick Barbarossa, or perhaps even the heavenly wingèd Archistrategos. You fought deliriously with these invaders for the freedom of your Tataria, for your people, for your beloved ruler, for your family hearth, for your beautiful wife, for your children, and for your elders ...

FOMA (*continuing to eat*): Until a base metal put an end to your noble impulse.

Roman looks at Foma furiously.

FOMA (*sadly and apologetically*): Believe me, my friend, I pronounced those words without a hint of post-cynicism. (*He sighs.*) Yes! Two metals met in the head of this warrior—one noble and one not. And the head could not withstand their collision. The alchemical marriage of these two principles didn't come off. It's a tragedy. A sublime tragedy. 'Twould seem that the main battle didn't take place near Bugulma, but in the head of this unknown hero.

ROMAN (*unhappily*): He fought to the last! He fought! Fought with Wahhabi barbarians! With those demonically possessed invaders!

FOMA: Yes. The possessed. And the sad paradox lies in the fact that these barbarians didn't have to beat anything metallic into their heads in order to become heroes, for their heads had been beaten with heroic ideas since they were children. But those opposing them couldn't get by without nails. That's why they lost.

ROMAN (*growls in disagreement, raising his half head like a mug*): He triumphed! He's a knight! He's a Nibelung! He triumphed!

FOMA: Certainly. And I propose to honor his memory with a sip of the drink so well known to you.

Foma takes a flask out from the rucksack and hands it to Roman. After a brief moment of immobility, he takes the flask and drinks.

ROMAN (*twitches, barks*): O-o-o-o-of!

Foma takes back the flask, pours it between his jaws, swallows, and squeals.

ROMAN: I must admit, I've lost my appetite.

FOMA: I'm also stunned. This head has reminded us of the ultimate goal of our dangerous journey.

ROMAN: No! It's more than that: who we are, where we're from, and where we're going.

FOMA: We, the victims of anthropomages, having escaped from Countess Yusupova serf theater, are headed for Telluria.

ROMAN: Telluria . . . How distant! How desired! My God! For how much longer must we torment ourselves? For how many nights must we travel? For how many days must we hide ourselves in ravines and bushes? Life! What exactly are you?! In sooth—the boundless world is filled with tears!

FOMA: Don't lose heart, old boy. (*He holds the nail out in front of him.*) Yon nail is not the skylarking or the japery of Providence. It's a compass. It shows us the direction of our path. Southeast! Lift up your head! We're on the right track, my dear! Just a little longer and we'll have reached the Ural Mountains, then past them—the Ishim Steppe, Barabinskian forests, the Salair Ridge, and then—Telluria!

ROMAN: I so don't want to lose faith in our dream.

FOMA: Our dream is always with us. Our dream is our Altair!

ROMAN: Shall we take this nail with us?

FOMA: No! (*He drops the nail into the grass.*) It's *empty*. For it has already done its duty and given the warrior a *dream*. And we need new, shining nails! Our tortured brains hunger for these nails!

ROMAN: Shining nails, carrying joy and power within them.

FOMA: Joy!

ROMAN: Power!

They sit motionlessly, as if they were afraid of destroying something enormous, distant, and desired.

FOMA (*shaking off his paralysis*): My friend, I beg you, before sleep hurls us beneath these bushes—sing.

ROMAN: Sing?

FOMA: Yes, yes! Sing. Something uplifting and classical.

Roman throws back his head and begins to sing. Foma wordlessly howls back at him, looking up into the murky sky.

ROMAN:

> And in the capital city, in Moscow,
> Three homeless dogs were off to drink their fill
> Of water right round noon.
> One dog was white,
> Another was black,
> The third was red.
> They came to the Moscow river,
> Found themselves a quiet place,
> Right round noon.
>
> The white dog drank—and the water went white.
> The black dog drank—and the water went black.
> The red dog drank—and the water went red.

The earth shook and the sun disappeared,
Lobnoye Mesto entirely collapsed,
Collapsed and broke apart,
Sprinkling forth scarlet blood,
And from the heavens, a thunderous voice rang out:
"He who was an executioner, shall now be the victim!
The hour of retribution, oh it is approaching!"

They sit silently for a little while; then, having calmed down and without much appetite, they return to their refection. Foma suddenly begins to chuckle. Roman looks at him as he eats.

FOMA: I just remembered ... for some reason ... m-m-m ... I don't even know why ... past deliriums ...

ROMAN (*warily*): What?

FOMA: Just don't get offended ... I suddenly remembered your performance as Artemon in *The Adventures of Pinocchio*. (*He waves his hand.*) Forgive me, old boy, forgive me ...

ROMAN (*looks furiously at Foma*): And I remembered you as the little dog in *The Blue Bird*: Hello-o-o-o, hello-o-o-o my little deity! Woof! Woof! Woof!

FOMA (*bares his teeth, laughs, and barks hysterically*): O-o-o-off! Oy, my friend ... that's really one for the books ... I don't have enough tears left to shed ...

ROMAN (*flinging away the bowl with the remains of the head*): I'm ready to forgive our foolish princess all but one thing!

FOMA (*nodding*): That she didn't let us play werewolves? Yes! They only used us in dreadful children's matinees.

ROMAN: I would forgive the drubbings and the chain and the humiliations and the dry food. For a single role. Just one! But that chicken-brained broody feared high art as if 'twere fire. Foolish woman!

FOMA (*sighing*): Foolish, foolish ... I didn't even play the poodle who gets a cameo in *Faust*. Not to mention *A Dog's Heart* or *White Fang* ...

ROMAN: The closest we got was arguing about *A Dog's Heart* before falling asleep... (*barks hysterically and laughs.*) The sinny or the play, what's more organic?!

FOMA: The book. The book, my friend. A work's literary context can't always be transformed to suit the cinema or the theater. Think of *Lolita*.

ROMAN: I would've played Sharikov brilliantly.

FOMA: I don't doubt it. But no real sinnyma, as Sashka the coachman used to say, would've come out of it.

ROMAN: It would've! I would've stretched forth my performance like the boat at the head of an armada! Like a *flagman*!

FOMA: Yes, my friend... Although... "Flagman" is quite a word. Isn't it also a Jewish name?

Roman looks at Foma angrily. He begins to bare his teeth threateningly. Foma raises his hands conciliatorily.

FOMA: Don't growl at a sick, old tramp, old boy. You and I are in the same boat—a boat called *Escape from Shameful Past*. Theater! What is theater to us now? And what is sinnyma? What could be more absurd and immoral than our actorly profession? To walk out onto the scaffolding, ape faces, cry with others' tears... No wonder they had to bury our brother beyond the fence... as if his end would corrupt the surrounding dead... And, yes, the fate of a serf-actor, one with a dog's face at that, is simply...

ROMAN (*baring his teeth angrily and resentfully*): A horror!

FOMA: Precisely. A horror. Or as the unhappy, indecisive Sergei Efremovich would have said, "It's simply *White Bim, Black Ear*."

ROMAN: Yes, for some reason he always said that whenever something terrible happened. (*He laughs.*) White Bim! (*He sighs.*) Sergei... poor Sergei... Why the devil did he stay? We'd be traveling in a trio right now.

FOMA: There turned out to be a timid heart in that formidable mastiff's body. He was a coward—nothing to be done.

ROMAN: Whippets turned out to be bolder than mastiffs.

FOMA: Thanks be to Dog…*ptooey*, pardon me, thanks be to God! (*He scratches himself drunkenly.*) Generally speaking, old boy, there shall be no sinnyma until we get to Telluria … And there … they shall beat a shining bit of tellurium into your head and, moments later, you shall walk out onto a crag hanging above the raging sea, not the miserable scaffolding of a stage. You shall read your great poems to the Ocean!

ROMAN (*declaiming*): Roar, oh mine ocean, roar as a free beast!

FOMA: And, shaken by your verses, the ancient Ocean shall cease its raging, lie at your feet, and reverently lap at them.

ROMAN: I have come here to rule over you from now on!

FOMA: And I shall become the new Nietzsche—Nietzsche-2—shall take an alpenstock and go up into the mountains, going higher, higher, and higher so as to meet the sun of the new millennium. The Millennium of Truth! I shall say to this sun: "Shine for us, oh luminary of life's new meaning!" Then, I shall enter my alpine hut, sit down at my desk, pick up a pen with a steel tip, dip it *into* my left hand, and, with my own blood, shall write of the new zoomorphic Zarathustra, he for whom a spiritually impoverished humanity has been waiting for so long.

A pause.

ROMAN (*sighing wearily*): I have come here to rule over you from now on…

FOMA: You're tired, my friend. Dreams don't only inspire, but also exhaust.

ROMAN: Yes… Especially those which are already not that far away… isn't that so? Already not so far? Hmm? Isn't that so?

FOMA: Not far at all. But you must save up your energy so as to continue overcoming inhospitable space, old boy. We'll need our strength for this night's nocturnal passage. That's enough dreaming. Let's sleep.

Roman nods exhaustedly and yawns with his entire snout, letting out a little howl. It's obvious how stupefied he's been by food and drink. Foma wipes the bowls and pot off on the wet grass and puts them away into the rucksack. Folds up the camping tripod. The travelers lie down beneath a birch tree in each others' arms. Fall asleep. A light rain begins to drizzle down. The coals in the extinguished campfire hiss weakly and emit smoke.

23

On a late July morning, Jean-François Trocard, the president of the Republic of Telluria, awoke in his palace, L'Edelweiss Noir, which towered up on the south face of Mount Kadyn-Bajy, the crown of the Altaian mountains. Here, in the mountains, Trocard always woke up late, probably because the summer sun, having crawled out from behind the snowy eastern peak, didn't reach the windows of his palace before eleven. Or perhaps because his sleep in the mountains was invariably as deep and calm as the glaciers of White Mountain and, like the five mountain rivers flowing reluctantly from these glaciers, he never wanted to leave its embrace.

Without opening his eyelids, Trocard threw off his thin camel blanket, put his hands over his head, felt for his bed's low headboard made of solid Altaian cedar, grabbed on to it, and stretched out his entire body, throwing his head back even farther onto a small, flat pillow filled with Altaian mountain herbs. He arched his back and stretched until his cervical vertebrae cracked. This habit had remained entirely unchanged for three decades, having taken root in the barracks of his flight school in Istra. Back then, as an eighteen-year-old, he would cling to the plastic back of a cadet bed and stretch, stretch, stretch with his whole young, muscular body, thirsty for life, flight, and adventures.

Despite his fifty-two years, his current body was still just as strong and mobile. Trocard worked hard to stay in shape.

He always slept naked. Sitting for a little while on his high, spacious bed, he then stood up and walked across the warm marble floor of the bedroom and into the bathroom. It was enormous and had a view onto the mountains. Drenched with sun, these mountains greeted the president with calm dignity. The weather was fantastic.

Trocard spent half an hour in the bathroom, swimming in a small pool filled with glacier water and bits of ice, taking a contrast shower, shaving, and rubbing his face with a special curative cream. A handsome, courageous physiognomy looked calmly and confidently out of the mirror at the president: broad cheeks, a coarse, crooked nose, full, authoritative lips, heavy eyelids, a stubborn chin with a slanting scar, and slightly graying temples. His face and body were covered in an even, beautiful tan.

Having put on a black silk robe, Trocard walked barefoot out of the bathroom and found himself in a small dining room, also overlooking the mountains. Barely had he sat down at the empty round table, when an Altaian girl in a gray pantsuit silently came in through a narrow door, walked over to him, and began to massage his shoulders and neck. The president's heavy eyelids fluttered. Even without smiling, the girl's narrow-eyed, wide-cheeked face exuded quiet joy. Her thin, strong fingers ably did their work. The energy of the girl's hands penetrated into the president's body. Ten minutes later, she went away just as silently as she'd come and a wide door immediately opened, light jazz music began to play, and two exquisitely dressed young Altaians in white gloves pushed the breakfast cart in. For Trocard, breakfast was always exclusively French, made up of foodstuffs from his once native Normandy, which were regularly delivered to Telluria by direct flights.

A marble plateau decked with cheeses, grapes, red currants, Bayonne ham, a decanter of orange juice, coffee, cream, croissants, a crispy baguette, salted butter, fromage blanc with fresh strawberries, and cleansing white rosemary honey from Narbonne in Languedoc—the last of which was a gift from the grand magister of the Templar order to the president of Telluria—appeared in front of him on a linen tablecloth embroidered with meadow flowers.

Having wished the president "bon appétit" in their excellent French, the servants departed. There were three official languages in Telluria: Altai, Kazakh, and French, the last of which was used primarily by elites and officials. In schools and universities, students were taught in all three languages. The president barely spoke Altai, but had mastered Kazakh quite well over the last twenty-two years. He read out his presidential messages to the parliament and appealed to the people in Kazakh. Communication with his subordinates and elites was conducted exclusively in French.

Having unhurriedly finished his breakfast, the president retired to his dressing room where two young servant girls helped him to put on his *home-for-the-weekend* ware. It was Saturday and no state affairs were in the offing. On this day, as on Sundays, the president was unavailable for reports, requests, and proposals.

In a light-blue suit with a yellow handkerchief in its chest pocket and a blue shirt with small yellow spots, Jean-François Trocard went up to the second floor, which was entirely occupied by his enormous office, in the elevator. A huge window, which took up a whole semi-circular wall, contained views of both peaks of White Mountain, part of the Kadyn Ridge, two glaciers, a river, and a bluish-emerald valley with the tiny boxes of peasant homes. This was a view that shocked the imagination. But the president, glancing briefly at the mountains as if they were an old friend, walked over to his massive desk, its size and shape reminiscent of the fossilized rhinoceros that had once trod on this land before it had become mountains. Barely had he sat down in his extremely comfortable leather armchair when a hologram of the latest world news for this fine Saturday morning arose and hovered in front of him. A gaze from beneath heavy eyelids wandered across the hologram. And didn't linger on any single bit of news. The president *put away* the hologram, picked up a thin Altaian bone pipe already filled with Dutch tobacco, lit up, blew a stream of smoke, and looked around at the space of the office with his habitual gaze. In addition to the desk, there was a long, low table surrounded by flat leather divans, an antique grandfather clock from the home of the Trocard family in Rouen, Chinese vases, a human-size crystal candelabra from Versailles, two tapestries dating back to the time of Louis XIV, royal chests of drawers inlaid with ivory, paintings by Magritte, Klimt, and Matisse, sculptures by Arnaud Brecker and

Rodin, a cabinet of old French weapons, a large photograph of Trocard in the uniform of a colonel of the wingèd legions surrounded by fellow soldiers immediately after the capture of Ohlàlà,* and eternally hovering next to the photograph was a holographic blue hornet the size of a mountain eagle. A highly detailed globe bristling with dozens of tellurium nails like a deep-sea pufferfish loomed by the window.

The president's gaze still didn't linger on anything in the office. With the stem of his pipe between his teeth, he made a tangential motion with his finger and two holographic women appeared before him. One had the head of a lynx and the other of a doe.

"Bonjour, Monsieur le Président!" Lynx sang, drawing out each word and squinting.

"Bonjour, Monsieur le Président!" Doe bowed her head very slightly.

"Hello, my little beasts." The president spoke without the calmly confident expression of his face changing. "Our meeting has been moved to this evening. I'll be ready for you just after eight."

Lynx and Doe opened their mouths to express their gratitude, but he quickly *put away* their holograms. Having sat at his desk and smoked his pipe for a little while, the president put the pipe down into the ashtray, stood up, walked out of the office, and went up to the third floor. Putting his palm to a lock, he walked into a large room that resembled a library. An evenly illuminating overhead light flashed on. This was the repository for the President of Telluria's coin collection. There were no windows here, only identical cabinets standing along each of the four walls. There was a small desk with an old-fashioned green lamp on it in the middle of the room. There were also three little wooden boxes on the desk—new arrivals. The president sat down at the desk and turned on the lamp by flipping its creaky, antediluvian switch. And immediately, the three boxes opened up. In one, there were two silver coins from ancient Olbia, in the second, a Chinese cast-iron coin from the Liang period, and in the third . . . in the third was the currency he'd waited the longest for, stone coins

*The capital of the Republic of Telluria

from ancient Novgorod—six round pieces with holes in the middle, in a package from the Novgorodian republic.

"*Très beau . . .*" Trocard muttered, took out a magnifying glass and napkins from a desk drawer, called up holograms of reference books, and occupied himself with these six flat monetary units from ancient Rus' that'd been hewn from pink slate ten centuries earlier. Without interrupting his work, he pressed a button at the edge of the desk. An old-fashioned screen came out of the ceiling, the light on the ceiling went out, and only the lamp on the desk remained lit. Music began to play and on the screen appeared the opening credits of a black-and-white French sinny. It was a comedy that'd been filmed before World War II.

Busying himself with the coins, the president hardly looked at the screen. This had already become a tradition. There were only *flat* black-and-white sinnys in his filmorary. And he watched them only when he was busying himself with his coin collection. The foundation for this coin collection had been laid by his great-grandfather, a major-artilleryman.

Jean-François came from an old Norman military family. Starting in 1870 with the Franco-Prussian War, his ancestors had managed to actively participate not only in the two world wars, but also in the Balkans, Algeria, Haiti, and Guiana. But, unlike Jean-François, they had all been *down to earth*. He was the first to throw a gauntlet to the heavens by becoming a pilot and then the leader of the "Blue Hornets" legion, which was already renowned by the time he joined up. But it was he who brought fame to the legion on the world stage.

More than an hour passed. The president was busying himself with his new coins and looking at the screen out of the corner of his eye. A new comedy had started to play on it. Suddenly, the "message of extreme state importance" alert rang out and three red exclamation marks flashed over the table. The president touched them with his finger. The exclamation marks unfolded into a hologram of the face of his first assistant, press secretary Robert Leroux.

"Mr. President, I wouldn't dare disturb you during your time of rest, but a message of extreme importance has forced me to take this step," Leroux began to speak in his old-fashioned, ornate manner.

"I'm listening, Leroux," Trocard pronounced, turning off the sound of the sinny with one hand and not letting go of a silver coin with a depiction of the goddess Demeter and an eagle sitting on a dolphin's back that'd been cast in Olbia five centuries before the birth of Christ with the other.

"The Baikalian Republic has officially recognized our state."

The president put the coin down onto the table.

"When?"

"Just now, Mr. President."

Leroux *unfolded* the text of the BR's decree. Trocard read it attentively, the expression on his face not changing, then made his pronouncement.

"That's good news, Leroux."

"Wonderful news, Mr. President."

Trocard got up from his desk, began to pace, then stretched so as to make his neck vertebrae crack.

"That's ... that's simply ... devilishly good news, Leroux."

"Yes, devilishly good, Mr. President! Konashevich signed the decree last night. And they held an emergency vote this morning in parliament. The decree was approved almost unanimously."

"So the Baikalian Communists triumphed."

"Yes, Mr. President! Sokolov and Hwan got their way. Our three years of aid did their work. From now on, Baikalian liberals shall no longer shove sticks between our spokes."

"Yes, into our wheels ... the wheels of trains filled with tellurium," the president added and smiled for the first time that morning.

"Going east along the Trans-Siberian," Leroux affirmed.

"Yes, yes ..." The president stuck his hands into his pockets and rocked back and forth on his blue socks, the same color as his suit and shoes.

"With your permission, I'll prepare a text addressing our citizens."

"Of course, Robert. And I owe you one for the good news."

"I was unspeakably happy to inform you of it, Mr. President." Leroux was shining.

"Now...no, in the evening, we'll have an emergency meeting of the Cabinet of Ministers."

"Sir, yes, sir, Mr. President."

"See you soon." Trocard nodded at him slightly.

The hologram of the press secretary disappeared.

The president walked across the wide parquetry of the coin-storage room, turned sharply, then froze, his arms crossed across his chest. His gaze came to rest on the screen. There, a soldier with a horsey smile was trying to kiss a girl.

"*Très bien*," the president pronounced.

Then he suddenly let forth a sharp, guttural cry, jumped up, pitched his legs out to either side, slapped his hands onto them, and got down onto the floor, crouching and spreading his arms. Frozen in this posture, he made a sound that resembled a restrained growl.

On the screen, the girl pushed the soldier away.

The president straightened up, exhaled, fixed his suit, left the storage room with his slow but energetic gait, and went down into his office. At this hour, the office was completely flooded with the sun's rays. The president pulled out a drawer of the rhinoceros desk, removed a box of tellurium nails and a small hammer from it, picked out one nail from the box, walked over to the globe, turned it toward the sun, immediately found the capital of the Baikalian Republic—Irkutsk— put the tip of the nail to it, and lightly beat it in. The sun shined onto the head of yet another tellurium nail. Having put the hammer down onto the marble windowsill, the president walked over to the globe and gave it a spin. It swam round in a circle, the heads of all the nails sparkling.

"A path to the east..." Trocard muttered, staring intently at the spinning globe.

Now this path was clear. Which would allow for the exportation of tellurium not only to the Far-Eastern Republic, which so yearned for it, but also to Japan, Korea, and Vietnam. No more winding air corridors, roundabout paths, and dangerous mountain roads. There was no longer any need to hide. The Trans-Siberian! The trains shall push off from the station—armored trains decorated with the coat of arms of Telluria and filled to the brim with nails. And nobody shall stop them. Nobody!

The day had begun wonderfully. He would have to remember it: Saturday, July 15. A wonderful day! And on such a day, one certainly couldn't sit in an office, sort through coins, or engage in foolish conversations. He would meet with the ministers in the evening. Now he wanted flight. Flight! The president turned to the desk and called up a hologram of the majordomo.

"I want to leave now, René. Prepare everything."

"Sir, yes, sir, Mr. President."

The president moved to the exit. Then remembered his debt to the kind messenger. And again called up the majordomo's round face.

"René, send Mr. Leroux a case of 1982 Château Lafite Rothschild from my cellars. Right away."

"Thy shall be done, Mr. President."

A quarter of an hour later, a helicopter with Trocard on board rose up from the launchpad of the presidential palace. The president was outfitted in a black jumpsuit with an intricate backpack and had a helmet equipped with an oxygen mask over his head and ski boots on his feet. The helicopter began to rise up. The slopes of Kadyn-Bajy stretched out all around him, becoming even whiter. The sun was shining onto their spurs. There wasn't a single cloud in the bright-blue sky.

The president's palace was located at an altitude of two thousand meters above sea level and the helicopter was rising up above it higher and higher until it hovered over the peaks of one of the two mountains—the western mountain. The door opened up and they helped the president out onto the peak and gave him his skis and poles. He made a gesture of farewell to the helicopter and the iron dragonfly with an image of a blue hornet on its side flew away. Trocard fastened his skis, grabbed the comfortable handles of his poles, which were cast from sticky self-generating rubber, stuck the poles into the hard snow, and froze. He was standing on the peak. A strong northern wind was blowing at his back and the thermometer on his wrist showed −12 degrees Celsius. But the president wasn't looking at the thermometer. His gaze was filled up by the magnificent vista spread out all around him. Mountain spurs towered up and sparkled with snow, fog-filled grayish-blue chasms gaped, and an abyss opened up, ornamented with the white snakes of four glaciers crawling into the valley and beckoning with greenery and turquoise lakes. He glanced to the left. There stood the sharp spire of the eastern peak of Kadyn-Baji. A small cloud was resting on it—as if it were seeking protection. He glanced to the right. There rose up the Kadyn Ridge, extending off to the west and to the east for one hundred and fifty kilometers. Beating into his eyes from the southeast, the sun was so strong that the mighty ridge appeared to be steaming beneath its rays.

The president stood on the peak. These moments were incomparable. He was alone. The world was at his feet. And this world was wonderful. Nearby, on the wind-compressed snow, he could see the traces of poles and boots. It had been him standing there two weeks earlier.

A gust of wind pressed at his back. This was a signal. The president abruptly pushed off with his poles, then again, and again—and tore into the welcome abyss. The wind hummed, roared, and howled into his helmet, the fresh snow rustled beneath his skis, the thick crust creaked, the ice squealed, and the black figure of the skier rushed downwards in a complicated zigzag.

Colonel Jean-François Trocard could ski and snowboard just as magnificently as he could fly his hornet. Perhaps even better. His passion for extreme descent, which had come to possess him at the age of sixteen, had never let him ago. It was stronger than him.

He knew his route and conquered the formidable space with professional fury. Flying over chasms, sliding along icy fault lines, leaping over exposed granite blocks, and slaloming across planes of snow, he cut into the abyss with the blades of his skis. And the disturbed snows fell indignantly from its perches, flying after Trocard with a growl, rising up in waves of sparkly, snowy dust, chasing, threatening, and buzzing. But he was faster than it was.

Two dips of dark ice flashed, rushing past, rustling quietly, a gentle fell, a crest rose and fell and an almost-vertical, kilometer-wide wall loomed before him, crushing in its detail, while far below, the presidential palace flashed forth, a black flower hewn from granite. From above, it was the size of an edelweiss. A black edelweiss growing in the abyss—offering comfort, sigils of authority, and the joy of human warmth . . .

Now began the most complicated part. The icy wall plunged down menacingly. It demanded the impossible. But he was so familiar with the impossible! Ice screeched indignantly beneath his skis, the points of his poles pierced it, and it was as if the black figure were mounted to the wall. His skis rattled across the exposed granite, cutting and sketching out an incredible zigzag. The wall rose from below like a wave, sparkling with ice and trembling with strength. He went down, slaloming and sliding, as if he were selecting the proper place to fall. It seemed there would be no end to it, but suddenly, it began to obediently bend, was subjugated, fragmented into crests, drooped, and, now three hundred meters away from the palace, Trocard flashed into a jump, glided, landed, and slid through a long, wide saddle full of deep, loose snow. He unfastened his respirator. Cold mountain air burst into his lungs. The saddle twisted in waves, cradling and rocking him. He dropped his poles and pressed a button on his wrist. Something clicked in his backpack and narrow black wings spread out and unfolded evenly from his back, two solid-fuel engines coughing as they started up. He grabbed onto the wing mounts with his hands. A draft carried him up and he pushed off from the snow, taking off and letting his skis fall. At just the right moment—immediately after the saddle was cut off by a gorge. He took off, rushing forward through the air, down toward where there was no more snow, where meadows blazed with green, where cedars and pines cast shadows 'gainst the ground, and where lakes shone with blue. He'd left behind the world of icy silence. Ahead of him lay the human world. And it was *waiting* for him. The engines carried him and he cut through the air, getting warmer every second. Having flown over the two tongues of glacial ice, he rushed down into the valley. The mountain river crawled out from beneath one of the glaciers and twisted around underneath him, gaining strength as it did. Peasant houses appeared in the valley and smoke, smoke, smoke rising upwards, smoke that had only one meaning: We're waiting for you and we love you. They *were* waiting for him. And they *did* love him. Hundreds of plumes of smoke from hundreds of campfires. This was worth an awful lot. These plumes of smoke were incomparable—neither with rounds of applause nor with distinctions awarded by the worldly elite, neither with guards of honor, nor with wealth and power... And he always smiled joyfully as he flew down into the valley.

The peasants were waiting for him. He flew exclusively on the weekends and only when the weather was good. Those living around the mountains knew that. They also knew that, after a flight, their president loved to eat a bowl of *ketche*—Altai mutton soup cooked over a campfire. And hundreds of peasant herders looked up at the sky from beneath their palms all day—will it be clear today? And if it was—they chopped firewood, made a fire, hung a cauldron of clear mountain water over the fire, went to the sheepfold, chose the youngest and most beautiful lamb, slaughtered it, flayed it, made the *ketche*... and waited for their president. Because of his eternal black jumpsuit and wings of the same shade, they nicknamed him the Black Stork. The Black Stork flew down from White Mountain, becoming the guest of any family for an hour and bringing great joy with him.

He flew down into the valley. The river flowed into a lake of whitish water. The second lake was turquoise. The third—black. The meadows swam past and the tops of centuries-old spruces and larches flashed by. The greens became more toneful and everything else became somehow *juicier*. The plumes of smoke approached, as if they were the columns of an invisible temple of Popular Love. The engines ran dry and, now empty, shot back and flew down. He continued to fly, soaring by inertia. Now he had to choose; he descended upon a new family every time. He tilted right toward the lake of turquoise water, flew over it, and prepared to land. Green hills with little houses on them swam past beneath him, approaching as he got lower. The smell of campfires penetrated his nostrils. And, with it, the cries of small children reached his ears.

"Black Stork! Black Stork!"

He planed even more to the right, flew out over the forest, then over two hills, and saw a lone plume of smoke ahead of him beyond the rows of fir trees. He had never been there before. Having glided over the tops of the spruces, he found himself above a hill with a miraculous meadow, a wooden house, and a sheepfold. A campfire was burning next to the house and people were visible around it. Having noticed him, they began to cry out and wave their hands. He made a circle, easing down and landing gracefully in the meadow near the fire.

They ran over to him. He unhurriedly unfastened his wings, took off his helmet and gloves, threw them into the grass, and unzipped his jumpsuit. The sensation of coming down to earth was very peculiar, but Trocard, a professional pilot, had long grown accustomed to it. And still, after everything, to be standing on this lush alpine grass was extremely pleasant.

An Altaian family stood before him—an old man, an old woman, a young man, a woman, an adolescent, and two little boys. They beheld him with silent delight—as if he were a miracle. And he was a miracle—the president of the republic that had given tellurium to the world, the Black Stork that dwelled in the Black Edelweiss and who'd now flown down to this campfire from the highest mountain in Altai.

"Peace be to your home," the president pronounced in Altai.

And the family came to life, bowing and mumbling joyful greetings. The chatter of helicopters was audible up in the air and two silver machines landed near the hill, guards beginning to jump out of them.

The president shook hands with all members of the family. It wasn't just the little boys who couldn't restrain themselves, shaking their heads, smiling, muttering, and whinging, but also the old man and old woman. The president proffered his hand and they each stated their name. When it was the young woman's turn, she also stated her name and greeted the president in bad French. Trocard replied and asked if her children spoke French. It turned out that they did. And significantly better than their mother. The older boy said that a Frenchwoman was teaching at their school, one Mademoiselle Palanche. *Très bien! Très bien!* The president was happy that more opportunities were presenting themselves to this new generation of Tellurians. Was their school far from home? *Oh non, Monsieur le Président, très proche! Juste une demi-heure à vélo!* Wonderful! Studying in today's complicated world is more important than ever. Do the children help their parents out at home? *Oui, bien sûr, Monsieur le Président.* Fantastic! Are the parents content with the successes of their children? *Très, très satisfaits!* Terrific! Not understanding, the old man and old woman nodded joyfully. The president addressed them in Kazakh, as all Altaian understood this language.

"Are the cattle healthy?"

"*Mal aman! Mal aman!*"* They nodded even more violently.

"Wonderful! If the cattle are healthy, that means the health of your children and grandchildren. The clean air of Telluria, its bowels, that means ecology, the guarantor of the health of us all. However, isn't it time for us to partake of the soup? Your president has become slightly peckish in the mountains." His Kazakh wasn't quite perfect.

The family bustled about joyfully, and soon the president was sitting with the Altaian family at a table that had been brought out to the meadow and eating *ketche* soup accompanied by freshly baked flatbread kneaded in sour milk. The taste of this soup, cooked from young lamb and lentils over the fire, had been as important for Jean-François Trocard as the descent from White Mountain and the flight over the valley for a long time. All of it was a tradition and it was impossible to separate one part from the whole. Sitting at the wooden table in the meadow with this pleasant family, sharing a simple refection with them, breathing in the clean air with a hint of campfire smoke, talking about ecology, grain prices, and new mountain tun-

*[Kazakh] The cattle are healthy

nels...what could be better after such a dizzying descent? And the great mountain he'd once again conquered, this White Giant, confirmed with the sparkling of its age-old snow: nothing.

Having finished their refection, the president took a tiny hourglass filled with tellurium sand and with a Tellurian coat of arms on its exterior out from his pocket and gifted it to the head of the household. He made this gift to everyone he flew down to visit. The hourglass measured exactly one minute.

Having warmly bid the family farewell, the president got into a helicopter and returned to his mountain palace. Having taken a bath and drunk a calming tea, he went into his bedroom, lay down in bed, and slept until seven. Sleep after descent was always distinguished by its particular depth and duration.

After he woke up, Trocard took a shower, put on his evening suit, drank a cup of not-very-strong coffee, smoked an Egyptian cigarette, and went into his office. The sun had already disappeared behind the western spurs and the office was evenly and pleasantly illuminated. The mountains turned gray and moved off into the distance, hidden away by mist here and there. The globe lit up and illuminated the corner of the office with a pleasant bluish-green light. The president made a motion with his hand and the holograms of all twelve ministers of Telluria began to hover around his office. They already knew the main news of the day and looked at their president with friendly smiles.

"Congratulations, gentlemen," the president said. "Our path to the east is clear."

Congratulations and joyful exclamations rang out in response to him. And the emergency meeting of the Cabinet of Ministers began, dragging on for more than three hours. It ended unusually: the president asked for champagne to be brought in and stood up with a glass in hand. The ministers also had glasses of champagne in hand. The president walked up to each hologram and clinked glasses with each minister. The leaders of Telluria drank to their country.

When the holograms were extinguished, the president left his office and went down to the basement floor. There, in a spacious living room decorated in a Moroccan style, two women with enchanting figures wearing dinner dresses had already been waiting for him for a long time. One had the head of a lynx and the other of a doe. Doe was smoking a thin cigarette inserted into a long mouthpiece and Lynx was cutting lines of cocaine on a mirrored table. When they saw the president, the two women stood up and walked over to him.

"Jean-François!" Doe bleated, hugging him and kissing his right cheek.

"Jean-François!" Lynx purred, pressing her fur to his left cheek.

"Hello, my sweets." He smiled slightly. "Have you been waiting long?"

"We've been wa-a-a-aiting!"

"Wait-ing and wait-ing!"

When they'd finished embracing, they walked over to the low sofa, sat down on it, and leaned back onto colorful cushions. Doe handed the president a glass of champagne and Lynx brought a little porcelain spoon of cocaine to his nostril. The president snorted the powder into one nostril, then immediately snorted another portion with the other nostril. This was his evening norm. But the president did not abuse narcotics. Doe wiped his solid, world-famous nose with a handkerchief of the finest batiste.

"*Très bon* . . ." the president muttered and took a sip from his glass.

"They say our path to the east is clear?" Lynx purred.

"No more obstacles, huh?" Doe squinted.

"No," he replied without looking at the women.

"Our country will get even richer?"

"And even mightier?"

"Yes."

"Shall we celebrate that today?"

"Yes."

"Does a celebratory dinner await us?"

"Yes."

Even under the influence of cocaine, Trocard didn't become more talkative. His gaze passed over a carved cigarette case. Lynx pulled out a cigarette and inserted it between his lips. Doe brought a flame to the cigarette. The president lit up, taking sips of champagne as he did. They sat in silence. When he'd finished his cigarette, Lynx took the butt from the president's lips and put it out in an ashtray.

The president finished his champagne and put down his glass. Looked at the women. And slapped them on the knees. "Time for our savanna, you little beasts."

The women laughed tenderly and helped him up. They embraced, then passed through the living room and over to a door. The president put his hand to a lock and the door opened. They entered a dim, round room. The door closed behind them. There was a low square podium glowing with pinkish light in the middle of the room. Four charming teenagers of both genders in turbans and loincloths were frozen at the corners of the podium. They were holding palm fronds and smoothly fanning the podium. The room was hot, cicadas were singing, and it smelled of the south. The president walked over to the podium and tumbled down onto his back. The podium was soft. The president lay down, spreading out his arms and legs into the shape of an "X." He stared up at the pink ceiling. His courageous face exuded confidence and élan. Lynx and Doe threw off their dresses quickly and easily. Doe was slender with small breasts and had a very fine plant tattoo on her stomach and a bare pubis. Lynx was plump, with large white breasts and a pale body, and had reddish fur on her pubis. Her long, thin phallus was erect. The women sat down next to the president and began to slowly unlace his shoes.

"Is Jean-François ready for a safa-a-a-ari?" Doe bleated.

"Did Jean-François load his r-r-r-rifle?" Lynx growled.

"Yes!!!" the president cried up at the pink ceiling and clapped his hands together loudly.

24

OH, HOW fine the horse fair is in Konkovo!

Horse traders hurry on over here from every corner of the world with their live product.

Not just from PodMoscow, glorious Yaroslavl, Saratov incubators, and Voronezhian and Bashkirian cart-horse factories; herds also trickle their way to ZaMoscvorechye from distant states—for example, a van of little blue ladies' horses just arrived from Espanish Córdoba much to the delight of Moscow beauties, and what more can be said about strong-chested Chinese xiaomi standin' in groups of five, waitin' for their masters and shakin' their shaggy manes. Pavlodarian, Circassian, Mongolian, Tatarian, Ivanovian, Provençal, and Bavarian horses—bring 'em all down to Konkovo! Step right up, the market occupies six square versts of land and the traders still complain: Ain't enough space no more, no place to walk our lil' horses proper 'n show off how strong and beautiful they are.

Vanya arrived at the fair with his roan horsphere before dawn. Came up from the subway, tossed the box with the horsphere over his hump, and got to walkin'. Walkin', lookin', and feelin' joyful. So many horses round that yer eyes set to runnin'! At the fair, there're normal horses of all possible colors, ponies, cart horses, *corroded* little horses, funny 'n spirited horses, fastuns, and *calmuns*. Herds of *tinies* of every possible dimension in their stables. Crowded up and clompin' round so much it makes ye wanna laugh.

And Vanya did laugh, lookin' at a little herd of mottled horses— it was real funny all right! White as can be, but with spots of dark, as if someone'd spattered paint on 'em. Forty of 'em crammed into a stable, clompin' round, eyes like black currants, and barin' their tiny teeth at their owner. And their owner, a healthy and rotund fella, stands with his arms crossed and smokin' importantly, as if they wasn't his herd.

"How much ye goan trade this herd for, old man?" Vanya asks.

"A thousand five hundred," the horse trader answers without lookin' at Vanya.

"Hot damn!" Vanya clicked his tongue.

But that's how much a herd of mottled horses costs, o' course. Vanya keeps walkin'. The fair is buzzin' all round, nevermind the early hour. They're tradin', bettin', and bristlin' *domes*. And a flood of horses all round! After the *tinies*, he got to the *sizables*. Cart horses! They tower up, each one bigger'n the next. Some're two times as big as a man, some even more. They stand there real calm, not payin' no mind, and people are fussin' all round 'em and tradin' 'em. Cart horses don't give a damn about little people! As if they weren't gettin' talked about—trade us, that's fine, but we ain't goan look at ye.

Vanya looked further on and sized up the biggest horse at the fair. A light-bay cart horse the size of a three-story house. And he stands like a house too without movin' at all. A red mane like a midday cloud and shaggy pasterns two times wider'n a man could hold. Pigeons and crows are sittin' on his back as if it were a roof. Vanya walked over, mouth open wide, looked way up, and the hat fell off his head.

And the cart horse snorted 'n sparrows flew forth in a flock from his ears. Then the horse sighed with its wide chest, farted like a cannon goin' off, and dropped a turd so big ye couldn't take it away in one go with five wheelbarrows.

Vanya picked up his hat and bowed at the waist to the cart horse.

"Glory be to ye, oh knightly horse."

Right then, the horsphere in the box neighed: Don't forget 'bout me! And rightly so—that horsphere was the main thing for Vanya. He set off to find a spot and found one 'mong the other horsphere traders real quick. Paid the Kyrgyzian guy in charge twenty kopecks, got up, opened the box, and prayed to himself: "Send a buyer real soon, oh holy Frol and Laurus!"

And Vanya got real lucky—a half hour hadn't even passed when a businesslike secondhand dealer wearin' lots of gold, in a silk brocade, with three smartypantses and a tellurium nail stickin' outta his dome, approached. He got the price down to ten with the box included. Vanya crossed himself and put the tenner under his hat. Thinkin': Now I'll buy my wife a self-generatin' shawl, sweetnesses for the kids, pastila for Mama, then hurry on home to Aprelevka. He set off through the fair toward the subway, but right along the way was a tavern. Beautiful, new, and opulent. An enormous livin' picture above the porch—a red-faced floor cloth gesturin' at a table, winkin', and cryin' out, "Your work is done, now have your fun!" And on the table . . . Vanya's already droolin': hams linin' up, pies blushin', cucumbers all green, kvass chillin' in a jug, vodka sweatin' in its decanter, and, in the middle of the table, a roasted goose steamin'.

And Vanya couldn't understand how he ended up in the tavern— his legs walked in of their own volition. Sat down at a lil' table, ordered a half *shtof* of Smirnov and a pie to go with it. He'd just had a couple drinks when they waved 'im over from a big table: Come sit with us, home slice! He gave 'em a good look—ord'nary people 'n horse traders. He joined 'em and they drank up and got to talkin'. First they bought drinks for Vanya, then he did for them. Then the singers came on over and set to playin's Vanya's favorite song: "Stop Scoldin' Me, Darlin.'" And Vanya had such a fine time he came to his senses only at night when a Tatarian guard was shovin' an' pushin' him out through the gates of the fair. Vanya sat down beneath a streetlight, his head was buzzin' and he couldn't remember nothin'. Got up, wandered over to the pump, and drank his fill of water. He remembered that he'd come to the fair and sold his horsphere for a tenner. Turned out his pockets—empty. Thought to himself: How am I goan go home with empty pockets? We were goan use that money for a new bathhouse. That's why they raised, 'n groomed, 'n fed that horsphere with oats and clover for a whole year. His wife, a warmhearted woman, plaited a birch bark box for the horsphere; his girls wove multicolored ribbons into its mane; and his momma tinted its lil' hooves with silver. And at the end of the day—no box, no horsphere, 'n no tenner...

And our Vanya set to weepin' hot tears.

25

CHÈRE fillette,

As an individual deeply beloved by me, you know well not only my weaknesses, but also my sins. And all that which is tied to Ali represents my gravest sin. Am I ashamed of it? Without question. Do I regret what happened? No—I regret only the pain I caused you. That which happened might not have caused any pain at all. It depended solely on me and not on Ali—simpleminded and infinitely kind to us both—ready as he was to cut our torturous knot. Unlike you and me, he is a consummate and courageous individual, who knows not only how to give in to strong feelings, but also how to burn bridges. And so, my beloved, my sin consisted in the fact that when Ali found out about *everything* and burned the bridge of his feelings for me, I began to extinguish the fire with my tears and lamentations, flying over it like Rukh the bird, fluttering my sensitive wings and finally putting it out; it smoldered, smoked, and swayed over the abyss for these last two months. This smoking, charred bridge of our feelings for each other brought suffering into your heart. That is very painful to me. Then, when the bridge collapsed, it pained me doubly to think of how I could not take back my initial attempts to *not* let the bridge collapse. And I am prepared to atone for this sin. Tomorrow, I am purchasing a piece of silvery metal born in the bowels of distant mountains so that I might retrieve what you and I have lost. You know *whom* I shall meet in the city of your childhood and *what* I shall ask for on your behalf. If I am destined to perish, know that you were, are, and always shall be the person most beloved by me on earth. There is no one dearer to me than you.

I love you!

Eternally yours,
Fatima

P.S. Whatever happens to me, I pray that you hold no rancor in your heart for Ali. In addition to his enormous spiritual and emotional capacities, he also liberated our native Groningen from crusaders. His young, gorgeous body was scourged by the bullets of Christian barbarians and his left shoulder was scorched by napalm. You and I are indebted to him for our peaceful life and well-being more than we are anyone else. Remember that.

26

RUSSIAN ORTHODOX BROTHERS AND SISTERS!
COMRADES!
CITIZENS!

The usurper who seized power in your native Podolsk is drinking
your blood. He sits like Moloch upon the throne so untimely abandoned by Prince Stanislav Borisovich. The usurper's feet trample the
backs of working people and his hands clutch at the prince's throne
with a death grip. The prince is surrounded by the bloody oprichniks
who brought him to power by way of a secret coup. 'Tis God alone
who knows how much Russian Orthodox blood these monsters of
human nature spilled as they cleared a path for the usurper. The arms
of these bipedal animals are covered in blood up to the elbow. Having
fooled our gullible metropolitan Sophronius, seduced the widowed
Princess Sofya, bewitched the heir to the throne Sergei Stanislavov-
ich with his demonic beguilements, bribed the regional committee
with tellurium nails, and arranged a shameful purge of the apparatus
of the city party committee, the usurper and his oprichniks organized
a secret ballot in the city duma on the second of December, as a result
of which they rose to power in our native Podolsk. Neither church
hierarchs and party activists, nor the nobility and the city duma could
resist the devilish pressure of the usurper and his clique. For verily,
Satan himself helped these fiends as they disguised themselves behind
crosses and party membership cards. Immediately after the passing
of our prince Stanislav Borisovich, the usurper and his faithful oprichniks began their devilish attempt to seize power in Podolsk. The

assistants to the city governor Stepanov, Friedmann, Boykov, Zhang Mo Waen, Kozlovsky, Berkutovich, Lieutenant Colonel of State Security Smirnov, and the duma clerks Volkov and Pak were arrested on false charges and the entrepreneurs Rakhimov, Swan Wei, Rinder, and Mr. and Mrs. Khloponin, the merchants Zalessky, Popov, Alikhanov, and the Ivanov brothers were thrown into prison. The nobleman I. I. Akhmetyev died under mysterious circumstances on a hunt while in the process of actively resisting the seizure of state power in the city duma. As a result of the "purge" organized by the usurper and his oprichniks in the city party committee, such distinguished Communists as Comrade Wet, Comrade Volobuev, and Comrade Chrysoprazis were expelled from the party. Nineteen Communists were also withdrawn from the leadership of the city and regional party committees. A criminal case was opened against the Communist Comrade Vorotnyuk, who opened his veins at a shameful "cleansing" meeting of the new city party committee and smeared his blood all over the face of the new secretary of the city committee, Count Kvitovsky. For bold and honest denunciations of the usurper and his gang, the intercessor of the people Father Nikolai Abdulloyev was deprived of his parish and imprisoned in a monastery. The gang of crooks could not abide the cleansing flame of his accusatory sermons. Father Nikolai's wife, Zulfiya Rakhimovna, fell into a fever from the grief and sorrow for her husband and gave birth to a stillborn child. Having seized power in Podolsk, the usurper and his henchmen began to seize our natural and industrial resources. Therefore, in September they concocted the sale of 62 percent of the stock of Podolsk Industries to the comradeship of Matvey Norstedt, who was stained by his friendship with the enemy of the Podolskian people, the former chairman of the city duma D.A. Alekseyev. As a result of the devilish fraud perpetrated by the duma clerk Volodin, our deposit of porcelain clay was acquired by Mosgovsalk, despite the fact that the initial owner of the deposit was a Podolskian cattle farmer, one N.A. Mokshev. The question is: Why did Comrade Mokshev hastily sell his holdings at the Beaver Plant and leave Podolsk in August of this year? And where might Mr. Mokshev now be found? The hair of honest citizens stands on end when imagining the sheer scale of arbitrariness and lawlessness created by the usurper and his gang upon our native soil. The PodMoscovian earth moans and bleeds beneath the boots of monsters. For how long shall us Podolskians have to withstand the mockery of the usurper? For how long shall our hard-working people have to bow to the oprichniks occupying the Podolsk Kremlin like fascists? For how long shall Russian Orthodox people have to contemplate the whorishness, drug abuse, and perpetual fall from grace of this bloody clique? For how long can they make peace with witchcraft and devilish beguilements? For how long shall honest Communists have to raise their hands and say "aye" in the city party committee, so tellurized and shellacked by the usurper's gang?

Brothers and sisters, 'tis time to put a stop
To this lawlessness in our native land!
Down with the usurper and his gang!
Come to the rally on December 15!
Meet at the cathedral at 14:00.

27

TELLURIUM—a chemical element of the sixteenth group of the fifth period located on the periodic table under number 52 and in the metalloid family. A delicate, silvery-white metal. Also a rare-earth metal, as autogenous deposits of tellurium are incredibly uncommon, with only four of them in the world. It was first discovered in 1782 in the gold-bearing ores of Transylvania. There are 120 known minerals of tellurium, the most renowned of which are tellurides of lead, copper, zinc, gold, and silver. Tellurium and its alloys are used in electrical engineering, radiotechnics, in the production of heat-resistant rubber, chalcogenide glasses, as well as in the production of semi- and superconductor materials. The special properties of autogenous tellurium were discovered rather recently. In 2022, in the mountains of Altai, near the hamlet of Turochak, an ancient Zoroastrian temple founded in the fourth century BC on top of a deposit of autogenous tellurium was discovered by Chinese archaeologists. The temple had been built in the form of a cave hidden away from the outside world. The cave, which was later named Maktulu (or "Glorified") was decorated with rock inscriptions and an image of the sun engraved with pure tellurium. Judging by the evidence, the Zoroastrians worshipped this image. Forty-eight skeletons with their arms crossed across their chests were discovered in the cave of Maktulu. All of the skulls had small (42 mm) wedges of autogenous tellurium beaten into their skulls at a single point. In an altar niche beneath the image of the sun bronze hammers and tellurium wedges were arranged in a semicircle. The wedges of tellurium had been beaten into the skulls of the forty-eight skeletons with these hammers. The entrance to the temple cave was walled over from the inside. In the wake of this discovery, scientists from the Peking Institute of the Brain along with their colleagues from Stanford University conducted a number of studies on volunteers and received phenomenal results: when beaten into a particular place on the head, the tellurium wedges of the Zoroastrians caused a persistent euphoric state and a feeling of time's disappearance in the volunteers. However, a fatal outcome was not at all rare. In 2026, experiments with tellurium wedges were forbidden at a United Nations convention and wedges of autogenous tellurium were declared to be a hard drug, the manufacture and distribution of which would be punishable by law. After a military coup organized by the Norman wingèd legion "The Blue Hornets" ("Les Frelons bleus") in the Barabinskian province of Altai, a referendum was conducted in the province, through which the majority of the population declared themselves in favor of the secession of the province from the Republic of Barabin. It was in this way that, on the seventeenth of January, 2028, a new state, the Democratic Republic of Telluria (DRT), was proclaimed on the former territory of the province of Altai. Colonel Jean-François Trocard, the commander of the legion of "Blue Hornets," was elected as the first president of the DRT. Telluria is recognized by twenty-four states in the world community. In addition to cattle breeding and the export of tellurium and other rare-earth metals, the principal occupation of Tellurians is that of the so-called tellurium healer, which is to say the trepanation of the skull with autogenous tellurium following the method of ancient Zoroastrians, a technique used to treat various ailments, including cancer of the brain, schizophrenia, autism, multiple sclerosis, and Alzheimer's disease. Telluria is the only country in the world where tellurium wedges aren't considered to be a drug. Attempts to impose international sanctions on the government of the DRT have been heretofore unsuccessful. A number of states (Australia, Great Britain, Iran, California, Prussia, Bavaria, Normandy, Albania, Serbia, Wallachia, Galicia, Moscovia, White Sea, the Uralian Republic, Ryazan, Tataria, Barabin, and the Baikalian Republic) have yet to establish diplomatic relations with Telluria. The citizens of these countries are forbidden from entering Telluria.

28

"Isn't it time to, so to speak, *bivouaquer* as we're able?" Mikitok asked in his lazily drawn-out voice, flexing his well-groomed white hands, on which he was wearing two rings—one was platinum with a black sapphire cut through with the hieroglyph for "well-being" and the other was gold with a diamond monogram of an "M."

Dozing in deep chairs of pinkishly marbled leather, the brigade began to move sluggishly. The last bivouac had been at noon near Bobruisk and had naturally coincided with the lunch prepared by the brigade chef, Du Zhuan—an abundant, seven-course lunch, which culminated in dessert, cognac, hookah, and an after-lunch stroll through the spring forest. Now the old-fashioned clock inside the cabin indicated that it was a quarter to six.

"It's too early for dinner." The thin Laertes, almost entirely covered with *living* tattoos and mormolon scales, stretched out.

"We must needs drink some tea." Arnold Konstantinovich brutally slapped himself across his hollow cheeks.

"Which is precisely what I had in mind, my good gentlemen." Mikitok put his hands languidly to his chest, threw back his beautiful head with its curly hair and its gracefully trimmed beard, and let forth a quiet moan. "O-o-o-o-o-h . . . my dea-a-a-athly anguish . . ."

"Shall I wake the brigadier?" The hunchbacked, narrow-faced Latif folded up a smartypants made to look like an old book.

"Wake him." The slender, high-cheeked, and narrow-eyed Serge nodded, unfastening his seatbelt and pressing the button to call the steward.

With Caucasian complaisance, Latif lay his beautiful hands with their thin layer of black hair on the elbow of the brigadier who was dozing in a neighboring chair. Witte's broad, noble, and intelligent face, which always displayed an expression of confident and business-like calm, even when he was sleeping, still preserved this expression now. His eyes remained shut.

"Someone has need of something?" the brigadier asked in his pleasant, confident voice without opening his eyes.

This confident voice forced everyone to begin to rouse himself and unsnap his seat belts—everyone except for the sleeping and snoring Ivan Ilyich.

"Yes, Brigadier," Latif pronounced with an almost filial smile, as he gently squeezed Witte's elbow.

"And this need is devouring us, as if 'twere the Leviathan." Mikitok called up a mirror on his smartypants, looked into it, and straightened his crooked, peach-colored bow tie. "My members have gone numb!"

"Everyone should stretch!" Arnold Konstantinovich announced in his imperative manner.

Serge looked out the window.

"Yes, the terrain should allow for that."

A singular landscape had been dragging on outside the window for three hours already: a mixed forest touched by spring on the right and the ruins of the Great Wall of Russia on the left.

A steward elegant in every sense of the term, Antony came in with drinks and refreshing napkins.

"A bivouac," the brigadier pronounced and opened his brownish-green eyes.

The interior of the cabin rocked slightly, the motion of the train began to slow, then it stopped.

"Wonderful!" Arnold Konstantinovich got up quickly—he was small, lean, and invariably cheerful—put on his pince-nez, fussed about in a businesslike manner, removed his suede jacket from a cabinet, and began to dress himself nimbly.

Mikitok threw the warm, wet napkin over his face and pressed his palms together with great pleasure.

"Oh death! Oh my dea-a-a-a-ath!"

"A tea party *en plein air*," Witte ordered the steward, taking a sip of lime-flavored water.

"Sir, yes, sir." Antony nodded with a sly, charming half smile.

Quiet orchestral music floated through the interior of the cabin. Everyone began to prepare for a picnic. Only Ivan Ilyich continued to snore sweetly, his burly body drowning in his maximally reclined chair.

"Oh, lucky man!" Mikitok maneuvered around him toward the bathroom with an envious smile.

"Wake up, Ivan Ilyich." Serge patted the sleeping man on his plump shoulder.

The sleeping man didn't react.

"Let him sleep—don't wake the lion." Laertes went over to the cabin's oval door, turned the handle, and the door moved off to the side, opening up a view onto the May forest filled with loudly chirping birds. A staircase began to descend from the side of the train.

"Wake him! Certainly wake him!" Arnold Konstantinovich shook his head decisively. "If he wakes up on his own later, he'll get offended and rebuke us endlessly."

"And we'll make excuses for ourselves like dickheads." Laertes grinned, wiping his silvery eyebrows with the napkin.

Serge walked over to the sleeping man again, bent over, and spoke into his large, childishly pink ear with its fleshy lobe.

"Get up, Ivan Ilyich, we're going to go drink some tea."

But Ivan Ilyich's large, round, very pink face had an expression of such deep relaxation and happiness, his full cheeks were trembling so juicily, and his full lips were blowing out air with such careless negligence that Serge, shaking his shaved head, walked away and headed for the exit.

Latif smiled at Witte, whom Antony was helping to put on a mustard-colored Schwarzwald jacket with oak leaves and acorns on its dark lapels.

"Brigadier, your decisive action is decisively required."

Smiling condescendingly, the brigadier walked over to the sleeping man, quickly bent over him, and loudly kissed him on the cheek.

Surprisingly, this managed to rouse Ivan Ilyich. Smacking his lips together, he let forth a loud nasal sound, opened his small, swollen, but also lively and quick eyes, and looked around the cabin uncomprehendingly.

"What . . . already?" he pronounced, his voice juicy and sonorous even after a deep sleep.

"Not yet," the brigadier replied.

"We're going to drink tea, Ivan Ilyich." Latif smiled.

"And sma-a-a-a-ash the cu-u-u-ups!" Mikitok sang in his tenor voice, throwing a creamy cloak over his shoulders.

Ivan Ilyich's wide, chubby chest rose as he inhaled, breathing in as if he wished to draw the fresh spring air vigorously tearing its way in through the oval door into himself and not just the cabin's air-conditioned oxygen.

"That's so . . . wonderful!"

Everyone chuckled, walked toward the exit, and took turns leaving the cabin and going down the narrow stairs as they held onto the railing. The stairway rocked slightly, as if the passengers weren't walking down to earth, but onto a pier attached to a moored ship. Serge was the first to place his foot onto the dried-out, long-uncut grass, which was backlit by young grass growing up from underneath it, then to notice the four guards who'd gone down before them with ropes, break off a dry stalk of hogweed, and, whipping it against the tops of the wild grass, walk over to the ruins of the wall. Mikitok, Arnold Konstantinovich, and Laertes jumped down into the weeds.

The stairway swayed again, as if it'd been intoxicated by the spring wind, forcing the brigadier, Ivan Ilyich, and Latif to cling to the railing. A heavy, rough, and rudely drawn-out exclamation came from below them.

"Stay still, you ro-o-o-ough-fo-o-o-o-oted de-e-e-evil!"

The three men descending the stairway turned. Danube, an enormous bay horse eight and a half meters tall at his withers, with a short-cropped mane, a tail trimmed at the root, powerful, shaggy hooves, and clomping about in place, snorted and shook his head, which was the size of a seven-seater car. The cabin in which the brigade had been riding was mounted onto the horse's back and, together with the combat kitchen, luggage compartment, and security berth, occupied his entire, spacious back, while a box with a backrest on top of it, on which was enthroned a bigun who went by the nickname of Lash, was mounted to the mediastinum of his mighty neck, right by the body. He held the reins. In comparison with the horse, the three-meter-tall Lash was a Lilliputian.

"Spring bothers the bay." Arnold Konstantinovich nodded at the horse and pulled out a cigarette case.

"And again he'll beat about impetu-o-o-ously!" Mikitok sang out in his tenor.

"Whether he gets impetuous or not, Danube won't find any damn mares out here . . ." Laertes spat onto the grass as he looked around.

The horse smashed his hoof against the ground as if he'd understood Laertes. The earth buzzed. A gray hen rose up out of the wild grass and flew into the forest clappingly. The horse shook his head, which set the steel rings of the reins to tinkling menacingly, bared his yellow teeth, and neighed thunderously.

"Who-o-o-o-oa!!!" Lash cried out from the depths of his belly with a menacing howl and, with a practiced motion, grabbed the impressively sized whip attached to the hood of the box.

Danube exhaled noisily through his nostrils and grinned silently, as if the horse were laughing at this Lilliputian postboy.

The rest of the brigade went down the pacified stairway, followed by Antony and Du Zhuan, who were carrying boxes.

"Clear a clearing," the brigadier ordered quietly.

One of the guards ran over, grabbed a radial cutter, knelt down, and, with three handy circular motions and an accompanying crack, mowed down the wild grass in the area necessary for the bivouac. In Witte's brigade, all of the guards were clones and absolutely identical to one another: tall, broad shouldered, shaven headed, dressed in chameleon overalls, and loaded up with the most advanced tools for detecting, discerning, and destroying their enemies.

The guard began to collect the grass he'd cut into his arms, but Ivan Ilyich stopped him with a light kick.

"No, no, my dear, let it be. We must needs roll around on cut grass! Yes! On cut grass!"

The guard dropped the grass in his arms and walked over to his post.

Antony and the cook spread several thin, colorful rugs out over the cut grass, dropped pillows onto them, got down onto their knees, and started to take everything necessary for a tea party out of the boxes—this included sweets, preserves, and oriental treats.

"Ah . . . devilishly good!" The rotund Ivan Ilyich fell back onto a pillow, rolled over onto his side, and propped up his large, round head with its wide, beautiful forehead and trembling pink cheeks with his hand. "What a fantastic idea, Brigadier! All of this swinging and swaying and losing our fulcrums . . . O! Listen to this, gentlemen! What a dream I had today!"

"Doubtlessly something about young Armenian pussycats." Laertes winked his mormolon eyelid, deftly sitting down cross-legged onto the rug.

"No, no!" Ivan Ilyich waved his hand at him. "I dreamt I was fly-ing on a plane!"

Everyone laughed.

"A wonderful dream, Ivan Ilyich." Witte sank down to the rug. "And where were you flying?"

"To Yerevan," Laertes suggested, winking *loudly*.

"Why the hell would I be flying to Yerevan . . . no, I was flying to . . . to Argentina and traveling with a suitcase full of . . . can you guess what?"

"Nails?"

"I often have that dream, but not today. No! A suitcase full of smartypantses . . . dried ones at that! They'd been specially dried so's to take up less space, and, upon my arrival, I was to lower them into a *smart* brine so that they would, so to speak, swell and grow to their normal size."

"Like Armenian sheep's cheese . . ." Laertes grinned.

Ivan Ilyich weightily slapped his heavy hand on Laertes's scaly knee. "Hey! Amigo! That's enough about Armenia! Yeah, I beat in a couple of crooked nails there, but that's no reason to disparage me, devil take it!"

"You are most monotonous in your japery, Laertes," remarked Arnold Konstantinovich, who was crouched down on a pillow with a cigarette between his lips.

"I'm only joking, gentlemen!" Laertes spread apart his multicolored hands.

"Joking meanly," Latif remarked. "Our profession requires delicacy."

"Then what, did you put the smartypantses into the brine?" Mikitok asked, standing up with an open cloak and breathing in the spring air with great pleasure.

"It didn't come to that... a pity!" Ivan Ilyich lay down onto his back and yawned. "O-a-a-a... spring weakness. Make the tea a little stronger, Antosh, otherwise we'll sleep like gophers the whole way."

"I can brew Iron Goddess if no one minds," Antony replied.

"No one minds," the brigadier replied.

Serge walked over with a rusty trowel in hand and showed it to everyone.

"Fuck your Bodega Bay..." Laertes snapped his eyebrows.

"A trowel!" Ivan Ilyich reached for his pince-nez.

"How charming!" Mikitok threw up his hands as Serge approached.

"An instrument of production." Serge nodded his round head. "There's other stuff lying around too. A wheel from a block and tackle, scaffolding..."

"Artifacts of the great *unfinishment*." The brigadier took the trowel from Serge, examined it, then tossed it behind his back. "Convicts used to work here. The most hopeless sector on the European part of the wall, as my deceased grandfather used to say."

"My God! They worked day and night, they suffered, they didn't sleep properly, didn't eat prop-er-ly...!" Mikitok shook his curly head of hair. "And for what?"

"For the sake of Mother Russia." Arnold Konstantinovich puffed at his cigarette. "One final imperial illusion."

"That was when there were those... what's the word... oprichniks?" Serge asked.

"You're so young, you don't even know the word!"

"And why would he? Serge isn't from Moscovia." Laertes yawned. "They've got a democracy in the Baikalian Republic."

"Forgive me!" Serge sat down onto the rug with a grin.

"Mhmm, the Great Wall of Russia was never completed." Ivan Ilyich looked up at the sky as he lay on his back. "But what an idea."

"An entirely utopian idea," Arnold Konstantinovich muttered, squinting up at the sky.

"Why didn't they finish it?" Serge asked. "Were there not enough bricks?"

"The bricks were plundered," Arnold Konstantinovich explained.

"And still, how regrettable it is! How absurd!" Mikitok threw up his hands as he looked at the wall. "Millions of people worked, labored sore, and destroyed their bodies so as to bring something sublime and beautiful to fruition ..."

"The grand idea of reviving the Russian empire fell apart because of bricks," Ivan Ilyich pronounced with obvious pleasure as he stretched out. "Listen, gentlemen, when shall we have our tea?"

"It's already being prepared," Antony reported.

Du Zhuan, the brigade cook, deftly set down and filled porcelain cups on a slotted, lacquered tea board.

Standing entirely still, Danube the horse suddenly passed gas. This was equivalent to the test-starting of a decrepit but once powerful jet engine. After two weeks of traveling west, the brigade had already grown accustomed to their horse and his salvos. They called them "Taganrog aerial processions." Chewing something and sitting atop the box, Lash stirred after the horse passed wind, unfolded the rope ladder, and, still chewing, nimbly lowered himself to the ground. Swinging and waving his long coachman's arms, which almost reached down to the ground, he walked over to the brigade, took off his cap, and bowed at the waist.

"What do you need, oh *knight-that-could*?" Witte asked.

"I gotta feed the horse, milord," Lash roared.

"Feed him while we drink tea."

"He needs an hour, milord."

"An hour then. We're in no rush."

"I thank ye, milord."

The bigun bowed and walked over to the horse. Having scrambled back up to the box, he threw down a bale of self-generating hay, clambered down himself, and sprayed the bale. The bale began to grow and soon became a whole stack. Danube perked up his ears and moved toward the haystack. Lash leaped up, grabbed Danube by the bridle, and, with obvious effort, pulled the weighty bit from the cart horse's grinning jaws. The horse then shook his head so much that Lash was thrown and fell into the weeds. Not paying any attention to his groom, the horse took a good armful of hay between his lips and began to chew, letting forth the sound of ancient millstones grinding together. Rising up without any particular resentment, Lash shook himself off, slapped the horse on the mouth, walked off toward the forest, let down his pants, and crouched between two young oaks.

"For whatever reason, Lash just feeds him tons and tons of hay." Latif squinted at the horse chewing loudly.

"Oats are expensive," Arnold Konstantinovich explained. "In White Rus' especially. It's their second year of crop failure."

"Everything's expensive there. Fucking Europeans . . ." Laertes put out his hand and Du Zhuan gave him a cup of tea.

"*Merci bien*," Laertes muttered.

Still lying down, Ivan Ilyich proffered his hand. The cook put a cup into it.

"*Xièxiè*," Ivan Ilyich thanked him and began to speak Chinese. "Du Zhuan, do you know that your name is reminiscent of the name of the great womanizer Don Juan?"

"I know, sir," Du Zhuan replied imperturbably as he filled and served the cups of tea. "This isn't the first time someone's told me that."

"How's your relationship with women?"

"In my youth, I preferred men."

"Do you have a boyfriend?"

"No, sir."

"Why?"

"There's a Chinese saying: If you want trouble for a day, invite guests; if you want trouble for your whole life, find a lover."

"'Tisn't solely a Chinese saying!" Laertes laughed.

"You mean to say men don't interest you anymore?"

"Only as consumers of the food I prepare."

"You've a strong will, Du Zhuan." Ivan Ilyich took a loud sip of tea.

"It's not will, but pure calculation," Arnold Konstantinovich began to speak in his poor Chinese. "Is money more important than pleasure?"

Du Zhuan was silent.

"Money and pleasure are synonyms," the brigadier answered for him in his brilliant Southern Chinese. "Profession and pleasure are too."

"I don't agree." Arnold Konstantinovich shook his head.

"Our profession is both money and pleasure," Latif pronounced in his old-fashioned Mandarin.

"And a massive responsibility," Serge added in his young person's Pekinese.

"And responsibility is the greatest of pleasures." Ivan Ilyich handed his empty cup to the cook. "A fine tea."

"Wonderful! Wonderful!" Mikitok moaned, savoring his drink. "Tea *en plein air*, my God, how wonderful, how fantastic for the stomach and the soul . . ."

"By the way, about the soul"—the brigadier looked at his watch—"we need to kill an hour while Danube gets full."

"The hike is canceled." Laertes looked Lash over gloomily, crunching back out of the forest. "Everything's overgrown in there; impossible to tear your way through."

"We could simply sleep outside, give ourselves to the zephyr, and have wonderful dreams." Mikitok half closed his eyes languidly.

"After Iron Goddess, sleep might be problematic," Arnold Konstantinovich replied.

"We could play a round of torque?" Serge proposed.

"There's not enough time," Witte objected.

"Then a round of blind fool?"

"Boring."

"Perhaps a round of nail-puller, gentlemen?" Arnold Konstantinovich recollected. "Last time we didn't get to the end."

"Yes, nail-puller," Ivan Ilyich also recollected and began to laugh. "You really amused us last time Laertes...ha-ha-ha...wasn't it, 'Take my mommy out of me'?"

"Take my mommy out of me!" Serge also recollected.

"Hey, listen, take my mommy out of me!" Latif made a characteristically Caucasian spinning motion with his fingers.

"It's unbelievable." Arnold Konstantinovich shook his head. "It's hard to believe such wild *game* exists."

"And I didn't make it up." Laertes sipped his tea.

"Who went last?" Latif asked.

"I did," Arnold Konstantinovich replied. "My tale was entirely unbeautiful, you've all probably forgotten it."

"In Saratov? The guy with the dog meat? Yeah, yeah..." Ivan Ilyich recalled reluctantly. "If you were the last one to tell their tale, then Mikitok is next. Then me, then the brigadier."

"Oy, nail-puller..." Mikitok rocked back onto his pillow, grimacing affectedly. "It's so raw...so torturous..."

"*Ku bi le!*"* Serge clapped as he got into a more comfortable position. "It's nice to listen to some nail-pulling before our seasonal *shabashka.*"

"What does *shabashka* mean?" Arnold Konstantinovich asked as if he hadn't heard properly.

"Well, we're an artel off to do some, so to speak, seasonal *shabashka* work in Europe." Serge smiled.

Everyone exchanged a look.

"I'm going to do...*shabaska* work?" Mikitok asked fearfully, clutching his palm to his chest.

Arnold Konstantinovich removed his pince-nez and his face seemed to have instantaneously become drawn and serious.

"Young man, you be careful with the expressions you use, sir."

*[Chinese] cool

Latif grunted in a way that was uncharacteristic, smiled nervously, then shook his head, raising his eyebrows as he did.

"Going to *shabash*? And we're *shabashers*? Is that right, Brigadier?"

Witte was silent, calmly sipping at his tea.

"I'm a *shabasher*, my dears! And I'm going to Europe to sha-*bash*, sha-*bash*, sha-*bash*!" Mikitok imitated a hammer beating in a nail with his right hand. "Ivan Ilyich! Have you registered for the *sha-bashka*?"

Ivan Ilyich glanced reproachfully and indifferently at Serge, then turned back to his cup, which was being filled by Du Zhuan.

"Never mind, gentlemen, I was only joking … I just wanted to … it was only a joke …"

"It's not a joke," Laertes pronounced, snapping his scales threateningly. "During the Second War, jokes like that could get you court-martialed."

"Gosh … *shabash* … sha-*bash*!" Latif shook his head.

"I'm no *shabasher*, young man!" Arnold Konstantinovich put on his pince-nez and looked at Serge in such a way that the smile fell right off of his high-cheeked face.

There was a heavy pause. Interrupted only by the menacing sounds of Danube's chewing.

The brigadier put his empty cup down onto the notched board, took out his cigarette case, pulled out a cigarette, and lit it slowly.

"You see, Serge," he began, "we're professionals. Experienced people with history and authority. But that's not all. There are quite enough professionals in the world already. Perhaps now, after all of the wars, there are even more professionals than there are amateurs …"

He fell silent, blew out smoke, then continued.

"We're honest carpenters. And that distinguishes us from a lot of other professionals. We ended up together only partially because of our authority, experience, and professionalism. For the most part, we're together because we're honest. An honest artel. And you, Serge, ended up in this brigade not only because you beat in three hundred straight nails and only twelve crooked ones. There are carpenters who have beaten more and better. You're with us because you're honest.

You're a responsible, ethically adequate individual. Otherwise, you wouldn't be here."

The brigadier fell silent. Serge was also silent, his Kalmyk eyes fixed on the ground. The entire brigade was silent.

"We're a carpentry artel. We're headed for Europe," Witte continued. "Europe is the cradle of civilization. An old woman. She's been having a hard go of it. The Wahhabi hammer hit her. Hit her mercilessly and brutally. But Europe withstood the blow and her spine didn't break. Though many of her bones did. She's crushed and shattered. But still alive. Her wounds are healing, she's bandaged up, she's been prescribed bed rest. She needs good care . . . good nutrition. And good sleep. *Schlafen ist die beste Medizin*, as my Black Forest ancestors used to say. And they were right. Even a healthy person needs good, proper sleep. Which implies the maimed need incalculably more. So there, my dear Serge, the Old Woman of Europe had invited us carpenters from the East so that we might give her good sleep and good dreams. With our hands. Our hammers. And our honesty."

And, as if illustrating the brigadier's words, Mikitok took an elegant golden hammer with the coat of arms of Telluria embossed on it out of an interior pocket of his tailcoat, squeezed it in his plump fist, and thrust his hand forwards. The sun flashed onto its golden edges.

"We're not going there to *shabash*, but to do our work honestly," the brigadier concluded his monologue. "And we'll not tolerate jokes that cast doubt upon our ethics. Got it, Serge?"

"Got it," he answered with a tense expression.

"No, my friend, you didn't get it. You just said 'got it' in a formal tone, I can *feel* that. You've never approached our common labor as if it were a *shabashka*. You've long grasped and incorporated our moral principles. You share them with us, as you are also an honest carpenter. But you still don't understand: Why did we react to this joke so seriously? Am I right?"

"Yes, brigadier." Serge nodded.

"As an ethnic German, I have always been guilty of excessive scholasticism." The brigadier extinguished the butt of his cigarette in a malachite ashtray brought over by Antony. "Can one of you explain the issue to Serge?"

Everyone exchanged reluctant looks. Clearly no one wanted to.

"Nobody?" The brigadier looked them over.

The brigade was silent.

"I'm prepared to explain," Latif suddenly pronounced.

He unzipped his leather jacket and took it off, which left him wearing only a tight greenish-steel-colored shirt. After unhurriedly unbuttoning the shirt, he took it off and was left wearing only a white mesh undershirt. He took the undershirt off and turned his back to Serge. On his swarthy, muscular back, there was a large brand that covered almost all the skin—the coat of arms of Telluria—that had been burnt into his back three years ago by interrogators in an Omsk prison. Judging by the scars, the brand had been burnt into the skin gradually, the branding process combined with an interrogation that'd lasted several days. Serge stared at Latif's back. The coat of arms, made up of burns of different thicknesses, was deeply familiar to him: mountains with the rising sun behind them, the Maktulu cave surrounded by two palms, a wasp on an edelweiss, and the inscription in Altaian: "PEACE AND POWER TOGETHER." On the official coat of arms, the wasp was blue. Serge had always appreciated the sight of this blue insect sitting on a mountain flower very much—he could feel something that was *to come* in it, something strong and spacious. The sun flashed onto the golden hammer still in Mikitok's hand and fell into Serge's eye. He involuntarily shifted his gaze onto the second coat of arms—small and embossed in gold—of the country that had given him not just a profession, but a reason to live.

Everyone except for Latif was staring at Serge. His cheeks, pale before this, went pink and his lips parted into what looked like a helpless, almost childish smile.

"I . . . got it," he sighed.

Latif turned around and looked him in the eyes.

"I got it," Serge repeated, firmly this time.

"How wonderful." The brigadier nodded, reached out, and squeezed Serge's narrow wrist.

Latif began to get dressed. Mikitok put away his hammer.

"Now let's move on to nail-puller," the brigadier said loudly.

The brigade began to stir with relief.

"Your turn, Mikitok."

Mikitok rubbed his sleek hands together as if he were about to eat, clasped them together, and cracked his knuckles.

"Yes … nail-pulling … I can't say that it's particularly pleasant for me to recall nail-pulling, my good sirs, but that seems to me to be entirely natural, in keeping with the very rules of the game, isn't that so? It's about time I get used to the subject after ten years of *practicing*, to calm down and perceive it as something essentially quite ordinary, right? Like slipping on spring ice, for example! A man was walking and walking, a quite decent, smart, charming, handsome, and well-dressed man—a dandy, one might say—and suddenly, a puddle, thin ice, he slips, and—bang! Sits down into a puddle. Then what? Tears? Curses? Not at all! He swore, got up, laughed, and shook himself off. Kept walking. But for us … that is to say for me … it's not like that. Not at all. There's no lightness in the *crooked*. No lightness at all! I don't manage to just get up, shake myself off, and keep going. I don't manage at all. And I can't do anything about it! I get ready, get in the mood, meditate, pray, persuade myself, make a deal with myself that when things go *crooked*, I must needs begin to sing some life-affirming operatic aria in my head, or perhaps something lighter—an operetta even: We'll go-o-o-o to Varazdin / where I'm the bo-o-o-oss of all the pigs / and I'll groom yo-o-o-o-ou like a swineherd. Just like that … But it doesn't work out. Neither opera nor operetta. Nail-pulling! It's such a hypersensitive little moment in the practice of every carpenter: *oro*,* complication, little nightmare, then devil take him and all of his guts! We're not robots, not knot-headed morons with nerves of rope, and not cynical narco-dealers, that's as clear as day, my good sirs! The carpenters' craft demands not hypersensitivity and precision alone. It also demands ethics. Not that that's any guarantee! And nobody's ever insured, not even if you're a most honorable

*[Altaian] pit

carpenter or have golden hands, still, still, still sooner or later, the damned thing'll wobble and go crooked. Fatum! Yes! Well, that's enough of a preamble. Six months ago, I was invited to a single-homestead settlement to beat in a couple of nails. The journey, I must say, was not a short one. Not at all! A distant call, you see, happens with some regularity, of course that's so. I never, never neglect distant calls. It's fundamental, gentlemen, fundamental! Noblesse oblige. Not to mention it was a moneyed homestead and the fee in question was substantial. So, as it happened, we prepared the carriage, then I got together my little instruments, took the plunge, and gave Andryushka a kick: Let's go. We were riding for eight hours. With stops, bivouacs, and samovar breaks... The way there was gorgeous. The war didn't make it to Bryansk, as everyone knows: cleanliness, hospitality, new robots, and healthy zoomorphism. By the evening, we'd arrived at the place. Such picturesque curtain walls, buckwheat fields in bloom, bees buzzing, a state of plenty, if you know what I mean, clouds, sunset, nice weather, and a willful wind. The customer's steward comes out to meet me, a quite decent, civilized gentleman who speaks English and has a guard, and takes me to the homestead. We arrive and... goodness gracious me! An excellently constructed wooden manor house, not in the bast-built, moth-eaten style of Rus', but a kind of bungalow, outbuildings, a stable, decorative gardens, vegetable gardens, a shooting range, a little aerodrome, three pools, and a waterfall. They conduct me to the proprietors. A father and son. The father is American and the son Californian. They spend spring and summer in the Bryanskian Republic. And why not? It's obvious their love for each other is strong, they don't hide their feelings, for why why why should one hide one's feelings?! The son is a bona fide pretty boy, a sort of Californian Apollo, tall, gray eyes, dangling curls, quite an ensemble. The father is no monster either: affable, simple, and smiling. 'Wouldn't you like a bite to eat after your journey?' he asks in English. 'With great pleasure, sir!' They sit me down at a table, regale me with veggie steak and an ear of corn, while they drink cucumber water and prepare themselves. It's their first time. Which is why they've called for an experienced carpenter from afar. How fantastic! I finished my chow, clarified the conditions, and we began to begin. We walked into the room, changed clothes, and they began to embrace and kiss each other's hands, an avalanche of tenderness, tears, wishes, and parting words, a wonderful, wonderful scene. They were anxious, of course. I calmed them down, prepared them, and laid them out. I beat it into the father as if his head were made of butter. Everything's clean, it went whitely, oh joy, excellent fields, a new world, words, *bosorogos*,* an avalanche . . . I beat it into the son. And it went in crookedly. Grievously so, a real tornado,† the fields darken rapidly and in the most beastly way, my good sirs! The father lies next to him: joy, penetration, and benevolence. And the son—straight into the abyss. I tell Andryushka: Get me the nail-puller right away! He rolled it in, we opened it, picked it up, and hoisted this Californian Apollo inside, but I didn't have a spacious one back then, it was an old, homemade thing from Shanghai, I could barely squeeze him in, a big boy, his bare feet were sticking out of it. And the father—the orbits of electrons, the Heisenberg uncertainty principle— it'd turned out he was a physicist—becoming a free particle, a photon, cutting across orbits, and longing to meet with his son for an *energetic fusion*. He'd figured out that he and the son were a pair of *entangled* photons, a single, so to speak, quantum grouping. With enviable pomp, he declares that they're one quantum family emitted by a single source and that they must needs overcome time alone . . . But I'm no good at nuclear physics, my good sirs: the son sustains an *esten tanu*.‡ I begin to pull at the nail, it goes badly, slips out of my hands, the fields darken, the chamber roars, suction, pulse . . . I barely barely pull the nail out and, suddenly—agony and trembling legs. *Zhurektyn toktauy*.§ Okay, then, the *tebene*,¶ top adrenaline straight into the heart, that's

---

*A carpentry term indicating the successful penetration of the nail into the client's brain
†An unsuccessful penetration of nail into brain
‡[Kazakh] loss of consciousness
§[Kazakh] The heart's stopped
¶[Altaian] a long needle used for injections into the heart

what I gotta do. I lowered the pressure, put him into the *argada*,* and turned on the inductor. In general and on the whole, gentlemen, I start his heart back up right when I pull the nail out. We pull Apollo out of the nail-puller, then shock and cauterize him. And he came to his senses. And the father, still lying down, stood up joyfully and said, 'I'm waiting for you in the photon stream, my son.' Then walked out of the carpentry room. So that's my nail-pulling story, my dears."

"*Zhurektyn toktauy* happened so fast?" Laertes asked. "What luck."

"That happened to me twice." Arnold Konstantinovich stretched out and stood up. "The fields darken and, immediately, *zhurektyn* . . . Catastrophic."

"*Esten tanu* doesn't necessarily imply *zhurektyn toktauy*," Witte objected. "If the fields immediately go dark, that's still not a *chirik zhalan*."[†]

"I agree, Brigadier, I agree entirely, but some people are *alsyz*[‡] by nature." Arnold Konstantinovich spread his hands apart and began to walk toward the forest. "*Toktauy* is hardly *toktauy*, but a loss of speech is easy. Easy! Congenital weakness, what can you do, even if you're Apollo himself, as you implied."

"Apollo, a pretty boy, and a Nibelung!" Mikitok also stood up, pressing his hands to his chest. "Arnold Konstantinovich, my dear, are you off to take a piss, I wonder?"

"Not to take a piss, but to siphon off the excess fluid . . ." he muttered as he walked without turning around.

"I'll come too! I'll come too!" Mikitok hurried after him.

"Mhmm, you have a new Danish nail-puller now." Latif nodded after him.

"His feet wouldn't have been sticking out of that." Laertes grinned and cracked one of his eyebrows.

---

*A carpentry term referring to a special device that resembles a helmet, which the head is put into in emergencies
†[Altaian] rotten field
‡[Kazakh] weaklings

"It's good and big, but it takes up a lot of space in my luggage."
Mikitok waved his hand toward the chewing Danube.

Still chewing, the cart horse perked up its ears. Its enormous penis
with its glossy plicate skin jerked and a thick, powerful stream of
urine with the circumference of a log hit the earth noisily.

"The actions of others are contagious!" Arnold Konstantinovich
cried out as he entered the forest.

The brigade heard an echo from within the forest.

"My inductor bit the dust a long time ago," Ivan Ilyich recalled.
"If a nail goes in crooked, I'll need to think of something real quick..."

"You don't need an inductor for that," Serge spoke up. "Pressure
plus fields."

"There you go..." Ivan Ilyich stretched out and began to sing.
"You place all your trust in the fields, fields, fi-i-i-ields!"

"You can't straighten a *tartyk kadu** with fields alone." Laertes
stood up and stretched out with a snap.

"An *ak sorguy*† always helps," Serge retorted.

"Yes, it helps!" Laertes nodded mournfully and ironically. "It
stopped swinging and—it's a *chakly*!‡ It's not a nail-puller you need
now, but a grave."

"The *ak sorguy* depends on the strength of the carpenter's field."
The brigadier sipped at his tea and sucked on a licorice candy.

"If the field is powerful, no inductor is needed." Latif nodded with
categorical delicacy.

"Not everyone was born strong." Laertes made several flat motions
with *dancing beasts*.

When Mikitok and Arnold Konstantinovich returned, the brigadier made a sign to Ivan Ilyich.

"Your go, colleague."

"My go." He put his empty cup down onto the notched board, sat
down cross-legged with some difficulty, and laid his hands to rest on

---

*[Altaian] crooked nail
†[Kazakh] white pump
‡[Altaian] trap

his thick, spherical knees. "This story didn't come to pass too long ago."

He fell silent and began to concentrate. It was as if his broad, thoroughbred face with its plump, almost childishly pink cheeks, small, sensuously full, stubborn, and self-confident lips, and lively, intelligent, and quick eyes had suddenly turned to stone and become a marble statue; something heavy, emotionlessly immobile, and unwelcomingly menacing appeared in it, as often happens in the faces of state dignitaries or commanders. "The world of people that has been entrusted to me is not at all consummate," the face seemed to say. "It is a world of chaos, entropy, petty passions, and egotistical impulses. In order to direct this world toward the good, to civilize and cultivate it, having made it meaningfully useful for humanity and consciously constructed it with reference to the history of world civilizations, one must know how to engage with this homogenous mass and be able to subjugate it. And for that reason, it is necessary to defeat in oneself the desire to see particulate individuals in this great mass; one must strive to see the mass as a singular individual; one must understand and accept this truth—that man is only a mass."

However, the carpenters in Witte's brigade had grown used to Ivan Ilyich's face and did not see this train of thought being expressed at all, but something entirely different, something known to all those who have attached themselves to a difficult and dangerous profession: a carpenter must never *test* tellurium.

Ivan Ilyich's petrified face seemed to spell out this maxim letter by letter.

"We're all so sure that we know exactly what we want in this world," Ivan Ilyich began and his face lost its marble-like inexorability just as suddenly as it had gained it, becoming an ordinary human face. "We've learned to convince ourselves of this, in any case. We want happiness. And in order to achieve it, we choose our paths, often impossibly winding ones. There are not and cannot be two identical people. There are not and cannot be two identical paths to happiness. Everyone has their own path. And everyone is happy in their own way. So, a *womanly* story. A lonely, middle-aged lady, a quite beautiful and enchanting one, ordered an experienced and expensive carpenter. I arrive. A modest apartment in the suburbs of Ufa, signs of compulsory loneliness. A widow. A hologram of her deceased husband and something like a shrine of the deceased's possessions. The apartment delicately and tastefully set up. Old books, paintings with elements of ethnomysticism, Shinto attributes, but not overdone. A woman of culture, but enslaved, enchanted, and subdued by her husband's strong personality. Naturally, I get right down to business. I ask the three main questions and it becomes clear that this is her third time *testing* tellurium. Local carpenters had already beat it into her. Why this terribly expensive carpenter from a faraway kingdom? It turns out they beat it into her five years ago when her husband was still alive. They *tested* it together. But back then, she says, with her husband, it was entirely different. As if it were an entirely different kind of tellurium to be used with entirely different goals in mind. And now she has a very particular, very important goal, which is why she needs an Oop.* Yes, madame, I am an Oop. I named her the standard price for a long-distance trip. She didn't even bargain. I can tell that she'd scraped this money together with some difficulty. But, we shouldn't pick at the *torsok*† of others, as they say in Altai. Without asking any extraneous questions, I begin to prepare. But she won't stop: Hold on, Mr. Carpenter, I want to tell you about myself. I reply: Madame, our professional ethics insist on our ignorance of our clients' biographies. She insists. I'm categorical: I cannot and do not want to overload my fields. She's in tears. Me: I can't, it's impossible, it's the codex. She's on her knees. Sobbing, almost hysterical. Yeah, it's a womanly story, I warned you, gentlemen!"

"Sounds familiar…" Latif nodded with a sad smile.

"Oh, how familiar!" Arnold Konstantinovich exclaimed, straightening his pince-nez.

"Yes, yes, familiar! A charming woman is hugging my knees and

*[Altaian] craftsman
†[Altaian] callus

sobbing. A heartrending scene, gentlemen. But despite my external softness, I'm a hard person when it comes to my profession. I remove her hands from my knees. Inform her of the penalty rate for a deceptive call and the sanctions that will ensue from all artels; I pick up my suitcase and push my nail-puller toward the door. Then she rushes to the shrine with the hologram, grabs a black velvet box out from underneath it, runs back toward me, and drops down to her knees once again. Opens the little box. And in the box is a golden nugget. Decently sized too, slightly elongated in shape, about a pound and a half. Well, a nugget is a nugget! I'm indifferent to gold, you know. I say, madame, this golden nugget is not capable of swaying my professional principles. And she just says: Listen! Listen! Listen! It's not a nugget at all. It's the gold that was poured into my husband's throat on the orders of the despot. It's all that's left to me of my husband."

Ivan Ilyich fell silent. Without meeting the eyes of his listeners, he fixed his lively, clever gaze onto a lonely young pine tree, which had grown apart from the forest, not far from the ruined wall.

The brigade was silent.

"A casting," he began to speak again. "A throat casting. That sounds more precise than a nugget. But . . . broadly speaking . . . Broadly speaking, dear colleagues, I couldn't refuse her. Don't judge me, I simply couldn't. Human, all too human! I couldn't. And I ended up paying for that . . . Hers wasn't exactly a trifling tale. As it turned out, her deceased husband had been an akyn. He sang ballads of his own composition, playing along with himself on a three-stringed instrument. He was extremely popular in his state. They called him the 'Golden Throat.' But his ballads didn't only have a mystico-philosophical meaning; he also denounced the immorality of the elites. And, gradually, this theme began to prevail, as one benefit of decomposing despotism proved to be the procurement of rich satirical material. The people praised this akyn to the skies. And not just figuratively. They blocked his passage when they saw him and showered him with flowers, caresses, and gifts. But it all ended deplorably—one night, the state security service came to take him away and, several days later, his wife received the velvet box with the casting in it. The akyn's body was burnt in secret and the ashes were scattered. By the will of the cynical, merciless authorities, the akyn had finally earned the name bestowed on him by the people. His throat was cast in gold. I finished listening to this heartrending story and asked the widow an entirely logical question: Why did you tell me all of this? It turns out she wanted the nail beaten in so as to meet with her husband. If the meeting went well, she would start to save up immediately for the next nail and live in expectation of their next meeting, and if she accidentally died, then I would have to testify to the fact that she'd died attempting to meet with her eternal love. Otherwise, her soul would never be pacified. That was the beautiful widow's logic. I agreed. I arrived without an assistant in a coach. I got her ready, laid her down, and beat it in. Crooked. *Esten tanu*. Tornado. *Chirik zhalan*. The nail-puller didn't help. Twenty-four minutes later, she was dead."

Ivan Ilyich took a narrow box of cherry cigarillos out from his jacket pocket, lit one, and let forth a stream of aromatic smoke.

"I of course set fire to the apartment. I had to lose the nail-puller too. I returned to Khabarovsk in stagecoaches, taking a very circuitous route. Covering my tracks cost a pretty penny. And that's my nail-pulling story, gentlemen."

He sighed.

"And when I was walking out of that burning apartment, I took one final look. I'm not sentimental, but I'll always remember the holographic akyn's gaze cutting through the smoke. It seemed as if the widow had managed to meet with him once again."

Ivan Ilyich fell silent and smoked.

"How important it is not to violate the codex!" Serge pronounced with conviction.

"And what was the cause of death? *Zhurek* or *méé**?" Laertes asked.

"*Méé*," Ivan Ilyich replied.

"Women have more problems with *méé* than with *zhurek*." Latif nodded.

"Men's hearts are weaker, that's obvious." Arnold Konstantinovich

*[Altaian] brain

reached for his cigarettes. "Yes, Ivan Ilyich, a noble tale. A carpenter's harsh everyday, so to speak."

"You burned the nail-puller?" Laertes asked, loudly stretching out.

"I burned the nail-puller." Ivan Ilyich nodded.

"And you didn't take the casting with you, of course." Laertes chuckled.

Ivan Ilyich looked at him with great hostility. Laertes raised his scaly hands.

"A stupid joke, *pardonnez-moi*."

"Only chumps joke like that," Latif remarked sullenly.

"I agree . . ." Laertes made several smooth, beautiful movements with *dancing beasts*.

"A horrible and uncanny story, gentlemen!" Mikitok threw up his hands. "I can imagine it perfectly—the apartment, the fire starting, the smoke spreading, and, we all know it, the beautiful lady, lifeless, already lifeless, and this image, the image of her beloved husband, his gaze cutting through the smoke, this silent reproach . . . how horrible! One could never grow accustomed to that, never . . . You know, gentlemen, despite all of my experience with my *practice*, with blood, and with moans, every time someone dies beneath my hammer, I feel myself to be a murderer. And I can't seem to do anything about it! I understand that it's stupid, that it's idiocy and sentimentalism, but I feel it all the same! I can understand it with my intellect, but this . . ."

He poked his finger into his plump chest, then fell silent and shook his beautiful head.

"My dear Mikitok, on that day, I also felt myself to be a killer." Ivan Ilyich squinted at the lonely pine tree, blowing out the smoke that smelled of blossoming cherry trees. His full cheeks were flushed and it was obvious that he was reliving this tale anew.

"You should have felt yourself to be a killer when you said yes to that woman, colleague," the brigadier spoke up.

Serge, Laertes, and Arnold Konstantinovich nodded silently. Ivan Ilyich continued to smoke without saying anything.

"Did you fulfill the contract?" Latif asked.

"Of course," Ivan Ilyich dropped his cigarillo, quickly pulled a folded smartypants from his breast pocket, stretched it out, and activated it.

A hologram rose up over the smartypants—a beautiful Bashkirian narrator told the story of the deceased in her own language. During the story, images of a tellurium nail, the akyn, the "Golden Throat," the burning apartment, and Shinto deities rose up.

"Now, all admirers of her husband's talent know that the widow's last wish was to join her beloved in another world," Ivan Ilyich translated and clarified, even though Serge, Witte, and Arnold Konstantinovich knew Bashkir decently well and even sometimes allowed themselves to make fun of each another with that famous line of poetry about a dandyish carpenter named Eugene: "Bashkir he spoke and wrote with ease." Laertes and Mikitok also more or less understood Bashkir.

"Ivan Ilyich's story is a harsh lesson to us all," Arnold Konstantinovich began. "It's important to be conscious of that especially now, as we enter Europe. We must needs remain professional and remember the codex in every possible situation. What do you have to say, Brigadier?"

Witte crossed his arms across his chest.

"I'll say that I agree with you entirely, Arnold Konstantinovich. But it has nothing to do with Europe. The codex is the codex. It must be the same for us everywhere. In Bashkiria and in Bavaria."

"A carpenter must remain a carpenter everywhere." Latif nodded. "Clients have *wanted* me twelve times. And all of them were beautiful, decent, and respectable people, men and women, as if I'd selected them myself . . . But I always refused them harshly. There was umbrage and even tears, one Georgian man kissed my knees, but I found the words to stop him. If words didn't help, I would use forceful means of convincing. And they would understand."

"Wanting is a somewhat different subject," Ivan Ilyich spoke up, as he lay back and clasped his hands behind his head. "It's easier to cope with wanting than with a situation like the one I described. Much easier."

"There's no need for any sort of categorical imperative here." The brigadier stood up and walked across the rug with his arms folded across his chest. "Practical reason: your proposition is unfulfillable, for it shall harm you first of all, valued customer."

"If I'd been a robot, that's how I would have answered her."

"In our profession, we should be like robots." Serge stood up.

"Not everyone manages to."

"A carpenter shouldn't be like a robot."

"Sometimes he should!"

"I don't agree. Robots don't have free will. *Ak sorguy* implies total free will."

"One must be a robot when dealing with matters of the codex. Man creates *ak sorguy*."

"The separation between man and robot has grave consequences for the *sin*.*"

"If you don't like the idea of the robot, use another thought experiment: the surgeon."

"That helps sometimes. But only sometimes."

"A surgeon shouldn't *sentimentalize* with the sick."

"We're not surgeons and our clients aren't sick."

"We're not surgeons, that's right." The brigadier stopped across from Ivan Ilyich, who was still lying down. "We don't heal people, we bring them happiness. Which is much *stronger* than abdominal surgery to remove a late-stage tumor from a wretched beggar—for deliverance from the fate the tumor threatens does not necessarily bring happiness. Deliverance is simply relief. But it is *not* happiness. Happiness is not medicine. Nor narcotics. Happiness is a condition of the soul. And that is what tellurium offers."

"Yes, a nail beaten into a beggar's head makes him happy," muttered Ivan Ilyich, looking up at the sky that had gradually cleared of clouds. "So there's no point paying any attention to his late-stage tumor."

"*Genau!*" Witte hunched over Ivan Ilyich.

But Ivan Ilyich was looking around the brigadier and into the

*[Chinese] soul

clear spring sky, in which the first signs of sunset had already quite noticeably appeared.

"We must not take anyone else's karma upon ourselves, not even in small matters," the brigadier continued. "Especially now in our renewed, postwar world. Take a look at the Eurasian continent: after the collapse of ideological, geopolitical, and technological utopias, it was finally plunged back into the blessed and enlightened Middle Ages. The world returned to human scale. Nations *found themselves*. Man ceased to be the sum of the technology around him. Mass production is living out its final years. There aren't two identical nails beaten into humanity's head. Man regained a sense of the *thing*, started to eat healthy grub and ride horses again. Genetic engineering helps man to feel his true size. Man has regained his faith in the transcendental. Regained his sense of time. We're not rushing anywhere anymore. Most importantly—we understand that there can be no technological heaven on earth. And, in broader terms, no heaven at all. Earth has been given to us as an island of overcoming. Everyone chooses what to overcome and how to overcome it. And they make that choice themselves!"

"Yes. We must not deprive anyone of their choice," Arnold Konstantinovich spoke up.

"That would be a sin," Latif pronounced.

"False compassion is also such a sin," the brigadier summed up before falling silent.

Having done away with the haystack, Danube stood there calmly, half closing his eyes and breathing quietly. As it inclined itself toward its own setting, the sun shone onto the horse's dark-red back and the trunk of the lonely pine. The coachman was slumbering atop his box.

"Yes, I have something to overcome," Arnold Konstantinovich pronounced with a sigh, sitting up on the rug. "By the way, Brigadier, it seems to me that it's your turn now?"

"It is," Witte responded without a hint of surprise, as if he'd been waiting for this question for a long time.

"We're listening."

"It's quite a simple story. Montenegro. An old man. Not terribly well-to-do. A pensioner. Saved up for a nail and gave me a call. I beat one in. Crooked. The nail-puller did its thing. Which helped. I pulled out the nail. The old man came to. And said two words to me in Serbian: '*Nema Boga*.'* That's all."

The brigadier coughed briskly and set off toward the pine tree.

The artel accompanied him briefly with their unsatisfied gazes.

"Brevity is the sister of talent…" Arnold Konstantinovich smirked and shivered. "However, the air's become rather chill."

"The cold's blowing over from the ruins." Laertes lifted up a dry blade of grass, put it into his mouth unhappily, and began to chew.

"I'm off to take a snooze." Mikitok got up from the rug with some difficulty and walked toward Danube.

With even greater difficulty, Ivan Ilyich got up, grunted, and followed after Mikitok.

The brigadier reached the pine and began to urinate onto its trunk. Three crows flew up over the ruined wall. Then two more.

Latif stood up easily and did a somersault forwards. A smartypants squeaked in his pocket.

"And where are the *details*?" Serge asked in a sotto tone as he glanced at the urinating brigadier.

"Where?" Laertes snapped his eyebrow. "In the nail."

*There is no God.

29

UNCLE Yurek the carpenter beat it into me that morning I lay down drank a touch of herbal tea woke Pirate checked the arsenal leaped through the window got to the subway made it to the place Kazimish came in reports from the air they had him surrounded at House No. 7 I lay low pinpointed the fuck with the GPS and leaped there right away I was thinking he would go down to the bottom through the heating networks and the thundertron was already loaded and it was like he sensed Lil' Pirate and me moved along the brim of the ruins so quickly that cement dust flew up me with the thundertron over my shoulder Pirate jerks the shotgun out of its case I let Pirate forth c'mon Lil' Pirate c'mon and sniff the air so's the fuck doesn't get away along the brim otherwise we know he'll tear off to the auto-mobile showroom they're so lousy he'll get past 'em and go off into the park and nobody'll get him there and we'll cut him off cut off the fuck he'll start goin' round in circles with Kazimish coming from above and the surrounder from behind he won't have anywhere to go Pirate gave voice and started to work that bitch gloomming off along the brim making everything shake I rush along the bottom Pirate keeps his voice out ahead rushes and he darted to the left and from above all the way from the fourth floor from the laundry room down to the burnt-down supermarket sprinted all the way I riddle the charred bits with a bank shot as I go bang bang right past him and how to get down there the big guy caught a glimpse of the 1.5-ton claws they flashed they make you wanna shit Pirate and I go into the supermarket through a window and I immediately fan off six charges in every direction and he's in the far corner where there were canned goods

and tears through the walls like cardboard going going going away
from us Pirate's behind him and I cry back you can't follow him on
your own and I just see the fuck flash and go underground what to
do they're bitches they smell holes right away then I got an idea bomb
through the hole bang and I jump outside flank it on the right and
the bomb detonates Pirate and I are flanking it on the right I pull
out the thundertron through the cracks bang bang bang and hear a
roar beneath the ground that means I got him and I see asphalt puffing up behind the tobacco counter think I got it the reptile is slither-
ing up pulled out the shotgun inserted the clip heel Pirate heel he
tears forward my carbine pointed straight at him sit Pirate you get
to work when the fuck shows his face and asphalt floods in from
every direction and the fuck jumped up so high right to the center
of the prospect where'd he get the strength I'm in the lead bang bang
bang and once he fell and bellowed out so loud all the glass on the
street set to singing let Pirate loose around the corner I'm behind him
see the jump he heads up for the balconies again and I just bang bang
bang and caught him again and he smashes into an apartment and
goes silent and I prepared a noise bomb and Pirate restrains his voice
I start to run from the end and on the sixth floor I threw one at him
from the bomb-hurler a little gift a hoot and he flew away I hear all
the way on the balconies again Pirate choked I just jump around the
corner and I see him glomming along the alley to the boiler station
to the little shops to McDonald's and already the bitch isn't moving
so fast never come across such a maaaasssss where'd he find so many
corpses to eat not in the bombed-out cinema I don't think I immediately start to bang away in his direction and smokily through the
trees everything all milky now Pirate caught up to him and he's
straight through the window and into a boutique sit Pirate sit so's he
doesn't go in after him I run up see blood on the windowsill and
realized he got hit pretty bad Pirate barks I flank on the left banged
a cracker from the bomb-hurler through the window then a second
right away bang and jumped back he's out through the same window
and I'm behind him and I see he's twinkling and already not as fast
the piece of shit got tired turns out sets off through the courtyards

and I flank and jump around through a gateway and come out at him Pirate's nearby and I see on the GPS that he's rushing toward us and we're gonna meet in that gateway Pirate's tearing forward I squeeze his jaws shut shut up don't move he's one tooth away from us here and I knelt down so's to shoot more handily and he rushes toward me and I let him come a bit closer to my chest bang a bursting bullet didn't even take him out a bull like him and he roared and rushes forwards his snout sticking halfway through the gateway all covered in fur aim between his eyes and bang missed bang bang missed three meters from him reaching for my pistol and his claws all out half-a-meter long while I jerk the pistol from my holster stumbled over fell down I think that's the end for you František your time has come and you lean back and then Pirate jumped in and grabbed at his hand and the corpse-eating nit is at Pirate's throat and I jumped up ran over to them and point blank at his dome from my pistol a whole clip bang bang bang bang bang bang bang bang bang bang bang bang his brains splash all the way onto my mug and he toppled over and Pirate's whining underneath him I grab the reptile by the head to get him off of Pirate but can't move such a zoomorphic mass Pirate I wheeze Lil' Pirate hold on I look around there's a pipe lying there grabbed it lifted it propped up the reptile pushed him aside so hard almost ripped his gizzard Pirate's layin' there whining and I see his guts coming out of his belly the reptile managed to tear him apart Lil' Pirate I say Lil' Pirate undo my spacesuit tear off my undies bind up Pirate's guts with my undies pick up Pirate in my arms feel his ribs are broken the reptile managed to crush him too and I shoot a help-spark to Kazimish up in the sky and I jump jump jump along the prospect with Pirate in my arms I can already hear Kazimish winging his way over Pirate whines I'm thinking we'll take him to the hospital they'll sew him up and heal him I jump up behind Kazimish I cry out fly faster there's a German hospital the Martin Luther Hospital to the southwest flying up through the gateway Kazimish glanced all the way over grunted how'd you take this one out Grzes he shouts and I saw Mihas owes me a bottle and 1.5 nails and then Kazimish is flying whistlingly at full speed to the hospital Lil' Pirate needs sewing up we took off started to fly Pirate still breathing and looks down below at the city we got there quickly landed I jumped up with Pirate in my arms didn't keep jumping but brought him to the hospital carefully so's not to shake him around and my Lil' Pirate yawned and hung his head and stopped breathing and that was that my Lil' Pirate is no more.

30

"How is it you think you can remember those times when they had passed by the time you were born, my dearest?! I can still remember being a boy in Moscow when it was *the* capital city, the cars running on gasoline, oh, there were so many of them, it was impossible to even walk through the city, not to mention drive. Throngs and throngs of cars, you understand, and all of them were always dirty for whatever reason, yes, yes, for whatever reason always dirty."

"Why?"

"It's a mystery, I don't know why! I can remember it perfectly, we were living on Leninsky Prospect back then and every morning I would go out to walk our spaniel Bonka and stroll alongside these dirty cars—past the Moscow department store and into the park by the Palace of Young Pioneers."

"What a beautiful name. And did these young pioneers live in that palace?"

"You know, I'm not at all sure who lived there, but I can remember the lawn in front of it, a kind of concrete obelisk, plus the dog lovers. I remember the stores too. So much of what was in them was bright and superfluous. Suckers on a stick had a funny name: 'lollipops.' You know, I can even remember the last rulers of Russia. They were so little, with a strange way of speaking, as if they were schoolboys, so young and cheerful, one of them played an instrument, perhaps it was an electric mandolin, and another was fond of sports, that was fashionable back then, once he even flew with cranes."

"With cranes?"

"Yes, yes, with cranes, precisely with cranes, can you imagine!"

"You already had *pro*-wings back then?"

"No, no, of course not, no one had *pro*-wings back then, he flew with some kind of apparatus and, I think, broke something...a leg or an arm, I can't remember."

"That's strange."

"Back then, many things were strange. A receiver was called a television, and for some reason they always used it to show either people getting killed or funny stuff. I remember there was this fat guy, his name was Poet Poetovich Citizeninov, an entertainer and a merry fellow—he would always come out onstage with a swimsuit and a bow tie, recite his funny poems in a chant, then jump around, do his best entrechats, his fat thighs clapping together so's they rang out like bells. And for some reason, they called this clapping-together of his thighs the 'opposition.' And his legless partner with a sort of hollow-cheeked, heavy face, if you know what I mean, would roll out onto the stage in a cart, drink vodka straight from the bottle, and curse everyone and everything."

"I'll come right out and say it—that's super weird."

"I also remember there were a lot of different holidays back then, they were strange too—Day of the Polar Explorer, for example, or Day of the Brown Bear—but it was absolutely necessary to celebrate them, have guests over, make Olivier salad, drink vodka, dress up like a bear, and roar out songs: 'I live in my de-e-e-en, I have shaggy le-e-e-egs...' Holidays, holidays, holidays, both frequent and strange...I remember an enormous poster: 'Long Live the Glorious Victory of Stalin's Cholera over Hitler's Black Plague!'

"And I know that people didn't bow to each other back then and didn't address their bosses as one might expect."

"Oh yes. And they didn't wear head coverings in the summer!"

"They say that this was done on purpose, so they wouldn't have to bow. Wild, huh? And women dressed in a beastly way with exposed belly buttons that were sometimes even pierced. Do you remember those beauties?"

"With pierced belly buttons? What's so strange about that? In White Sea, we would also go around half-naked in the summer. We're

not Moscovians, you know...well, then, my dear, help me get up...
like that...thank you, thank you...it'll be better if I stand a bit like
that...easier to breathe..."

"So, what was Moscow really, like, *like*?"

"You know, it seemed to me to be an enormous city, so loud, so
rude, and always bustling; my aunt lived off in the suburbs, my parents
and I would go and visit her, such long journeys to get there, and a
sea of those filthy cars all around, a sea, you understand, and the sea
itself was swimming, we're going, going, going, almost for a whole
day..."

"And were there horses?"

"Not one!"

"That can't be!"

"I assure you, my dear, not a single horse! Back then, we only ran
on gasoline. Today, in your Moscow, it stinks of manure, but back
then it stank of gasoline."

"You ran on gasoline?"

"Yes, everyone did."

"How excessive...and what about the city itself?"

"Yes, Moscow...Moscow...You know, it was a densely populated
city, extremely so."

"Were there any walls?"

"No walls, no walls at all."

"Everyone settled wherever they wanted to?"

"Wherever they could. They bought an apartment where their
resources allowed them to. There were no estates. Only rich and poor."

"Do you remember the Moscow Holodomor?"

"Fortunately, we went away to our grandma's in Kharkov right at
the beginning of the Troubles. If my father hadn't made that decision,
then I could tell you all about that Holodomor! Without leaving
anything to the imagination! Or perhaps I wouldn't have anyone to
tell!"

"And then you left Kharkov, but didn't go to Moscow?"

"As soon as the First War ended and White Sea became a democratic republic, we moved there from Kharkov."

"And why not to Moscow?"

"They'd already crowned your Sovereign there."

"You were afraid of constitutional monarchy?"

"No, no, not the monarchy... my parents had a more general wariness of Moscow. They were afraid of it. In any case, a lot of stuff had happened there, there were rumors, cannibalism for example, everyone had witnessed these awful scenes..."

"But that all ended, the Sovereign put everything in order. Cannibals and marauders were hanged in the city squares."

"Yes, of course, everything worked out, but still, you know... my parents didn't want to move there for some reason. All this talk of the beastliness of the oprichniks, of their red cars and brooms..."

"Those rumors weren't entirely true. There was no *especial* beastliness."

"All of those public executions and floggings..."

"Those were indispensable. How else could one put everything in order?"

"Well, I dunno... in White Sea, we got by without oprichniks."

"The Germans and Finns helped you, but Moscovia had to raise itself up on its own."

"Yes, they helped, of course... The Neubert-Malinen Plan. That was decisive... that, so to speak, saved us... and Murmansk rose up from the ashes and the Islamists were booted out of Arkhangelsk..."

"And your aunt? Did she stay in Moscow?"

"My aunt... kinda disappeared... I can't remember... I haven't ever seen her since I was a kid. Mom said that she called a couple of times from Moscow, then went silent. For good."

"And you've never been to Moscovia since?"

"Never! Not once! If I went to Moscow, I wouldn't be able to tell..."

"ZaMoscvorechye from PodMoscovia?"

"Yes! Yes! I wouldn't be able to tell, I wouldn't recognize it... my dear... now help me... to sit down here..."

"Of course."

"Thank you. Wonderful... But, speaking frankly, I'm pleased with your current Sovereign. I listened to his speech when he came to visit White Sea. He's a serious guy, you know... And he seemed to me to be an intelligent man."

"Our Sovereign is a wise ruler. We love him very much. You can't imagine how Moscow has blossomed under his rule, all of Moscovia too, what PodMoscovia has become overwhelms the eyes."

"I've heard that you don't have any more problems with supply chains reaching the city."

"Yes, for a long time now! The markets are seething! And such fairs! You don't have fairs like that in White Sea."

"But we do have fish. Moscovians eat up our herring, yessir they do!"

"But it's hardly free, is it?"

"No, it isn't! And you know, my dear, I hear that littluns are oppressed in Moscovia?"

"Nonsense! Slander and libel!"

"But weren't all of them simultaneously resettled out of Moscow and ZaMoscvorechye and into PodMoscovia? A few thousand people in the middle of the night, right? They caught 'em with special nets... they even wrapped the homeless littluns up in mesh?"

"There must be order in everything. There must be no epidemics or unsanitary conditions in the city. And how many burglars were there among these littluns? Disgusting! The Sovereign provides everyone with equal amenities and equal rights. But the law is the law."

"Yes, yes... *Dura lex*... But I was watching, I've noticed that, for whatever reason, your Sovereign definitely doesn't like littluns. He has some kind of complex, they say... something to do with his wife..."

"That's a lie. A deliberate lie about the Sovereign spread by Europeans, Ukrainians, and your people from White Sea. His mercy is boundless."

"They also say that there's never not a nail in his head."

"I'm not even gonna *comment* on that!"

"Rumors, huh?"

"Think about it, how on earth could you rule a state with a nail in your head?!"

"But a lot of people live like that now… it's the Age of Tellurium, so to speak…"

"Addicts and people with pathologies live like that, you mean. What a fine example they are! How can you compare them to our Sovereign? He doesn't have a nail in his head, it's already filled to the brim with care for the state and his loyal subjects. You know, my wife is a rather cynical and pragmatic individual, but even she often just comes out and says, 'Darling, what a blessing that we have our Sovereign.'"

"And I would say the opposite: what a blessing that we don't!"

31

"FIRST ye help me prop 'er up an' get round it, an' then, after that, so's t'get yon job done." A bigun who went by the nickname of Pigeon scratched at his arm, which looked like the root of an oak tree twisting up from the ground.

"Yeah, we'll help ye, we'll he-e-e-e-elp ye!" Losing patience, Sophron pressed his cap to his chest for a third time.

"And where ye goan prop 'er up to get round it?" The bigun raised his voice, as if he were about to burst into tears.

"Hey, look, they're rollin' it in! They're already rollin' 'em on in!" Sophron raised his voice too, waving his cap at the wide-open gates of the threshing barn.

Sitting in the corner of the threshing barn, Pigeon stared at the gates, as if, after the red-headed Sophron's exclamation, something was taking shape out of the warm July air. But all he could see through the gates was the same wedge-shaped view of ripening rye, bushes, and behind them—a potato field, and behind the potato field—a strip of forest with the setting sun behind it. The bigun's swollen little eyes goggled malevolently and resentfully at the evening landscape.

"And where on earth . . . where on earth ye goan set it?!"

And, as if by magic, three guys appeared between the gates rolling in a wooden barrel. One of them was carrying an empty bucket.

The bigun went silent and his face, reminiscent of a hyperpotato tuber, still carried its previous expression of furious resentment.

"There ye go, motherfucker." Sophron hit his cap against the top of the crumpled facade of his boot with malicious relief.

The guys rolled the barrel in over the dented floor of the threshing barn. The bigun stirred noisily in the corner and raised himself up to his full four-meter height. Pigeon was dressed in a long kosovorotka woven from rope, woolen trousers, and leather bootees on his bare feet. There was a plastic burse fastened with a snap tied round his waist and a wooden comb the size of a rake dangling from his belt. When the bigun saw the barrel, he immediately became more cheerful and serious.

"There we go... and ye didn't believe it." Sophron poked at the barrel with the toe of his boot.

"And yer goin' to..." Pigeon pointed his enormous finger at the barrel.

"We'll open 'er up in a sec," one of the guys spoke up, pulled out a knife, and began to cut off the barrel's hoop.

The other guys took out their knives and set to helping him. Having calmed down, Sophron thrust his cap over his cowlicked forehead, pulled out a cigarette, and lit up.

"And so's all and that—t'get round it." Grazing his long-haired head on the rafters of the threshing barn's thin roof, Pigeon moved toward the barrel threateningly.

"All of it's yers, o' course, nothin' to conversate about." Sophron nodded as he exhaled smoke.

The guys tore the hoop from the barrel and took off its lid. The barrel was full up with moonshine.

"Come on, Gray, scoop it out!" Sophron ordered.

One of the guys carefully lowered the bucket into the barrel, let it fill up, then pulled it out. Pigeon's hand immediately reached out and grabbed the bucket as if it were a glass.

"Be befuckt for yer health." Sophron fixed his red cowlick.

Pigeon carefully brought the bucket all the way up to his mouth with its uneven, pinkishly flaky, almost ragged lips and drained it easily, throwing back his head and ruthlessly breaking part of the roof. His head stayed like that for some time, as if he were thinking about something *higher*. Then he sighed, grunted, and proffered the empty bucket to the guys. They began to fill it up again.

Pigeon only really calmed down after drinking three buckets, bunched his lips up into a trumpet, and exhaled noisily, which caused the sweet smell of moonshine to swim up over the guys' heads.

"And but this, so's such slighter?" Pigeon asked.

His cheeks were crimson with blood.

"Chasers," Sophron translated for the guys.

The guys began to take large pieces of bread and lard wrapped in paper out from the pockets of their jackets. Throwing the bucket off into the corner, Pigeon proffered his open palms to both of them. The guys filled them with pieces of bread and lard. Pigeon put his palms to his mouth and began to eagerly gobble down the chasers. Once he'd finished, he licked at his palms with his enormous pinkish-white tongue, wiped his hands on his trousers, and burped so forcefully that ripples passed across the surface of the moonshine.

An accordion played off in the distance. Then a second and a third.

"Woah!" Sophron raised his finger. "Ye hear that?"

Pigeon nodded. His little eyes had become drowsy.

"Don't let us down, Pigeon." Sophron scooped a pitcherful from the barrel, drank it, and, taking off his cap, wiped his hand off on the back of his head.

"And this, I . . ." Pigeon nodded reassuringly.

"Don't let us down!" Sophron threatened him with his finger smilingly.

Pigeon winked at him.

"Lez go, shy boys." Sophron fixed his cowlick and disappeared through the gates.

The guys followed him out.

Pigeon watched the setting sun. His lips drew into a smile. He took the comb off of his belt and began to comb his long, fair hair.

That evening, at the new club in Big Souloukh, it was the third night of the dancing competition. The last evening of the competition pitted dancers from two villages against each other: Big Souloukh and

Little Soloukh. It was three versts and change from one village to the other, not to mention the shoals of the Zhurna River, where they all fished for perch and gudgeon. In Big Soloukh, there were one hundred and five homes, and in Little Soloukh, there were sixty-two. In Big Soloukh, they worked as carpenters, and in Little Soloukh, they worked as joiners. In Big Soloukh, there were many drunkards, and in Little Soloukh there weren't as many. There were two kulaks in Big Soloukh—Nikita Volokhov and Pyotr Samsonych Gubotiy—and in Little Soloukh, almost half of the residents lived in the lap of luxury. In Big Soloukh, there was only one old auto-mobile for everyone, and in Little Soloukh, there were seven! The Little Soloukhians hired the Big Soloukhians to mow and scythe hay, to harvest and thresh rye, and, in the fall, to dig up taters. And the maidens of Little Soloukh tended to be finer, spiffier, and statelier. And, as for the dancing competition, Gramma Agafya would always put it real ambiguously: every year round the Apple Feast of the Savior, there's a dancin' contest, an' who's goan outdance whom ain't never clear. The Big Soloukhians were crowned as winners for three years, but then the shy boys from Little Soloukh struck such sparks beneath their boots that all the devils in the guts of the earth of the Yaroslavian Principality got to feelin' real sick. The prize samovar flew from one village to the other. And got filled up with pure gut-rottin', hoochin', bathtub-brewed moonshine on the third and final night. In which state the winners carried it home. Well, the Little Soloukhians were sick of dancing *honestly* and, the previous summer, they'd decided to *angle* the competition: at the fair in Vladimir, they hired a dashing dancer, molded a living mask over his snout, and, yeah, they made him look exactly like the youngest of the Khokhlachev brothers, the most famous of the Little Soloukhian dancers. So "Serenka Khokhlachev" came, danced for three nights, took home the samovar of moonshine, and that was that. The elderly judges from Wet Farmstead didn't bat an eye. And the Little Soloukhians were practically buzzing with joy for three days in their tavern. But murder will always out—in the tavern by the station, the lame water-carrier

Sashka let it slip and the Big Souloukhian guys understood that they'd been had for fools. And they decided to take revenge.

The accordionists finished playing and shook their sweaty forelocks and earrings made of *empty* tellurium nails so's drops flew up into the stale air of the packed club. Having taken a final knee, Nikita Sramnoy, the last of the dancing Big Souloukhians, shoved his finger behind his cheek, made a popping noise—as if he were opening a bottle of champagne—and spread out his arms: the end of the dance. Then, staggering off in a silk shirt that was wet through, he walked over to his guys accompanied by whistling and applause.

Maidens hastened to bring the dancer kvass.

Six old men from Wet Farmstead sitting beneath icons nodded approvingly and talked amongst themselves. A very short time passed and the oldest among them waved a white handkerchief: 'twas to be the Little Souloukhians last dance.

The accordionists stretched out their bellows and burst into song. The Little Souloukhians made way. And Serenka Khokhlachev jumped into the middle of the club. Whistled dashingly, scissored up his light legs, managed to clap twice beneath his crotch, crouched down, jumped up, crouched down again, jumped up again, stretched his legs out like compass needles, put his hands behind his back, threw back his *dry ass*, and began to walk around in circles like a cock chasing after hens, then marching on the Big Souloukhians in time to the beat, smirking, winking, and making it understood with his entire aspect: We'll take it away! Today we'll take away the samovar of moonshine!

But he didn't manage to complete two circles before the bright, new floor made of thick boards of spruce swayed beneath his feet. The dancer was stunned and lost the beat.

And the floor swayed again. The windows clanged and the icons fell.

The maidens squealed.

And again—rock-a-bye-bye!

The log building cracked, swayed, and set to lurching.

The old men from Wet Farmstead set off across the floor in their chairs as if it were made of ice.

The crowd screeched and roared.

Sitting dumbfounded on the floor, the dancer was tipped toward the other wall, right into the Big Soloukhian shy boys. There, the flea-bitten Lil' Sophron grabbed him. And wordlessly caromed his hand into the dancer's mug. A living mask lay in Sophron's hand. And beneath the mask—the face of the dancer from Vladimir.

The floor stopped swaying as if nothing at all had happened.

"Take a look at what kinda Serenka's been dancin' front of y'all for three days already!" Sophron shook the dancer by the scruff of his neck, showing him to the old men.

And in his other hand—holding the mask.

Everyone gasped. The old men goggled. And the Little Soloukhians quickly mastered their dumbfoundedness, heading for the door, for the door, for the door . . .

The entire village noisily escorted the Little Soloukhians all the way to the river. Some saw them off with clubs, some with fists, and some with kingpins. Voices in the air and boxes on the ears rang out long into the night.

And, having finished the second half of the barrel after his great feat, the drunken Pigeon slept in a ravine behind the old threshing barn with the sleep of the dead, shaking the nettles with his knightly snoring and frightening the nocturnal birds and beasts.

32

"The original! Give me the original immediately, *zum Teufel*!" Stein cried out, menacingly banging his beer mug against the table and beer foaming up around its rim like the sperm of a Titan. "Oh, putrescent Volokhov! Oh, Volokhov, weaver of mysterious worlds and woes! Oh, Volokhov, ye shredder of virtue! The original! Give me the original here and now or I'll tear you apart like a fish!"

Gloomy even in moments of cheer, Volokhov waved his hands around as if he were an orangutan savages had skinned before releasing it back into the humid jungle.

"The original's in *your* memory, Stein; rummage through that snorted-to-shit brain of yours!"

Stein splashed beer onto him with a roar.

"The origina-a-a-a-a-l-l-l-l-l-l!!!"

Nastenka squealed like a pregnant pythoness and clapped her hands together.

"Well, mother-fuckin'-fountain-pen-fucker, Volokhov! Don't undermine the hierarchy!"

And she burst into laughter as if she longed for only one thing— to turn into a giggling marble statue and stay there in Volokhov's studio. For the last month, she'd taken to squealing infernally and swearing floridly.

"We're all longing for the original, Andrei," Priscilla pronounced seriously on her knees in front of the puffy and sweatily silent Apothecary, from whose head protruded a tellurium wedge. "You mustn't trust your memory. Especially not these days."

Coming out of the bathroom, Terminal silently raised his middle finger, proffered it to everyone, poured himself a glass of green liquor, and drained it in a single gulp.

"The origina-a-a-a-a-l-l!" Stein growled.

"The original!" Nastenka squealed.

"The original . . ." Priscilla rolled her eyes, touching Apothecary's impressive genitals.

Volokhov lost his patience.

"You're a miserable bunch of Platonists masturbating to shadows in the cave! Shadows! Your originals are nothing but shadows! You can have 'em!"

He ran over to a smartypants and jabbed at it with his bony finger. The studio was plunged into semidarkness. And a hologram of Edvard Munch's painting *Kristiania Bohemians* rose up in the middle of the studio. Yes, this had been the last *idea* voiced by Spot, even before Poet's burial. The burial had been all mixed up, like a hell turned inside out, and everyone had been enthusiastic and unsheltered. But Spot, that rubber of sweaty palms and collector of monstrous ideas, reminded and disturbed. The time had come for the incarnation. Volokhov supported it gloomily, Nastenka waved inwardly to her long-armed deity, Priscilla joined in enviously, and Stein was always up for *anything*. They all confirmed and picked a night. And that night had come—quiet to the point of insensibility and unhinged to the point of senselessness.

Munch's painting occupied the entire space of the studio: six bohemian characters at a long table and, at the end of the table, a laughing prostitute. Spot's blood began to slow in his veins at the sight of this painting—so cherished and adored by him—and he collapsed onto the studio's beer-covered plank floor.

"You don't have the right! You don't even have the right to faint!" Stein began to rumble, kicking at Spot.

"He's dying at the possibility of incarnation, dying from the stunning possibility of losing himself for even a moment!" Nastenka squealed and clapped. "Oh, centaurs gettin' fucked in the goddamn mouth, how wonderful!"

Priscilla pulled vodka into her mouth and sprayed some of it onto Spot's face. He came to his senses with some difficulty.

"*Sois sage, ô ma Douleur, et tiens-toi plus tranquille…*" Priscilla recited.

"Since my childhood, I've never liked the oval, since my childhood, I've killed for approval," Spot replied to her, lying on the floor with the irreproducible smile of fulfilled desire. "Lift me up."

Stein and Volokhov raised him up roughly and shook him, as if they enviously wished to shake the sweetness of anticipated incarnation from Spot's heart.

"Let's get into position," Spot muttered, his lips having completely lost their color.

"I'm here! Here!" Nastenka squealed and stood in the place of the prostitute, her hands resting on her hips. "This is my spot, you dark hookers!"

"Who could doubt that," Terminal grunted as he burped.

"Apothecary! This is your spot!" Stein's finger pointed at the gentleman with his walleyes bulging into the abyss.

Apothecary obeyed sweatily.

"And I'm here," Priscilla chose for herself an obscure character of indefinable sex who was squinting at the sad bearded man sitting next to them.

"I'm next to you, oh wise Priscilla! Even though I don't have a beard!" Stein rumbled, taking the bearded man's place.

"Your place is in the first row, Volokhov!" Spot laughed hysterically. "Oh, how much you resemble him! Oh, those sunken and ravaged eye sockets! Oh, the wormy face of a coke head!"

"It's all the same to me." Volokhov shuffled into the painting as if he were entering the next world and took the place of the coke head.

Terminal became the chubby gentleman with a blot of mustache beneath his snub nose, and Spot, trembling at the possibility of incarnation, slid *into* the figure perched at the corner of the table and looking off somewhere past the prostitute.

"Confirmed," he muttered in delight.

Everyone froze. The smartypants captured them.

"Release!" Stein roared.

The group broke apart. Only the unhappy Spot didn't want to leave the incarnation under any circumstances. He sat and sat, his head drawn down into his shoulders, and stared tensely off into a corner, as if there, among the cobwebs and bunched-up tubes of paint, a black crack were opening up and spreading and breathing the nonexistence of void out onto him, but perhaps images of new and wonderful worlds as well...

"Show us both paintings!" Volokhov ordered the smartypants.

The holograms of the two bohemians rose up in the space of the studio—Kristiania from the end of the nineteenth century and Saint Petersburg from the middle of the twenty-first.

Having served themselves their favorite drinks, everyone except for Spot, who was completely paralyzed, started at the images.

"I don't see any fundamental differences," Volokhov took stock gloomily.

"Identical!" Stein laughed, splashing beer out onto the holograms. "My spirit burned helplessly in the flames of perverse desire!"

"Glory to the Fallen Star, we're indistinguishable!" Terminal hiccupped after taking a gulp of absinthe.

"I'm more infernal! More authentic!" Nastenka squealed, then hurled her glass of wine at the Norwegian hologram. "Oh, fuck me with the Neva, how beautiful I am!"

"I want to go there..." Priscilla whispered into her glass. "How very possible it is...the shore of a mirage..."

"I've come to this world to see the sun," Apothecary pronounced sweatily, then passed gas noisily.

"And now—an orgy!" Stein dropped his mug and clapped.

"Orgy! Orgy! Orgy!" Nastenka shrieked.

"Orrrrr-gyyyyy...." Terminal opened his yellow cardigan.

"If there's got to be an orgy, there's got to be an orgy." Priscilla grinned into her glass.

"Orgy-porgy..." Apothecary sweated, farted, and undid his fly.

"An orgy..." Volokhov nodded his bald head with doomed energy.

And only Spot just sat and sat in the same uncomfortable position, his head drawn down into his shoulders and staring unblinkingly into the dark corner. Tears rolled down his unshaven cheeks. What had he seen in that dark corner? 'Twould seem that he himself didn't know yet.

33

VIKTOR Olegovich woke up, slid out of his case, put on his narrow sunglasses, stood in front of his mirror, beat a tellurium nail into his head, put on a Mongolian bathrobe, walked into his meditation room, and meditated for sixty-nine seconds. Then he walked into the kitchen, opened the refrigerator, took out a packet of red liquid, poured a glass of it, and drank slowly, looking at daytime Moscow through the violet window. Entering his fitness room, he threw off his robe, jumped onto a spinning bike, and pedaled for sixty-nine minutes listening to the music of falling drops. Then he went to the bathroom and took a contrast shower. Having pulled a steel-colored leather jumpsuit over his sinewy body, he walked out onto the balcony, locked the balcony door, spread his wings, and flew out over Moscow. Having flown over Vozdvizhenka Street and Gogol Boulevard, he planed to the left, riskily and dashingly flying between the crosses of the Cathedral of Christ the Savior and frightening two crows off of them, swooped down toward the river, striking one wing against the surface of the water as was his tradition, climbed up again, and hovered over Bolotnaya Square for a long time, planing, circling around, gaining height, then planing again. He noticed the discharge of the *manifes*-dough begin at precisely 15:35 Moscow Time. Previously sold in whole rows of metal cells of the approved and agreed-upon shape, the softened and thoroughly mixed-up *manifes*-dough flowed out onto Bolotnaya Square, stuck together into a homogenous mass, and ended up occupying almost the entire space of the square. The fermentation process had been activated in the *manifes*-dough, as a result of which it began to swell and rise up as it approached. At this critical moment, representatives of the Kremlin began to intensively infuse it with loosening agents, inhibiting the rebellious growth process of the mass of *manifes*-dough. Prepared and tested in Lubyanka laboratories, the liquefiers of the *manifes*-dough lay dormant in the innards of the rebellious mass until they received the command to liquify and proceeded to act. Occupying positions along the perimeter of the mass of *manifes*-dough, the beery *manifes*-dough softeners activated their softening mechanisms. Sensing the danger of *diminution*, the *manifes*-dough began to peacefully resist the diluents, softeners, and leaveners. Only the front section of the mass of *manifes*-dough actively resisted. Rapid-rotation action metal augers were put to use against the active part of the *manifes*-dough, dividing it into neat bits of dough for frozen pelmeni and pirozhki, which were then sent to freezer cells for further processing. Having removed the actively rebellious section of the *manifes*-dough's mass, the augers changed their rotation speed from fast to slow and began to knead and squeeze the rest of the mass of *manifes*-dough out of Bolotnaya Square toward Yakimanka, the embankment, and adjacent lanes. After the last of the residual rebelliousness, the *manifes*-dough lost its yeast activity and was *diminished*. The leaveners and softeners provided hidden, yet still effective aid to the augers. By 16:45, the *manifes*-dough had been entirely squeezed out of Bolotnaya Square, dismembered, softened, liquefied, and successfully poured into the Moscow Metropolitan reservoir.

"Dissolved!" Viktor Olegovich said aloud.

Circling around over Bolotnaya Square for a little longer, he then flew toward Triumfalnaya Square, planed down to the veranda restaurant of the Peking Hotel, passed into a separate office, dimly lit and connected to the restaurant, then, as usual, ordered an empty plate with a thin garnish of reddish-gold dragons. Placing his own tail onto the plate, he began to chew at it unhurriedly, reflecting on what he'd just seen. But suddenly, his reflections were interrupted by a tiny sesame seed lying on the snow-white tablecloth. This seed forced him to unexpectedly remember that this was the second week he hadn't been sleeping alone in his encasement. A bloodsucking insect had moved in with him. Every night, it crept out of its crack to gorge itself on Viktor Olegovich's blood. As a Buddhist, he wasn't *against* this—on the contrary, it brought him great pleasure to feel the bites and subsequent loss of blood through the Veil of Maya that is sleep. *As it sates itself, this being makes me more consummate*, he would think in his sleep. *I let this younger being suck at me. That ain't no* managerial style… During the day, he would sometimes pray briefly for his new blood brother. But, one thing remained unclear: each time it finished gorging itself on Viktor Olegovich's blood, the insect let forth a particular noise, something like a discontinuous chirr. It was rhythmic in its discontinuity and, as it *spoke* tonally, the sound was also organized in a particular way. The insect made this noise every night. It was the sound of satisfaction and perhaps even gratitude. *He's thanking me, I'm thanking him, and together, we are necessarily thanking the Great Wheel of Samsara because, for as long as we are dependent upon it, we must be its spokes. Humility is the lubricant of these luminous spheres*…Viktor Olegovich thought. But the insect's chirring was somehow stuck in his head. He wanted to understand it. And, as if at the bidding of the Buddha's Little Finger, it was at this moment, chewing on his own cold tail and peering at the lonely sesame seed, that he suddenly recollected and deciphered the collapsed buzzing sounds, that they shined out into one long phrase in his brain:

"Crownedwithawreathofroseswhiteaheadofthemgoesouroboros."

That was unexpected. Blok being devoured by a snake. But the cold-blooded Viktor Olegovich didn't stop chewing his tail. *I understand what this sentence means, but what does it signify?* he thought, continuing to stare at the sesame seed. *For, verily, between the signified and the signifier, there lies an abyss of, not only conventional, but also often ontological unfuckability. Exactly like the gulf that separates* Technology for the Youth *from rejuvenating techniques. An abyss lies between them! And only a real tightrope walker can overcome it, a lawful hermeneutic who's so fluent in morphosyntactic nunchucks that the blonde beast of the signified he dicks all over falls from the tightrope all the way to the very bottom of the deepest gorge.*

But suddenly he noticed another sesame seed. It was lying at the very edge of the tablecloth and, for that reason, wasn't terribly conspicuous. That was the second surprise. But he didn't stop chewing his tail this time either.

A second seed, he thought. *That changes everything. There are two of them? Why does only one thank me? And if there are two of them, there must also be a Third . . .*

Viktor Olegovich wanted to reflect on this Third One, but stopped himself in time.

No, I'm not going to think about the Third One. And therein shall lie my humility for the day.

34

PAPA BOUGHT a smartypants at the bazaar.

Varka'd been waiting for this day for a long, long time—for as long as she could remember herself. She and her friends exchanged complicit winks, whispered amongst themselves, dreamt, and prayed to the Mother of God that She might send Varka a smartypants. And how could they not pray, dream, and whisper round in corners? There were solely two smartypantses in the whole village—the kulak Mark Fedotych had one and the lector had the other. Neither one of 'em ever let their smartypants escape from their hands. The first was greedy and the second was a bore.

Polinka Sokolova asked the lector if she could use his smartypants to stop by the World Exposition of Dolls and he just said to her:

"You can watch your dolls on the radio, my smartypants wasn't made for larks."

And that was correct—every hut in the village had a radio now and you could watch it all day—till they turned off the electricity. But there were solely three programs on the radio and they only showed a *droplet* about the doll exhibition. And what's the use of a *droplet*? It drips down, then it's gone, all it's done is set your desire alight...

And so the young maidens were sitting in a crowd by the radio and waiting for Sunday's program to come on again. And it did, they caught a glimpse of the *living* dolls, then wandered off back to home with great sadness in their hearts: the elbow was near, but they couldn't bite it...

But 'twasn't for nothing that Varka'd prayed: that summer, a miracle fell upon Varka's papa. He and Semyon Markov had set to burning out charcoal on the Tarnations; they got to work, chopped down a birch deadwood, sawed it up, and started to dig a pit, but— hold on!—they saw something metallic down in the pit. They dug it up and it turned out to be a whole gas-run Mercedes auto-mobile with three headless skeletons inside it. Sixty years before, highwaymen had killed those people, robbed 'em, cut off their heads, driven the auto-mobile into the forest, dug a pit, and buried it so that no one would ever find it. This was during the days of the Second Time of Troubles—when the Three-Fingered Thief had already entered Moscow in a tank. Varka's papa hadn't even been born back then and Grandpa Matvey was only ten.

The auto-mobile had rusted, but the motor in it was untouched— her papa and Semyon dragged it out, loaded it up onto a cart, and brought it to the village. They took out the motor, looked it over, cleaned it with moonshine ... and it was good as new. They took that motor to Shilovo and sold it to auto-mobilers for 165 rubles. A lotta money. Papa and Semyon split it in half—Semyon immediately set to building a new hut with his share and Papa bought a cow with its calf, all kinds of clothes for everyone, a moonshine machine, plus a smartypants. The most expensive purchase was the smartypants. It was a jewel. Six times more expensive than the cow and calf together. That's just the kind of papa Varka had. He brought the smartypants home, took it out of the box, and held it out to Varka.

"Check it out, Varka!"

Varka looked over ... and was stunned: a smartypants! How many times had they shown these on the radio, how much had she talked and talked about 'em, how many times had she peeked through that bore of a lector's window just to see the thing out of the corner of her eye—and now she had her own. It was soft, pleasant, and smelled like the city. At ten years old, Varka already knew everything about smartypantses. She touched it with one finger and received a swift reply.

"Hello, Varvara Petrovna."

"And hello to you, smartypants." Varka bowed.

"What form will you have me take, Varvara Petrovna: a book, a picture, a bun, a cube, a cylinder, a stick, a bag, a belt, a shapka, gloves, or a scarf?"

"Be a bun," Varka commanded.

And Varka's smartypants became a round bun with a cheerful li'l face, rosy cheeks, and affable li'l eyes.

And Varka began to live with this bun.

The Opilovs' hut became more cheerful—as if the sun had settled 'tween their bunks. The wooden cuckoo doesn't even manage to cuckoo at six o'clock in the morning before the bun releases a hologram of a rooster (no one has kept chickens in the village for a long time and eggs on tap are cheaper than bread at the store); the rooster flaps its wings, shakes its oily head, and starts to sing together with the cuckoo. Often, it starts to sing even before the real bird—Grandpa's cuckoo is old and is starting to run slow.

All the Opilovs wake up, Mama lights the stove, they sit down to breakfast, the bun plays songs for 'em, gives 'em the news, and shows 'em what's happening in the world and where. Grandpa Matvey drinks tea and quacks from time to time.

After breakfast, Varka kisses the bun on the crown of its head, puts on her little shoulder bag, and sets off for her ecclesiastical parish school. You can't take your personal bun to school: the school has its own smartypants. It is a very very strict one, which hangs from the board like a sheet, neither japing nor playing songs. The children are afraid of the school smartypants, it gives no quarter and sees everything. Should someone be naughty or copy someone else's answers, the smartypants immediately speaks up in its stern voice.

"Thirty minutes kneeling in peas after class, Pastukhov!"

"Sixty minutes in the corner after class, Lotoshina!"

There can be no mischief with this smartypants around. The director locks her up in an iron cabinet every night.

Varka sits through her three required lessons, returns home, has a nibble—then straight to the bun.

"Bun, bun, oh my little bun, show me far-off lands and wonderful planets and *living* dolls and beautiful kings' sons!"

Her friends would come over and sit round the bun and it would show them *everything*. And it would release bubbles all over the place—here's the sea for you and a desert and oversea cities and wonderful forests. The bun is solely forbidden from showing that which is sinful and seditious. The bun helps everyone in the family: it tells Papa the correct prices for arboreous charcoal and where to sell it, it tells Mama where to buy chintz, and gives Grandpa a hand with his gout and his tobacco. When the Opilovs' cow strayed from the herd, the bun immediately showed 'em: the wanderin' tramp is in Wet Beam devouring juicy grass. The bun helped plant potatoes, calculating everything down to the last seed and showing 'em exactly what to do. It also gave 'em a hand with their moonshine and calculated all the proportions—Papa's rotgut came out pure as a teardrop and burned with a clean blue flame. And when Grandpa set his mind to weaving new bast shoes for her brother Vanya, the bun indicated where best to tear the bast. That surprised Grandpa. For all his life, Grandpa'd been tearing in Burnt Grove, but, this time, the bun sent him to Paninsky Fold. Grandpa cursed it, but he went all the same— it was a verst closer, but linden trees didn't grow there, just a willow tree and a hazel tree. He arrived, looked around, then gasped: a little island of linden trees had shot up in the middle of the brush. Grandpa joyfully tore off seven wafts and barely managed to drag 'em home. That evening, he got drunk, set to singing, and clinked glasses with the bun. Everyone had fun laughing at Grandpa that night...

In the winter, the bun would spin sinnys about hot countries, play cheerful music, and arrange performances with a variety of voices. It was real cheerful!

And so, the Opilovs lived out a year with the bun.

Then came trouble. Chinese gymnasts were passing through and, as luck would have it, ended up in Varka's village. People gathered together in the town square for a performance. The Chinese started to twirl and twist around their pretzel things and the people stared and clapped. Varka stared with everyone else. But when they got home, the bun was gone. All the locks were whole, the windows were shut, but no bun.

Papa wanted to set off after the Chinese, but what was the point—y'think ye can catch an auto-mobile on a horse?

Varka cried the whole night through. And in the morning, before the cuckoo had even cuckooed, she got ready, took seven rubles and a piece of bread for the road, and went to look for the bun. She'd heard word that the Chinese were headed for Morshansk. But maybe they lied on purpose, who the hell knew. There was nothing to be done, she had to find the bun. Varka set off straight through the forest for the highway so's to catch a ride to Morshansk. She hadn't even made it halfway there when suddenly she sees a little old man sitting on a stump and smoking a pipe. Varka hadn't seen very many littluns in her life, solely in farces at fairs. Varka walked over to the little old man and bowed.

"Hello, gramps."

"Hello, oh vexed Varyukha," the old man replies.

Varka was surprised the old man knew her by name.

"Don't be surprised, Varyukha, I know a lot of things, and not about ye alone," the old man says to her. "Yer lookin' for yer smart bun?"

"I am, grandfather."

"Give me a lil' bit of bread to eat and I'll tell ye where to find yer bun."

Varka took out her hunk of bread and proffered it to the old man.

The old man closed his eyes and set to gobblin' it down. It seemed he hadn't eaten for quite some time. The old man finished the hunk of bread and spoke to Varka.

"Once ye get to the road, get on the bus and go to Bashmakovo. That's where yer bun abides."

"The Chinese went to Bashmakovo, then?"

"The Chinese are eatin' and drinkin' in a roadside tavern right now and soon they're gonna sell yer bun to a bigun, the town miller. He's from Bashmakovo. He has a mill right near the town. He'll return there this evening with yer smartypants. Should ye want yer bun back, ye must needs go there now."

Varka was stunned.

"How d'ye know what shall come to pass, grandfather? Could it be ye have a supersmarty?"

"Here's my supersmarty, girl!" The old man took off his felt hat and tilted his head forwards.

A shining nail was protruding from the old man's head. Miracle of miracles! Varka didn't say anything, yeah, she simply bowed and set off on her way. She reached the road, waited for the bus to Bashmakovo, got onto it, paid three rubles for a ticket, then they were off. She rode for a half day before arriving. She got off the bus and there was a market right there. She walked over to a broad and asked how to get to the mill. The broad showed her how. And Varka set off for the mill. She walked through the entire town, then through a field and a copse, and saw the mill from some distance away. She walked toward the mill where there was a line of carts filled with grain and muzhiks fussing about next to 'em. Varka walked even closer. Made of hefty logs stacked on top of each other, the mill was enormous. She could hear the millstones spinning and grinding inside it. Varka was surprised—there was no stream with a water wheel, no wind wings, and no diesel engine—just millstones spinnin' about. She looked inside through a crack and could see an enormous giantess twirling one of the millstones. As tall as a tree. But she didn't see the *big* miller. Varka listened in on the muzhiks' conversations and realized that the miller still wasn't back and that this heifer was his wife—the milleress. So Varka decided to sneak into the miller's hut while the millstones were still spinning, hide, and take her bun back during the night. And that's what she did. While the milleress was grinding, she made her way into the hut. The miller's hut was huge and everything in it was made from logs—the chairs, the table, the wardrobe, and the bed. And all these things were so very big. Varka started to become afraid in the hut, but then she remembered her bun, its smile plus its little eyes, and she overcame her fear. She clambered under the bed and set to waiting. An hour passed, then a second, then a third. The millstones had ceased spinning. The muzhiks had set off every which way on their carts. The milleress came into the hut, drank a barrel of water, and began to set the table. Soon, the earth shook, the doors flew open, and the miller walked in. He and his wife kissed, then she sat him down at the table and began to feed and *water* him. The miller ate and drank his fill, belched, farted, then began to speak.

"I've brought ye an expensive li'l present, oh wife of mine."

He took the bun out of his pocket and put it down on the table. His wife gasped, took the bun, stuck a finger into it, and it began to speak.

"My mistress is Varvara Petrovna Opilova, I serve and obey her alone."

The miller and milleress laughed so loud the whole hut shook. Then the miller spoke again.

"Tomorrow, I'll bring a handyman from the city and he'll reconfigure yon bun so's it'll serve ye. Ye'll be my little queen of the world!"

The milleress laughed with joy. She and the miller tumbled down onto the bed and set to fornicatin' and philanderin'. The bed above Varka's head set to shakin' and she was one step away from callin' out for help. But then she remembered her little bun and gritted her teeth. The miller and the milleress came to the peak of their fornication, then began to snore. Varka clambered out from under the bed, climbed up onto the table, grabbed the bun, then got out of the frightening hut as fast as she could.

And in the courtyard, the night was already dark as could be and Varka couldn't see anything—an owl's hoot alone for company. Varka pressed the bun to her chest, kissed it, then touched it with her finger.

"Hello, Varvara Petrovna," the bun says to her.

"Hello, my dear li'l bun!" Varka replies. "Help me to find my way home!"

"Thy shall be done," the bun replies.

The little bun lit up and showed Varvara the way home. And brought her right out to the highway. There, at that very moment, the night bus to Serdobsk was rolling past. Varka took her seat and paid three rubles for her ticket. And, by morning, she was already in Serdobsk. From there, she went home on foot.

She walks through the fields, tossing the bun up into the air and singing little songs. And the bun plays music for her and releases rainbows. She arrived in her village and, there, everyone was looking for her, Papa already having *puzzled* the police with her absence. Her people saw her and were delighted. And she shows them the bun and boasts that she stole it back from giants. Her mama and papa were surprised, they weren't expecting to have given birth to such a brave girl.

And Varka put the bun onto a shelf, covered it up with an embroidered napkin, and made a declaration: "From now on, lil' bun, I won't let anyone have ye, neither biguns, nor littluns, and neither people, nor robots."

And the Opilovs again began to live, fare, and make *good*.

35

IT ALL started with the crusaders in the early morning three of them
came to us in Mittenwald with bollards to investigate the murder of
the neighbors they investigated it and investigated it so well that by
the end of the day they'd taken twenty-one calves a tractor and two
trailers full of potatoes from Frau Schulze as if it was she who'd killed
them I don't give a damn about the potatoes or the tractor it just
makes me sad to think the calves will be sent to slaughter or to a farm
to Füssen or to Schwangau and then their heads will get beaten in I
guess and I had to leave Frau Schulze but the crusaders gave Angelika
all that remained of the murdered neighbors' estate it was properly
passed on to her a fridge three smoked hams a bench a churn a heap
of clothes everything fit I even got a dress and a coat with a bit of a
bloodstain but I washed it and it went away and a cardigan and snow
boots and two little rings with turquoises and a scarf with Paris
embroidered onto it and pants that didn't fit I got a little chubby
during the war it's funny how my behind spread out I drank milk at
the farm and ate *knödel* in sauce too so the nice pants didn't fit but
the bad boots with heels how am I supposed to walk around in them
the snow boots are better and a jug and a little watch and a computer
it works I washed the calves maybe they didn't get their heads beaten
in they got given away to grow up into beef Frau Schulze didn't want
their heads to get beaten in and she screamed at the crusaders but
they unfolded a smarty and showed her a papal bull with a seal and
she pushed them off of the farm crying but the main one says you
should be thanking us that we're not arresting you and they took
away the twenty-one calves and a tractor and two trailers full of

potatoes to Neuschwanstein and I was crying for the calves let them take the potatoes and the tractor it's too bad I raised them like my own children Angelika stayed silent she could've given them something better'n calves the slattern with my donkey ears and hairy snout how could they want me but Angelika's busty and young she could've given it to 'em in the hayloft next door they obviously liked her if she was awarded the neighbors' goods and sundries the foolish wench wouldn't have died from giving it up to the three of them I bet and I winked at her and made signs with my fingers and tongue and she turned her mug away as if she didn't understand as if she weren't a woman even before the war she'd had men and Frau Schulze is crying no money to buy our things back the crusaders don't even need nice things she offered them a pricey fur coat six pairs of boots beautiful shoes twelve pairs of shoes that'd been her deceased husband's three pairs of leather pants three nice new tasseled hats and the bastards turn their noses up we don't need nice things of course you don't need them in a single year you rob enough to last ten they're obsessed the bull this the bull that give us the calves the tractor and the potatoes they loaded it up and the bastards drove off Urban says the crusaders are worse than the Salafis those guys would just cut off your right hand for playing chess and flog you on the main square for drinking alcohol or smoking tobacco but they always bought the meat they took from the people but the crusaders just take it drag it away on the authority of a new papal bull they occupied Neuschwanstein they say there are heaps of gold there from all of Europe all they're missing is Smaug the dragon and maybe they didn't beat the calves' heads in right away maybe they dragged 'em off to Füssen there are three big farms there and maybe they just sold 'em maybe the crusaders don't even need meat anymore they'll sell 'em and take the money and maybe our calves are in Schwangau there's a big milk farm there too and even three big geldings who haul wood they'll put 'em in stalls hopefully they keep the red ones together but what can I do Frau Schulze had nothing left she told me right away you saw how I got ravaged donkey I don't need a cowgirl anymore and what am I to do go wherever you want to and where am I to go wherever you want to go be a cowgirl for the crusaders yes yes they don't have any of those all they have is six thousand bollards and I say of course they have cowgirls and they're probably all beautiful not like me with my donkey ears where am I gonna go I don't know Frau Schulze also doesn't know she just whimpers what am I to do I asked Urban and he said there's a place where there's a big farm it's in Switzerland in Ascona it's called Monte Verità pagans live there who worship the moon naked at night they don't obey anyone they have their own garrison and a big farmstead they only drink milk because milk is a gift from the moon they need a lot of milk and they can only get it milking the cows by hand Catholics won't work for them you see but you're a zoomorph so go to Monte Verità and go work for them as a cowgirl you'll get shelter and a hunk of bread you'll have cottage cheese and sour cream every day and I set off what else to do I have to do something no one gives something for nothing I'm a donkey and asking for alms is no good and I'm not exactly gonna start work as a porter I have to stick with my speciality I got ready packed up two suitcases lay them over my shoulder with a stick and set off on foot what now I need money for a bus or for a train Frau Schulze only gave me room and board I only ever saw money before the war she couldn't even give me anything for the road she weeps that she doesn't even have a single mark to spare she gave me some baked potatoes baked apple and rhubarb pie for the road well then I bowed and set off and what am I to do it's so far though there'll be good work when I get there I'll milk cows I'm no stranger to them I would even say I'm on friendly terms with cows I know everything about them I walk walk and walk and while I walked I was thinking so's it wouldn't get boring and trying to take careful steps so's not to wear out my mountain shoes they're practically new Urban gave them for me for doing some work they were his oldest son's shoes the one who didn't come back and I was always barefoot at Frau Schulze's and wooly feet don't get cold in the summer or the winter but I decided to wear the boots so's not to tear 'em up on the rocks and so's they wouldn't make fun of me they already made fun of me so much donkey ears a wooly snout donkey donkey boys used to chase me and throw pine cones at me donkey donkey and when I would wear proper boots they wouldn't make fun of me as much and they'd respect me more and they'll treat me more seriously at the border if I'm wearing boots and it's true I crossed the border with no questions asked I have a zoomorph passport and then I walked walked walked until I reached a village and there were Austrian soldiers there and here's what happened I could tell they'd just eaten they were sitting and smoking and I'm walking past and as luck would have it I walked over to the fountain to take a drink I started to drink and one came over to me asking where I'm coming from and I say from Bavaria from Mittenwald and he laughs isn't it hard for you with two suitcases not too bad I say you're strong he says I'm strong I say and what's your name strong-ass donkey he says strong-ass donkey you guessed it I say and he bursts out laughing and when I started to drink again he came up from behind and grabbed my ass and screamed I've never fucked an ass before I kicked him away and kept walking and five of 'em come after me chirping various bawdries about fucking an ass and about my ears and about my behind and saying that whatever I've got between my legs is probably deep as a well and it's probably cool up in there and then they started to argue about my legs are they smooth or are they wooly let's take a look they say one ran over and lifted up my skirt and they saw that I had wooly legs and they started to hoot and holler and I keep walking not paying any attention then suddenly they fell behind well good I thought and kept walking I left the village set off down along the highway thinking soldiers and crusaders always want everything for free peasants are more honest they always give you something for what they make use of you for if not money then food I keep thinking and not too much time passed and I hear a car coming up from behind me I walk over to the roadside and the car brakes I look and see a military jeep and the same five soldiers are inside of it they jumped on out grabbed me and dragged me into a fir grove and they're all silent not laughing or anything nothing without talking they began to kick me pushed me knocked me over backwards tore off my skirt lifted me up by the legs two of them are holding onto one leg and two onto the other I have strong legs and the fifth lay down on

top of me and began to rape me and I had a tellurium nail hanging
from my neck I found it in the city once on Albert-Schott-Strasse it
was just lying there on the pavement and I picked it up and decided
I'd use it to clean my big ears a lot of wax builds up in 'em and flies
go inside of 'em too when you're working on a farm I'd wrap the nail
in cotton wool at the end of the day dip it in vinegar clean my ears
and go to bed so I started wearing it around my neck on a piece of
rope so's not to lose it and then when this soldier started to rape me
I grabbed the nail and jammed it into his neck with all of my strength
he screamed and fell off of me with the nail in of his neck all the way
up to its head and the other Austrians rush over to him and I sprint
across the fir grove they were screaming then they drove off probably
headed for the hospital then I put my skirt back on put the suitcases
over my shoulder and set off again but not along the highway this
time but straight through the fir grove I walked walked and walked
until it got dark then walked out onto the road walked for two days
all the way to the Swiss border and there I had to sit in quarantine
they checked me over for illnesses and parasites they fed me twice a
day then they let me go I managed to hitch a ride with a nice man
driving a truck he took me all the way to Schwyz then I made it to
Bellinzona on a freight train then I walked and walked and made it
to Ascona and found Monte Verità it's on a mountain and they didn't
let me in they have their own border barbed-wire fences cannons and
machine guns they're fenced off from everyone else I showed them
my passport and said I'm a professional cowgirl I want to work I came
here from Bavaria they let me in and we went straight to the farmyard
and there a woman with white hair comes up to me and between her
breasts there's a silver moon she took me over to the cows without a
word and their farmyard was big there were a hundred and twenty
cows there and horses and calves and turkeys and guinea fowl and
ducks in a pond with geese and chickens and it was exactly time for
the evening milking and other cowgirls had already started to milk
the cows they only milk 'em by hand and this white-haired woman
tells me well show us how a Bavarian donkey-cowgirl knows how to
milk and they gave me a bench and a pail and took me over to a cow

I washed its udder I say give me some Vaseline to rub onto the nipples and they give me some butter that's how rich the living is here I rubbed butter onto the nipples then I set to milking the pail was ringing like a church bell and the pail's full two tugs later okay the white-haired woman says I'm satisfied with you donkey my name is Jyotsana I'm your boss you're going to live and work with us first she took me off to the shower where a woman washed and disinfected me then they took me into the cafeteria where they stuffed me to bursting with cheesy polenta and salad and then they took me to the communal bedroom where the cowgirls live they showed me the bunk where I would sleep and told me to rest from my travels I say I'm not tired I can milk as much as I need to and they just say sleep sleep you're not gonna work today and they went off I was left alone in the bedroom there were thirty-two bunks in there and it's only for cowgirls and there are cowboys here too I saw three guys with bears' heads in the barnyard they were cleaning up the dung and also some beautiful horse-headed guys and one boar-headed guy with the geese but I didn't see any donkey-headed people yet so I sat and sat I tumbled over into bed and wanted to sleep right away and as I was falling asleep I thought now because of those Austrian morons I don't have anything to clean my ears with at night.

36

ANFISA was no more ready to let the last drop *fall* than the first; she caught it in a spoon, licked it up—it was still so warm—and pronounced, "Let it not be the last!" loudly enough so that her husband and Mars, sitting behind the partition of drying sheets, might hear—then, for herself, in a mysterious whisper: "Oh, ooze into our pockets, ye creeping fog, so's they might become like bogs." And it was only then that she turned off the faucet. This had been her custom for three years already: her husband drank the first drop and she would lick up the last. The first drop, a masculine drop, burned with strength and purity—this was the head of the hooch, born from fusel vapors, cutting a liquid path for itself into these PodMoscovian stomachs—and the last drop, muddy, weak, feminine, the miraculous apparatus completing its six-hour task on the precipice of exhaustion.

Having molded the smartypants over the kitchen table in the form of a checkerboard, Mars and her husband were playing checkers for the right to flick each other on the forehead. The smartypants burred and beeped. They each lost and won in equal proportion.

"How much dripped out, Anfis?" her husband asked as he became a king.

"Fourteen whole ones," Anfisa responded happily, dexterously corking the final bottle.

"Legit." Her husband moved his king. "We goan set ourselves up real good!"

The smartypants rang out approvingly, like the Sugar Plum Fairy from *The Nutcracker*, and one checker shined with blue light.

"You'll get set u-u-up, of course…you'll set up such a shambles that we'll have to call in the priests..." the bald, bearded Mars mumbled as he scratched himself.

"Fourteen," Anfisa repeated, as if she were justifying herself before herself.

"Fourteen, that's leg-i-i-it, no doubt..." Mars mumbled, losing his third checker in a row.

"That's how it is nowadays." Her husband poked his finger with its tobacco-stained nail into the shining board.

"Well, what am I gonna do now?" Mars stooped over, squeezing his hands to his stomach.

"I'm not gonna rack my brains about what *you* gotta do..." Her husband moved a checker at the edge of the board, hopelessly trapping Mars's checkers.

"Which piece am I gonna move?" Mars exclaimed in a womanly voice.

"Move whatever piece you wanna move." Her husband hung over the board with a victorious smile and twisted his mustache. "Howbeit, it occurs to me that you shan't be moving any piece, Mars Ivanych, but preparing your lil' brow for a blow!"

"Ah, you're a terrorist." Mars clicked his tongue and plunked his five fingers down onto the board. "I give up, may your mother be fucked by the Taliban!"

"A-hem." Her husband straightened up, puffing his chest out valiantly and stretching forth the middle finger of his right hand. "Mars Ivanych, are you ready to *receive*, my lord?"

"Sir, yes, sir."

Mars squinted, clasped his arms at his sides, and proffered his forehead.

Her husband gave him a juicy flick. Mars made a silent exclamation of pain, as if he were blowing a fly away from his lips in his sleep.

With a bottle of warm moonshine in her hand, Anfisa ducked under the sheets and out toward the men.

"Hey there, fellas, I know you're busy, but want a swallow of some fresh yield?"

Her husband squinted penetratingly at the murky liquid in the bottle and touched it.

"Any way we can palm off a little more of the tail and drink a little more of the head?"

Anfisa thumped the bottle angrily against the table.

"We only got eight bottles of head, Sashok, it didn't ferment that much!"

"So because you didn't leaven it enough, the dignity of Mars Ivanych and me has to suffer? I don't understand your philosophy, Anfisa Markovna."

"We're not gonna be in the green if you suck down all the head, Sashok!"

"We're not gonna suck it *all* down." Her husband and Mars exchanged judicious looks. "We'll just have a *drop* of it to kick things off. Right, Mars Ivanych?"

"Right!" Mars straightened up and stroked his beard.

"I know what you mean when you say 'kick things off'!" Anfisa waved her arms around as if she were fighting off invisible devils.

"Instead of yapping your head off, you should throw together some chasers." Her husband folded the smartypants into the shape of a pipe, stuck it into a beer mug, took three glasses from the shelf, then began to clean them off with a dirty towel.

"Come on, Sashok, have a glass of the head, then a glass of the tail, okay?" Anfisa begged, before internally muttering, "May you drink water alone from now on, oh ye Buderusians."

"What are we still talkin' about?!" Without rushing, her husband wiped off the glasses like an executioner polishing his ax, taking occasional glances at the lamp as he did. "*Jiaoshe!*"*

"The head isn't the only fish in the sea," Mars concluded reasonably. "But we must needs begin with it."

"We must needs begin with it," her husband repeated seriously.

"My-y-y Go-o-od . . ." Anfisa rifled through the refrigerator by the

*[Chinese] We made a deal

window and began to throw chasers out onto the table: sour pickles, cabbage, lard, tofu, and mushrooms.

And, suffering much as she did so, she set out the head for the two men.

Her husband lauded her.

"Now we're talkin', wifey."

And began to pour their drinks.

"Give me tail!" Anfisa insisted.

"Don't break the chain of command, Anfisa Markovna." Anfisa's husband pinched the fat of her ass. "A proper day's work must be washed down properly, isn't that right, Mars Ivanych?"

"That's right!"

"Tail for me...tail for me..." Anfisa whimpers.

"I cannot allow such a woman to drink dregs," Anfisa's husband takes her by her detergent-mauled hand and looks her in the eyes. "Not a woman like you, Anfisa Markovna."

"No sir!" Mars affirmed, chewing at his beard.

"Sit down!" Anfisa's husband brought a chair over with his foot and pulled her down into it by the shoulder.

"Oh you..." Anfisa laughed exhaustedly, her flabby ass flopping backwards into the chair.

"To the Sovereign!" Her husband raised his little glass.

"To the Sovereign!" Anfisa and Mars repeated.

They drank, then fell upon the chasers.

"Don't rush to sale, Mars Ivanych," Anfisa immediately began to sing her old song. "We've still got a few kopecks in our pockets, there's no reason to rush, it'd be better to sell it for more, ride over to Butovo and sell it to the invalids by the station..."

"I'll sell it how I sell it," Mars snapped back.

Her husband poured them a second round. Of head.

"Sashok?" Anfisa twisted her lips weepily. "You promised!"

"The second must also be pure, for we are drinking to our dear Communist Party," her husband reasoned. "You and Mars are unaffiliated, but I'm a Russian Orthodox Communist with good standing. And I will not permit such fuckery."

Mars and her husband drank up, while Anfisa took only an offended sip.

"What the he-e-ell is that?!" Her husband stopped chewing his cabbage, poking his finger threateningly into the side of his wife's glass. "Ideological sabotage? A provocation by piece-of-shit Ukrainian plutocrats? A sortie by militant atheists?"

"Terrorism!" Mars, already drunk, shook his goatee like a goat.

"I'm not gonna drink the head," Anfisa snapped, her face becoming stony.

"Anfis…" Her husband spread out his hands, almost knocking the bottle off the table. "Do you respect us?"

"We're saving up for a new stove, Sashok, you know the kind of needs we have!" Anfisa pronounced pleadingly and offendedly.

"We'll still save up," her husband promised sternly. "We'll drink up, then we'll save up."

And he flicked his tobacco-stained fingernail against the bottle of head.

Anfisa sighed powerlessly, took a pickle, and crunched into it.

"Glory to our dear party!" Her husband picked up his full glass in his left hand, stood up, crossed himself sweepingly, then gulped the head down in a single go.

As unaffiliated persons, Anfisa and Mars drank sitting down.

They began to eat the chasers.

"Anfis Markovna, you say we should sell to the invalids by the stations…" Mars crunched into a pickle. "A year ago, we sold there with no problem. But now, no one goes there, not even Chinese fugitives, it's a different kind of invalid there now. They'll cut you up like a dog, drink your moonshine, and use you as the chaser."

"Why would they do that?"

"Because you're behind in current affairs, you don't see anything other than the personal," husband reproached wife as he chowed down on cabbage. "Social custody. Public will. The country's old wounds take a long time to heal. The Sovereign and the party do everything they can. But the di-a-lect-tics of the present moment end up being more powerful."

"A year ago, who was sitting there beneath the platform?" Mars started to explain it in his own way, bending his fingers around as he did. "Invalids of the Uralian War. Guys who'd been fucked up with ordinary weapons and, y'know, burnt 'em with napalm too. And now who's flooding into Moscow and wherefrom? Krasnodarian veterans. The Salafis fucked them up with a new weapon there, a more deadly weapon—"

"Paralytic-vacuum bombs," her husband interjected.

"After dealing with those, the soldier's mind begins to falter. In my opinion, it's better to lose both your legs than your reason."

"So that's why you won't sell beneath the platform anymore?" Anfisa chewed with growing resentment.

"Well, I would go down there and wouldn't even be afraid if they at least paid me in rubles. But look at what they pay you with down there nowadays!" Mars stuck his hand into his pocket and pulled out a heap of *empty* tellurium wedges bound together with a rubber band. "*Empty* tellurium nails! Three nails per bottle. And what can I do with those? You heard about the decree?"

"Decree Number Forty." Her husband scratched himself smugly. "To be purchased through the pharmacy alone."

"Through the pharmacy alone!" Mars spread out his hands, hitting the sheet as he did. "And half goes to the state!"

"A new policy, of course..." Her husband scooped up some sauerkraut, threw back his head, and lowered the sauerkraut into his mouth.

"So where are we gonna sell it now?" Anfisa stopped chewing.

"I'll try my luck in Yasenevo and swing over to Bitsa, to the factories." Mars put away the wedges.

Anfisa sighed unhappily.

"There's not much demand among the factory workers—they make it themselves," her husband objected.

"I don't agree." Mars pushed off of the table with his fists, as if he were getting ready for a fight. "Only country people brew their own, but they still buy it in the Slobodka settlements. That's why I've never tried my luck with country people in Medvedkovo and Sokolniki."

"That ain't right," her husband declared admonitorily.

"What do you mean—ain't right?" Mars pulled at his beard.

"Let's have another drink, then I'll explain it to you."

The little glasses were filled with head.

"To a peaceful sky!" Her husband picked up his glass and glanced at the lamp. "Pure as a teardrop!"

Anfisa chewed with an expression of pure doom: the head was disappearing.

"To no more war!" Mars added.

"That the thunderstorm of war may ne-ver a-gain cover the Moscovian sky!" her husband pronounced weightily, raising his finger threateningly.

They drank. And ate.

Her husband sighs, lights a cigarette, it goes beneath his teeth, elbows onto the table.

"And now, Mars Ivanovich, I'll tell you why you're wrong. You're unaffiliated, right?"

"Well, yeah."

"And why?"

"What the hell do I need the party for?"

"There"—husband jams elbow into wife's side. "You hear that? Why the hell do I need the party! Infantile apoliticism."

"Maybe he's right, Sashok, what the hell does Mars Ivanych need the party for?"

"What, the invalids'll pay extra to get your moonshine if I just show 'em a party membership card underneath the platform?" Mars hiccups and throttles his beard. "They want moonshine, not a party member. And they can't use party membership cards as chasers; they can only sniff at 'em like bread as black as party boots to lick at!"

Anfisa laughs.

Her husband sighs and glances up at the leaky ceiling.

"Mhmm . . . there we go: what the hell do I need the party for . . ."

Mars spread his hands apart victoriously.

"Yeah! What the hell do I need it for!"

Anfisa interrupted them.

"Come on, Sashok, your party membership card helped you with your work, now no son of a bitch can fire you, but how would it help Mars Ivanych? He was, is, and shall always be a parasite."

"Yep, and shall always be." Mars jammed a fork into the tofu. "So, Sashok, what the hell do I need your party for? I've got enough moola for my bread and butter without it."

Her husband blows smoke into Mars' visage.

"And you, Mars Ivanych, who the hell are you?"

"A free man! That's who the hell I am."

"And what kind of con-vic-tions do you possess?"

"I've only got one conviction, Sanya: two rubles are better'n one. Nothing more than that."

"Do you respect the sovereign?

"Of course. I respect him."

"And the party?"

"What the hell do I need your party for?" Mars pushes off of the table and gets up. "Okay, we've had a good sit and now we're up. Give me your bottles, Anfis."

"Where to?" Her husband reaches for Mars's frock coat.

"Thereto!" Mars hits her husband's hand.

"Sashok!" Anfisa grabs her husband by the shoulder.

"You're fre-e-e-e-e-ee?!" Her husband begins to shake Mars by the collar.

"And you're not!" Mars shoves at her husband's chest.

"Guys!!!" Anfisa grabs their hands.

"You drunk faggot!" Her husband gives one to Mars on the kisser.

"You boot-licker!" Mars gives one to her husband on the ear.

"Guy-y-y-y-y-ys!"

Mars is through the sheet and over to the door.

"Stop! Stop!" Anfisa's husband reaches out his arms to grab Mars, but she belts her arms around him.

Mars fumbles with the lock and spits blood onto the sheet.

"I'll be back, you fucks, ask solely…"

"Stop already!!!"

"Sashok! Sasko-o-o-ok!"

"I'm out!" Mars slammed the door so hard that the smartypants in the beer mug squealed out an alarming red: "Possibility of earthquake!"

"Never trust a pig that tells you it's done eating shit!!!" her husband barked at the sheet as he struggled with his wife.

37

TATYANA got off of the electric train at Sokolovskaya Station. The clock on the station platform showed eleven in the morning. Tatyana looked at her own watch—12:12.

What on earth is this . . . she thought.

She'd recently noticed that whenever she looked at a clock, she would see two identical numbers.

Symmetry . . . the numbers so comely, all like me, so yummy . . .

"And the moon has fallen away," she pronounced, drawing in the spring air with great pleasure.

The platform was almost entirely empty—there were only two or three human figures around her. A wet wind made Tatyana's blond hair rustle and rocked the still-naked branches of beheaded poplars. The spring was late in coming; despite the fact that it was the end of April, there was still dark snow on the ground in some places.

Tatyana walked down from the platform by way of a dirty staircase. A monument to Stolypin towered up on the station square where a sluggish trade trudged along: sunflower seeds, sauerkraut, honey cake, cheap chatterers, self-generating boots, *soft* batteries, and candles. The square was entirely covered over by the hulls of sunflower seeds.

"Young woman, give me somethin' to feed on, for Christ's sake." A hunched-over old woman proffered her mittens to Tatyana.

Giving her a five-kopeck coin, Tatyana quickly walked past, crossed the entire square, and set off briskly down Lenin Street in her high blue-leather boots. She was wearing a short black cloak; a purse the same color as the boots hung from her shoulder; and her gloves were the same shade as both of the other accessories. The frames for Taty-ana's glasses were also blue.

The rare passersby were, for the most part, elderly, but a group of four factory guys were stamping around with cigarettes between their teeth outside a watering hole.

Having passed by a grocery store and a hardware store, Tatyana smiled at a shaggy stray dog, walked around two concrete blocks of unknown purpose that had grown into the earth, and turned onto Miklukho-Maklaya Street.

Not too far, 'twould seem... She looked around and saw a water tower ahead of her at the very end of the street.

"Very close indeed," she pronounced aloud and, looking around at random, noticed that two of the factory guys she'd just seen outside the watering hole were walking behind her.

Walking quickly. Too quickly.

Well, hello there... Unpleasantly surprised, she quickened her step.

The ice on the uneven street crunched beneath her heels. There was no one ahead of her. Only the tower stuck out among the roofs and naked trees. Jackdaws cried out to each other and a dog barked somewhere behind a fence.

Straightening her shoulders, Tatyana took quick and sweeping steps along the street.

Why am I doing this? Some guys are walking behind me—so what? She calmed herself down. *They're going about their business. It's day-time—it's totally light out.*

She glanced up into the sky. A faded blue was visible in the gaps between the clouds.

Where the air is blue, like a bundle of linens being carried by a man discharged from the hospital... she recalled, thinking: Pasternak.

Behind her, one of the guys coughed.

Where the wind is empty, like an interrupted tale... the wind is empty... and it's daytime now... still thinking: Pasternak.

Tatyana was walking past an unremarkable fence. The dog was

barking behind this fence. And two more dogs joined in—both next door and across the street.

Give me that paw for luck, Jim ... I've never seen such a scaffold ... never seen such a paw ... thinking: Esenin.

Keys jangled in one of the guys' pockets. A lighter snapped. Four jackdaws were sitting on a linden tree and exchanging cries with a crow, who was sitting on the crown of a fir.

Dew atop the evening fields ... no, snow ... crows above the dew ... thinking: Tsvetaeva.

One of the guys spit and coughed.

I bless you to all ... to all four corners of the world ... still thinking: Tsvetaeva.

The guys quickened their step. The crow took off and flew away. The jackdaws followed behind it with a caw.

And crows about him ... the horror of cold already within them ... again thinking: Pasternak.

Tatyana began to run.

The guys rushed after her. Clutching onto the purse that was almost flying from her shoulder, she ran down Miklukho-Maklaya Street. And heard one of the guys slip, fall, and swear. The other helped him get up.

"To all four corners, to all four corners ..." Tatyana muttered, desperately trying not to slip.

It was a straight road to the water tower. But it was still far away. And the road was slippery, bumpy, nasty, vile, beastly ...

I won't make it!

A passage appeared on her right, something like an alleyway. Tatyana rushed into it, noticing out of the corner of her eye that the guys had rushed after her again.

The coat of the one who'd fallen was open and fluttered behind him like short black wings.

"Crows ..." whispered Tatyana.

She ran down the alleyway and a dog behind a picket fence choked out a bark and ran alongside her. And the alleyway turned out to be a dead-ennnnnDDDDD! All of Tatyana's insides tightened up. But on her left there yaaaaawwwwned a passageway—redemption! She rushed into it and fell into a dirty snowdrift, then, moaning and waving her hands, she burst out of the wet snow, ran down the narrow road, turned to the right, rumbled across some rusty sheets of tin, and saw an old barn with a broken door in front of her, and through that door—another door, open and feeding out onto a neighboring street demarcated by a brand-new street sign. This sign gave her hope. There was a path to the street through the barn.

Tatyana rushed toward the barn, ran into it, and, her heels crushing into the rotten floor, tore toward the half-open door on the other side.

That door swung open on its own. With a shriek.

And the guy with the open coat stood in the doorway.

"Where to?" he hissed.

His face was dark and frightening, something about him—and not just his coat—was foresty and crow-like. Choking for air, Tatyana backed away from him.

There was the sound of iron banging behind her, a crack, and . . .

"Where to?"

This time, the question came from behind her. Tatyana turned around. The second guy was a redhead with a wide, big-lipped face. His face wore a good-natured expression.

Trying to come to her senses, Tatyana exhaled and pleaded in a strangled voice.

"What do you want, young men?"

In response, Crow closed the door with the same nasty shriek. The redhead closed his door as well. The barn became gloomy, light beating its way in only through holes in the walls and gaps in the roof.

"Where do ye think you're headed, huh?" Crow asked as he approached.

His swarthy, unshaven face exuded anger and his eyes glittered unwholesomely.

"Ye wanna to play cat and mouse with us?" the redhead pronounced both mockingly and good-naturedly.

"What do you want?"

It seemed to Tatyana that she was not the one asking these questions, but some faraway woman from distant isles in a limitless ocean full of mysterious depths and sunken ships and kind dolphins and wise whales and coral reefs with beautiful and bewitching fish—Technicolor and indifferent.

Crow pulled his swarthy hand out from the pocket of his jacket. A short but wide blade snapped and leapt out into his hand. He brought the blade up to Tatyana's face.

"Ye just try it, cunt!"

The redhead came up from behind her.

Tatyana held out her purse to Crow. Crow took it and held on to it, staring into Tatyana's eyes, then, with a sharp motion, threw the purse into the corner of the barn.

"We don't need yer fuckin' junk," Crow snapped, approaching Tatyana and grabbing her by the lapels of her jacket.

The redhead hugged her around the shoulders from behind and snuggled up to her, his breath reeking of tobacco, vodka, and sunflower seeds.

"We've conceived of fornicatin' with ye, milady!"

Through his pants, she felt his erect penis and went cold. A suffocating wave constricted her throat.

"I'm preg…nant…" she muttered with great difficulty.

"Pregnant?" Crow confirmed evilly.

"Ye can't really tell…" the redhead grabbed at her stomach.

"I'm beg…ging you…I'll give you anything…" she babbled, becoming increasingly cold and numb.

"We won't fuck with yer pregnancy," Crow grabbed her by the neck and bent her over.

The redhead pulled her down by the hips.

"I'm beg…ging you…" she cried out in a strangled voice as she fell to her knees.

Lifting up her short cloak, the redhead grabbed her panties, pulled at them, and tore them. Holding the knife in one hand, Crow undid his fly with the other and let free his long, swarthy penis.

Tatyana jerked, struggling to get up. But the knife's blade kissed her cheek.

"Ye just try it."

The redhead's strong hands lifted her hips up and his fingers pulled apart her buttocks.

"Look at that sugary asshole..."

His penis pressed into her anus.

"I'm begging!" she screamed.

"Shut 'er up, Petyun," the redhead ordered.

Crow grabbed her by the head.

"No! No! No!" she shook her head.

"I'll cut your throat, whore!" he growled, hunching over her.

And she realized that he really would. Her mouth fell open helplessly. The guy's penis went into it. The redhead thrust into her anus. When he was fully inside her, her body shuddered and trembled. Tatyana moaned.

"Well, will ye look at that...and ye were afraid of us..." The redhead grinned good-naturedly.

The guys began to thrust in total silence. The redhead gripped onto Tatyana by her hips. Crow held her by the hands. Tatyana's heel hopelessly scraped and thrashed against the rotten floor of the barn, scraped and thrashed, scraped and thrashed, scraped and thrashed, as if it'd begun to live a life completely apart from Tatyana's body.

A gentle shudder seemed to pass across the redhead's squat body and his head twitched, as if he were shying away from a cold wind.

"Ugh, cunt..." he exhaled and his broad smile became helpless.

Hunched over, Crow thrusted for a little while longer, then dropped the knife, groaned loudly, grabbed onto Tatyana, crumpled, and snuggled up to her.

They pulled out of her body almost instantaneously and she collapsed helplessly to the floor. The guys silently put away their penises. Tatyana just lay there, breathing greedily and hiccuping.

"There ye go..." Still gasping, Crow raised the knife, folded it, and put it back into his pocket.

The redhead spit, turned away, walked over to the door with an unsteady gait, kicked it, and left the barn.

"Ye can relax now…" Crow muttered exhaustedly and hurried after the redhead.

Tatyana remained lying on the dirty floor of the barn. After lying entirely still for several minutes, she turned onto her back and raised herself up, pushing off from the ground. Something happened to her face: not only did her narrow glasses stray to one side, but her features also seemed to slide out of place. Catching her breath, she wiped off her mouth with the back of her hand, took off her glasses, and threw them off to the side. Then she slid over to her purse, opened it, took out a smartypants folded into the shape of an envelope, and poked at it with three fingers. The smartypants lit up and jingled with the sound of bells. Tatyana tumbled over backwards again. The sun appeared through the gaps in the barn's slate roof.

Tatyana smiled helplessly. Her lips began to move and she spoke almost inaudibly.

To the sun of the coming day…thinking: Vertinsky.

From the street with the new sign, she heard a car drive up, doors slam, and people run over. The door of the barn shrieked open. Two big, strong men in black came in, one of them immediately picked her up, as if she weighed only as much as a feather; the other picked up her purse and glasses, a third ran in wearing a coat and hat and the second man handed him the purse and glasses.

Tatyana was quickly taken out to a large black car and laid down onto a wide leather seat in its spacious white interior. The men in black also took their seats in a part of the cabin separated from the passengers' area with an opaque partition. The man in the coat and hat remained in her section and sat down across from Tatyana.

"How do you feel, Your Highness?" he asked.

His face expressed nothing.

"Wonderfully," she pronounced in a weak, but satisfied voice.

He handed her a wet antiseptic wipe. She cleaned off her hands and threw the wipe onto the ground. He handed her another. She placed it over her *rumpled* face, then pulled it off. The mask made of self-generating plastic sagged off her true visage. The man took it and put it into a garbage container together with the napkins and the glasses. And handed Tatyana a hot, damp towel.

She pressed it against her face with great pleasure, leaned back into the chair, and froze.

"Your Highness," the man began, "I'm begging you, I conjure all of the saints in asking you to never henceforth deviate from the confirmed route. Wherefore did you go down Miklukho-Maklaya Street and not Sunny Street? We almost lost you. And why did you go so fast? For whatever reason, you always deviate from the intended plan."

"And you always reproach me with exactly the same words..." Tatyana pronounced without removing the towel from her face.

"Your Majesty... I carry personal responsibility for your well-being before the state, and I—"

"Am the only one who does," she interrupted him, jerking the towel from her face. "That's enough, Nikolai Lvovich. Don't be so predictable."

Tatyana's face had gone pink. She grabbed at her blond hair, pulled at it, and removed the wig. Beneath the wig was her enchanting black hair, known to all of Moscovia and neatly wrapped round her head. Tatyana pulled a barely distinguishable film off her hair, and it fell beautifully across her shoulders. Without rushing, she took off her cloak and dirty boots. The man in the coat helped her put on a long cloak made of black silk and with a hood, which she immediately threw over her head. He then opened up a bar, poured some whiskey into a glass, and put ice into it. Tatyana picked up the glass, took a drink, and, putting her legs up into the corner of the row of seats, froze for a long time with the glass between her knees.

Forty minutes of swift driving down the red state lane later, the car drove into the walls of the Kremlin and over to the mansions of the heir, then went into the garage. Sliding out of the car with her hood over her head, Tatyana practically ran through the door opened for her by the ever-present Mother Stepanida. Chubby and round-faced, she let Tatyana inside, then closed and locked the door. Her cloak rustling, Tatyana turned right, then right again, bent down to go through a low, vaulted door, and began to climb a narrow stone staircase. Having closed the ancient door with its huge forged hinges behind Tatyana, Stepanida leaned her back against it, her arms crossed across her high chest.

When she reached the top of the stairs, Tatyana entered a small prayer room with a luxurious and ancient iconostasis. Here, candles were burning and lamps were glowing in front of dark faces in their expensive frames. Getting down onto her knees, Tatyana crossed herself and bowed to the icons.

Then she got up, walked down a dark little corridor, passed through two vaulted rooms, and ended up in a similarly vaulted third room, which was occupied by a large triangular bathtub filled with pink-tinted water. She took her smartypants out from the pocket of her cloak and threw it into the water. Then she took off her cloak and panties and got into the bath.

On the tub's marble edge was a glass of celery-apple juice. She picked it up and took a drink.

When it *felt* the water, the smartypants became a small, potbellied boat.

As she drank, Tatyana felt at her anus with her left hand, stuck her middle finger inside it, took her hand out of the water, and attentively examined the finger. There was nothing on the finger.

She remembered the redhead's strong hands first grabbing at her belly, then her buttocks.

"The total mercilessness of desire," she pronounced, squinting, smiling, and shaking her head.

And the dark guy in his torn jacket ... a ragged guy ... a ragged crow, a black crow, a ragged raven, you've stolen, crow, you've stolen or untruth you've spoken ... how he squeezed me, how he squeezed my wrists ... and the knife fell, his little knife fell, the cutie pie dropped it and moaned, as if he were about to weep, and all of his evilness evaporated in an instant, all of his blackness flew away, flew away, blackness passed through the eye of a needle...

"The shattering helplessness of pleasure," she pronounced, resting her head back against the plastic headrest.

The vaulted ceiling was painted with ancient Russian iconography: with Sirins and Alkonosts—birds with beautiful women's heads and full, perky breasts—plus sturgeons and dogs.

How they ran across the ice, how they rushed, the one falling, the poor guy, they were rushing to the fatal affair, to the fatal and mysterious, criminal and sweet petite *affair...*

"Where to?!" she pronounced loudly with Crow's precise intonation.

Her voice echoed loudly against the vaulted ceiling.

"Where to?" she pronounced with benevolent menace like the redhead.

And she laughed, shaking her head with delight and slapping her palm against the pink water.

The smartypants, in the shape of a little boat, gave forth a hoot. Putting down her glass, Tatyana touched the smartypants with two fingers. A hologram with the face of Princess Apraksina arose above the boat: shaven head, beautiful face, and a tellurium nail sticking out from just above her right ear.

"Hello, Tanyusha!" Apraksina greeted her with a smile.

Tatyana tilted her head deliberately and, glancing sullenly at the princess, began to speak.

"Marfinka did it again today..."

"Oy..." Apraksina sighed and shook her head. "Tanyush—"

Tatyana pressed her finger to Apraksina's holographic lips.

"Not a moan from her chest!"

"Tanyusha, my darling..."

"Shall I expect you this evening?"

"Certainly, but Tanyusha, our sweet, darling Tanyusha...you force me and all of your friends to suffer every time you do this! Every time!"

Apraksina's voice rang out against the ceiling with concern.

"If you only knew how good it was today, Glasha." Tatyana's eyes fluttered shut with pleasure.

"It's a risk every time, Tanyusha. And not just for you."

"Don't frighten me, my friend."

"I'm not frightening you, Tanechka, I just can't understand, oh heart of mine, how the hell you got a taste for these half-breeds! And where this PodMoscovian debility came from! Right next door you've got the Kremlin regiment, handsome guys—in the bloom of health and each one of them—"

"Guardsmen are for the sovereigness. I have a different status, my friend."

"You're skylarking again, Tanyusha, listen . . ."

"Ah, Glasha! How good it was!"

Squinting, Tatyana leaned back onto the headrest and clasped her hands over her bosom with its tiny nipples.

"And if something happens?"

"Nothing's happened yet."

"You must needs decisively break this habit, Tanyusha."

"Just as you do with tellurium."

Apraksina sighed and held a pause.

"Tanya. You're making all of us suffer."

"Suffering purifies. Remember Fyodor Mikhailovich."

"This isn't a joke, Tanyusha! I'm so afraid for you and so exhausted! My God! I don't know what to do! Perhaps I must needs come with you!"

Tatyana raised her head and opened her eyes.

For a moment, the two women looked straight at each other. Then suddenly began to laugh. Tatyana splashed water onto the hologram of her friend's head. The spray passed through her round, beautiful face without even remotely altering it.

"I shall take you anon—without question!" Tatyana pronounced as she laughed. "Just no nails—so the guys don't get scratched, my friend."

"*D'accord!*" Apraksina wiped away tears of laughter.

Tatyana leaned back onto the headrest again and sighed.

"Ohh, Glashenka, but how important it is to give oneself to one's people. You must admit how important that is..."

"So that they don't betray us?" Apraksina asked with a lascivious grin.

Glancing up at the painted ceiling, Tatyana thought for a moment, then answered seriously.

"So that they love us."

38

ANDRZEJ Pomorats, a twenty-four-year-old Serbian Pole who had left Sofia on the eighteenth of November after the so-called Wahhabi Spring, had a breakfast of oat flakes with milk, coffee, and a croissant, left his small apartment in Kremlin-Bicêtre, a Parisian banlieue, walked two blocks, entered the barbershop owned by the *soft*-legged Hottab, and bought a tellurium nail from him for 145 postwar francs. Hottab's youngest son, Farukh, shaved Andrzej's head, then Andrzej went down into the basement of the barbershop and lay down onto a couch. Hottab's oldest son, Nasrullah, beat the nail into Andrzej's head. Having thanked him with a two-hundred-gram lump of smart dough, Andrzej left the barbershop, bought apples and a bottle of hibiscus tea at Sobar's vegetable shop, returned home to his little apartment, and composed the following text on smart paper:

Living furs from the Barguzinov and Sons Trading Company shall both warm and delight your loved ones in ferocious frosts. What could be more charming than an enchanting woman in a living fur? For thousands of years, our beautiful companions were forced to wrap their charm solely in dead fur ripped from the bodies of dead animals. Such furs preserved and carried within them eternal leptons of dolorous death and quarks of agonized suffering, negatively impacting the health and character of the possessor of the coat. The world of new technologies has given us the unique opportunity to present our wives, sisters, and mothers with living furs, unconnected with the deathly murder of the wordless creatures of God's kingdom. Leather proto-furs grown in the laboratories of Barguzinov and Sons are sold in our stores at very reasonable prices: from 50 to 450 rubles. During their first winter, they sprout with a magnificent first fur, which will already be 2–3 centimeters long. And what a fur it is, my dear ladies! Is it even possible to compare it with dead fur? That which you used to wear? Arctic fox, she-fox, mink, sheared mink, or, in the best possible case, sable. But is it even possible to compare the most luxurious Siberian sable with our living furs, which, in the process of growing, are capable of not only changing color, but also texture? Sable from Barguzinov and Sons can be blue, violet, or fiery red, it is able to grow more *actively* on cuffs and collars, the very texture of each strand changing. It's a real miracle! And, miladies, you may also notice that you're not wearing last century's faux fur upon your shoulders, but a living organism reaching for light, a living organism loving and warming you. It feeds on light and moisture, absorbs snow, and turns molecules of water into growth energy. For that reason, your fur shall always be dry. And one more stunning quality inherent to the furs from Barguzinov and Sons: they're companionably tactile. You press your palm to your furry beauty and it answers with the gentle surf of a furry ocean. Four years after you buy it, the living fur sheds. You can continue to wear it after the shedding, for the fur shall begin to grow again, but not quite as quickly or effectively, it's true. No wonder the people have informally dubbed these coats as "self-generating." Instead of allowing the fur to grow in this way, we advise you to partake of the genetic-renewal process. With us, in the Baikalian Republic, it will cost you anywhere from 40 to 80 rubles. And the luxurious fur shall then play and shimmer upon your shoulders for four more years!

Dear women! Respected chevaliers! Come pay us a visit! Buy living furs from the Barguzinov and Sons trading company!

When he'd finished writing, he sent the text off to the Baikalian Republic. Then drank some tea, got undressed, anointed himself with coconut oil, lay down in his chamber, and turned on some show.

39

WE DROVE down the highway for two hours, then turned into the forest. Gramma got all upset and worried right away: Where are we? I explained everything to her and she calmed down. Generally speaking, our gramma is pretty darn well preserved both internally and externally given her age. I'm not gonna rattle on about her lively soul and worldly ingenuity—just know there's no one remotely like her. Sonka and I've got a *supergramma* in every sense of the term. And it's got nothing to do with tellurium.

We went four versts through the forest, then stopped and got out. The forest around us was all old fir trees—you could make a pretty penny cutting 'em down and selling 'em. Gramma immediately remarked that back when it all happened, the trees were barely taller than my sister and me. Dope! Sonka bristled up at this and talked back in her usual absurd way: We were taller than all the fir trees back then, Gramma, you just didn't notice us, your holographic guests from the future. What a thing to say!

In short, I molded a GPS over my eye and we set off. The forest was dense—untrimmed fir trees. Getting lost in trees like this would be a piece of cake. Without a GPS, you couldn't do anything—just shout "Hell-OOO!" But we were fine—we easily followed the necessary path, going deeper and deeper into the woods and Gramma muttering the whole time: I don't recognize anything, she says, I can't remember and I can't understand.

Sonya amused and distracted us while we walked in her particular way: she pretended to be a wood goblin, molded the smartypants over her head, made it turn red, and came up to us from behind the trunk of a fir tree like Little Red Riding Hood—eat me up, gray wolves, just make sure it's slow and painful! I laughed and Gramma smiled.

Overall, we stomped out our merry way to the place for a long time, Gramma keeping up her good spirits all the while.

And finally, we made it. The trees seemed to part very slightly, like we were peering into a clearing, and in this clearing was a rock. An enormous boulder as tall as two humans. You can find boulders like this only in forests in northern countries. This one must have rolled here from God knows where during the ice age. And Gramma immediately threw up her hands: There it is, my children! We approached the boulder and took a lap around it—there was a niche inside it that looked like a cave. And in that niche were three busts hewn from the granite of the boulder. Sonka's and my mouth dropped open in awe. Three busts! Hewn right out of the stone as if they'd just beetled out from the wall of the cave. Not to mention they were detailed and filigreed. For some reason, I thought of the statue of Khafra, the pharaoh, which had so struck me with the artistry of its creation; that pharaoh had also been hewn from granite and he had a falcon perched on the back of his shoulders protecting the nape of his neck from enemies. I could use a falcon like that these days! So Sonka and I were standing there in a mild state of astonishment and our gramma immediately walked up to the busts, bowed to them, and loudly pronounced: Thank you, oh you Three Great Ones! We came to our senses, walked over to the busts, then began to touch and examine them. And Gramma says: Hold on, my children, let me tell you everything in order. My dear grandchildren, here stand the three statues of the three *fatal* rulers of Russia; in other words, before you are the Three Great Baldies, three great knights who crushed their own dragon-like country. They say that the first of them, this sly fellow over here with the beard, destroyed the Russian Empire, that the second, with glasses and a birthmark on his bald head, tore down the USSR, and that this third one, with his tiny chin, buried a frightening country that was called the Russian Federation. And all three of these busts were hewn sixty years ago by my deceased husband—a democrat, pacifist, vegetarian, and professional sculptor—during the summer when the dragon that was Russia decisively expired and forevermore ceased devouring its own citizens. Gramma approached each bust and lay sweets and gingerbread onto their shoulders. And she said: This is for you Volodyushka, this is for you, Mishenka, and this is for you, Vovochka. Sonka and I just stand there watching her as she spreads out her offerings, muttering affectionate words all the while. How unusual! I should add that our gramma has always been an atheist, she's never worshipped anyone or anything. And now, we were in a temple with three deities. Always the smart one, Sonka stayed silent. I, of course, couldn't hold back my questions: who, what, when, where, why, Gramma? She told me everything in great detail, but then she drew a line in the sand, as it were. She says: Russia was a frightening, antihumanist state at all times, but the monster was especially beastly during the twentieth century, when blood simply flowed like a river and human bones crunched in the dragon's snout. In order to crush this monster, the Lord sent three knights marked with baldness. And each of them performed great feats in their own time. The bearded man crushed the dragon's first head, the four-eyes crushed the second, and the one with the little chin cut off the third. The beardy managed to do this thanks to his courage, they say; the four-eyes because of his weakness; and the third one thanks to his cunning. And, of the three baldies, Gramma seemed to love this third one most of all. She muttered something very tender, stroked him, and lay a great many candies across his shoulders. She shook her head as she did this: How hard it was for this final third one, he had it the hardest of the three. For, she says, he did what he did secretly and wisely, sacrificing his honor and reputation and calling fury unto himself. How many insults he endured, she says, the hatred of a foolish people, dumb anger, and slander! And she strokes and kisses and embraces him, calling him a "little crane" and beginning to weep. Sonka and I were kinda stunned. Then she says to us: He suffered a lot, my children, but still performed his great feat.

Gramma categorically forbade us from shooting the cave with our

smartypants—photographing and duplicating shrines is inappropriate, she says. Too bad! We agreed to come back here in a year.

On the way back, we stopped by our family's favorite restaurant,
Snowman, and, I gotta say, we had a great lunch.

40

QUELLE horreur! As everyone knows, we don't get to choose our parents and relatives, but to make peace with this determinism is still incredibly difficult. I'm not talking about Grandma Liza, but about Pavlik. The higher powers gifted me with the unspeakable joy of a two-year separation from my brother, but it was only yesterday, when I first saw him again, that I was able to appreciate the true greatness of this gift. Yesterday finally came to pass the landmark trip that we have been discussing for the last thirty (!!!) years. While under the influence of tellurium, Grandma's consciousness was *enlightened* and, glory to the Cosmos, she remembered the *place*. Pavlik did some research with a GPS and found a stone of appropriate size in the forest. I must admit that this whole story, which I've been hearing since I was a child, has become much like the actual boulder—grown over with the moss of rumor and speculation, in which we, the Dolmatovich family, were doomed to wander and lose ourselves. And all because of the gaps in Grandma Liza's memory. But everything was restored, the neural puzzle was solved, and the GPS led the way to the stuff of legend. It's difficult to articulate the feeling I had sitting in my brother's car; the expectation of the fulfillment of a childhood dream is always fraught with the expectation of wreck and there's never any escape from wreck, just as there's no escape from the Apocalypse rolling up into the scroll of sky. Alas, we're all always carrying our own pocket-size apocalypses with us. But what I was dealing with inside that car for the one hundred and thirty-two minutes of our trip turned out to be more frightening and delicate than all other fears, apocalypses, and forebodings. My brother's vulgarity. Nauseating in its vile variety and terrifying in its infernal depths. The devil is, as everyone knows, vulgar. For the entire journey, Pavlik didn't gift us with a single minute of silence. That fat-faced, self-satisfied bastard successfully *cunted up* the whole trip. His vulgarity reminds me of a big, fat caterpillar, colored by the law of reverse evolution in hideous shades of green and pink. This carnivorous animal is unbelievably active and gluttonous—it slides into your brain, then devours it. Talking about the weather, about taxes, about the advantages of gasoline engines over potato engines, about his "dope" wife, about how to treat hemorrhoids, about his boss's favorite hobby (collecting *twink*-lers), and about the third clone of his cat Vasily, my brother ate up almost all of my perfectly nacreous brain. Stepping out of his damned gasoline car with my newly emptied skull, I lay my feet onto the coniferous carpet of the fir tree forest in a state of total exhaustion. And only the forest—lively, magnificent, created by the Great Demiurge, and filled with the aroma of resin and the songs of birds—brought me back to my senses. We set off for the place. My hope that the fountain of Pavlik's speech would dry up among the fir trees turned out to be a vain one; in there, the mandibles of his pinkish-green monster began to work with renewed force. So's to avoid being utterly disintegrated into molecules, I decided to defend myself with good ole' carnivalization: chuckling, remaining aloof, and philosophizing. Yon oft-tested shield against external idiocy helped this time too; we successfully reached the place without any hysteria or self-mutilation. And, by that time, the stone helped too, or should I say the *stone*—perhaps best to say the Stone—the size and shape of which were reminiscent of a kneeling elephant. Pavlik finally shut his yap when he saw the three statues in the belly of the sleeping elephant. They stunned us. The surfacing childhood memories of Grandma's story about a mysterious monument forgotten in a forest crumbled when they came into contact with its granite reality, something that came to pass in my life for the first time, as, typically, the myths of our childhood years end up being stronger than their corresponding realities—and not just for me; we might also recall the poet's preference for discussions about Christmas trees to actual Christmas trees during his adolescence. I was expecting to see three stone giants like the four American presidents hewn from stone on Mount Rushmore, but the power of human scale turned out to be much mightier when the three granite men looked out at me from inside their stone niche. Their *unblinking* gazes shattered the giants of my childhood imagination into little pieces. My previous assessment of my grandpa's skill as a sculptor collapsed along with them, as I'd always found it lacking before this. Here, in the forest, I understood *for what* my grandpa had so mastered the art of sculpture. Without doubt, this was his magnum opus, executed with truly miraculous craftsmanship. Grandpa's *peak*. Mount Everest. How could one even conceive of what these three men had done in order to be immortalized in such a way! Staring at them, I lost all sense of time and any desire to ask Grandma about anything. *Silentium!* Now I knew everything... And Grandma was really in fine form, as if she'd been there very recently, just like the Russian Orthodox people always in the cemeteries in front of the Trinity on Saturdays. She walked around the statues, bowed, stroked them, muttered something emotional, sobbed, and showered them with sweets and gingerbread, which didn't look at all ridiculous, as I might have expected. The majority of Grandma's warmth and sweets were diverted to Russia's final ruler. "How much suffering you endured, how many humiliations, how many condemnations and curses, but you endured everything, endured it silently, my dear, my little one, my modest one..." she muttered, kissing the granite of his bald head. The final chord in Grandma's piece was insisting we not photograph the sanctuary. Unlike Pavlik, that unhappy extrovert, I completely supported Grandma's embargo—here was an unshakable rock of values towering over the dull mistakes of the centuries. In this case: over the history of the Russian state.

A miracle came to pass on the way home—Pavlik was silent. Grandma, on the other hand, was excited and talkative and chattered incessantly about Grandpa, about their love and their tribulations, about their great friends who'd passed away, about the summer when Grandpa, hidden away in the forest for three months, sculpted those three knights, about her own heartless mother, and, of course, about

Moscow, about that Moscow, which Pavlik and I had never seen, the Moscow that "bloated up like an evil frog over the course of centuries, stretching its skin from Brest to the Pacific Ocean, before bursting from three pricks of a fatal needle."

I fell into such a pleasant state of stupefaction from Grandma's talking, the long road, and that which I'd seen that I even allowed Pavlik to take us to his favorite restaurant—Snowman—a pretentious and undelicious place. I even had some white wine there.

I came back to my apartment late and with a single productive idea: to sleep. Without pillows, smartypantses, or dreams.

41

July 12

TODAY, I finally went to see the Trinity with Sonechka and Pavlik. At first, I was worried and afraid. But when I saw them, all my fears faded away. I was left with only gratitude to all of the Three and to my Marik. And to the little nail that helped me to remember.

May they all rest in peace: Volodenka, Mishenka, Vovochka, Marik, and the little nail.

42

ALL CENTAURS getten brands. All centaurs getten brandethed.
They gettethed brands pon two places. The first place beeth the groin.
The second place beeth the left shoulder. My first brand gotteth
brandethed when I wæs hardly three months eald. The second brand
gotteth brandethed when I wæs hardly ten years eald. And I wæs
sellethed to the prince gavrilo gavrilovits. The prince he buyethed me
in the fall from a brooden ground and bringethed me to a fair in
voronezh. And I wæs weepen. I wantethed not to goeth away from
the brooden grounds. There wæs lots of centaurs at the brooden
grounds. We hadethed much fun at the brooden grounds. They wæs
goode at the brooden grounds. At the fairs, they wæs so so yfel. At
the fairs everyone bith screamen and shoven. And there beeth bigsie
horsies and smallsie horsies. And yfel people screameth and sweareth.
And I wæs so so verray afearen. The prince wæs belooken at me. The
prince buyethed me for twounded an fifty rubles. And the prince
madeeth the horseleech to brandeth me pon my left shoulder. When
he brandethed me I settethed to weepen most bitterly. Thanne they
puttethed me on the train to his estate. It wæs loud and afearen on
the train. I ridethed on the train for al the night. And I wæs most
afearethed and weepen most bitterly. Prince gavrilo gavrilovitsa pos-
sethed an estate that wæs most large. In yon estate wæs a pond and a
forest and a garden and a meadow. First they washethed me in a
bathhouse. Thanne they feedethed me and I refusethed to eateth.
Thanne the prince takethed me to the stable. And I settethed to
sleepen and weepen. Thanne they leadethed me out and the al prince's
familiary wæs belooken at me. And the prince's bearns settethed to

clappen and sayen how goode I wæs. And the prince's wife settethed to stroken and combessen me. And sayen goode words. And given me apples. But I refusedeth to eateth. And gavrilo gavrilovits wæs thinken that I wæs tired and afearethed. Thanne his bearns settethed to stroken me and sayen goode words. And I stoodethed there and saidethed nothyng. And the prince's wife settethed to stroken my cockcomb. And the bearns puttethed apples in my mouth. And I eattethed the apples. And the bearns clappethed and sayethed that I wæs goode. And they tookethed me to walketh in the gardens. And the prince's gardens wæs goode. And we walkethed around in the gardens. And the bearns walkethed with me and feedethed me apples. And thanne they puttethed me into the stables. And givethed me more to eateth. And I settethed to eatten verray verray much. And thanne I settethed to sleepen. And I settethed to liven with the prince. And every day the groom takethed me out of the stables to walketh. And I walkethed pon the meadows and runnethed verray much. Thanne they waterethed and feedethed me. And on holidays they adornethed me and dressethed me and sprinklethed gold in my hair and curlethed my hair and givethed me a golden bow and arrow and I gallopethed and shootethed and I carryethed the bearns to go playen pon the meadows. And everyone beeth belooken at me. And everyone beeth so nice and given me tasty mete to eateth. And gavrilo gavrilovits beeth prideful of me and sayen that I beeth so precious. And life bycamethed goode. And I livethed with gavrilo gavrilovits for two years. And I waxethed bigger. And I runnethed fast and shootethed from a bow and givethed the bearns goode rides. And pon a holiday there wæs many guests and I drinkethed and eatethed verray much and I givethed the bearns rides and I shootethed arrows verray straight and everyone settethed to stroken me and feeden me. And thanne in the evening wæs fireworks. And there wæs many flames and stars fallen into the ponds and everyone beeth standen and belooken at the fireworks and at the stars 'sif they wæs trothful stars fallen into the ponds. And I just stoodethed and watchethed. And a lady comethed to me. Her name beeth Columbina. And she takethed the diamdem from her head and puttethed it over my arm. And there wæs a nail sticken out of her head. And I wæs afraid that she wæs dead. And she laughethed and sayethed that it wæs a maygical nail and it pleasedeth her. And she laughethed most hardily and huggethed me and sayethed to me into my ears centaur centaur givest thou me a ride. And I sayethed I only giveth rides to bearns. I am reservethed from given rides to grown-ups. And she sayeth if thou giveth me a ride I shall showeth thee an invisible pouch. And I askethed what prithee be an invisible pouch? And Columbina sayeth that in the invisible pouch are magical küsschen. And I asketh what prithee be these magical küsschen? And Columbina sayeth when thou shalt tasteth of the magical küsschen thou shalt verray happy beeth. And I wantethed to beeth verray happy. So I agreethed. Columbina gottethed pon my back and I givethed her such a ride so far away and it wæs verray dark and I wæs tired and we wæs standen near an oak. And Columbina sayethed here's the invisible pouch with the magical küsschen. And there's nothyng better than yon küsschen in al the world. And shes showethed me yon pouch. And I can't seeth the pouch and I sayethed where where where beeth pouch? And Columbina sayethed and showethed me here here beeth the pouch. And Columbina takethed the magical küsschen out of the pouch and stickethed them pon my lips. And I settethed to fearen. And my legs sat to tremblen and I fallethed to my knees. And I wæs tremblen all over. And I beeth so afearethed of the küsschen. And Columbina strokethed me and sayethed to me goode words. And I calmethed down. And thanne she takethed out one invisible küsschen and puttethed it pon my lips. And I feelethed goode. And Columbia takethed out another invisible küsschen and puttethed it pon my lips. And I feelethed verray goode. And thanne I feelethed verray verray verray goode. And thanne I feelethed verray verray verray verray verray verray verray verray verray verray verray verray verray goode. And I jumpethed up and wæs overjoyethed and she sittethed pon me and laughethed and singethed a song. And we rideethed and ridethed and I carryethed Columbina through al the forest and I feelethed verray verray verray verray verray verray verray verray verray verray verray verray verray verray goode. And I feelethed so goode goode goode

goode goode goode that I gottethed tired and fallethed asleep. And when I wokethed up Columbina wæs gone. I wende around seeken Columbina. And thanne everyone wæs belooken for me and the groom yellethed at me and hittethed me with a whip and puttethed me on a leash. And I settethed to weepen and callen for Columbina. And they punishethed me and puttethed me in the stables with no mete. And I standethed and weepethed and callethed out for Columbina and her invisible pouch and her küsschen. And the younger groom sayethed to me Columbina already wende to saint petersburg. And I weepethed so much and shoutethed and callethed for Columbina. And they punishethed me and puttethed me on a chain. And I eatethed and drinkethed not for two days. And I callethed for Columbina and weepethed verray much. And thanne when it wæs night I tearethed my chain and out through the gates of the stables and I runnethed to saint petersburg to findeth Columbina.

43

LATE FALL. Late evening. Alexei's one-bedroom apartment in Kolomna, in PodMoscovia. Having turned out the light, Alexei pulls a smartypants over his pillow as if it were a pillowcase. He places the pillow down onto his double bed next to his regular pillow, lies down next to it, and strokes the smartypants-covered pillow with four fingers. The pillow begins to glow. The image of a girl's face rises up onto the surface of the smartypants. The girl is lying on her own pillow. Her name is Shan. The girl smiles at Alexei.

SHAN: Hello.

ALEXEI: Hello.

SHAN: Is it already way past midnight there?

ALEXEI (*nervously*): Yes. Usually... in November it gets dark fast. Super fast. Is it morning there? Morning? Morning? (*He kisses Shan's image.*)

SHAN: Hold on, baby.

ALEXEI: Baby... (*He kisses her.*) ... I'm all... I've been waiting for so... long...

SHAN (*putting her hands over her face*): Alyosha, baby, let's not... don't rush like that...

ALEXEI (*kissing the image of her palms*): Baby... oh, baby...

SHAN: Hold on, please. There's no reason to rush.

ALEXEI (*nervously*): I... you... I...

SHAN: And I you. (*She moves her hands from over her face and looks at Alexei.*) Talk to me.

ALEXEI (*restraining himself, he rubs his reddened face, shakes his head, and sighs loudly*): *Hao!** *Ni hao ma, Shan?*†

SHAN: *Hao tzila!*‡ It's morning here.

ALEXEI: You lucky duck.

SHAN: But it's still super early. The street sweepers aren't even up.

ALEXEI: We don't have street sweepers anymore.

SHAN: What a great way to start a conversation!

Alexei and Shan laugh.

ALEXEI: Forgive me, Shan, I'm behaving stupidly, I always ask stupid questions and give stupid answers, I'm sorry...I dunno. It's 'cause I always get nervous at the beginning of our calls...always...

SHAN: I know. I'm used to it.

ALEXEI: It's just...I really want you.

SHAN: I want you too, baby.

ALEXEI: No way you do...I mean you're always so calm. So calm! How beautiful and calm you are. I'm jealous of your...well... your ability to stay calm.

SHAN: That's just how I look. It only seems like I'm calm. I'm not actually calm at all. Really not. Don't you realize I'm not sleeping even though it's super early?

ALEXEI: It's cool that you're not sleeping. I'm not sleeping either. And I doubt I'll fall asleep tonight. I'm not sleeping, you're not sleeping, they're not sleeping, nobody's sleeping! Yay!

A beat. Alexei touches Shan's image with his hand. She holds out her hand to him. The image of her hand meets with his hand.

ALEXEI: I feel pretty...bad. Really bad.

*[Chinese] Good
†[Chinese] How are you, Shan?
‡[Chinese] Terrific

SHAN: No need for that, baby.

ALEXEI: What do you mean "no need"? Need—no need...I feel bad. I feel really bad without you.

SHAN: Baby. I'm starting to get upset.

ALEXEI: No need for that, I'm begging you. (*Annoyed.*) I'm not telling you that I feel bad so that you feel bad!

SHAN: I can feel that you feel bad, baby.

ALEXEI (*very nervous now*): I feel bad, but not because I lay down next to you just now, lay down like a selfish, sinful log only so's to mewl like this: I fe-e-e-el so ba-a-a-ad, Shan! He-e-e-elp me-e-e-e! That's not why I'm here. Don't think of me like that.

SHAN: That's not how I think of you at all, Alyosha...

ALEXEI: You better not, Shan! I'm just saying: I feel bad without you! I feel bad without you! I feed ba-a-ad witho-o-o-out you!

SHAN: I feel really bad too, baby.

A beat.

ALEXEI: Well, there. It's all turning out stupidly again somehow... All we feel is bad, it turns out. That's crazy! Listen, Shan, no, it's not like that, not like that at all! I feel great, I feel awesome, all 'cause you're here now. You're next to me and I can see and feel you.

SHAN: And I can feel you. I can even smell you, even though I've never actually breathed you in. Were you drinking beer?

ALEXEI (*laughs nervously*): Yes! A little...how did you...ah, you saw the bottle?

SHAN: No, I didn't see it.

ALEXEI: Yeah, I drank some beer. I dunno why...I was waiting for you to wake up and I drank some beer. You judging me?

SHAN: Not at all.

ALEXEI: Don't you have a dry law for young people there?

SHAN: Yes. All alcohol is prohibited to anyone under eighteen.

ALEXEI: And we can only drink beer, dry wine, and champagne. That's PodMoscow for you!

SHAN: PodMoscow sounds cool.

ALEXEI: Vladik sounds cooler. You have a casino, an *eszunhui*,* game emporiums . . . All of that got banned here a long time ago. Back when the first sovereign was in charge.

SHAN: You want to play roulette?

ALEXEI: No, no, I'm just saying. You have more freedom than we do.

SHAN: But you have less criminality, I know. And more polite people.

ALEXEI: They still love to jostle each other in public . . . And you've got the ocean. I've never seen it in real life.

SHAN: It's beautiful. I swim every summer.

ALEXEI: Cool. Tell me, do you go to *eszunhui*?

SHAN: No. It's expensive. I go to the disco. I even did back when I was in school.

ALEXEI: Western music was forbidden in our school. Now it's allowed, but not everywhere I guess. Back then, they were called "depraved dances."

SHAN: That's funny. Depraved dances. Depraved dances—one, two, three! Dance, dance, dance!

ALEXEI: I can't say I like the way you dance in the DR.

SHAN: Well, your Moscovian dances are slow. You're used to it, of course. And your songs are so sluggish and melodious. You have a lotta sad songs.

ALEXEI: No . . . I mean, we can dance well too. Russian jigs. I was in the jig club at school, but not for long . . .

SHAN: I've seen lots of Russian jigs. That's dope!

ALEXEI: And your mom doesn't do jigs?

SHAN: For whatever reason, no . . . I've never seen her do one. She remembers Russian songs and sings all the time when she and her friends drink. Dad sings Chinese songs and Mom sings Russian songs. Overall, like, we have a lotta different songs here in

*[Chinese] nightclub

Vladik and a lotta different kinds of music—the Japanese sing their songs and so do the Chinese and the Russians. Someone's got some holiday pretty much every day. It's a noisy life! The sound of a far-eastern symphony! (*She laughs.*)

ALEXEI: Shan, can I . . . may I kiss you?

SHAN: Yes.

Alexei kisses Shan's image on the pillow. She kisses back. Then puts her palm forward with a smile, pushing him back.

ALEXEI (*displeased, stops*): Listen . . . could we ever meet in the DRU?

SHAN: We already talked about this, baby. They'll only let me go to the DRU in eight months, when I turn eighteen.

ALEXEI: And they won't let me into Barabin.

SHAN: Yes. It's terrible . . . So stupid . . .

ALEXEI: Well, come on, we can still dream!

SHAN: Yeah, okay.

ALEXEI: What about Tataria? Maybe there?

SHAN: We talked about that too. You've forgotten. There're no direct flights between Tataria and the DR. And the train is dangerous. Don't you remember the movie? *The Red Robbers of Tataria*?

ALEXEI: A dope sinny, I'm sure, but it's banned here . . . Yeah, the train's dangerous. And takes a long time. Through Barabin, the DR, and Bashkiria . . .

SHAN (*strokes Alexei's face with her hand*): We'll just have to wait for eight months.

ALEXEI: Yeah, I remember now. Eight months. It's already been decided . . . How awful! (*he lowers his face into his hands.*)

SHAN (*sighs*): Awful . . .

ALEXEI: Fuck 'em all . . . Where are we gonna meet? (*With a furious grin*) I guess it'll have to be Telluria.

SHAN: We don't have diplomatic relations with them in the DR.

ALEXEI: Moscovia does. Our friends were there.

SHAN: Did they *test* it?

ALEXEI: One did. The tellurium's cheap there, not like here.

SHAN: I'm against drugs.

ALEXEI: I am too. But tellurium is more than just a drug. It helps people open up.

SHAN: People should be able to open up on their own. Like flowers.

ALEXEI: You're my flower.

SHAN (*sighs*): Telluria's a mysterious country. A lotta things get said about it here . . . Everything's free there . . .

ALEXEI: It's just another country. But one that got lucky.

A beat.

SHAN: You really are sad, Alyosh! There's no need for that!

ALEXEI: Shan.

SHAN: What?

ALEXEI: I'm not sad. It's just . . . hard for me to talk to you when I *want* you. You're torturing me.

SHAN: I'm not torturing you, Alyosh, I . . . I always just want to stretch this moment out like a holiday. My parents are still going to be asleep for a long time, the door's locked, and I'm alone with you.

ALEXEI (*embraces the pillow with Shan's image*): I want you!

SHAN: Okay, baby, whatever you say.

Shan's image is extinguished. Alexei throws the blanket off of the bed, takes the smartypants off of the pillow, and pulls it over the bed like a sheet. He gets undressed quickly and nervously, gets down onto his knees in front of the bed, and touches it with three fingers. The image of Shan, naked and lying on her own bed, rises up onto the smartypants stretched over Alexei's bed. Alexei begins to kiss her body, then lies down on top of her and takes possession of Shan's image. They moan.

SHAN: Baby . . .

ALEXEI: Sweetheart . . .

A beat.

SHAN: Alyosha...
ALEXEI: I lo-o-o-ove yo-o-ou.
SHAN: I love you.
ALEXEI (*rolling over to get up*): I ...you're ... such ...
SHAN: Don't get up—hold on. Lie on top of me. Please.
ALEXEI (*freezes*): It's just I ...want to see you ...
SHAN: And I want to hear you. Your heart. Lie down. So that, like, together...(*She turns up the sound.*) Don't you hear?

The sound of Shan and Alexei's beating hearts.

ALEXEI: Yes.
SHAN: Yours is beating harder.
ALEXEI: And yours is beating faster.

A beat.

ALEXEI: Good. You feel good with me. Is that true?
SHAN: It's true, baby.
ALEXEI: I feel so terribly... so terribly good with you ... (*He squeezes the bed forcefully in his embrace.*) Baby... my... most... most...

They lie down, stroking each other's images. Some time passes.

SHAN: Sea, forest, or mountains?
ALEXEI: Sea. You're my sea.
SHAN (*issuing a command*): Goa.

A hologram of sea surf and white sand rises up around Alexei's bed. Still embracing, Alexei and Shan lie down as if they were in the surf. Doris Day's song "When I Fall in Love" begins to play.

ALEXEI: What are we gonna do, Shan?

SHAN: Baby. I wanna say something.

ALEXEI: What?

SHAN: Just don't get me wrong.

ALEXEI: I'll always get you right.

SHAN: You see, I really love you. And I'll always love you. But I have . . .

ALEXEI: Someone else?

SHAN: Of course not! I have this fear.

ALEXEI: A fear? Of what?

SHAN: A fear that when we actually meet, we'll lose something.

ALEXEI: Why?

SHAN: I dunno, maybe it's stupid. But it happens a lot with *vertu lovers.*

ALEXEI: That's crazy talk. Crazy talk! (*He laughs as he strokes her image.*) It's the other way round! We'll start to love each other even more.

SHAN: I'm afraid.

ALEXEI: Don't you dare. Don't you dare! I'm gonna sit up now and I'm gonna marvel at your beauty. To cure you of your fear!

Alexei gets up from the bed, takes a chair, and sits down. He looks at Shan's naked body. The gentle surf rolls over her.

SHAN: There we go. Why the hell did I say it? I'm such an idiot!

ALEXEI: You're so . . . it could drive me insane . . .

SHAN: I'm yours.

ALEXEI: I want . . . (*he lies down on top of Shan.*)

SHAN: Baby.

They kiss. Suddenly, Shan's image begins to sway.

SHAN: Oy, Alyosh, we're having an earthquake again . . . Damn . . . This would happen right now! So dumb! Everything's shaking again . . . (*There's a knock at her door.*) I gotta go, baby, my parents are knocking!

Shan's image vanishes—all that remains is a hologram of the beach and the surf. Alexei lies in the surf for a little while, then lifts himself up and sits. Sits tensely. The waves pass rhythmically through his body.

44

AGAFYA Viktorovna, the wife of the neighborhood warden charged with the supervision of the Novoslobodskaya nanomarket, dreamt that she beat a tellurium nail confiscated from a semitranslucent Hindu by her husband into her own head and turned into an Ammophila wasp. This metamorphosis gave Agafya Viktorovna great pleasure; her body, having shed its usual plumpness, contracted, lengthened out, and filled up with incredible strength and mobility, light and powerful wings growing out of her back and beginning to flutter. Frozen with delight, the warden's wife flew out through her bedroom window and began to cruise over her native ZaMoscvorechye. She immediately wanted to visit her friend Zoya Fedorovna, the wife of another warden, and boast of her fantastical metamorphosis, but her heart began to pound and she felt a certain *higher* duty inside her: her blackish-yellow stomach was bursting with eggs. This sensation was not at all burdensome; on the contrary—Agafya Viktorovna's soul was filled with even greater delight. And the most significant thing was that she felt as if she'd been impregnated in the actual Kremlin by none other than the sovereign himself. With the whole of her new body, she suddenly felt and understood that she must accomplish something elevated, important, and state related, something demanded by the sovereign and by the country as a whole, but it was also something very pleasant and very tender, something that would bring her great pleasure. In expectation of this pleasure, she felt a sweet sucking in her heart. The wings roaring on her back brought her to her goal of their own accord—the maternity hospital on Lesnoy where, four years earlier, she'd successfully given birth to a boy. Having flown in through a small ventilation window, she flew over the heads of the midwives drinking tea, passed by the prayer room, went down a hallway, and ended up in a spacious "bedroom" filled with sleeping infants. Trembling with overwhelming emotion and delight at having been entrusted with this state business, she began to land on each of the sleeping infants and implant the whitish-pink larvae of loyalty into their delightful little bodies. The larvae poured out of her long ovipositor in nacreous swaths—like pearls. All the infants were sleeping sweetly and quietly, as if they'd been internally prepared for this procedure. The beautiful eggs disappeared into their tenderly sleeping little bodies. And this sweet infants' sleep, the white silence of the bedroom, the soft pearls popping out of the ovipositor, the intoxicatingly pleasant feeling of relief at each egg she laid . . . all of this filled Agafya Viktorovna's elastic body with bliss. Her enormous faceted eyes, which saw all around her, filled up with tears of pleasure. She noticed Ravich, the chief physician of the maternity hospital, the senior midwife, and an elderly nun quietly walk into the bedroom. They smiled reverently and the nun crossed herself. And Agafya Viktorovna understood that they all knew, that they'd all been waiting for her arrival for a long time, and that they were prepared for this most important procedure. Upon making this realization and at the sight of the people who had come to behold the process of the laying of these deeply useful larval eggs, eggs from which something bright, big, and useful for the state, something exaltedly loyal, would eventually hatch, Agafya Viktorovna began to feel even better. Choking up with tears of tenderness and emotion, she carried, carried, and carried these eggs until the last one had passed through her long, thin ovipositor with torturous sweetness and into the body of a little baby named Arseny. But barely had this come to pass and barely had Agafya Viktorovna's striped belly been emptied out when the face of the chief physician Ravich darkened with fury; he slammed the door and threateningly pulled out a hand holding a flyswatter from behind his heavy back. There also turned out to be a mop in the hands of the senior midwife and the nun pulled out a smartypants rolled into a tube from her sleeve. Silently and ominously, the three of them began to approach Agafya Viktorovna, who was still overwhelmed by what she'd just experienced. Feeling that something wasn't right and struggling with the languor that'd come over her after laying the eggs, she took off and flew for the windows, but they were all securely shut—hermetically, even. The flyswatter whistled past her head, Agafya Viktorovna dodged off to the side, the mop cut through the air in front of her such that turbulent streams of air knocked her off her flight path, she flew toward the floor, noticed her salvation—a crack beneath the door through which she might slide—but, at that very moment, the nun's smarty-pants knocked her onto the linoleum floor with a sweeping blow. Agafya Viktorovna had been beaten down onto the smooth and shitty gray floor, she tried to take off, but the sole of the nun's shoe came down like a gravestone, squashing her, then crushing her.

Cr-r-r-r-r-r-u-n-c-h!

Agafya Viktorovna woke up covered in sweat and gasping for air. It was already a quarter past nine; her husband had gone off to his service a long time ago, and the sun was shining in through the tulle of the curtains. Familiar sounds came to her from the kitchen: her mother was feeding her son.

"My God . . ." Agafya Viktorovna muttered, sitting up.

Coming to her senses, she moved her feet off the bed and down onto the floor, located her slippers with them, stood up, crossed herself in front of an iconostasis, stretched out, yawned, walked over the window, and opened the tulle curtain very slightly.

The Gorlov cul-de-sac was, as always, chock-full of the auto-mobiles of traders who'd come to Novoslobodskaya.

Nasty poplar fluff flew through the air.

"What'd they crush me for?" Agafya Viktorovna asked the cul-de-sac, turned away, then, scratching herself, shuffled into the bath-room.

45

BIGUNS OF THE REPUBLIC OF BERNE!

THE SCOURGE of the Chinese wingèd legion has definitively usurped power in the capital. The parliamentary elections were conducted with monstrous falsifications and manipulations. Not one bigun became a senator. We have been shamelessly removed from power. Five months ago, when the Chinese legionnaires and the Army of the Resistance drove the Salafis out of Berne, we were used as cannon fodder. It was us advancing on the tanks in Nordring, us breaking the gates to the cathedral under machine-gun fire, and us being incinerated by flamethrowers on Bubenbergplatz. Our innate heroism, kindness, and responsiveness are to blame. Now we've become a burden to Berne and its new rulers. With the support of the littluns and a small group of pro-Chinese citizens, the Chinese have conducted a great deal of covert work and turned the citizens of the republic against us. According to them, 'twould seem, the biguns are guilty of looting and pillaging! The biguns are to blame not only for the humiliating plunder of the Mövenpik wine shop and the paltry abduction of twenty-eight cheese heads from Chäsbueb, but also the notorious penetration into the gold depository of the National Bank. Even though everyone knows it was the littluns from the Furious Bilbo gang who slid into the bank through liquid gaps under the leadership of a bandit who betrayed his homeland and collaborated with Volpe the carpenter, a bandit able to get in touch with executed Salafis—those responsible for running the bank before the war—while under the influence of tellurium. The gold stolen by this gang was used to bribe voters to the benefit of Chinese candidates. Now the full weight of state power in the capital and the republic is in the hands of Chinese legionnaires and their *little* accomplices, who received the majority of seats in Parliament. Even as the true heroes of the war, we are now destined to be second-class citizens. They still want to use us only for heavy labor, like cattle. That cannot be! It is time to begin the Big Campaign of Biguns for Berne! Biguns! We are gathering tomorrow at 12:00 in the bunker of the Federal Assembly. We ask you to come only with clubs and not with steel weapons or firearms. Our campaign must be of an especially peaceful character.

DOWN WITH THE CHINESE USURPERS
AND THEIR ACCOMPLICES!
Mutig, mutig, liebe Brüder!
Mir werde gwinne!

46

"MY DEAR friend, Nadezhda Vasilievna, drop those dolls of yours, drop the televisioning, get on an avion, and fly to me. You can't even imagine how fantastic spring is here in Poshekhonye!" Elizaveta Pavlovna had managed to write in her even, clear, almost schoolgirl-like hand when the doorbell rang.

"Who could that be . . ." she muttered, shifting her *light* pen down to a fresh line, then suddenly recalled with disappointment that it must be the milkman, who'd returned after disappearing for two weeks because of his "illness"—really he was just drunk—and now she would have to interrupt her writing, count out the money for Varvara, tell her for the hundredth time that she didn't even remotely need cottage cheese or eggs and that she'd take no more than a single bottle of baked milk.

Something's been distracting me constantly all morning, some kind of darkness . . . Elizaveta Pavlovna thought, pushing her pen off to the side and closing the smartypants on which she'd been writing to Nadenka Sumina in far away Medyn by hand, as she always did with all of her letters.

She straightened up in the creaky Viennese chair, clasped her hands together, and began to knead them, as if she were getting ready to play that same piano behind which Grandma was, judging by the sounds that reached her, hopelessly attempting to teach Rita Schumann's "The Merry Peasant."

The clock in the living room struck noon.

Twelve! Elizaveta Pavlovna thought disdainfully. *I'm not managing to get anything done, my day off is passing me by . . .*

She stood up and walked into the living room, accompanied by the torturous sounds of the old "Xinghai."

There, everything was as it had been before: Grandma and Rita were behind the piano, Volodenka was doing geography at the table, and their old cat was on the old sofa.

"Ritulya, my golden one, stop yawning, and one, two…" Grandma's thin, slightly trembling hand touched the keys, as if she were groping for the right ones with a blindfold on.

"And… one and two and three and four…" the six-year-old Rita counted out, shaking her neatly combed light-chestnut little head of hair with a braid emerging from it and knocking her leg against one of the legs of her chair.

Elizaveta Pavlovna sank down into another Viennese chair, this one just as creaky, and positioned herself across the round table from Volodenka, who was decorating the middle of the island of Sakhalin with two Japanese characters on a smartypants stretched out over the table. Paying no attention to his mother, the son *swamped* the island's outline in yellow. His face had a painfully focused expression as it always did when he was engaged in something precise and serious, a stubborn *TR*-spiral cowlick stuck out over his swarthy forehead, and his full lips protruded in almost maudlin fashion.

I really must somehow contrive to get them to the lakes this summer if it doesn't work out with the Black Sea … Elizaveta Pavlovna looked tenderly at her son's stubborn, pimply, adolescent forehead. *Volodenka won't even look at me … He's so sick of all my advice and instruction … Mothers have a hard time being the authority for teenagers … it's almost impossible … especially for someone like me … What am I? Who am I? A medical student who didn't finish school … a singer who never made it … a woman with a weak character … with an eternal lack of consistency, character, and backbone …*

She remembered the drunken milkman.

He and Varvara probably already have their tongues down each other's throats … it's unbearable … insanity growing up all around us like a crust of ice, the insanity of our daily life is unbearable at times, it overwhelms all that surrounds us, it becomes more and more difficult

*to break through that ice, but one must grapple with it, one must make
an effort, one must wish everyone well, everyone, everyone, yes, even
Varvara and this drunken milkman...*

"The insanity of being," she pronounced aloud.

Son glanced briefly over at mother, then lowered his head once
more.

The door opened. Varvara's bulky figure appeared in the threshold
wearing a long gray dress and a whitish-red apron.

"The milkman," Elizaveta Pavlovna anticipated her announcement
with a hint of irritation in her voice.

But Varvara made an uncertain gesture back behind her with one
arm—bared to the elbow and puffy from washing clothes.

"Lizavet Pavlovna, some kinda strange man's here to see ye, he
won't...deign to wait, he's comin' in...says ye've been waiting for
him for a long time..."

"And who is this man?" Elizaveta Pavlovna began to get up.

But, at that moment, Varvara was pushed slightly off to the side
and a dark, masculine figure wearing a rough gray long-skirted gar-
ment of some kind that was spattered with filth from the road stepped
through the door and into the living room. This man with his swarthy, unshaven face and painfully brilliant, sunken, insomniac eyes,
which were so bright, they seemed not to see anything, took two
steps, took his worn little hat off of his head with its closely cropped
hair, pressed it to his chest, and just stood there.

Elizaveta Pavlovna froze, now unable to get up. Grandma brought
her pince-nez to her folded, always guiltily preoccupied and eternally
wrinkled face, glanced at the man, and exhaled.

"Lord Almighty..."

Having stopped playing and tapping her little leg, Rita stared
sullenly at the man. Giving the figure an inhospitable once-over,
Volodenka paused on his weathered, tanned face, suddenly opened
his mouth helplessly, and, his face changing, whispered:

"Dad..."

Elizaveta Pavlovna stood up, pushing off the table with her hands,
as if the table had been her life for these last four years, a difficult life

that had tormented her with constant waiting, a life from which there was nowhere to run or hide.

She put the palms of her hands to her mouth. The man's brilliantly dark eyes met her eyes. The man's dirty, swarthy hand, still clutching at his hat, unclenched. The hat fell to the floor.

"Seryozhenka!" Elizaveta Pavlovna cried out in a stifled, frightening voice.

The May wind rocked the branches of the blossoming cherry tree, so old this was probably its sixtieth time in bloom—its motley shadow also swayed as it swam out and rippled across the detailed embroidery of the festive Vologda tablecloth, across the plates, cups, and samovar, across the faces of the adults and children sitting here in the garden at a round table, and across Sergei Venediktovich Lukomsky's face. His thin, intelligent face was still just as restlessly tense, though he'd just shaved with his old Brown electric razor, which had been waiting for its master on a shelf in the bathroom for these four years, his eyes, sunken into their deep, dark sockets, still shone just as deliriously and sleeplessly, as if he hadn't yet seen the nearest and dearest people to him in the world, people whom he'd been dreaming of day and night and who were now sitting around him in this familiar garden, under this old familiar cherry tree, which had become wildly unkempt during the infinitely long time he'd been away.

Dressed in a white kosovorotka, Sergei Venediktovich was sitting holding his wife's hand with one hand and his son's hand with the other, squeezing them too strongly at times as if he were trying to affirm that these people were now no longer the torturous ghosts that would come to him at night during those four whole years of separation.

He spoke. And his family listened.

"For, verily, man's craving for narcotic substances is immeasurable. Its roots go back into the distant past, to the Stone Age, when people were living together *with* nature and animals; even then, they chewed coca leaves, they inhaled smoke, they drank the juices of strange roots, and they ate hallucinogenic mushrooms. Oh, my darlings, I can see that distant time so perfectly, that time when, surrounded by the virginity of nature, at night, around a campfire, dressed in the skins of the beasts they'd killed, our primogenitors ate plants that made them hallucinate. It might seem as if, unlike us, they should've been content with the material world, with the visible and tangible world, would've been in total conformity with the world of nature, would've taken from it only what they needed for their survival and for procreation, only the meat of animals, only the sweet roots of plants, only pelts, roots, and rocks to help them hunt, make clothes, warm up in the cold, make hunting weapons and fishing rods, but, even then, they were attracted to *illusion*, for man has been expelled from paradise, and, therefore, can never be in harmony with the world that surrounds him or, in the case of ancient people, with the world of nature. The abyss that existed between man and the world was fatal even then, when mammoths and saber-toothed tigers still filled up the virgin forests with their roar, when man himself was more like a beast than a human. And, already, that shaggy man wrapped in a goatskin with his strong jaws and small forehead was taking a mushroom into his rough hand and bringing that mushroom to his mouth, not as food, but as an opportunity to discover other worlds."

Lukomsky fell silent, gazed on the overgrown, neglected garden, and lifted his gaze upwards to where the May sky was visible in the gaps between cumulus clouds.

"All of that fades, goes pale, and is extinguished next to the divine tellurium. That product has no equal in the world of narcotic substances. Heroin, cocaine, LSD, and amphetamines are mere squalor next to tellurium's consumateness. Put a stone ax next to a violin and the distance between them can only be measured by a millennium. The *Homo sapiens* develops, his world changes and becomes more complex, it is overgrown with masses of new technology, and he is able to extract atomic energy from matter. The substances that allow him to survive in the world change too. The sphere, cube, pyramid, cylinder, cone, truncated cone, torus, and spiral are products of a new era and of new technologies. At one time, they seemed to us to be *super-products.* Many people *testing* these products said the same thing, their voices merging into a ringing chorus: This is the peak, the consummation, we desire nothing more, we are sat-is-fied! And that period lasted for almost twenty years. Until the discovery of divine tellurium. Knock all of the plates, cups, and forks off of the table, my darlings, put an enormous scale here instead, cover their copper pans with black velvet, lay out all of the products I listed on the left scale, and on the right—just one silvery, shining tellurium nail. And you shall bear witness to a miracle—the right pan shall move triumphantly downwards, for a tellurium nail outweighs the entire geometry of modern narcotic technologies, all of those pyramids, tori, and spheres shall float ingloriously up, for they turn out to be light, for they are not equal to the great tellurium, for their faceted faces are powerless against the nail!"

After almost shouting the final sentence, he froze for a minute, calmed down, then continued.

"And, along with them, so too shall all of the laboratories crammed full of equipment, people, and drugs float up like hot-air balloons, puffed up by their own ignominy; all of the scientists with their formulas, the mages and alchemists who created these beastly pyramids, cubes, and cylinders, hoping that humanity might play in these cubes and pyramids like babes, might squeal, fart joyously, and let forth grateful drool, as if to say 'Glory be to you, oh wizards of these new miracles!' But humanity is no suckling child. Man is that which longs for truth. Man is that which must be overcome, not once, but constantly. Every day, every hour, every minute, and every second . . ."

Sergei Venediktovich fell silent, turned his closely cropped head of hair and exposed its right side, where there was a tiny scar visible above the ear.

"Touch it," he pronounced.

His family reached out their hands and took turns palpating the scar.

"My journey *toward* the divine tellurium lasted for four years," Lukomsky continued. "And I don't regret a single minute of that time, even as I also understand how you must've suffered. I also suffered at my separation from you, I suffered terribly... monstrously... I spent so many sleepless nights, thinking of you, my family! Just a single radio-kiss from you ... Just a single *splinter*... But I wasn't just suffering at this separation; I was also rejoicing that, upon my return, I might tell you about this miracle, which would make your life meaningful, fulfilling, which would *exalt* it. And it was this realization that helped me to endure an endlessly long and difficult road, our separation, deprivations various and sundry, to endure all that I was fated to, and all that which I crossed paths with on my long path *toward* tellurium. Oh, such a path, a road *toward* a dream ..."

Lukomsky closed his insomniac eyes, as if he were internally moving down that road once more. He began to speak without opening his eyes.

"I passed through Ryazan in a horse-drawn carriage, having bought my liberty from Tatarian bandits with blood and sperm, worked as a porter in Bashkiria, stole my living in Ural, humiliated myself panhandling in Barabin, then spent three months in a filtration camp in Telluria, where I was raped four times. And I endured all of this only so that I might have tellurium nails beaten into my head nineteen times. Which came to pass."

He opened his eyes.

"Do you know what the power of tellurium is? It awakens the brain's inmost desires and its most cherished dreams. And these, I might add, are fully realized, deep, and long-lived dreams, not mere momentary impulses. All famous narcotic substances have always led us down the garden path, substituting our desires for the desires of the substance, our will for its will, and our idea of pleasure for its idea of pleasure. I remember when I first tried regular acid, I was only eleven. I saw images that stunned and frightened me in equal measure. I'm sure you know what I'm talking about, my darlings. Subsequently, we learned how to cope ... how to subtract the fear from the pleasure. Other, more consummate products acted according to the same principle. But tellurium ... divine tellurium doesn't produce euphoria, spasms of pleasure, a high, or a banal rainbow trip. Tellurium gifts you with an entire world. A solid and plausible world, a living world. And I ended up in the world that I'd been dreaming of since my early childhood. I became one of the disciples of Our Lord Jesus Christ."

It seemed as if Lukomsky's eyes had filled up with tears, but they were only sparkling with a new, especially bright and deep brilliance.

"All of my childhood and adolescent dreams, all that which I'd thought about the life of Our Lord, about His deeds and His *feat*, all of it came into being. I became one of the apostles. I was with Him, I walked through Palestine, I heard the Sermon on the Mount, I drank the wine of Cana in Galilee, I sailed across Lake Gennesaret, I saw the resurrected Lazarus emerging from a cave, saw the lepers cleansed and the herd of swine hurling themselves off of a cliff and into the sea, slept in the Garden of Gethsemane, wept impotently on Golgotha when the Roman pierced the side of the crucified Savior with his spear..."

He fell silent. His family was also silent.

"I saw everything," Lukomsky said in such a way that his wife and son shuddered. The face of Lukomsky's wife's mother was distorted into a helpless grimace and tears flowed in a river from her damp, elderly eyes. But she didn't raise her hands so as to wipe away these tears. Wife held husband by the hand and stared at him with such focus that it was as if she were together with him in Cana and on Golgotha. The son's face, flushed and ready to burst into tears, exuded bitter reproach: Why wasn't I with you, Father? And it was only the six-year-old Rita who was still sitting just as motionlessly as before—she was utterly paralyzed, her blue eyes wide open, as she seemed to be looking straight through her father.

"My darlings," Lukomsky continued, "now, we all have a goal in this life. We know what to do. We know how we're to live from now on. And that for which we're to live."

He stood up suddenly, knocking over his chair, which fell unexpectedly quietly onto the young May grass, picked his daughter up from beneath her arms, and set her on the table. Not at all surprised by this, the girl continued to look ahead of her with wide-open eyes.

"Tell me what burns within our hearts, oh my daughter," Lukomsky pronounced and got down onto his knees.

The wife, the son, and the wife's mother also got down onto their knees.

Lukomsky's daughter lifted up her face and, peering at the sun through the branches of cherry blossoms, began to speak.

"Our Father, who art in heaven, hallowed be Thy name, Thy kingdom come, Thy will be done, on earth as it is in heaven, and give us this day, our daily bread, and forgive us our trespasses, as we forgive those who trespass against us, and lead us not into temptation, but deliver us from evil. For Thine is the kingdom, and the power, and the glory, forever and ever."

"Amen," Lukomsky pronounced.

And he smiled with relief for the first time on this endlessly long and difficult day.

47

THE STEPPE opens up. Stretches out submissively before me.

Beneath the hooves of my white mare, the boundless steppe creeps past. Who shall measure the steppe? What shall be used to measure its breadth? Only the arrow of my faithful crossbow. The gait of my frenzied mare. And the flight of my desires.

Heiya!

Carry me, oh mare, down the path of my desires. Spread out, oh steppe, as an endless carpet 'neath my feet. Whistle out, oh wind. Ring forth 'gainst my tellurium wedge.

Heiya!

I am a free woman. Neither people nor the city have caught hold of my freedom. I was born into a dark city and my father and mother conceived me in a stone coffin. My mother gave birth to me in that same stone coffin. All city people live in stone coffins. They are born into stone coffins, they live in them, then they die in them. And those who have died are transferred into wooden coffins so that the earth shall swallow them for all time. Is it worth living only so's to be transferred from one coffin to the next? Is it worth living only so's to satisfy one's slow stone-coffin desires? Is it worth living only so's to deafen our desires in the stone coffins of our cities?

Heiya!

Tellurium revealed the simple truth to me. I ran from the dark city—from its stone coffins. I exchanged my mournful mother and slow father for a mare and crossbow. The mare is my mother. The crossbow is my father. There is no one closer to me than my mare and crossbow. It is only them that I love, only them that I trust, and only them to whom I am loyal.

Heiya!

The wind, the stars, and the steppe are my friends. I cherish their friendship and keep it safe. The counsel of my friends is dear to me, I wouldn't exchange it for anything. The wind sings me a traveling song, sets my wedge to ringing, and whispers trusty words into my ear. The stars point the way, they caution and take care of me, direct and warn me. The steppe stretches out beneath the hooves of my mare, gives me a bed, and cradles me with herbs. The steppe grass sings me lullabies.

Heiya!

My world is the steppe's expanse. To track and to hide, to skulk and to attack, to pursue and to catch, to love and to kill—these are my desires. My eye is keen, my ear is sensitive, and my hand is true. I shall see and I shall hear, I shall catch and I shall overtake, I shall subjugate and I shall defeat.

Heiya!

My arrow flies faster than the wind. It knows not the act of missing, nor the act of mercy. Even faster is my desire. It carries me to my goal and helps me to evade steel bullets. I turn my back on human bullets, for I am quick and humans from stone coffins are slow. Their thoughts are slow, their desires are slow, their steel horses are slow—even their bullets are slow. How many of their bullets have whizzed past my quick body like sleepy drone bees? How many of their steel horses have tried in vain to catch up with my white mare? How many hunters who've come to hunt me have I turned into game?

Heiya!

The lath of my crossbow buzzes and arrows fly toward their slow bodies. They fall, penetrated by my arrows, toppling over onto the steppe with great surprise. A quick death overtakes their slow bodies. And they remain upon the steppe. A quick death snatches up slow people from city coffins. And they remain upon the steppe—then they are free. Instead of a coffin, the wind and stars—instead of a priest, a steppe eagle—and instead of a lector, a black crow. The grass sings out a funeral chant for those killed by me.

Heiya!

I kill those who hunt me. I snatch up whomever I desire. I desire men and I desire women. I love men *strongly* with my hot member. I love women *tenderly* with my hot tongue. Their hearts go cold with the fury of my love. But this love is fleeting. I leave these men and women after I've loved them well past the point of collapse. The bodies of those exhausted by my love also remain upon the steppe. They shall always remember the heat of my desire. And to think that any slow person is capable of loving as I am...I doom these men and women to longing and to tears. They shall long for my hot body and cry at night in their city coffins. But there's no one to love them in the stone city. And my goal leads me further into the steppe—toward new goals and desires.

Heiya!

The wind sings me a traveling song. The steppe buzzes beneath the hooves of my mare. The stars show me the way, guiding me and cautioning me. Time has perished in my heart. There abide only space and a thirst for desire. I am eternally content.

Heiya!

48

AND SO, Patrick and Engelbert decided to spend their honeymoon traveling to exotic countries. And the first of these turned out to be the USSR—the Ultra-Stalinist Soviet Socialist Republic.

The idea of beginning their travels in the USSR first occurred to Patrick—who else? Only his quick, superficial, and perpetually undoubting mind could have thought up such a thing. On the other hand, the phlegmatic Engelbert didn't bother to protest; it was basically all the same to him. In fact, only one thing set him to trembling: Patrick—his straw-stiff hair, his thin, permanently adolescent torso with ribs ready to tear through tender skin, and his perpetually cracking voice. And where—in what countries, on what continents and planets—he would see, kiss, and touch Patrick was all the same to him.

"The USSR!" Patrick pronounced in Russian, then laughed as he clicked his pterodactyl earring against himself.

Truthfully, there was no special meaning in Patrick's idea—only a personal motive: his grandfather had been born in Saint Petersburg on the day the first USSR had collapsed. That same grandfather had then emigrated out of Putin's Russia to France and married a French student—Patrick's grandmother. Patrick knew only three dozen Russian words and had hazy memories of his grandfather reading weird-ass Russian fairy tales about some idiot traveling around on a stove and talking to fish.

The calm and thoughtful Engelbert was interested only in whether this unusual country was safe. And, indeed, safety was guaranteed to tourists.

On the first of June, they arrived on a charter flight from Vienna into the only airport in the USSR: an airport that bore Stalin's name, like everything else in this tiny country.

"*On y est, Babar!*" Patrick said to Engelbert when the plane landed to the accompaniment of clapping Stalinist tourists.

"*Willkommen, mein Kitz*," Engelbert replied to Patrick.

They kissed.

Usually, they endeavored to communicate with each other only in English, which had again become fashionable. The lovers always had to choose which language to speak. And they had more than a few to choose from. When he was twelve, Patrick's parents had taken him out of France, which was in the grips of a Wahhabi revolution, to the safety of Sweden, where he grew up and studied at a technical school so's to work with *cold* machines after completing school. In Patrick's home, they spoke mostly Spanish, his father having been born in Córdoba and fled to France during his youth from the dolefully notorious Spanish Black Friday, which had destroyed any hopes for the future of the Spanish economy. He got set up as a waiter in a Parisian banlieue and, a couple of years later, married Patrick's mother, who was half-Russian and half-French and worked as a maid at the Waterloo Hotel.

Engelbert was born in Munich to an elite family with a rich history. His great-grandfather was a well-known Bavarian philologist and Germanist; one of his grandmothers was an opera singer; the other taught the history of the Middle Ages; one grandfather, a theologian, committed suicide in India by throwing himself from a famous cliff along with his lover; and the other studied ornithology and conceptual art for his whole life. A chemist by training, Engelbert's father fled with his family from a Munich gripped by Wahhabi turmoil and to the mountains—where his eccentric brother lived. After their father's suicide, his brother had decided to marry an Albanian peasant woman, settle down in Oberburhbihl, and to become one with nature. He'd changed professions from economist to farm laborer and taken to it in unexpected fashion. Forced to join his brother's household, Engelbert's father still had absolutely no intention of sticking around in the picturesque Alps, but, after the turmoil was quelled, Bavaria suddenly seceded from Germany and became an independent state, which, for whatever reason, threw his father into a deep depression. His brother, on the other hand—an anarchist and pantheist—rejoiced. Engelbert's father, mother, and both of his brothers remained in Oberburhbihl and never again returned to the city. Engelbert himself decided to go away to Munich to study philosophy, even though he'd been obsessed with plastic surgery and genetic engineering for his whole adolescence. He couldn't rationally explain his new desire.

"I want to *comprehend*," he pronounced at a family meeting.

These words had a hypnotic effect on his depressed father, who'd already become close friends with alcohol—he agreed immediately. In his son's choice of a profession that was so uncommon during those days, his father caught a glimpse of the prosperity that was to come after a time of troubles. He paid for his son's studies and daily expenses without any hesitation, freeing him from the need to work as a waiter. For four years, Engelbert had been occupying himself with only philosophy. And this occupation brought him great pleasure.

He and Patrick had met at a technological achievement fair in Frankfurt. Engelbert was convinced to go there, not by a love for technology, to which he was indifferent, but by a fashionable book of philosophy by Su Zheng entitled *Deus ex Machina*, which had crushed the European neo-deconstructionists and thrown a dozen weighty cobblestones at *Nichtsein und Postzeit* by Hector Mortimesco. Engelbert sought visual confirmation of Su Zheng's stunning ideas.

He noticed Patrick next to the fifth model of the famous machine that turned words into gastronomically refined dishes, which, if they so desired, the fair's visitors could obtain and taste. The curious Patrick, having paid a small sum, pronounced the Russian word *pizdets*—meaning "clusterfuck" or "cunted up"—into the intake valve and, with a little growl, the machine squeezed out a greenish-pink oval object with orangish protuberances and a burgundy hemisphere in its center. The dish smelled of uncertainty.

"Are you gonna eat that?" Engelbert asked curiously, observing Patrick.

"Duh!" Patrick shook his shaggy head so that his pterodactyl earring opened its beak and croaked.

Engelbert liked Patrick and his pterodactyl right away. He also put money into the machine, then pronounced the word *Dasein*. A beautiful, ivory-colored little cube slid out of the machine's semi-transparent, funnel-shaped opening.

Standing next to the machine and washing down their creations with bitter Frankfurt beer, they got to know each other. For Engelbert, Patrick's image was always connected with the taste of the cube: a light fish soufflé that melted pleasantly on the tongue.

Patrick couldn't really make out the taste of the *pizdets*. But he ate the whole thing courageously. He liked Engelbert's massiveness, calm, and solidity, immediately christened him as "Elephant," and intuitively felt that Elephant would have a big trunk. Which turned out to be true.

After spending the night in a lousy hotel, they were forced to separate the next day, each of them heading back home. They made virtual love six times. And decided to meet up for real that summer and go "to a dope place."

And so did it come to pass.

They were picked up from the airport with its five-meter-tall crystal statue of Stalin by a young, little fag (as they'd ordered), who was to be their guide, and driven into the capital of the USSR, the guide chattering away in good English the whole way.

The story of this state was a cool bit of exotica in and of itself: immediately after the collapse of post-Soviet Russia and the emergence of a dozen and a half new countries on its expanse, three Moscovian Stalinist oligarchs bought up an empty tract of land measuring one hundred and twenty-six square kilometers from Barabin and the Uralian Democratic Republic. Prosperous followers of the mustached leader poured onto this island of Stalinist dreams. The path was closed to poor Stalinists. The new state proclaimed its existence rather quickly, setting itself off from the surrounding postimperial world with a formidable electric fence and machine-gun nests. The construction of a Stalinist paradise in this specially chosen country proceeded at the Hollywood version of a Stakhanovite tempo and, six short years later, the country opened its doors to tourists. They didn't wait around: charter-flight companies couldn't manage to keep pace with all the people who wanted to see "the fairest state in the world," the population of which professed a new religion—Stalinism.

It was true—the oligarchs had brought their dream into being creatively and with the iron implacability of Stalinists. In addition to their grandiose constructions, they acquired almost all that remained of the Soviet dictator's reign, including the remains of the leader himself. In Stalingrad, the capital of the USSR, an enormous marble temple was erected where, beneath thick bulletproof glass, the relics of "the leader of all of progressive humanity" found peace. A new religion had been created and intellectuals and theologians far from the worst humanity had to offer occupied themselves with its first principles and elucidations.

What tourists didn't come to see the USSR during those years?! There were left-wing radicals, Trotskyists, anarchists of all stripes, insurgents with *living* tattoos of Che Guevara, veterans of the Partisan Wars, fashionable writers, big shots who were fed up with life and big shots who weren't, masochists, fetishists, lunatics, and, finally, just simple tourists—tireless devourers of images and information.

Stalinists, on the other hand, gathered here only *on business* for their regular congress, which was held in a specially constructed Palace of the Soviets, a copy of the three-hundred-meter-tall Cyclopean plans for the original that was five times smaller than the original would've been if it'd actually come into being in Moscow during the leader's life.

Each congress was conducted beneath the slogan "Stalinists of the world, unite!"

And they *united* once every five years, sharing their experiences, reading reports, spewing forth curses upon capitalism, monarchism, revisionism, and opportunism, reporting on yet another Stalinist Five-Year Plan, merging together into a collective orgasm of applause and toasts in honor of their immortal, mustached god...

The road from the airport to the capital passed through hills covered over in light forest and corpulent mansions.

"Are those dachas or houses?" Engelbert asked the guide as he trifled with Patrick's delicate fingers in well-practiced fashion.

"This is where our creative intelligentsia lives," the youth explained. "Basically only people employed in the service sector live in Stalingrad."

"And what's the population of the capital?" Patrick asked.

"Three hundred thousand," the solid Engelbert whispered into Patrick's ear.

"Three hundred forty-two thousand six hundred and four people," the guide corrected him with an enchanting smile.

"And all of them only work in the service industry? Dope!" Patrick snapped his pterodactyl and touched his finger to the tip of Engelbert's little nose.

"Temples, the Palace of the Soviets, museums, cinemas, restaurants, shops, bathhouses, pools, gyms, houses of tolerance—all of this requires constant care," the guide explained.

"And there's no industrial production." Engelbert nodded, deep in thought.

"The USSR produces only Stalinist souvenirs, books, and sinnys. We have extremely clean air."

Indeed, the air invigorated and delighted with its freshness. The lovers had gotten lucky with the weather—the sun was shining and the sky was blue.

Their program was to be an intensive one. After lunch, the lovers were expected to visit the main temple of the USSR—where Stalin's relics were kept. This majestic, pyramidal building was lit up from the inside; its expensive decoration was radiant and its combination of Russian Orthodoxy, constructivism, and classicism was striking. Its marble columns loomed, its chandeliers shone, and an enormous hammer and sickle blinded with their gold. In the center of the temple, there was an altar with an iconostasis depicting the life of their deity. In front of the altar reposed the suprematist glass coffin with the relics. The lateral faces of the temple pyramid were decorated with imposingly sized icons of the leader's associates depicted in an austerely classical manner. Patrick liked the icon of Yezhov in a red toga with white-hot tongs in his hands, while Engelbert committed to memory the painting of the handsome, white-bearded Kalinin in a birch grove with peasants and animals and also the one of Vyshinsky in a judicial mantle with shining scales in his hand. The first reminded him of Bavaria, cows, and his family, while the second reminded him of college and of an unfinished term paper on a "new anthropology."

In the temple, as in a movie theater, there were rows of soft chairs—they even reclined. It was very comfortable. From a reclined chair, one could easily survey the ceiling, which had been painted in the style of Michelangelo: a bearded Sabaoth wrapped in clouds and resembling Marx holds out his hand to the ascending naked, beautiful, and young Stalin, who's surrounded by seraphim.

In the temple, refreshing drinks were served by littluns. Their guide left them for a little while. On the temple pylons shone the text of the main prayer to this new saint in three languages—Russian, Chinese, and English.

"Oh holy Stalin, oh Steel One, oh consummate Sublime, have mercy on us..." the prayer began.

Half reclining in a chair and reading the prayer, Engelbert let his hand wander down toward Patrick's fly.

"Some not-so-heavy petting, Elephant?" Patrick asked, taking a glass of apple shot from a littlun scurrying among the chairs.

"It can't hurt." Engelbert sipped at a nonalcoholic beer.

During *caresses*, he became invariably taciturn.

From the temple, they were taken to a museum full of holograms, models, exhibits, and documents. In a separate hall, all the gifts given to Stalin while he was still alive were on display. Patrick was amused ("Dope! Dope!") by the grain of rice with a portrait of Stalin on it executed by Chinese Communists. A telephone given to Stalin by workers from the Polish city of Łódź made a particular impression on Engelbert: a globe, a receiver in the form of a hammer, and a cradle in the form of a sickle.

After the museum, Engelbert was, as always, exhausted, while Patrick was overexcited and wanted to swim. The guide appeared and they set off for the city beach, which was covered with sculptures of swimmers. Stalinist songs were playing loudly on the beach and boats filled with smartly dressed young people floated across the basin.

Despite the hot Siberian summer, the water was still quite chilly and Patrick got out quickly, while the stubborn Engelbert continued to swim, *overcoming* himself. Sitting in chaise-lounge chairs, the friends sipped at a pretty decent local beer.

"Don't forget you have a meeting with the One this evening, gentlemen," the guide reminded them.

"How could we forget?" Engelbert muttered relaxedly.

"Dope!" Patrick gave Engelbert a high five. "Are you ready to meet the Original, Patrick?"

"*Natürlich* . . ." Engelbert squinted out at the white boats. A young man sat in each of them with a girl carrying a bouquet.

He counted the boats. There were eighteen of them.

The beach and the water had awakened the travelers' appetites, and soon they were sitting in Gori, a Georgian restaurant, drinking *kindzmarauli*, tasting Georgian dishes rich in proteins, greens, peppers, and lipids, and listening to Stalin's favorite songs being performed by an ensemble in national dress.

After the meal, they were drawn into bed.

A short spell of lovers' intimacy gave way to sleep. Which was interrupted ninety minutes later by the guide's call informing them that it was time to meet.

Having taken a shower and drunk a cup of thick Georgian coffee, the friends got dressed and went down into the lobby, where the guide was waiting for them in an Emka with a smiling driver, dressed in the fashion of the 1930s.

"An amazing journey awaits you, gentlemen," the guide chattered articulately as he guided them into the car. "Our state gives tourists the right to one free tellurium trip so's to end up in the great, fearsome, and heroic era of developed Stalinism and personally meet Comrade Stalin. You enlightened Europeans, I hope, know the book by the famous European intellectual Suetonius Likuidas entitled *My Seven Meetings with Stalin*, which tells of his seven *trips* to the Soviet Union—all conducted here during a three-month visit to our state. That book became a worldwide bestseller, it's already been made into a movie, and Likuidas's dialogues with the leader are often quoted by the European left-wing intelligentsia."

"'No person, no problem, Comrade Likuidas,'" Engelbert recalled. "'But if there's a robot, now *that's* a problem.'"

Their guide laughed happily, his beautiful mouth curling up.

"Dope!" Patrick remarked, not really listening to the conversation about Likuidas.

"I'm sure that you've also come across other recollections of such trips; the actress Chloé Robbins, for example, who became the leader's mistress and discovered the unbelievable properties of his secretive, tormented, and lonely soul, so saturated in deep feelings; the media mogul Bukhweizen, who created the super successful television channel Stalingrad after his trip; or the car king Hopkins, who managed to save one of his companies from bankruptcy after conversing with the leader—"

"I know about that one!" Patrick interrupted him, grabbing Engelbert by the ear. "Can you imagine that dude getting a nail beaten into him, then deciding to modernize his two unprofitable car factories. Can you, Elephant? He did it and profit went up forty percent right away. But the dopest thing is that no one really knows what he actually did to drive up profits! The factories still produce the same cars, but, for whatever reason, they sell much better now!"

"For a mystical reason?" Engelbert asked, looking out the car window as it slowly slid down Stalin Avenue.

"God knows, maybe his brain just started to work better, that's what usually happens after a tellurium trip. I was telling you before how I got unexpected abilities in aeronautics and swimming. I got my flying license really easily and started to swim better—seriously! I used to be really damn scared of the water."

"Yeah, I remember..." Engelbert stroked Patrick's fingers.

A year ago, he'd tried tellurium himself, using the money he'd saved up from what his father had sent him. It was a *strong* experience; he spent an unforgettable spell in the great School of Athens and learned many new things. He hadn't been able to find a common language with Plato, they'd simply kissed torturously and wordlessly for a long time, Engelbert completely frozen with pleasure, then he'd allowed this philosopher of Herculean build to do whatever he wanted with him. Pythagoras had seemed to him to be the wettest of blankets, old man Plotinus had called forth mystical dread in him for whatever reason, and he'd managed to establish a productive dialogue with the vigorous and tolerant Parmenides, as a result of which the twenty-first century messenger was able to prove to the ancient Greek—not without the help of Hegel, Heidegger, and Sartre—that nonbeing was as real as being. Therefore, it was just as purely present, which implied that being was not eternal, for it rises up out of nonbeing.

But he hadn't acquired any new abilities after this trip and all that remained in his memory was the taste of Plato's imperious and persistent tongue.

The guide chattered on about European politicians flooding into the USSR "for ideological support after the Wahhabi hammer's blow." Allegedly, the French president and the Berlin prince-elector had also come here and spoken with Stalin about the national question.

Engelbert didn't really believe their guide. And, more generally, he wasn't all that interested in this touristic, contrived, thoroughly artificial state, in which they'd ended up at Patrick's behest. He also wasn't interested in Stalin. But he'd read the fashionable Likuidas— whaddya expect? His *Dochsein und Postzeit*, which polemicized with the great Mortimesco's *Nichtsein und Postzeit*, had been read by all the students in the philosophy department. Still, to the extent that he was already in the USSR, he had to stop by 1937. In his book, Likuidas devoted two chapters to that year, as he'd been there twice— the first time as an NKVD executioner interrogating the theater director Meyerhold, then as Meyerhold himself, whom the investigator tortured with insomnia and beat with a rubber club. Likuidas had turned this into an energetic, existential-philosophical essay entitled "A Machine of Violence Desired Both Compulsorily and Not," in which he shared the feelings and enthusiasms that had arisen as a result of the trip, which he described as "pro-upgraded psychomatics, formatted corporeality, and reloaded existentiality," then, during the next trip, having become one of the members of Stalin's Politburo, he got down onto his knees in front of the leader and kissed his hands. To which the leader grumbled, "Don't play the fool, Kalynich."

"A clean head . . ." Engelbert pronounced thoughtfully.

"I haven't washed mine for a long time!" Patrick admitted with a laugh.

In the spacious temple of the Meeting, they were awaited by charming girls in white who undressed them, shaved their heads, sat them down into a marble tub, washed them, anointed them with Altaian oils, and enrobed them in white clothes with delicately embroidered Stalinist symbols. Having drunk their fill of herbal tea from Gorno-Altaysk, the tourists signed the traditional contract regarding the state's lack of liability in the case of any damage to their health, after which they were handed over to a gray-bearded Tellurian with an expressively calm face. Having sat them down into special chairs and carried out the necessary manipulations, he beat two tellurium wedges into their smooth, aromatic heads.

Patrick died eight minutes later. Engelbert's brain fought against death for almost four hours.

It was curious that there had only ever been two lethal outcomes from tellurium trips in the USSR before Patrick and Engelbert: the first had been a thirty-year-old Englishwoman who'd come to the USSR with her Communist parents and the second had been a nineteen-year-old bio-rapper from Angola, who dreamt of meeting with the Soviet jazz pianist Tsfasman and recording a track with him back in 1930. Just like Patrick and Engelbert, these victims had not been Stalinists. The large tribe of the mustached Father of Nations' followers had not suffered in any way whatsoever: all of them had returned from their travels happy and rejuvenated, one ninety-three-year-old Chechen woman even wrote a book with the unsubtle title *I Spat in Stalin's Ugly Mug*.

But, for whatever reason, it hadn't turned out that way for Patrick and Engelbert.

Why? No one knows...

Their frozen bodies were delivered to their relatives at the expense of the USSR.

And that's how it all happened.

49

I SAW THE worst minds of my generation torn out of black madness by tellurium, minds

who overcame the quotidian morass of the swamp of an ordinary life,

who cast the concrete crust of idiotic self-assurance and dull complacency off from their souls,

who trampled the chimera of earthly predestination in an instant,

who shook the ashily shaggy mold of tired perception of the world off from their eyes,

who crushed the sticky shell of depression with their new hands,

who spat the hot magma of consummateness into the dull face of thousand-year-old spleen,

who breathed the new breath of life into the empty eye sockets of dusty libraries

who let thousands of schizophrenically hopeless books fall into the wind—books that had pushed readers either to suicide or the loony bin,

who beat a shining tellurium stake into the grave of earthly despondency,

who broke the backbone of the dismal dragon of humanity's disappointment in itself,

who rose up from the ashes of previous generations' weakness and lifted their shining bodies up to the heights of a New Reality,

who rent asunder the chains of Time, rusty with blood, sweat, and tears,

Time, the white-eyed executioner of hopes and expectations,

Time, which rolls billions of those humbled in their expectations and insulted by the collapse of their hopes beneath the wheels of its infernal machine,

Time, which has poured the merciless amber of the impossible over countless generations, as if they were gnats,

Time, which has saddled man and torn open his mouth with the steel bridle of the eternal thirst for the irrevocable,

Time, which has spurred its two-legged horse into a gallop for illusory success until its final breath, until the absolution of its sins, until the gas burners of the crematorium, until its burning nose and melting buttons, until warm ash fills up a cold urn,

Just what kind of metal has slipped into your drowsy brain and filled it with imaginings?

Tellurium! Dreams coming into being! Thoughts becoming real! Childish fantasies! A Christmas whisper onto thawing frosty glass! Drool and tears onto a pillow! Kind wizards! The Czarevna coming back to life! Prince Charming! Fairy tales! Entreaties! The impossible!

Tellurium! Memories of that which passed away long ago! Deceased loved ones coming into your bedrooms! Ghosts of the past embracing us! The scents of those who went missing without trace!

Tellurium! The might of incarnation! The torturous fantasies of homely women! The dreams of cripples! The inmost thoughts of beggars and idiots! The nightly prayers of the lonely! Hopes and requests! Parallel worlds encroaching 'pon reality!

Tellurium! New horizons of hope!

Tellurium! Shining like the vestments of the angels!

Tellurium! Shining like the prophet's lightning!

Tellurium! Plunging into the brains of millions as if 'twere a divine scalpel!

Tellurium! Redefining the limits of humanity!

Tellurium! Filling people with confidence in the past, present, and future! Confidence! Happiness! Joy! To the brim! To the point of overflow! Till the blood boils! Till the Great Calming of the Soul!

Tellurium, whose name is the Overcoming of Time and Space!

Tellurium, which has made us consummate!

Tellurium!

You sparkle in the nights of humanity's bygone centuries! You break through the fog of History! You are the lodestar Polaris! You dig up graves! You revive soldiers, suicides, and drug addicts, those who perished from their wounds, from bombs, from toxic substances, from overdoses, from disappointment in the unattainable! You gather their rotting remains and sculpt them together! You lead them to their families and loved ones! Those who perished! Choked on their own blood and vomit! Who lost their eyes, testicles, and heads! Those crushed by tanks! Dissolved by virtual-reality tests! Burnt up in the quick flame of war and in the slow flame of madness! Those who let free their blood into a thousand overflowing tubs! Flattened against the predawn asphalt of unbelief in miracles!

Tellurium!

You scrape together their remains with shining hands! Up from the asphalt! Up from the vomit-colored paving stones! Up from the sides of the tub! You sculpt together their new bodies—they're even more robust than their old bodies! The metempsychosis of drug addicts rotting in their graves! The reincarnation of incinerated soldiers! The resurrection of beggars devoured by dogs! The might of corporeality returned!

The tellurium bell has come to collect you! The return of departed souls! New lips! New eyes! They laugh joyfully and triumphantly!

Tellurium has brought them back to life! They embrace us! We're together! There's no such thing as death! We're cheerful, strong, and happy! We embrace our dreams! The time has come! We push up off of the flat earth! We jump, jump, jump higher! higher! higher! up from the filthy asphalt! from the paving stones! from wormy crypts! from burning houses! from morgues! from jails and concentration camps! from mass graves! from blown-up barracks! from biographies that didn't turn out! from nauseating offices! from mangled tanks! from the Hotel Imperial! from the ruins of cities! from exhausted villas! from gyms and swimming pools! from identity crises! from beneath the wreckage of love and concrete! from restaurants and cinemas! from warm family beds! higher and higher! gathered up by tellurium! higher! higher! toward true hope! toward the coming-into-being of the chimerical! toward relatives and friends! toward lovers! toward forbidden desires! toward the impossibly adored! toward the criminally cherished! toward the great! toward Mozart and Plato! toward Nietzsche and Dostoevsky! toward Christ and Buddha! Mao and Hitler! toward new symbioses! toward the triumph over Time! toward living gods! toward triumph over death! higher! onto the roofs! over the streets! over the river! over the rainbow! higher! to the clouds, oh telluric catapult! higher! toward fiery seraphim, toward wise cherubs, toward stern angels, to Thrones and Dominions, to Powers and Authorities, higher, higher, higher!

50

THERE were no more taters. An' that was that. Soon's it got light, I woke up, bowed down to the sun, had some bread 'n lard, an' got goin'. Drove thirty-four versts through the forest on two sacks. Cast the last tater into the motor, like come on, darlin', let's keep it goin'. We started up again, the motor sneezed, then we stopped. That's how it was. We had nothin' more to trudge along with. An' wherefore needed I to keep on trudgin'? I'd stopped in the right place. A good place, like I'd done it on purpose: a clearin' ahead, birches and oaks all round, a fir grove nearby, nice glades too... Got down from the auto-mobile an' looked about. Yeah, a good place. Walked round, had a think, then decided. Bowed down to the sun, 's if to say: Thank ye, Jarilo, for warmin' up an' cultivatin' yon place for me. I could get settled here. Sat down, made a fire, roasted some horse meat, ate it up, an' pissed over by a walnut tree. Afterwards, I looked round some more: Jarilo himself musta sent me to yon place. There was even a creek right up 'longside it! That's one big blessin'! First I thought— who's murmurin' like a badger? Walked over an' took a look—a puddle into which some source was flowin'. Had a drink—delicious forest water. An' that means there's already a well. An' if there's a well, well, I can build a house here too. That won't take long. I opened the box, took out sacks, a hatchet, a saw, a chisel, an' a drill. Laid 'em out onto the sackcloth, got down onto my knees, bowed down to the sun, an' said: Jarilo, oh light o' mine, send me strength to build a cabin here an' not get hurt. An' I set to work right away. Seemed like my hands'd been longin' for carpenters' work. I'd been scootin' for the princess for six lil' years. Not that lil' of a time. But what could

I've done—there weren't nowhere else to go. The work wan't tough or nothin', but there was a lot of hustle an' bustle to it. They fed me pretty good. There was just one problem—other people's feedin' ends up gettin' stuck in yer craw like a log. So I had to go eventually. I worked for that broad long enough, now I can work for myself. If yer born a carpenter, ye can't let yerself die a coachman! The first thing to do was get the tools all set: the handle into the spade, the bit into the drill, the sledge, the wedges, an' the spare ax. As my deceased pa used to say: The tools've always gotta be sound. So I sharpened the hatchet, saw, chisel, an' drill. Then I took off my shirt, took up the ax an' saw, an' went over to the fir trees. Oh, how the chips set to flyin'! That's how bad I missed this kinda work! I chose the best firs, felled 'em, cleaned 'em, an' hewed 'em. Even though I'm goan be livin' in the depths of the forest, my cabin's goan be white as snow! Beautiful. I'd hewed out four logs by sunset. I took a gander an' even surprised myself: well, Gavrila Romanych, yer sure a strongun! I bid the sun farewell, scooped a lil' water into a pot, boiled up some gruel an' lard, an' gorged myself in my fatigue. Then tumbled down to sleep in the scooter right away. I woke up with the birds, had a bit of horse meat an' bread, waited for sunrise, bowed down to the sun, an' took up my hatchet. I hewed out five more logs before sunset. An' four more on the third day. I didn't even manage to sharpen the hatchet. Then I set to makin' the corner posts: I fell an oak an' cut out four of 'em from a single trunk. I dug out pits in the clearin', chucked some stones into 'em, an' nestled in the posts. Then set to nestlin' the cabin on top of 'em. Logs ready to be bound together are a spiritual sight! There's enough moss here to do it—an' what else could I possibly need? Moss soft an' fragrant like an owl's feathers. I set down the moss, bind together the crowns, an' I myself set to singin', which scares away the birds. Beauteous! Birches're standin' all round wavin' their branches at me: Good day to ye, Gavrila Romanych, welcome home! I got the bottom of the cabin laid down, cut out the windows, an' enclosed 'em with self-generatin' glass. Made the door, hewed the rafters, cut some vines, an' dug out some sod. Got myself set up with a nice, thick roof. Put some boulders onto it. Jointed the floor together from half logs an' filled in the chinks with self-generate so's the wind wouldn't blow through 'em in the winter. I walk away, then look back—the cabin turned out real nice! So I gave myself a rest. Walked round the neighborhood with my rifle. Didn't see no big game. But I did see some boar tracks an' a moose's footprint, so there must be some round here. I missed a gray hen, but felled three thrushes with one shot. A damn miracle! That'll be a real fine addition to the gruel. An' all summer, I just got myself set up an' settled down. Dug out a stream an' laid in a well with boulders. Burnt out a clearin', dug it out, an' fenced it off from the boars with a stack stand; in the spring, I'm goan plant some taters and rareripe, I saved up the seeds, an', when they get grown, I'll throw 'em into the scooter an' get goin' on my iron horse! An' with an iron horse, not even the devil's goan catch me. I'll roll on through the woods. And go huntin' wherever I end up endin' up. I'll fell a boar or moose, bring it home, set traps for fur-bearin' beasts, an' sew myself some fine vestments. I got myself three poods of salt, enough for the time bein', I can salt the moose meat, build a smokehouse, an' smoke some wild boar brisket. First, I'll get myself set up with a black furnace an', next year, I'll go to the river for clay, cut bricks from the boulders, lay down the stove, and rub it over with yon clay. Then I'll put in a potter's wheel there so's to shape pots an' pitchers then to fire 'em. I'll fill 'em up with badger fat, boar lard, nuts, dried berries, sea buckthorn, an' pickled mushrooms. I'll dig out a spacious cellar with an icebox. I'll sow rye, y'know, 'cause I grabbed so many seeds. I'll bake bread, brew beer, an' warm up by the stove. 'Haps I'll even find myself a lil' furry friend for company so's I don't get bored or nothin'. We don't need nothin' superfluous—not broads nor sinnys, not bubbles nor pyramids, not nails nor war, and not money nor yer top brass. That's how I'll live out my century. I got a house, the roof don't leak, and I got plenty to chow down on. Ye don't must needs go to work an', if ye set to plowin', do it for yer own damn self. Sleep when yer set on sleepin'. Bow down to nothin' but the sun. Caress nothin' but furry creatures. An' bicker with nothin' but birds of the forest. What else's a man need?

TITLES IN SERIES

For a complete list of titles, visit www.nyrb.com.

J.R. ACKERLEY Hindoo Holiday
J.R. ACKERLEY My Dog Tulip
J.R. ACKERLEY My Father and Myself
J.R. ACKERLEY We Think the World of You
HENRY ADAMS The Jeffersonian Transformation
RENATA ADLER Pitch Dark
RENATA ADLER Speedboat
AESCHYLUS Prometheus Bound; translated by Joel Agee
ROBERT AICKMAN Compulsory Games
LEOPOLDO ALAS His Only Son *with* Doña Berta
CÉLESTE ALBARET Monsieur Proust
DANTE ALIGHIERI The Inferno; translated by Ciaran Carson
DANTE ALIGHIERI Purgatorio; translated by D. M. Black
JEAN AMÉRY Charles Bovary, Country Doctor: Portrait of a Simple Man
KINGSLEY AMIS The Alteration
KINGSLEY AMIS Dear Illusion: Collected Stories
KINGSLEY AMIS Ending Up
KINGSLEY AMIS Girl, 20
KINGSLEY AMIS The Green Man
KINGSLEY AMIS Lucky Jim
KINGSLEY AMIS The Old Devils
KINGSLEY AMIS One Fat Englishman
KINGSLEY AMIS Take a Girl Like You
U.R. ANANTHAMURTHY Samskara: A Rite for a Dead Man
IVO ANDRIĆ Omer Pasha Latas
HANNAH ARENDT Rahel Varnhagen: The Life of a Jewish Woman
ROBERTO ARLT The Seven Madmen
WILLIAM ATTAWAY Blood on the Forge
W.H. AUDEN (EDITOR) The Living Thoughts of Kierkegaard
W.H. AUDEN W. H. Auden's Book of Light Verse
ERICH AUERBACH Dante: Poet of the Secular World
EVE BABITZ Eve's Hollywood
EVE BABITZ I Used to Be Charming: The Rest of Eve Babitz
EVE BABITZ Slow Days, Fast Company: The World, the Flesh, and L.A.
DOROTHY BAKER Cassandra at the Wedding
DOROTHY BAKER Young Man with a Horn
J.A. BAKER The Peregrine
S. JOSEPHINE BAKER Fighting for Life
HONORÉ DE BALZAC The Human Comedy: Selected Stories
HONORÉ DE BALZAC The Memoirs of Two Young Wives
HONORÉ DE BALZAC The Unknown Masterpiece *and* Gambara
VICKI BAUM Grand Hotel
SYBILLE BEDFORD A Favorite of the Gods *and* A Compass Error
SYBILLE BEDFORD Jigsaw
SYBILLE BEDFORD A Legacy
SYBILLE BEDFORD A Visit to Don Otavio: A Mexican Journey
MAX BEERBOHM The Prince of Minor Writers: The Selected Essays of Max Beerbohm
MAX BEERBOHM Seven Men
STEPHEN BENATAR Wish Her Safe at Home
FRANS G. BENGTSSON The Long Ships
WALTER BENJAMIN The Storyteller Essays

LILLIAN ROSS Picture
WILLIAM ROUGHEAD Classic Crimes
CONSTANCE ROURKE American Humor: A Study of the National Character
RUMI Gold; translated by Haleh Liza Gafori
SAKI The Unrest-Cure and Other Stories; illustrated by Edward Gorey
UMBERTO SABA Ernesto
JOAN SALES Uncertain Glory
TAYEB SALIH Season of Migration to the North
TAYEB SALIH The Wedding of Zein
JEAN-PAUL SARTRE We Have Only This Life to Live: Selected Essays. 1939–1975
ARTHUR SCHNITZLER Late Fame
GERSHOM SCHOLEM Walter Benjamin: The Story of a Friendship
DANIEL PAUL SCHREBER Memoirs of My Nervous Illness
JAMES SCHUYLER Alfred and Guinevere
JAMES SCHUYLER What's for Dinner?
SIMONE SCHWARZ-BART The Bridge of Beyond
LEONARDO SCIASCIA The Day of the Owl
LEONARDO SCIASCIA Equal Danger
LEONARDO SCIASCIA The Moro Affair
LEONARDO SCIASCIA To Each His Own
LEONARDO SCIASCIA The Wine-Dark Sea
VICTOR SEGALEN René Leys
ANNA SEGHERS The Dead Girls' Class Trip
ANNA SEGHERS The Seventh Cross
ANNA SEGHERS Transit
PHILIPE-PAUL DE SÉGUR Defeat: Napoleon's Russian Campaign
GILBERT SELDES The Stammering Century
VICTOR SERGE The Case of Comrade Tulayev
VICTOR SERGE Conquered City
VICTOR SERGE Memoirs of a Revolutionary
VICTOR SERGE Midnight in the Century
VICTOR SERGE Notebooks, 1936–1947
VICTOR SERGE Unforgiving Years
ELIZABETH SEWELL The Orphic Voice
VARLAM SHALAMOV Kolyma Stories
VARLAM SHALAMOV Sketches of the Criminal World: Further Kolyma Stories
SHCHEDRIN The Golovlyov Family
ROBERT SHECKLEY Store of the Worlds: The Stories of Robert Sheckley
CHARLES SIMIC Dime-Store Alchemy: The Art of Joseph Cornell
CLAUDE SIMON The Flanders Road
MAY SINCLAIR Mary Olivier: A Life
TESS SLESINGER The Unpossessed
WILLIAM SLOANE The Rim of Morning: Two Tales of Cosmic Horror
WILLIAM GARDNER SMITH The Stone Face
SASHA SOKOLOV A School for Fools
BEN SONNENBERG Lost Property: Memoirs and Confessions of a Bad Boy
VLADIMIR SOROKIN Ice Trilogy
VLADIMIR SOROKIN The Queue
VLADIMIR SOROKIN Telluria
NATSUME SŌSEKI The Gate
DAVID STACTON The Judges of the Secret Court
JEAN STAFFORD Boston Adventure
JEAN STAFFORD The Mountain Lion